# Heart of the Hawk

# Justine Dare

A TOPAZ BOOK

TOPAZ
Published by the Penguin Group
Penguin Books USA Inc., 375 Hudson Street,
New York, New York 10014, U.S.A.
Penguin Books Ltd, 27 Wrights Lane,
London W8 5TZ, England
Penguin Books Australia Ltd, Ringwood,
Victoria, Australia
Penguin Books Canada Ltd, 10 Alcorn Avenue,
Toronto, Ontario, Canada M4V 3B2
Penguin Books (N.Z.) Ltd, 182–190 Wairau Road,
Auckland 10, New Zealand

Penguin Books Ltd, Registered Offices:
Harmondsworth, Middlesex, England

First published by Topaz, an imprint of Dutton Signet,
a division of Penguin Books USA Inc.

First Printing, October, 1996
10  9  8  7  6  5  4  3  2  1

 REGISTERED TRADEMARK—MARCA REGISTRADA

Printed in the United States of America

For Hal again,
this time for the Gunbiter Song.

You take your inspiration where you find it.

# Chapter 1

*Wyoming Territory, 1878*

He wished they'd just hang him and get it over with. Joshua Hawk paced the small cell, rubbing a hand over his unshaven jaw. He stopped at the barred window, looking out at the structure silhouetted by the full moon. For an instant, just a fraction of a moment, he felt a pang of regret, mixed oddly with gratitude. Gratitude that Gramps wasn't alive to see how the last of the Hawks was going to end.

He stared at the gallows, hoping the hangman they were waiting for was damned good at his job; he didn't relish the idea of doing a death dance for the fine people of Gambler's Notch. And all the others who would no doubt make the trek to this godforsaken place once they learned who was going to be hanged. Gambler's Notch was a stage stop, and if word got out that they were going to hang The Hawk, and given enough time, they'd turn it into a damned party. All the more reason to wish the executioner would get here in a hurry.

Afterward, when they would no doubt display him like some kind of freak, he'd be too dead to care. Not that he liked thinking about it now, just as he hadn't liked thinking about it when Charlie Curry had died in that fray down in Sweetwater last year. His bullet-riddled body had been displayed in a store window for days after his death, and folks had come for miles to pay a nickel for a peek at the famous gunfighter.

*Probably would have kept him there for weeks, if it hadn't been summer and they couldn't get enough ice to keep him from smelling up the place*, Josh thought grimly.

He walked away from the window and its ominous view, and sat down on the edge of the narrow iron cot that was a foot too short for his six-foot-four length. No, he amended silently, rubbing at eyes gritty from lack of sleep, the only godforsaken thing in this town was him. And it was his own damned fault. He'd only come here because he'd run out of supplies, and the diet of rabbit and questionable greens—and the lack of coffee—had begun to weary him. So he'd suspended his profitless contemplation of his life and come down out of the mountains he'd been holed up in for nearly a month.

"Hell of a price to pay for a cup of coffee," he muttered to himself.

He stared at the uneven plank floor beneath his sock-clad feet. No doubt his boots would get sold to the highest bidder after he was dead, someone who would get some gruesome pleasure out of wearing them. And maybe talking about it to men gathered in a smoky saloon. "Sure's I'm standin' here, these're The Hawk's boots. Got 'em right after they hung him over in Gambler's Notch."

Grimacing, he stretched out on the cot, his feet dangling over the end. It was a sad state of affairs, he supposed, that he really had so few matters to put in order. All he'd asked for was a promise from the town marshal that his horse and saddle would go to the kid at the stable who had taken such good care of the rangy buckskin, and his rifle to the blacksmith who had fixed the horse's off fore shoe for free, simply because he didn't want to see a fine horse go lame because his owner was tapped out. Beyond that, he had nothing to leave, nor anyone to leave it to.

Not even the book Gramps had told him about, that book about the Hawk family. He hadn't found it among his grandfather's things after his death, and Josh wondered where it was, if it even existed. Most likely not; the old man had been half out of his head, and most of his rambling words had sounded like the ravings of a crazy man. The disjointed story had sounded like the Hawk legends Gramps had told him on the long trip west from Missouri, only Gramps had sounded like he thought this book was real. But he'd never told his grandson where to find it, just raved on that when the time came he would find it. That it would come to him as it came to all the last Hawks, the Hawks who were the last of the breed.

His illness, Josh supposed. The book probably wasn't real, any more than the warriors and wizards Gramps had woven into such entertaining stories were real. But Josh'd never know for sure. He'd never gotten around to looking for the thing. And now he never would.

Dawn was streaking the sky, pale pink to the east, fading to indigo over the mountains, and somewhere close by an early rising meadowlark was pouring out a song when he heard the raspy voice of the marshal calling his name. He wondered if the hangman had arrived and this was it, if this was his last morning. Too bad he'd never appreciated the soft colors of the waking sky before. Or the sweet sound of the little yellow-chested bird. Then he nearly laughed aloud; had there ever been a man looking at his own death who hadn't thought the same thing?

"Hawk!"

This time the call was punctuated by the sound of booted footsteps. He rose slowly, watching the approach of the round-bellied man who was tugging at his long, curling mustache in a gesture that had become familiar. Caleb Pike was a jovial fellow, but Josh hadn't been fooled. Anyone who failed to see the steely glint in the man's blue eyes, or let the apparent softness of his body blind them to the unusual quickness of his movements, deserved what they got. He had a feeling he would have liked the man, had the circumstances been different. He had the look of a man to ride the river with.

Pike came to a halt outside the cell door.

"Mornin', Marshal," Josh said, crossing his arms over his chest as he leaned a shoulder against the bars. "You're up early. Hope it's not in my honor."

"As it happens," Marshal Pike answered, "it is."

Despite his inner certainty that he was resigned to his fate, Josh felt a knot form in his stomach. He glanced upward. *I'm sorry, Gramps,* he thought. *I know I was a disappointment to you. At least where I'm going, we won't be seeing each other. You won't have to know.*

"Hangman got here, then?" was all he said. At least he could try and die with some pride.

Pike blinked. "What?" Then, smiling so widely the tips of his mustache quivered, "Hell, no, boy. In fact, I got good news."

"If he's going to be delayed long enough for half the territory to gather, I'd rather you did it yourself, now," Josh muttered. He didn't have the stomach to ask if there had been invitations to this string party sent out;

it was a common enough practice that he didn't doubt it. Except that Pike didn't seem the type.

Pike shook his head. "You're sure eager to die, aren't you?"

"It beats being a sideshow."

The marshal looked him up and down, and for a moment Josh had the feeling the man was also wishing they had met under other circumstances.

"No chance of that, son. Not now."

He unlocked the door and it swung open with a screech. Josh lifted a brow in query. Pike tugged a revolver from his belt, holding it up so Josh could see it. An old, neglected Dragoon Colt, he noticed. Very neglected. He wondered if the thing would fire. Then wondered why he cared.

Pike waited, as if expecting Josh to speak. When he didn't, the marshal did.

"We found it," he said, as if that simple statement explained it all.

Still Josh said nothing, wondering what the man was getting at. Pike obviously thought this was important to him, and until he found out why, Josh decided he'd be better off staying quiet.

"Out in back of the saloon," the marshal elaborated finally. "Right where Arly Dixon jumped you. It was just like you said, he was armed, after all. I've already sent off a wire to Judge Edgerton. That hangman won't be hangin' anybody this morning, so we'll just feed him a good meal and send him on his way."

Josh stared at the man. "You found this—" he gestured at the battered old weapon he suspected hadn't been cleaned since it had been made—"in the alley behind the saloon? Where I shot Dixon?"

"Yep. It was wedged in behind the rain barrel. That's why we missed it in the dark. Must have landed there when Arly fell. Luke, the kid from the stable, he found it."

Josh drew back, studying Pike intently. True, he had thought Dixon was armed when he'd loomed up out of the shadows that night, but only because he assumed nobody would be fool enough to sneak up on him like that without a weapon of some kind. His reaction had been swift, reflexive . . . and lethal. Only when the man lay dead had he discovered he'd been apparently unarmed.

And not a soul in this town had believed any different. No one believed Arly Dixon had been armed. He didn't have to be around this town, they'd said at the trial; his sheer size and cantankerous disposition made people keep their distance. And the absence of any weapon found where Dixon had died had put the noose around Joshua Hawk's neck.

"I thought you didn't believe me," Josh said slowly.

"Well, what with your reputation as a fast shootist and all, and people looking to make a name for themselves comin' after you all the time, I figured you might be one to shoot first and look later."

Josh winced inwardly at the accuracy of the assessment, but he kept his outward expression even. And his mouth shut.

"But," Pike went on, "Arly was no prize when it came to holding his temper, either. Especially if he thought you were messin' with his wife. He was plumb unreasonable about that girl."

Josh shook his head ruefully. He barely even remembered the encounter outside the mercantile, picking up a fallen package for a tall, plain, brown woman in a baggy dress. He'd accepted her hurried, whispered thanks, barely noticing that her voice held a hint of Southern softness, reminding him of things long forgotten and better left that way. He had touched the brim of his hat, and gone past her toward the saloon, his mind already on finding a poker game to give himself a stake. He wouldn't have remembered the chance meeting at all, except that it had come out at the trial.

She'd been there, too, but so swathed in black mourning veils that he couldn't even be certain it was the same woman. He'd felt remorse then, that he'd deprived this woman of her husband, the owner of the store he'd seen her in front of. He supposed that was when he'd decided to just give in; he'd killed an un-armed man by sheer, gut reaction, and he was tired of living that way. Maybe he was just plain tired of living. He'd thought the township of Gambler's Notch was going to solve that problem for him. And now here he was, free again, and with no idea who to thank. Or even if thanks were in order.

"I barely even spoke to her," he said yet again, as he had several times at the trial.

"That's all it'd take, for Arly," Pike said. "He was a mighty possessive man. And a good-looking hombre like yourself, well . . . Anyway, when I found out he took this old piece with him that night, it put a whole different light on things. Makes it self-defense, I'd say. I'm sure the judge will agree."

Josh swallowed tightly. "Just how did you . . . find out he was armed?"

"Well, that's how I knew it had to be the truth, see? Person who told me had no reason to lie, and every reason to want to see you hang."

Josh straightened up. He knew nobody in this town, and certainly nobody who'd want to help him. "Who told you?"

"Mrs. Dixon."

Josh blinked. "What?"

Pike nodded. "Yep. Arly's widow."

His boots back on, his hat in his hand and his gun-belt slung over his shoulder, Josh sipped at the coffee the marshal had poured for him, thinking the man should use some of the powerful brew to grease that noisy cell door he'd been listening to the entire two weeks he'd spent here, waiting for the judge to arrive and then through the trial.

"Let me make sure I got this right," he said as he sat on the edge of the marshal's battered old desk. "The widow of the man I killed told you he'd been carrying a weapon after all, that night?"

Marshal Pike nodded. "She said she found it was missing when she was packing away his things last night. She sent word to me right away."

"Generous of her," Josh muttered skeptically.

"She's a generous sort of woman. Said she couldn't bear to see an innocent person punished any longer."

Innocent. It had been a damned long time since anyone had used that word about him. And a damned sight longer since it had been true.

"Very generous," Josh muttered, suspicion biting deep. Why the hell would the woman he'd made a widow want to help him?

"After I found out, I sent Luke over to look around. You know how boys are, he was excited as all get out to be lookin' for evidence. Done a real good job, too."

"Thanks to the widow." Josh's mouth tightened. This made no sense to him. "I'd like to . . . thank her personally," he said to Pike at last. "Where does she live?"

"Well, now, I'm not sure—"

"I'm not going to bother the woman, Marshal."

"It wouldn't be smart of you. Folks around here

didn't like Arly much, but that girl's a different matter. She's been mighty good to a lot of folks around here."

"Including me, apparently. I just want to express my . . . appreciation." His mouth twisted wryly. "It couldn't have been easy for her to do what she did."

Pike muttered something that sounded like "You might be surprised," but that didn't make any sense either, Josh thought. After a moment the marshal went on. "She lives over the mercantile. Arly liked to be close enough to stand guard over his store. Kept a shotgun handy to do it, too. He wasn't the trustin' sort."

*Including of his wife,* Josh added to himself ruefully. *What the hell would Dixon have done to a man who had genuinely paid attention to the woman?*

"Thanks," Josh said. "Want to come along, make sure I don't scare the good widow?"

Pike looked him up and down. The long mustache quivered as the marshal's mouth lifted at one corner. "I don't reckon you scare many women, son."

"Don't forget I killed this one's husband," he pointed out dryly.

"Fair fight," Pike said with a wave of his hand.

*Fair fight.* Josh suppressed the grimace that threatened. He didn't want to think about that, not now. He set down the tin cup and stood up.

"I'll be on my way to the mercantile, then."

Pike nodded. "You do that."

Josh's gaze narrowed at the man's tone. "Just what do you mean by that?"

Pike met his eyes levelly. "Just that. For now."

The warning was implicit, and the lack of fear in the older man's eyes told Josh he wouldn't hesitate to back it up if he had to. Even against The Hawk; Josh had little doubt the man knew exactly what his reputation was and how many bodies it had been built on. But whatever he knew, the man was clearly not intimidated.

Admiration sparked in Josh for a tough man in a tough job. Although they were a long way from Texas, Josh was tempted to ask if there had once been a ranger star where the town marshal's badge now rested against the man's chest; he had the look.

"I'm not looking for any trouble," he assured the man.

"As I recollect," Pike drawled, "you weren't looking for any the other night, either."

Josh stifled a sigh. "I can't deny that. But I'm still not hunting for problems."

"Son, some folks just attract problems, like a carcass attracts flies."

And that, Josh thought with wry humor, about summed up his life. Pike seemed to discern his whimsy, and Josh could swear the man almost smiled.

"I'll walk away if I can," he said, meaning it.

Pike considered this rather rash promise for a moment, then nodded. "I believe you."

Josh buckled on his cartridge belt and adjusted the holster that hung from the right side. The rig was plain, lacking the fancy leather carving some went in for, but the fit of the Colt .44 in the holster was perfect; it slid out smoothly, yet didn't bounce loose at a gallop. A box fit, some called it. Whatever the term, it was vital to his survival, and he'd take it over any amount of fancified tooling.

"Folks are thinking about a town ordinance," Pike said conversationally. "No firearms."

Josh put on his hat, settling the black Stetson comfortably. Then he looked at Pike once more. "Good luck if they do."

"Time's a comin'."

"But it's not here yet."

*Time's a comin'.* The words echoed in Josh's head as he walked outside, into the sunlight he'd thought he'd never see again, except maybe on that last walk. *Time's a comin'.*

He supposed Pike was right. Civilization was advancing westward. The railroad had been completed nearly ten years ago, the long trip he'd made as a child with Gramps was easy now, and it seemed every train disgorged more and more folks aghast at the sight of six-guns in public.

Josh walked to the front edge of the covered boardwalk in front of the marshal's office. He shoved his hat up, tilted his head back, and let the morning sun pour over his face. Odd, he thought. He'd been resigned to this being his final morning, had even welcomed the thought . . . yet now he was finding pleasure in as simple a thing as the warmth of the sun on his skin. He wondered briefly if the one had caused the other.

His mouth curved down at one corner; that had been Gramps's kind of question, one of those things he'd called "philosophical explorations." The old man had been able to hold forth endlessly on topics that had seemed pointless to his grandson. Only after he was gone had Josh realized how much he'd come to enjoy those continuous discourses.

He grabbed the brim of his hat and pulled it back to its normal position above his brow. Dodging a board in the walkway that had been warped at some point in the town's relatively short history by rain, snow, or heat, he started walking toward the big, two-story building that stood out both for its size and its slight list to one side.

A quick glance to his right made him smile rather cynically, the proximity to the marshal's office of the narrow, rather ramshackle building with the words ALEXANDER HALL, LAWYER in obviously newly repainted letters on the weather-beaten gray boards seemed a bit convenient. Marshal Pike had suggested Josh wait until the man returned to town and hire him for his defense at the trial, but at the time Josh had had little interest in defending himself.

That had been the conclusion he'd reached in those lonely weeks spent in the lower reaches of the mountains, surviving a month of unpredictable spring weather that had left him sweating and shivering by turns; he just wanted it to be over. He'd wanted this life he'd come to hate over, and letting the law do it for him had seemed like the easiest way.

Gramps would have seen his release as a sign, he thought as he continued to walk. He would have expounded at length on the portent of it all, that Josh had been given a second chance, that he'd reached a crossroads requiring some momentous decision. Josh smothered a rather wistful chuckle; Gramps would have embarked on another of his stories, the ones he called the Hawk legends, and somehow found a way to use it to impart some lesson he felt Josh needed to learn.

His amusement faded; he was sure Gramps would find him long beyond learning now. He'd come a long way from the fifteen-year-old boy Gramps had hugged with the last ounce of his fading strength. And all of it downhill. His grandfather had always said Hawks bred true. Josh doubted he'd say it if he could see his grandson now.

A woman came out of the mercantile just as he got there. He reached out instinctively and held the door for her; at least some of Gramps's stern instruction had taken root. She took a firmer grasp on her basket, filled with what appeared to be sugar, a crock of apple butter, a length of bright calico cloth, and, if he could trust his nose, cinnamon. Arly Dixon's death hadn't halted business for long, he thought. The woman looked up at him.

"Thank you," she began, then her words faded away as her eyes widened in recognition.

Josh stifled a sigh. "I don't bite, ma'am."

She smiled suddenly, lighting up warm brown eyes with an amused twinkle that made her look like a girl rather than a woman who'd seen more years than he had. "I shouldn't think you'd have to, Mr. Hawk."

Josh blinked. He'd been complimented by women on his looks before; something about his dark hair and blue eyes seemed to appeal to them. And for some, it was what he was, rather than his looks. There were women who liked, or so they said, the edge of danger he brought with him. But he'd become so used to women like this, respectable women, sniffing as he passed, assuming they didn't scurry to the other side of the street so that their skirts wouldn't have to brush over the same dirt he walked on, that this took him by surprise. Especially when she obviously knew who he was and, since she was coming out of this particular store, no doubt knew who he'd killed.

"Lovely morning, isn't it?"

Warily, he studied her for a moment, wondering if there really was a glint of teasing humor in her eyes, or if he was imagining it.

"Yes," he finally said; it seemed safe enough.

"Much nicer than I'd anticipated," she said, and this time there was no mistaking her meaning, or the jesting tone. Josh found himself smiling back in spite of himself.

"And longer than *I'd* anticipated," he agreed. He was oddly gratified when the woman's smile widened.

"I'm Deborah Taylor," she said. "I live down at the end of the street. Since my father died three years ago, I also provide what there is in the way of doctoring in this town, should you need it."

"Thank you, but I hope to avoid that," Josh said fervently.

Deborah chuckled. "I'd say you avoided a big piece of it this morning. Kate will be glad to see you alive and well. I assume that's why you're here?"

"Er . . . yes."

Kate. Short for the Kathleen they had called her during his rather abbreviated trial, he assumed. He'd almost forgotten that was her name; it had only been mentioned once; the rest of the time she'd been simply Arly's widow. His gaze flicked to the window of the store where, lettered by a slightly steadier hand than had done the lawyer's sign, were the words DIXON'S DRY GOODS—GROCERIES. He was still having trouble figuring this out, why the woman he'd made a widow would first save him from the hangman, and then be glad to see him as well. He looked back at Deborah.

"She'll be glad to see me?"

The woman nodded. "She was quite upset at the thought of them hanging you this morning."

At least someone was, he thought wryly. He hadn't cared much. "A lot more'll be sorry to miss it. A good hanging always brings people to town. And they spend money."

"Barbaric." Deborah sniffed. "And that business of sending invitations to executions . . . you'd think this land had seen enough of death without setting it up as a celebration."

Something dark and pained shadowed the woman's eyes, and Josh quickly decided not to point out to her that she was conversing quite easily with a man whose business was death. He knew she already knew that, but for some reason had chosen to ignore it.

"I do appreciate Marshal Pike's not inviting the whole territory," he said lightly, and the shadow vanished from the woman's eyes as if she'd long been used to burying the pain that had caused it.

"Caleb Pike is a good man," she said, as if that answered him. And perhaps it did, he thought. He nodded.

She glanced at the storefront. "I'll be on my way. Congratulations on your freedom, Mr. Hawk."

He thanked her, touched the brim of his hat, and watched her walk away, carefully skirting the leaky water trough in front of the store. Interesting woman, he thought as he turned and opened the door of the mercantile, to confront the widow who had bought him that freedom.

At first he thought the store was empty. It was quiet and cool. Morning sun spilled in from the front windows, but the light faded away into shadow as it reached the center of the long, narrow store. Two glass-and-wood display cases full of fancier items—tins of tobacco arrayed beside papers of pins and spools of thread and lengths of ribbon—sat parallel to the long walls. Equally full floor-to-roof shelves ran along all three walls.

A small doorway was set in the back wall beside shelves crammed with ready-made shoes and bolts of cloth, a wall he guessed was a good fifteen feet in from the actual back of the building. Over the door was a sign, rather grandly lettered OFFICE. Beneath that, in a more amateurish fashion, was ARLISS DIXON, PROPRIETER. Josh's mouth twisted wryly; he doubted anyone had ever pointed out the misspelling to the cantankerous Mr. Dixon. Especially if that shotgun he could just see the stock of protruding from under the counter had always been as handy as the marshal had said.

A sound from above made him tense, the creak of wood making him spin to his right. A ladder leaned against the shelves of groceries: Mason jars of fruits and vegetables, sacks of sugar, flour and salt, and a few cans of various sorts. At nearly the top of the ladder, reaching out to hang a large cooking pot on a peg fastened to one of the shelves, was a woman dressed in a faded black dress. Either it wasn't hers, or she'd thinned out some, Josh thought. It was too large for her slender frame, although from this angle, and bent over as she was, it outlined nicely the womanly curve of her hips.

"I'll be right with you," came a soft, feminine voice, one he'd heard before.

The widow. He felt a slight flush as he realized he'd been eyeing the woman whose husband he'd shot down less than a month ago. True, he'd been a long, long time without a woman, but that was no excuse for ogling her. Nor was the fact that that soft, sweet-sounding voice was balm to ears long used to the drunken growl of rough-edged men.

But somehow, as she finished hanging the pot, he couldn't make himself look away from the graceful sway of her movements as she began to come down the ladder. She reached the floor and turned to face him. And paled slightly. He was certain of that, because it was so noticeable beside the ugly bruise that marked her left cheek and jaw. It was beginning to yellow, and looked even nastier because of the fairness of her skin and her fragile-seeming features. She was tall, he'd noticed that before, but almost painfully thin; the Dixons, it seemed, didn't hold with eating their own inventory.

She wiped her hands nervously on the skirt of the faded black dress. A widow's dress, Joshua realized. Perhaps she'd had to borrow it, and that was why it fit her so ill. But the dress he'd seen her in the first time had fit no better, nor had it been any less faded. Arly Dixon apparently didn't believe in outfitting his wife from his stock, either.

"May I . . ." Her voice broke, and she swallowed, a visible movement of her slender throat, and tried again. "May I help you find something, Mr. . . . Hawk?"

"No."

She went a little paler at his abrupt answer, and Josh swore inwardly. He hadn't meant to alarm her, he truly hadn't. But now that he was face-to-face with her, he didn't quite know what to do. She was a woman, and a frightened one, because of him. In a quick movement that was a belated and purely habitual reaction to being in a lady's presence, he reached up and yanked off his hat. He ran his other hand over his hair, which was almost to his shoulders after a month in the mountains and even longer away from any town that had boasted of a real barber.

"You can tell me something, though," he said.

The fear that had seemed to abate at his hasty removal of his hat turned to wariness in her eyes. Rather striking, gold-brown eyes, almost the color of rich, thick honey straight from the comb. Amid the plainness of her other features, they stood out like some kind of gemstones.

"Tell you what?" she asked, wiping her hands on her skirt once more.

Josh glanced around, to be certain they were alone. When he looked back at her, the fear had returned, as if she, too, had just realized she was alone with a man whose reputation preceded him most places.

"Tell me," he said, figuring there was little to be gained by subtlety here, "why you lied for me."

# Chapter 2

Kate barely managed to keep from putting her hand up to her throat in the helpless kind of gesture she had so hated in her mother. Then self-disgust filled her as she remembered she had no right to hate anyone, for anything. But she'd had a lot of practice at hiding her feelings, and she needed every bit of it now, with the infamous man known as The Hawk standing here staring at her.

"I . . . don't know what you mean," she managed to get out.

Lord, he was tall, she thought. Even taller than Arly, who had been big enough. But where Arly had been burly, brawny, this man was lean and rangy, although she wasn't sure he lacked any of Arly's breadth in the shoulders. Shoulders she barely came up to, for all that she was a relatively tall woman. Tall enough to have borne years of teasing from male and female alike. Tall, plain, strange-eyed Kathleen Dayton. Who had become tall, plain, strange-eyed Kathleen Dixon.

"Truly, I don't know what you mean," she repeated when he just stood there, looking at her with those bright blue eyes that had mesmerized her into immobility the morning she'd first seen him.

She'd thought in that first moment that she'd never seen eyes so haunted, so shadowed, despite the vividness of their color. She'd been stunned when she'd learned who he was; she'd never pictured The Hawk like this—a tall, handsome man with eyes like that, and longish dark hair that brushed his solid shoulders. A man whose low, husky voice had seemed almost kind when he'd spoken to her so briefly that day when he'd picked up the dropped package of Arly's new, custom-made shirts just in from St. Louis.

She wiped her hands on the skirt of her worn black linsey dress; her palms weren't really sweating, but she felt as though they were.

"You don't need to be afraid of me, Mrs. Dixon. After all, I would hardly harm the woman who saved me from the noose, now would I?"

"You're The Hawk," she said simply. "Who knows what you would do?"

An odd expression came over his face, a combination of regret and resignation that made her feel something very strange, something that seemed almost like sympathy. She told herself she was being worse than foolish; The Hawk was a cold-blooded killer. What would he have to regret, and what would he want with her sympathy?

"Reputation," he muttered, "is a double-edged sword."

She blinked. His bitter tone matched her silly thoughts, and that startled her. "What?"

He hesitated, then shrugged as if it meant little. "Reputation," he repeated. "It keeps the more disagreeable folks out of your way, but it also makes decent people too nervous to be in the same room with you."

There were some, she knew, who would say he had no right to be in the same room with those decent people. And from his expression, she wasn't sure he wasn't one of those who thought that way. How very unexpected, she thought. Who would have ever thought a man like The Hawk would ever feel the loss of polite society? Or that he would look at himself with such feelings as doubt and distaste?

Her brow furrowed at her own thoughts. One had, she supposed, to have been used to some kind of polite society in order to miss it. Arly had cared little what the "decent people" in town thought of him. He had never held with "putting on airs," as he called any semblance of refinement or genteel behavior. His language and his manners had been as rough as he was. A far cry from the unexpectedly articulate and mannerly man before her.

"You needn't frown. I don't make a habit of intimidating or hurting women."

She looked at him for the long moment, then drew herself up with an effort. She searched inwardly for her lost nerve; no matter how refined he might seem compared to Arly or some of the local cowboys, he was still The Hawk, and it wouldn't do for him to know she was afraid.

If indeed that was true. She wasn't positive that she was afraid, which worried her. Surely she wasn't foolish enough to believe a good-looking facade couldn't hide an evil heart. And you didn't become a famous gunslinger like The Hawk without possessing the evilest of hearts, she was sure of that.

"Not intentionally, perhaps," she said.

He lifted a brow at her in apparent surprise, and one corner of his mouth lifted in what was almost an amused grin. She felt as if the breath had been knocked out of her; perhaps she *was* that foolish, she thought ruefully. But then again, perhaps not—that grin didn't reach his eyes; they were as shadowed as they had been that first time she'd seen him.

"I'm sorry if I've intimidated you," he said, that husky rumble even more evident as he spoke softly. It made her feel wary, like at the quiet before the storm. A second later she knew her instincts had been accurate. "But I still want the answer to my question. Why did you lie for me, Mrs. Dixon? After I killed your husband?"

She was steadier now, prepared, and answered evenly, "I didn't lie for you, Mr. Hawk."

He shook his head. "They looked all over that alley that night. The marshal, and that little bald man who came out of the saloon, the one Pike called 'Reverend.' That one even looked right behind that barrel where that boy says he found that old six-shooter."

"Reverend Babcock? Then I'm not surprised he didn't see it. His eyes aren't what they used to be, and he's always misplacing his spectacles. He's been known to tipple more than a bit, too."

He studied her for a moment, intently. She made herself hold his gaze. Then, slowly, he said, "That boy . . ."

She drew herself up even straighter. "Luke doesn't lie, Mr. Hawk. He may be an orphan, and a little wild, but he's a good boy. If he says he found it behind that barrel, then he did."

For some reason, either her defensive words or their vehemence, he smiled. She wasn't sure if he was pleased or was mocking her, and it didn't really matter which it was, not when he was having such an odd effect on her. Perhaps he'd been right, and she really was nervous just being in the same room with the notorious Hawk.

"Besides," she said quickly, filling a silence that was

rapidly making her very uncomfortable, "what you said at your trial was right. A man would have to be a fool to come after you without a weapon."

"Was your husband a fool, Mrs. Dixon?"

The soft—almost too soft—query warned her that she wasn't acting precisely as a bereaved widow should act. But she found it difficult; if she felt anything at Arly's death it was relief. Relief, and some uncertainty about her future. And she doubted that would come as a great surprise to most residents of Gambler's Notch. She searched for an answer that would satisfy him, but not tell him any more than he already knew. She settled on the truth, if not the truth he was after.

"Arly was just fool enough to try and sneak up on The Hawk in the dark."

He looked at her again, steadily, those bright blue eyes fixed on her with such intensity that she wondered what he could possibly be seeing.

"Odd way to speak of your late husband." His tone was mild, but Kate didn't miss the note of curiosity.

"I'll not lie about it, Mr. Hawk. My husband was not . . . the kindest of men."

She saw his gaze flick to her bruised cheek, and resisted the urge to cover it with her hand. Instead she held her head up, as if daring him to comment. She realized the foolishness of daring a man such as The Hawk as soon as she did it.

"He did that to you?"

"That is my concern, not yours."

"It's mine if he did it because I spoke to you. That's about two weeks old, judging by the color."

She felt heat flood her face as she realized how ugly she must look. On her best days she was nothing to buy a mirror for, as her father had been wont to say;

with this unsightly mark on her face, she must be truly uncomely.

"It's none of your affair, Mr. Hawk," she reiterated.

"Perhaps," he said, "but it makes me feel less guilty about killing a man I had no quarrel with, to know he was the kind of brute who would strike a woman."

Guilty? He felt guilty? The thought that The Hawk could feel such a thing astonished her. But she didn't dare linger on the revelation. Warning bells were clanging in her mind. She had to put a halt to this; he was treading too close to dangerous ground. She walked around the foot of the ladder, only stopping to turn and face him again when the solid bulk of the counter was between them.

"I don't care to speak any more of my husband, if you don't mind. Was there something else?" she asked in her politest merchant's tone.

He didn't answer for a moment, and Kate held her breath, wondering if he was going to accept her obvious change of subject. And her explanation. It would be very ill-mannered of him to call her a liar. Other than Arly, she'd become used to being treated with at least some amount of respect by the decent men of Gambler's Notch. But she wouldn't have expected the same of the man known as The Hawk. A killer for hire hardly fell into the category she would label decent men.

At last he spoke, and Kate gave an inward sigh of relief at his words.

"Only my thanks, Mrs. Dixon. Not many men would have done what you did. And most women would have let me hang and been glad to see it done."

"One death was enough. I had no wish to see more."

He didn't say what she suspected he was thinking, that it was indeed very strange that she didn't wish to see the killer of her husband punished, regardless of the circumstances. Instead he glanced around the store.

"What will you do now?"

That, she thought, was the very question she'd been tussling with since Arly's death.

"I will run the store," she stated firmly, as if saying the words for the first time out loud could make them true.

"By yourself? A woman?"

She quivered inside, then ordered herself sternly to stop. She would have to become used to such reactions. She knew that the idea of a woman alone running a business like this would cause consternation. At least until people got used to the idea.

"Of course," she said, proud that she sounded, to her ears at least, confident and composed. "I've done so often, when Arly was gone."

And frequently when he was here, she added to herself, remembering all the times when he'd been too unwell from a long night of drinking to open up the mercantile in the morning. All the times when she had borne the brunt of his drunken ill-humor, and worn the marks of it for days afterward. Just as she was wearing one now.

But no more. Never again. This was the last bruise she would ever watch people stare at, the last time she would count the days until the last of the mottled colors faded away, before the ache subsided so that she could move freely again. Never again would she have to cower in fear, wondering if this was one of the times when the blows would be followed by something even worse.

And all because of this man.

An emotion that she could not deny was joy welled

up inside her, but she knew she didn't dare let it show. She tamped it down, and said the words again, just to hear them.

"I will run the store."

Something flickered in his eyes, something Kate thought for one silly moment might have been admiration.

"I believe perhaps you will," he said. He put his hat back on, and touched the brim in what was nothing less than a salute. "My thanks again, Mrs. Dixon."

She didn't know what to say to that, so she merely nodded. And watched intently as he turned and strode out of the store, moving with a lithe grace that brought home to her what a ponderous man Arly had been. She stepped out from behind the counter into the center of the store, her gaze still fastened on that tall, black-clad figure as he crossed the street, headed for the livery stable.

This must be what that book about Shakespeare's plays had called irony, she thought. She'd spent a long time studying that book, trying to work out the difficult words and more difficult meanings, hoping someday to be able to read the plays themselves. She'd had to sneak it at night, when Arly was snoring noisily; he hated her wasting time reading, especially about silly things written by a man long dead in a foreign country.

But this had to be it, that irony she'd tried so hard to understand. Irony, that a man like Arly, a man most would call a decent, law-abiding, solid citizen, had been a lumbering, clumsy oaf who ran to fat and jowli-ness; while a man most people feared, a man consid-ered a heartless killer, a man who stayed in one place no longer than it took to kill whatever hapless soul was his target, looked like an angel come down straight from heaven.

More likely cast out from heaven, Kate amended silently. Lucifer, the fallen angel, perhaps, shunned by the righteous and fit only to reside in hell.

She nearly laughed aloud. A fallen angel with the grace and manners of a gentleman. She wondered if she'd perhaps gone a little touched in the head after Arly's death, thinking such fanciful thoughts.

Or perhaps it was simply the realization that for the first time in her life, she was free. There was no one to tell her what to do, no one to answer to, no meaty fists to dodge, no ugly, evil nights to dread. She was free.

She twirled around, her arms outstretched. A tiny giggle threatened to escape her. She clapped a hand over her mouth to stop it. Then she remembered she didn't have to, and let it out. It became a laugh, and she spun faster, feeling every uneven spot in the crude wood floor through her worn kid slippers, but not caring.

She was free.

She was free, and nothing could mar this joyous feeling. Nothing.

Except the memory of a man's eyes, and the words he'd so unexpectedly spoken. *It makes me feel less guilty about killing a man I had no quarrel with.*

She stopped spinning, swaying a little as she came to a halt. "Who would have thought it," she whispered to herself. The Hawk feeling guilty. How was it possible? He'd killed so many. A dozen, if Luke's excited, nearly worshipful stories were to be believed.

She stood there for a long moment, pensive, pondering . . . and just a little bit vexed at the pall that had been cast over her exultation.

Josh smiled in satisfaction as he slipped his poke into the pocket of his black frock coat and stood up from the table.

"Gentleman, thanks for the game," he said to the other three poker players, who looked just as happy to see him go. He'd stopped with the last hand because he'd seen a couple of the losers were on the edge of becoming testy about it, and he didn't want to push them over that edge. He'd taken some of their money, but not a lot, not enough for them to complain.

It had taken longer than usual, nearly two days, since he'd been playing very conservatively in order to not draw any more attention than he already had in this town. He'd intentionally spread his winnings out over as many different players as possible, and not many townspeople, but men from the surrounding territory who were passing through and stopped to wet their throats. And he'd never won or lost big enough to cause any dissension. Occasionally, a player would begrudge his withdrawing from the game a winner, but they seemed to quickly remember who they were dealing with and withdraw the objection; he knew they were thinking that the paltry few dollars he was walking away with weren't worth dying for.

But now he had enough for his immediate needs. Enough to pay for his own room at the rather rickety building called—facetiously, he had to assume—the Grand Hotel, a room given to him, he was sure, on the strength of his reputation alone. The clerk had been far too afraid to ask for the usual payment in advance. And he had enough now for Buck's keep, and the reshoeing the smithy had done for him. Rankin seemed a good man, and Josh was glad he'd be able to pay him.

And he'd have enough left to lay in a few supplies. Enough to get him on his way out of Gambler's Notch, a place he wouldn't be sorry to see the last of. Maybe even enough to keep him going for a while, until he decided what to do with the rest of the life he'd had handed back to him. Next to that chore, winning enough of a stake to move on seemed easy. It would take one of Gramps's allegories to show him the way. Or maybe that magical book he'd talked about, the one that was supposed to guide the Hawks, because this Hawk had certainly lost his way a long time ago. Probably the first time he'd taken a man's money for the use of his Colt.

With a final nod to the men who were already dealing the next game, he walked out of the dingy, dark building that served as a saloon. Someday, he thought, he'd like to see a building with real windows again, windows on all sides, to let in the light. He got mightily tired of the dimness of most of the places in the kind of town he frequented.

The afternoon sun sent the shadows of the buildings streaking from west to east across the wide dirt street. Soon it would drop behind the Rockies and be gone, but the warmth of the day would linger; in a few weeks spring would give way to the territory's short, hot summer on the high plains at the foot of the mountains. Still, he felt the coolness as he stepped into one of the shadows. A tall one, and he knew without looking— he'd been working hard at not looking—that it was the shadow of the mercantile.

He'd learned a lot in the past three days. Mostly from Luke, the slightly wild kid who lived, at the grace of Art Rankin, in the loft over the livery stable. The kid who'd found that battered old Dragoon Colt behind the rain barrel, and who had been more than willing to tell his story again, especially to the famous man he boasted of saving from the hangman.

Josh no longer doubted that Luke had indeed found the weapon exactly where he said he had. He supposed it was possible Dixon could have had it in his hand and he hadn't seen it. And he supposed in the aftermath of firing his own weapon, with the Peacemaker's loud report, it was possible he might have missed hearing Arly's weapon hit the back wall of the saloon and slide behind the water barrel. Possible, but not probable. His life depended on not missing details like that. True, he hadn't been expecting an attack—no more so than he always was, anyway—but the likelihood of him not seeing the Dragoon in Dixon's hand, not seeing it go flying when he was hit, and not hearing it land wasn't very high.

But Luke had found it there.

And Mrs. Dixon swore she hadn't lied for him. He believed her; when she'd stared up at him and said it, he'd known she was telling the truth. And Lord knew she had no reason to lie, not for his sake. No matter what kind of man Arly Dixon had been, life was hard for a woman out here without a husband.

"Mr. Hawk!"

He turned his head to see Luke running toward him. The boy had taken to following him around, and although he recognized the signs of incipient hero worship, Josh hadn't had the heart to send the boy away.

"You headed for the stable?"

Josh nodded. "I owe Mr. Rankin some money."

"Aw, he don't care if you're late, s'long as you pay him. He's a nice man."

"Yes, he is."

"I like your horse. He's a real good 'un, isn't he?"

"He's got enough bottom for any man," Josh agreed. "Thought I'd give him a little attention this afternoon. Think you could round me up a brush, maybe a currycomb?"

"You bet!" Luke yelped and headed off at a run. By

the time Josh reached the stable, the boy was already haltering Buck in the big corral.

He found Rankin, a man who had a strength in his powerful chest and shoulders that belied his short stature, out back at the forge, working on a pair of metal hinges. Josh paid what he owed for the work and Buck's board, plus another day in advance. The quiet man took the money and his thanks with a nod and nothing more; he was a man of less than few words, Josh had discovered.

He walked over to where Luke had tied the big buckskin up to a post at the side of the barn. The horse craned around to look at him, and whickered softly.

"Hey, you old sugar eater," Josh said, grinning as he did so; Buck was a long way from a pampered animal. He was tough, strong, fast, and loyal, and a man couldn't ask for more than that from a horse. He patted the golden-brown neck; then rubbed up under the shaggy black mane. Buck whickered again.

Josh shrugged off his coat and pulled off his string tie. Luke was there in an instant to take them and lay them carefully over the fence railing. Josh smothered a grin, rolled up his shirt sleeves, and picked up the currycomb Luke had found for him. He began to run it over the golden-brown coat, thinking rather inanely that it was nearly the same color as Mrs. Dixon's unusual eyes. Shaking off that foolish thought, he worked his way down to the buckskin's muscled rump. He didn't speak, teasingly curious about how long the voluble Luke could stay quiet. Not long, he soon found out.

"You're not leavin', are you?"

"Not today," Josh answered.

Seemingly relieved by this, the boy chattered on for a while. Josh only half listened as he curried the horse, at least until Luke started in about the widow.

"I don't see why a lady can't run a store, do you? Miss Kate's a lot smarter than old Arly was. She was usually the one workin' in there anyway. An' she's real good with numbers; does all kinds of addin' in her head."

"Did someone say she couldn't?"

"Aw, just ol' Reverend Babcock. He's always goin' on, telling people what they should or shouldn't do."

"I think that's what a reverend does."

"Well, he does it too much, if you ask me. He shouldn't be botherin' Miss Kate, not with her husband just dead and all."

Josh went very still for a moment, but Luke didn't seem to find anything odd in bemoaning the widow's state to the man who had put her in that circumstance. When the boy didn't go on, Josh resumed his task.

"Is he . . . bothering her?"

Luke shrugged. "Nah, not really. Just talking big words at her, like he does."

"Big words?"

"Yeah. Tellin' her the town's givin' her some time, because of her recent beriv . . . beave . . ."

"Bereavement?"

"Yep, that's it. But that it wasn't proper work for a lady to be in business. Old goat."

Josh managed not to laugh at Luke's sniffingly disdainful assessment, but he couldn't stop his grin.

"She told 'em to go do their business elsewhere," Luke said as he handed Josh a brush to take to the buckskin's legs. Josh smiled at the pride in his young voice; obviously the liking between the two was mutual. "Said she'd either run the place or sell every bit of stock and close it up forever, and they could go all the way to Rock Springs for their coffee and tobacco. That hobbled their lips right quick."

"Sounds like a determined woman."

"She's got more sand than most of the men around here," Luke said.

"Most women do," Josh said softly, fighting off another host of memories he tried to keep locked away. They'd been harassing him a lot of late, and he didn't know why. He supposed it had something to do with nearly meeting his maker—and having to account for his no-account life.

"She had a tough time with ol' Arly. He was a mean one. Really mean."

Josh stopped moving again, the brush poised for a moment over the black points on the buckskin's legs. Then he straightened up. "How mean? Did he hit her?"

Luke dodged the question. "Mr. Rankin says he don't hold with men hitting women."

"He's right. It's a cowardly thing to do."

Luke nodded. "That's what he says."

"He may not talk much," Josh said, willing to let the boy avoid a direct answer for the moment, "but he's a man to listen to when he does."

"He looks out for me, since my folks died."

"How long has that been?"

"I've been here since I was eight, an' I'm twelve now." He shrugged his thin shoulders. "My folks died of the cholera."

The boy had been alone since he was eight? Josh didn't know what made him say it, but before he could stop them, the words were out. "My grandfather died of it, too."

Luke looked up quickly. "Really?"

Josh nodded. "He was the only family I had left."

Luke's eyes widened. "You're an orphan, too?"

Josh drew back a little. "I never thought about it like that, but I guess you're right."

"Guess we're kind of alike, then, huh?"

The boy was looking at him so hopefully Josh nearly smiled. "Guess we are."

Luke smiled, and Josh instinctively reached out and ruffled the boy's hair. Then he nearly laughed at himself. He'd hated that when Gramps did it, and here he was doing it in turn.

Josh went back to brushing Buck's legs. He still wanted his answer, but he didn't want to push the boy. He cleaned out the buckskin's hooves, then straightened up again. Luke was staring across the street at the mercantile. The boy seemed to sense his gaze, and looked back at him. He seemed about to speak, then hesitated. Josh said nothing, figuring silence would encourage the boy as much as anything.

Gramps had known that, had known how hard it had been for him at this same age, to talk about the ugly things. He'd made it clear he was listening, then left Josh alone to talk or not as he wished. In the end, he'd always talked; it had been too much to hold in.

"She tried to run away once, a couple of years ago," Luke finally said. "He caught her. Nobody saw her for a couple of weeks after that. Talk was they thought he'd killed her."

Something in the boy's tone caught Josh's full attention. He saw it in Luke's face, too. He might not have recognized it had he not been wrestling with it himself recently. Guilt.

"But he didn't," Josh prompted gently.

"No. He just beat her real bad. She could hardly move. Miss Deborah, she went in there and faced ol' Arly down, made him bring Miss Kate to her place so's she could nurse her."

He didn't doubt that, having met the redoubtable

Miss Taylor. But that didn't explain Luke's unmistakable look of self-reproach. "What else, Luke?"

The boy's towhead ducked, and when he finally spoke, Josh had to strain to hear.

"I . . . tried to help her. Got her a horse and hid it out back. She was always nice to me, let me come in the store when it was rainin', snuck me hard candy now and then. She even gave me a pair of shoes one winter, said they were damaged and couldn't be sold, but I couldn't see nothin' wrong with 'em."

"And Dixon found out you helped her?" Another nod. "What happened?" Silence met his query. "Luke?"

The boy stole a glance at him. "He whupped me but good. Knocked out two of my teeth, but Miss Deborah said it was okay, they weren't my real teeth yet. Ol' Arly told me if I ever tried anything like that again, he'd kill me."

The lingering guilt Josh was feeling about having killed the man was rapidly fading. A man who would not only beat a woman nigh unto death, but also a child who couldn't have been more than ten at the time, deserved killing. But there was something he still didn't understand.

"Why do you feel guilty about trying to help her?"

"Not that," the boy said quickly. "It's just that . . . he hit her more, because of it."

"What do you mean?"

"He told me that because of me, he was going to make her sorrier than she'd ever been in her life."

Josh's stomach knotted. The world was indeed a twisted, out-of-kilter place when men like Arliss Dixon flourished and boys like Luke carried burdens far too heavy for their young shoulders.

"Luke, it wasn't your fault. He would have done it anyway, if he was that kind of man."

Luke looked at him with wide brown eyes far too old for his young face. "That's what she said. Miss Kate. Later, when she got well. I was afraid she'd hate me, but she just kept telling me it wasn't my fault. And thanked me for trying."

Josh took in a deep breath. Sand, he thought, was not enough word for Kate Dixon. She might be plain, but she was a survivor. A survivor with grit, who could sum up what had apparently been a brutally painful life with mild words.

*My husband was not the kindest of men.*

*It is not the kindest of times.*

His mother's voice, just as soft, just as gentle, and so long forgotten echoed in his mind. No, not forgotten. Suppressed, forced into that darkest corner of his mind, where he kept the memories that were too painful to look at. Or in this case, too painful to hear.

"Mr. Hawk? Are you all right?"

Josh exhaled, long and slow. "Yes," he lied. "I'm fine."

*Except that my family would be ashamed of me and I should have died this morning, and I don't know what the hell it all means.*

# Chapter 3

"There a barber in this town?"

Art Rankin rubbed a hand over his own unshaven chin. "Was. You killed him."

Josh blinked. "Dixon was the barber?"

"Close as we had. Cut hair okay, but not many trusted him with a razor. Arly was kind of surly."

"So I've heard." He gave the blacksmith a considering look. "Nobody seems to miss him much."

Rankin shrugged. "Most towns I've been in, general store's a friendly sort of place. Not Arly's. 'Buy something or get out,' that was his slogan."

Josh ran a hand through the tangled length of his hair. It had been longer, but not often. "Guess I'll do without a haircut before I pull out, then."

"You're pulling out?"

"In the morning."

"You're in a hurryin' mood."

Josh looked at the man. "What's that mean?"

"Nothing."

"You don't have any slack in your jaw, Art. When you say something, you mean to. What is it?"

"After you sayin' at your trial you was sorry about the widow, figured you'd want to stick around and see she was going to be all right."

Josh glanced over to the far side of the barn, where Luke was industriously cleaning his saddle, despite his protests that it wasn't necessary. The boy was far enough away, and so intent on his job, that Josh didn't think he could hear. He looked back at Rankin.

"Some reason you think she might not be?"

"Just thinking there might be some of Arly's suppliers not eager to do business with her, once they hear Arly's dead."

Rankin didn't say it—he wouldn't spend that many words—but he didn't have to; the implication was clear. If those suppliers refused to deal with her because her husband was dead and she was a woman alone, it was his fault. She could wind up losing everything and it would be his fault.

*Don't be a fool, Hawk. You've made widows before, and never felt responsible. And Dixon had asked for it as much as those other men.*

"I'm a gunfighter, not a nursemaid."

"Woulda been a dead one, 'cept for her."

"Right," he muttered, still not certain that was something to be thankful for. But Rankin had put his finger on the problem; Josh had made widows before, but none of them had ever saved his life in return. And that was a debt that needed repaying, one he wasn't at all sure he could ride away from.

But he was damn well going to try. He slung his coat over his shoulder. Rankin said no more, but then Josh guessed he figured he'd said all that needed saying.

"I'll be over for my horse first thing," he said determinedly. Rankin only nodded, as if he'd never expected anything else. For some reason that irritated Josh, and he turned on his boot heel and strode out of the barn.

By the time he reached his room at the hotel, he was thoroughly disgruntled. He didn't like this feeling. In fact, he resented it. Arly Dixon had brought this on himself, and he'd evidently done the town a favor by ridding them of a surly, razor-wielding woman and child beater. And then he'd escaped a date with the hangman. He should ride out of here first thing in the morning feeling satisfied. And damn lucky besides.

He yawned, then blinked, startled, wondering where this abrupt feeling of weariness had come from. He'd been so irritated he would have thought it would carry him through the night until he rode out.

And he *would* ride out of here feeling satisfied and lucky, he told himself. He shut the door behind him and locked it out of habit, as he tried to fight off the odd lethargy. In fact, he thought, he'd pack his things tonight, so he could save time tomorrow.

He yawned again. The way he was suddenly feeling, maybe he'd wait until morning to pack. Then he shook his head, trying to clear it of this strange fogginess. No, he thought determinedly, he'd pack tonight.

He walked over to the table that held the chipped chamber set, where he had laid his saddlebags. He'd pack now, then roll out at first light, slide on his clothes and boots, and be out of Gambler's Notch for good by full sunup. He picked up the bags. He took a step toward the dresser where he'd put the two shirts he'd just had washed at the town bath house and laundry. Then he stopped dead.

He looked down at the leather bags in his hand. Unlike his gunbelt, the bags were intricately carved, with a design featuring a hawk on the wing, a design custom ordered by his grandfather to represent the family name. Gramps had given them to Josh on his fifteenth birthday, presenting them with great ceremony and a retelling of the original Hawk legend, the mythical one about Jenna, the Hawk who long ago had saved the life of an unusual man and won unending life for the Hawk name.

Josh had carried the bags for ten years now. They were worn, stained, gouged, but still sturdy, and Josh knew every mark on them. And even as groggy as he was, he also knew exactly how much they weighed empty, which these were. Or were supposed to be. And they didn't weigh this much.

Adrenaline kicked through him, pushing away the fuzziness. He hefted the bags, testing the weight, acknowledging both that he'd been right, they were no longer empty, and that the unexpected weight was in the bag with the bullet scar on it, picked up in that fight up in the Montana Territory last year. Only Buck's speed had gotten him out of that canyon ambush alive, and only the fact that the big horse was the best rimrocker he'd ever seen had kept him from plunging back to the bottom in the process.

He looked at the scarred bag for a long moment. A memory flitted through his mind, of a man with a young lady's three brothers on his tail, a canvas sack, and a very angry rattlesnake. He lifted the leather bags, gave them a shake, listened, then grinned at himself.

"You're suspicioning all kinds of things here, aren't you?" he said aloud.

Still, he set the bags carefully down on the bed and drew his Colt out of the holster before he pulled back the flap with the scar.

Nothing happened. He holstered the Colt. He reached out to tilt the bag up so he could see what was inside.

A book.

He nearly laughed at the image of himself almost

shooting the thing, but his amusement didn't last; this book wasn't his, so someone had been in here. Locking hotel room doors and windows when he left was a habit he'd gotten into early, to save himself any surprises upon his return; careless gunfighters didn't last long.

But this door had been intact, with no sign of being pried or forced open. And there was no window in this room. He'd asked for it that way, although the desk man had expected he would want one of the better— and more expensive—rooms. But no windows meant one less way for anyone to get in.

That left only the door.

He walked over to check the door again, and found nothing amiss. He unlocked the door and opened it, checking the outer surface and the knob; it looked perfectly normal. He stood there for a moment, thinking.

The man at the desk had told him there was only one other guest at the moment, a whiskey drummer who'd be leaving in the morning now that he'd finished his business with Hugh Markum, the owner of the saloon. He'd seen the drummer in the saloon when he'd been building his stake—he was a dandified, mild-seeming man who wore spectacles and a bowler hat, and didn't seem at all the type to risk breaking into The Hawk's room, nor to have the knowledge to do it without leaving a sign.

He closed the door again, and locked it. As he always did. As he knew he'd done this morning, before he'd headed over to Markum's saloon in hopes of adding to his stake.

If not the drummer, he thought as he walked back across the small room, who? The young man at the desk? Meeker, the name was, Josh recalled, and it seemed appropriate. Josh remembered how he'd been rambling on about his father owning this place as Josh had checked in. He hadn't paid much attention; he was used to people chattering at him, nervous in the presence of The Hawk's reputation if not the man himself. Meeker would have a key, but he didn't seem the type either.

Josh paused beside the bed, thinking as he looked down at the bags, at the hand-carved work that, despite the intricacy of the hawk design, was as familiar as the weight of the Colt in his hand.

He supposed the father could be suspect, but he thought he remembered hearing that the man was an invalid confined to a wheeled chair in his room in the front corner of the hotel. That greatly lessened the chance that he was involved in this. Whatever this was. He couldn't explain that, and he didn't like things he couldn't explain.

And that was the real crux of the whole thing. He could think of no reason why any of them, or for that matter, why anyone at all, would go to all that trouble to slip a book into his saddlebags.

A book.

A chill swept through him, unlike anything he'd ever felt before.

A *book*.

How many times had Gramps told him the story? How many times had he listened, first, as a little boy, rapt with childish wonder; then, as he got older, with the patronizing patience youth showed to age? How many times had he wished Gramps would find something else to talk about besides wild stories of previous Hawks Josh cared little about? The last of the Hawks he'd ever cared about, except for his grandfather, had been dead since he was eleven.

He stared at the book, telling himself it was impossible. It was a story, a legend with no more truth than the incredible yarns cowboys told around a campfire. There was no such thing as magic, so there was no such thing as a magical book that appeared to every Hawk who was the last of the line.

Like him.

The book. The magical book of Hawk legend. The book that Gramps had mentioned practically with his dying breath, saying that Josh would find it when the time was right. He'd muttered something about Josh being the last Hawk now, had told him to do the Hawks proud, and with a final, feeble squeeze of his fingers around his grandson's hand, had died.

Josh swallowed tightly. He hadn't thought of Gramps's death in a long time, hadn't let himself. He'd let the man down so badly, it hurt too much to ponder what his grandfather would think of what he'd become.

And he couldn't think of it now.

Shoving the painful thoughts away, he reached once more for the bags. He lifted them and shook the book out onto the bed. He stared at it for a moment.

He hadn't seen anything like it in a very long time. He had a faint memory of books like this, elegant books, in the library of the big house back in Missouri, the big house that had once been his home. His father's library, where Josh had often retreated when he wanted to get away from the constant teasing of his older sisters.

He jerked his thoughts out of that painful scene as well, and tried to concentrate on the book before him now. The book that couldn't be here, but was.

It appeared to be an ordinary book, although it looked very old. It was beautiful, like those books he remembered and like them, bound in heavy leather. He wondered what the leather had been dyed with; the color was deep, rich, and dark blue. He cocked his head to one side, to see the edge of the book. The pages looked thick and heavy, and were gilt edged, shining in the lamplight. Oddly, there was no sign of a title, or an author on the cover or the spine.

After a moment longer spent staring at it, he at last reached out to pick it up. And immediately nearly dropped it again.

It was . . . warm. No, warm wasn't right. It wasn't really any warmer to the touch than anything else in the room, including the saddlebags, but somehow, holding it, *he* felt warmer. And he couldn't explain the strange sense of peace that seemed to have overtaken him. Peace was a state he'd had little experience with since he'd been eight and war had become the focus of his young life. But he couldn't deny this sensation was pleasant, this gentle warmth, this feeling that perhaps he wasn't as alone as he sometimes felt, that perhaps Gramps would even forgive what he'd done with his life. . . .

He did drop the book then. Hastily, as he wondered what in hell had ever made him think something as stupid as that. His grandfather had been a gentleman, a man of learning, and above all a man of peace. It had nearly destroyed him to watch his family splinter and die in a war that had pitted one son against another. But each of his sons had believed in his cause, and he'd often told Josh that was the only thing worth fighting—and dying—for.

To even imagine that he would ever condone killing for money was pure foolishness, and Josh knew it. What he didn't know was where the crazy idea had come from. For a moment it had seemed almost as if it had been generated by the book.

"And that's plumb loco, Hawk," he muttered as he

stared at the volume that lay on the worn, faded quilt on the iron bedstead.

Still, it took him a moment before he could reach down and flip open the leather cover. The pages were, as he'd thought, of heavyweight paper, even heavier than the books he remembered. Paper that was made stiffer by the bright gilt of the edges. The inside of the cover was lined with an even heavier paper that also made up the first page, a paper marbled with an unusual design in shades of blue that blended with the color of the cover.

He blinked as he looked at it, at the design that seemed to change as he watched it, seemed to flow and fluctuate, until he almost thought he was seeing something more than a random design, thought he was seeing images there, shadowy figures of people, seeming to move even as he looked. Quickly, he looked away. He felt an odd lightheadedness, shook his head sharply, and when he looked again the pattern had settled down into a merely intriguing flow of lines and ripples.

"I'd swear I've been drinking some of Markum's worst rotgut," he said to the empty room.

The book lay harmlessly on the bed, open to that design that now looked like nothing more than a colored paper version of kerosene mixed with water. Josh shook his head, then sat down on the edge of the bed next to the book.

After a moment, he reached out and turned the heavy inner page over, to be confronted only with a blank sheet of the heavy, gilt-edged paper. He turned it as well, looking for the title page. Or what should have been the title page. Instead he found a picture of a couple dressed oddly in clothing that for some reason made him think of the tales his mother had read to him of a faraway land with misty forests, castles, and high stone walls.

He stared at the picture. A daguerreotype, he thought, or one of those photographs he'd heard about, done with some new kind of glass plate. He supposed if they could do that, they could put the results in a book. Then the details of the picture began to register. The man had long, dark hair and a strong face marked with a thin but very visible scar that ran from his right temple down to his jaw. The woman had even longer, but lighter hair, a wealth of it, and eyes that he instinctively knew, despite the fact that he couldn't know it from this picture, were blue. Vivid blue.

It made no sense, this certainty about the eyes of a woman who was a stranger to him. He stared at the picture, only now realizing that it was a drawing, a drawing so finely done and so incredibly detailed that it seemed impossible that it had been done by human hands.

He shook his head again. Had he seen this before? Was this some kind of drawing for a painting he'd once seen, perhaps with Gramps, who had always had a fondness Josh had never understood for paintings, statues, and the like. Was that why he was so sure this woman's eyes were blue?

Impatiently he shifted his gaze to the man beside her, who appeared to be at least a foot taller than her, with shoulders to match his height, and a look in his eyes that didn't bode well for whoever had given him that scar on his face. The fierce, predatory look of the man was softened slightly by the protective curving of his arm around the woman at his side, but that only heightened the overall effect—this was a man who would fight to the death to defend what was his.

And she was his, Josh thought as he studied the pair.

No doubt about that. Both their postures declared it. He vaguely noticed the length and sheen of the woman's hair—red, perhaps?—and the shape of the slender body beneath the layers of some kind of flowing gown, but again he couldn't look away from her eyes. Wide and bright beneath arched brows, they were fringed with thick, soft lashes, and looked strangely familiar. It was like looking once again at something that had been seen so often it didn't register anymore.

It hit him then. It was like looking into a mirror, or the unruffled surface of a pond. And seeing his own eyes look back at him.

He leapt to his feet, as if the book had burned him. He stared down at it once more, swallowing tightly. He didn't know how long he'd been standing there when a sharp knock on his door startled him out of his seeming trance.

"Mr. Hawk?"

Luke's voice, muffled as he stood out in the narrow hall, completed the job of yanking him back to normality. Josh walked over to the door.

"You alone, Luke?"

" 'Course I am. Who'd be with me?"

Who indeed? Josh thought. Maybe whoever—or whatever—had sneaked this book into his room. And maybe, he thought wryly as he opened the door, you'd better ask if that beef Markum's been cooking up had been chewing on locoweed.

"I finished your saddle, Mr. Hawk," Luke said as he came in. "It looks good as new. Better, even."

"You didn't have to do that," he said again as he closed the door behind the boy.

"But I wanted to," Luke said earnestly. And shook his head fiercely when Josh offered him two bits. "I didn't do it for money."

Pride, Josh thought. A boy's pride, the hardest to hang on to, and the easiest to hurt.

"I know you didn't. But an honest man pays for work done." Even, he thought ruefully, when he can't really afford it; his stake was dwindling fast.

The boy hesitated, pride clearly battling with the desire for money he probably rarely had, even in these small amounts. "But you haven't even seen it," he said.

"You said you did a good job. I know you wouldn't lie to me, Luke."

"No, sir, I surely wouldn't."

"Then take what you've earned."

Another second's hesitation, then the boy grabbed the money and stuffed it into his pocket, as if afraid his benefactor would change his mind.

"And," Josh added, "you can stop calling me Mr. Hawk. Josh will do."

Luke stared at him. Slowly, a wide smile spread across the boy's face, as if Josh had given him some kind of medal.

"Yes, sir, Mr.—Josh."

Wide-eyed, he looked around the room, as if he expected it to be different somehow, because of who was in it. He spotted the book, and with the instant curiosity of the young, went over to look.

"Golly, I ain't never seen a book like this before," he exclaimed.

"I'm not sure I have, either," Josh said dryly.

"Who are they?" Luke asked, pointing at the picture with a grubby finger that still bore signs of his work cleaning the saddle.

"I'm not sure," Josh admitted.

Luke gave him a sideways look. "Can't read, huh?" The boy shrugged. "Neither can Mr. Rankin. Neither could I, but Miss Kate, she's been teachin' me. She says she don't read so good herself, and it helps her. So it's like I'm doing her a favor, see?"

Pride, Josh thought again. "I see."

"Bet she'd help you, too, if you asked her nice."

Josh doubted that, but didn't see any reason to disillusion the boy. "Actually, I can read." He gestured at the book. "I just haven't read that yet."

"Oh." Luke sat cross-legged on the bed and turned his attention back to the picture. "That's some tough-lookin' hombre."

"I wouldn't want to face him down," Josh agreed.

"She's pretty." The boy's blond brows came together. He glanced at Josh again, then back at the picture, then back at Josh. "She has your eyes," he said.

Damn, Josh thought. Even this kid saw it. His jaw tightened, and he watched silently as Luke reached out and turned another page in the book. The boy's brows lowered again as he stared at the next page.

"I ain't never seen writin' like this, either, all fancy and curvy like that."

He was the picture of concentration as he stared at the writing. Josh could see from here that it was just what Luke had said, fancy and curvy. And it didn't look like it had come off a printing press. It looked done by hand, although he couldn't conceive of anyone having the patience to do an entire book like that.

"Je . . . Jen . . . a. Jenna? Is that a word?" Luke asked as he hunched over the book, But before Josh could speak, Luke yelped. "Hawk! It says Hawk, right here!"

Josh forgot to breathe for a moment as the boy's exclamation confirmed his earlier crazy notion.

"Look, Mr. Ha— Josh!" Luke leapt to his feet, holding the book, turning it so Josh could see. "It's a name, isn't it? Jenna Hawk. She's some kin of yours, isn't she? That's why her eyes are like yours."

Josh wondered what the boy would say if he told him yes. If he told him that, if the legends were true, that the woman in that picture was indeed kin to him. An ancestor who had lived so long ago no one was really sure when. Or where.

And he wondered what Luke would say if he told him he was holding a piece of magic.

*Damn, you sound like you're believing this,* he thought as he stared at the boy, who was intently studying the book. He shook his head. This was crazy. It was one thing to hear about something all your life in fanciful stories you believed as a child, then realize couldn't possibly be true, no matter how sincerely your grandfather seemed to believe in them. It was quite another to be standing looking at the proof those legends hadn't been fanciful at all.

It couldn't be. And yet the book was here. It had appeared, just as Gramps had said it would.

And it had nearly been too damn late, he thought wryly. By all rights and reasons, he should be two days dead by now. The book was supposed to come to the last Hawk, Gramps had said, to help him find his way. He grimaced inwardly; if things had gone as scheduled, the only path that book would have been able to help him on was the path to hell, and he'd already gone halfway there himself. Maybe further.

*You really are loco,* he told himself. Believing in such things as wizardry and disappearing books. At least he assumed it disappeared just as it appeared, without a trace of evidence as to how.

The logical assumption was that someone had somehow gotten into his room and placed the book in his bag. But the evidence of his eyes was indisputable; no one had broken in. He would question the desk man, the whiskey drummer, and even the invalid owner of the hotel, but he knew with that gut-level instinct he'd learned not to question that they'd say they had nothing to do with it. And the final conclusion still remained; they would have no reason to have done it, or to lie about it.

Unless, he supposed, one of them had found the book, seen the Hawk name in it, assumed it was his and returned it. He supposed not many would have the nerve to keep something they thought was The Hawk's. This was a comforting thought—except for the still remaining problem about where the book had come from in the first place.

"This is a good story!" Luke exclaimed, jerking Josh out of his fruitless speculation. "Is there really a place like this?"

He walked over to the boy. "Like what?"

"Like this," Luke said, pointing to the pages open before him. "With wizards and magic and all that."

Josh looked, oddly relieved that the boy had turned past the page that had held the picture; looking at the woman with his eyes was a bit unnerving. He read the elegant script, lettering that seemed perfectly suited to the tale it told, of a long, long ago time and place, where written history didn't exist or was lost in some kind of vague mist. And the tale of an amazing woman who was responsible for a large clan of people who were in danger. She couldn't save them alone, so she found a champion, a warrior with no name . . . and in the end he took hers.

An image of the man beside the woman in the drawing flashed through his mind. A warrior. Yes, he could believe that. The man in that drawing was a warrior, of the bravest and most fearless kind. He would have had to have been, Josh thought with a wry twist of his mouth, if this Jenna Hawk was even half the woman the story said she was.

*Hawks breed true.*

He quashed the memory of his grandfather's words, not wanting to dwell on the fact that he was the Hawk that disproved the rule.

"So is there?" Luke asked again.

"A place like this? I don't know, Luke. Maybe it's all just a story that somebody made up."

"But it says that after they saved those people they got married, an' had kids. That's real, ain't it? It says they were the found"—Luke hunched closer over the book, struggling with the long word—"the found . . . ation of the Hawk . . . din . . ."

Frustrated, the boy shoved the book at Josh, pointing at the last line of the writing on the page.

"There," he said, "look at that."

Josh looked. "Jenna and Kane," he read aloud, "the foundation of the Hawk dynasty."

"What's a dynasty?"

"In this case," Josh murmured as he stared at the scripted lines, "it means a family. A family that goes on for a very long time."

"How long?"

"Centuries."

"How long is that?"

Josh glanced at the boy then; Luke was looking at him expectantly. "A century is a hundred years. Hawks have been around for more of them than you've got fingers and toes."

Luke's eyes widened and the boy whistled in awe. He looked down at the book, then back at Josh. After a moment, he said very quietly, "It must be . . . good to know all that. About your family, I mean."

Luke's wistful tone made something tighten in Josh's

chest. It was ironic, he thought. Luke had been on his own for a third of his young life. Kate Dixon had had a husband who beat her nearly to death. While here he stood with a book chronicling the history of a proud family, a book telling him he had ancestors worth being proud of.

Yes, ironic was the word. The only one of the three of them who had a family to be proud of was the one who deserved it the least.

Assuming, of course, he believed this book was what it appeared to be. He shifted his attention back to it. He turned to the next page, the one after the end of Jenna and Kane's story. His forehead creased as he looked at the page. It took a split second for him to realize what the intricate network of lines and names and dates, printed at odd angles, were. He turned the book sideways and the names came into focus, confirming his guess. It was a family tree. The Hawk family tree stretching unbroken through the centuries from Jenna and Kane and their children to . . .

A chill swept through him, like the chill that had shot through him when he'd first connected the appearance of the book in his saddlebags to the stories he'd heard all his life. He was surprised his hands were at all steady as he straightened the book, then turned it over in his hands to look at the pages in the back.

Blank. At least half the book was blank pages.

He began to riffle through the gilt-edged paper, going back toward the front of the book. He stopped the instant he saw more of the intricate network of lines and names, and opened the book all the way.

On the page before him, the lacework net of lines, once wide and varied, suddenly narrowed. An old, familiar pain shot through him as he looked at the last page, at all the names of his childhood, all of them registering dates of birth—and death. Early death. So few years between those dates, name after name after name. He thought bitterly that from 1861 on, the ink should be red, the color of blood, for the blood had surely been drained from the Hawk dynasty. Drained until what had been a mighty oak had dwindled to one small offshoot, one tiny branch that was all that was left.

One small, irrevocably twisted branch that bore the name Joshua Hawk.

He stared at his own name, the single name left on the tree, the only one with a birth date not followed by the date of death. He stared at it for a long time, at that entry, at that "1853–" followed by the empty space that should have been filled in two days ago here in Gambler's Notch.

A sort of nausea filled him, and he had to close the book. He couldn't look at it anymore. It no longer mattered where it had come from, or who had put it here. The only thing that did matter was the truth it had laid out for him: He was the last Hawk. The last of a long line, a proud line.

A line he'd brought shame to, a line he didn't deserve to belong to. Those ancestors no doubt would just as soon not claim him at all. And he couldn't blame them for it.

If he was the only, and thus the best, thing the Hawks had left, then perhaps it was time to let it end.

Perhaps Joshua Hawk should indeed be the last Hawk.

# Chapter 4

"You're going to hurt yourself, trying to lift things like that."

Kate let out a tiny, startled sound and nearly lost her grip on the keg of nails she'd been trying to lift from the floor to one of the shelves behind the counter. Strong, masculine hands shot out to steady the small barrel; then lifted its weight out of her hands.

"Here?"

She nodded, staring at the man as he easily lifted the heavy keg up to the shelf she'd indicated.

"I expected you'd be long gone by now, Mr. Hawk," she said, thinking as she said it about Luke's excitement at being allowed to call him by his given name. Josh, Luke had told her. Short for Joshua, she supposed. A biblical name for a hardly biblical man. Of course, Luke had also told her he was a kind, patient man a fellow could talk to, an unlikely description of The Hawk, which she credited to the blindness of the hero worship of an impressionable young boy.

"So did I," he said. He pulled off his hat and shoved his hair back with his left hand, sharply, like a man not used to having his hair so long.

"So why aren't you?"

His mouth twisted wryly. "I'm not exactly sure."

She saw his eyes linger for a moment on her cheek, where the bruise was at last beginning to fade. Every morning she looked in her piece of broken mirror and rejoiced that when this one was gone, there would be no more.

As if he'd read her thoughts, he said quietly, "Pick a kinder man next time."

Kate laughed, a bleak, humorless sound. Next time? Not likely there would be one. "I didn't *pick* this one," she said pointedly.

"No?"

Her chin came up. "No, Mr. Hawk. When we first came to Gambler's Notch, we'd only been here three days, and already heard that Arly Dixon was the most mean-spirited man in town. Do you think I would *want* to marry a man like that?"

"Then why did you?"

Life was so simple for men, Kate thought. If they didn't want to do something, they didn't do it. No one forced them, or if they tried to, a man could leave and make his own way. Even if the only thing he could do was kill, he could make a living at it, she thought sourly as she looked at The Hawk. While she, as a woman, was merely a possession to be passed from an indifferent father to a brutal husband without a second thought.

He was staring at her oddly, almost embarrassedly, as if he somehow realized he'd somehow said something wrong. Or very foolish.

"My father gave me to him," she said abruptly, not sure why she'd said it, when she never talked about this to anyone.

He blinked. "What?"

"He wanted new boots. He couldn't pay. So Arly took me in trade."

He stared at her, so clearly astonished that she almost forgave him for being male. Almost.

"Was there something you wanted, Mr. Hawk?"

"No. I mean yes," he said, and she nearly smiled at the thought of having flustered the mighty Hawk. "I need some .44 cartridges."

*I'm sure you do,* she thought. But she merely walked over to the shelf where the boxes of ammunition were stacked, glad of the chance not to have to look at him. She paused with her hand on the top box of cartridges.

"How many?"

"Four."

Startled, she glanced over her shoulder at him. "Four boxes?"

He nodded. Lifting two of the boxes at a time—they were fairly heavy for their size—she moved four of them to the counter.

"Going . . . hunting?"

If he noticed her pause, or understood her tacit insinuation about the kind of hunting he did, he didn't react. She supposed he'd heard it too many times before.

"Practicing," was all he said.

"Practicing?" *You had to practice being a hired gun?*

"You think it happens by . . . magic?"

As he said the last word, a very odd expression, half bemused, half cynical flitted across his face. She wondered what he'd thought of that had caused it. Then he shrugged and went on.

"You don't practice, your aim gets rusty."

"Aim? I thought who is fastest was the most important."

"Been reading dime novels, have you?"

Kate colored; she had, on occasion, read a few of the little books. They were easier to read than some of the other books she tried, and made her feel less stupid. Then, reminding herself of her resolution to never again be ashamed, she lifted her chin and met his gaze.

"Sometimes," she said. "But everyone says the quickest draw is the best."

He smiled at her, as if he was sorry for embarrassing her. "Quick is fine, but accuracy's final," he said. "Second proverb of a fighting man."

She knew he expected it, but couldn't help asking anyway. "And the first?"

" 'God didn't make men equal, Colonel Colt did.' "

He grinned, flashing even white teeth, and she felt that odd sensation inside again; how could a cold-blooded killer make her feel this way? How could he make her smile back at him before she even realized she was doing it, even when that shadow never left his eyes?

"You . . . practice a lot?" she asked hastily.

"Only if I want to stay alive."

*When men like Arly jump you in dark alleys, you mean?* she wondered. For the first time, she looked at what had happened that night from his viewpoint. What had it been like, walking through the darkness, unsuspecting, and having a beast like Arly loom up out of the darkness at you? Even as accustomed as he was to fighting, had there been a moment when The Hawk had been scared? Had he felt, even for a fraction of a second, the kind of fear she'd always felt when Arly's brute force had been turned on her?

She sighed. Probably not. The Hawk was more than able to take care of himself, and his talent with a sixgun would more than make up for any difference in size between him and his opponent. And for any advantage surprise might have given his assailant.

It was true, she thought. Only a fool—like Arly—would try to take The Hawk. No matter what the reason, or what encouragement he got.

She shivered, and quashed the thoughts that had been threatening to engulf her of late. She couldn't change anything now. She had to get on with her life.

"Anything else, Mr. Hawk?"

"Yes."

"What?"

"Call me Josh."

She drew back warily. "Why?"

He sighed. "Because of the way you say Mr. Hawk."

"What do you mean . . . Mr. Hawk?"

He grimaced. "You say it like you're afraid of me."

Her chin came up again. "I'm not afraid of you, Mr. Hawk," she said firmly. She meant it; she would never be afraid of a man again.

"Then maybe you just mean to insult me, repeating it so often like that." Then, to her surprise, he added quietly, "But I guess you have a right to that."

"To insult you? Whyever would you say that?"

"I killed your husband, Mrs. Dixon," he reminded her, his voice quiet.

"In a fair fight," she reminded him in turn. "Marshal Pike says so."

She said it in tones of determined finality; she wanted the subject of her husband's death closed. Preferably permanently. "Now, if there's nothing else, I have a great deal of work to do."

He glanced around the store, his gaze pausing on the boxes she'd laboriously dragged out this morning from the small storage room in the back next to the office. Then he glanced at the keg he'd helped her lift before he spoke.

"Looks like you could use some help."

"I'll get by. Luke helps when he can."

"Luke's just a boy. He can't move some of those heavy things."

"He tries. And he needs what little I can pay him."

"You still need more than just his help."

Irritation sparked through her. She put her hands on her hips and glared across the counter at him. "Are you joining the line of people telling me I should give up the idea of keeping the store open?"

He drew back as if she'd startled him. "No. I just said it looked like you could use a strong back."

"What do you suggest?" she asked, still irritated. "All the married men have their own work to tend to, and the few unmarried ones who would work for Arly's widow at all have other things on their mind, even with me."

His dark brows rose. "*Even* with you?"

Her mouth twisted. "I have a mirror," she said, "and plain is the kindest of words for what it shows me."

"Maybe you need a new mirror," he said mildly.

Pain at his obvious teasing stabbed through her. And surprised her; she'd thought herself used to such things. She clung to her irritation as a shield.

"Maybe I should hire *you*, Mr. Hawk," she snapped. "You seem to have an answer for everything."

"All right."

She blinked. "All right, what?"

"I'll work for you."

Now he was teasing her about this. Her irritation grew. "That's a very poor joke, Mr. Hawk."

"That's because it wasn't intended as one."

Kate let out a laugh anyway, albeit a humorless one

again. "I doubt I can afford your rates, Mr. Hawk. I hear you're very expensive."

"Right now, what I am is broke." He nodded toward the office at the back of the store. "All I need is room to lay out my bedroll. In there will do. And maybe a meal or two, if you're cooking anyway."

She stared at him in disbelief. She glanced at the boxes of cartridges on the counter. "I need someone to do honest work around here, not . . . a killer."

"In spite of what you may think, I've done my share of what you call honest work."

"And you want to do more here?" she asked, her tone incredulous.

"Why not?"

"The Hawk working in a mercantile?"

"Why not?" he repeated.

"Why?"

It was a moment before he answered her. "Maybe because it's my doing that you're alone here."

She caught her breath. The revelation that had struck her when he'd first come to her after his release, the revelation that she'd managed to ignore since, came back now with stunning force. Was it really possible? Could the notorious gunfighter really feel . . . guilty?

She nearly laughed at herself for even considering the idea. Why would a man who'd killed a dozen men feel guilty over one more? One who had attacked him first? Especially when the record showed he'd been armed?

Still she stared at him, with no idea of what to say. She didn't believe he was serious, yet he was looking at her as if his only goal in life had been to take a job in this little store in this little town. Why was he doing this? If he was truly without funds, why wasn't he looking for a job—his kind of job, however one went about that? Or why wasn't he back at the saloon, playing poker as Luke had told her he'd been doing, getting his money the easy way?

Playing poker. It came to her then, a memory from one of Arly's drunken nights of boasting. *"I bluffed 'em, bluffed 'em all, and nobody called me. Anybody can play poker, but it takes a real man to bluff 'em all like that."*

Bluffing. The Hawk was bluffing. Maybe he really felt some twinge of guilt over killing her husband. Maybe he was offering because of it. But he knew she'd never agree; he had to know that. He expected her to say no, she didn't want The Hawk working here. And he would walk away, his conscience eased at very little cost to himself.

She wondered what he'd do if she said yes. What had Arly said it was? Calling the bluff?

"Fine," she said, not quite believing she was saying it. "I need someone to stock the high shelves." She saw him glance at the few cans of peaches and vegetables that were already there. "Oh, don't worry, there's a big shipment coming in soon. Big enough that those shelves that are splitting will need fixing. And the roof needs repairing. And I need someone to sweep the floor every day. Luke's got too much pride to do that. Still interested?"

"I said I'd do it."

The image of The Hawk sweeping her floor threatened to send Kate into gales of laughter. And suddenly she was enjoying this too much to stop. "I'll provide supper, breakfast if you're up in time. I won't wait the meal on you. And I won't pay you more than your keep. I can't afford both, and I won't take the money away from Luke."

That ought to do it, she thought. But the infuriating man simply nodded.

"He needs it more than I do."

What was it going to take to get him to stop this? "You'll have to sleep on the floor. There's no room for a cot in the storeroom, and I won't have you sleeping in my kitchen."

He shrugged. "It's dry, level, and it's clear of rocks. Better than a lot of places I've slept." He glanced at the doorway at the back of the store. "Storeroom?" he asked. "No more office?"

"Arly wanted to have an office to hang his name over. I want a storeroom, so I can carry more stock."

She looked at him steadily, daring him to comment on the unseemly speed of her changes with her dead husband's store. She didn't care if he did—the store was hers now. But he merely nodded.

"What do you want me to do first?"

"You can't really be serious about doing this," she exclaimed.

In a tone so solemn she suspected he was doing exactly what he was denying, he said, "I never joke about sweeping floors, Mrs. Dixon.

"I'm sure you realize this isn't wise, Mrs. Dixon."

"What might that be, Reverend?" Kate asked, knowing perfectly well what the little man meant.

"Why, you know what I mean. Now I know you're not thinking clearly, what with poor Arly going so unexpected—"

"I'm thinking quite clearly," Kate said sweetly. For the first time in my life, she added silently, I'm thinking clearly. She paused in her sorting of the tangled mass of ribbons before her on the counter to look up at him. "But thank you for your concern, Reverend Babcock."

The man's pale, watery eyes blinked behind his spectacles. How anyone could look at those eyes and, say

Joshua Hawk's, and call them both simply blue, was beyond her. Babcock's were a washed-out, faded blue barely worth the name, compared to the blazing vividness of The Hawk's.

Josh, she corrected herself. He'd asked her again this morning, very nicely, to use his Christian name, and she was trying, but she'd thought of him as The Hawk for so long, it was difficult. And calling him by his given name didn't seem to make him any less intimidating.

"Well, that is my job, dear. I'm concerned about the welfare of all the residents of our fair town. Those in need most of all, naturally."

"Naturally. So perhaps you should go tend to them?" she suggested, turning back to her sorting. She drew out a yellow ribbon and set it aside, trying to stifle her irritation at how her day was going. Facing The Hawk—Josh—had been nerve-wracking enough. But then she'd spilled the tray of thread and ribbons. And then, to her dismay, the reverend had arrived.

The garrulous man had entirely missed her implication that she didn't need him. Or else he chose to ignore it. She decided it was the former, as he wasn't clever enough for the latter.

"Oh, but I know you need guidance right now, child, and it's my godly duty to provide it before you stray down an ill-advised path."

Kate's fingers stilled. "I am not," she said carefully, "a child."

She was shaking inside, and she fought not to show it. For four years she'd been waiting for this time, the time when she would be free of Arly's cruel domination. And for sixteen years before that she had chafed under her father's careless neglect, knowing, somehow, deep in her soul, that there had to be another kind of

life, that this couldn't be all there was. That if there
was nothing better to look forward to, she would surely
die of despair. Or become like her mother, a pale, fragile woman who seemed nothing but a shadow of her
father.

And Kate had been planning for this day, planning
the things she would do, the way she would act when
she was at last free, at last accountable to no one but
herself, for a very long time. She had thought she
would have to do it all herself, and had been saving
what money she could, cent by cent. She'd had enough
once, but Arly had caught her before she could get
away. But she'd begun to save again as soon as she
was well enough, certain only that she could not live
like that for the rest of her life. But now she had a
chance she'd never expected. All she had to do was
what she'd been doing for a long time: run the store.

She would be free. Free of Arly's brutality, free to
come and go, free to have her own thoughts, make up
her own mind.

And the one thing she was most certain of now was
that she was through with being bullied.

"I am twenty years old," she told the reverend with
firm courtesy, "and I have been married since I was
sixteen. If I feel I need your guidance, Reverend, be
assured I will ask for it."

"But, my dear, trying to run this store by yourself,
having that man here, letting that wild, troublemaking
boy spend so much time here—"

Anger kicked to life within her. "Luke is not wild.
And he's not a troublemaker."

"Mrs. Dixon, everyone knows he's behind all the mischief in this town—"

"I know he gets blamed for it," Kate corrected. "He's
just a boy, and he's alone in this world. But he had

the courage to try and do what the fine men in this town were too scared to do, go against my husband. He did it to help me, and I'll not hear a word against him under this roof!"

Reverend Babcock backed up a step, as if her fervor were a physical thing pushing at him.

"It's . . . good of you, to t-take an interest in the poor orphan, of course," Babcock stammered. Then, recovering his pulpit poise, he added sternly, "But that man is another matter. You must see that having Arly's killer working here is hardly the thing. The whole town's buzzing."

The Hawk hadn't even been here one day yet, and already the word had spread like wildfire, Kate thought wearily.

"Would you like to order him out, Reverend?" she asked, her tone deceptively mild.

"Yes, Reverend, would you?"

The little man gasped and whirled, paling when he saw The Hawk in the doorway, his left shoulder—calculatedly keeping his gun arm free, Kate supposed—propped against the doorjamb as if he had been there listening for some time.

She had to admit he was an intimidating sight. Tall, lean, and clad in solid black, the only break in the darkness of his clothing the smooth brown leather of the gunbelt strapped around his slim hips. The dark sleekness of his hair only added to the overall effect; it brushed over his shoulders, blending with the black of his shirt, and making the vivid color of his eyes even more of a shock.

"Was there something you wanted to take up with me?" Josh asked pleasantly.

Babcock went even paler, for once seemingly incapable of speech.

"That's all right," Josh said in an exaggeratedly soothing tone. "I'm sure you didn't mean for me to leave before I . . . paid my debt."

"Your . . . debt?" Babcock said, squeaking.

"I knew you'd understand, you being a preacher. Why, I'm sure you preach this very thing in your sermons, don't you, Reverend? That a man should own up to his responsibilities? Pay his debts, especially those of honor?

"Of . . . course," Babcock said, sounding only slightly less squeaky as he eyed Josh warily.

"Then I'm sure you'll pass the word that I'm merely doing *my* duty. Through an unfortunate set of circumstances, I made Mrs. Dixon a widow. I'm sure you, and your congregation, will understand that I feel it's my responsibility to help her until she's on her feet again."

He said it so smoothly, so convincingly, that Kate almost believed him herself. Just as his actions all day long almost had her believing him. He'd been prompt, polite, and productive, doing everything she asked, and a few things she hadn't realized needed doing. He'd not complained at all about the cramped quarters of the storeroom, and when she'd brought him some leftover corn bread at noon, he ate it with manners better than she'd ever seen from Arly, and thanked her graciously rather than embarrassing her by pointing out that this wasn't in their agreement.

In short, he acted exactly like a man might who felt genuinely sorry about having left her a widow. Like a man who felt guilty over what had been an instinctive act, committed to save his own life.

"You do understand that, don't you, Reverend?" Josh said, his voice as smooth as a snake's tooth, and about as deadly.

"I . . . of course. Of course. Only thing a man can do," the reverend sputtered.

Josh moved out of the doorway, and the little man darted through it like a rat making its bolt hole just ahead of the cat. Kate stifled a giggle, then nearly gasped at her own temerity; she barely recognized herself anymore in this irreverent woman she seemed to have become.

"That should keep him out of your way for a while," Josh said as he pulled the door closed behind him and walked over to her.

"Yes," she said, examining the next ribbon in her pile carefully, "thank you."

She sensed rather than saw him shrug. "I figure cleaning out the no-accounts is part of my job."

Her head came up sharply. "Reverend Babcock, a no-account?"

Josh grinned at her. She was almost getting used to it, this odd sensation that seized her whenever he did it.

"I don't have much patience with folks who spend their life telling others how to live theirs."

She couldn't stop herself from smiling back at him. "He's surely good at that," she said.

When his grin broadened, and her heart seemed to lose track of its rhythm, she hastily turned her gaze back to her ribbons and resumed her sorting.

After a moment, because she couldn't seem to stop this, either, she said with a sigh, "I doubt anyone ever told you how to live your life."

"If they did, it clearly didn't take."

Something, some undertone of seriousness made her look up at him. His expression was distant, his eyes unfocused, as if he were looking inward. Then his jaw tightened, as if he didn't like what he saw. She quickly

he'd been doing was talking about . . . trees. And agreeing she wasn't the frills-and-ribbons type of woman.

"I . . . have to go start supper," she said desperately, even though she knew it was a good hour early.

For a long moment he didn't move, didn't pull his hand back, and she felt the heat of his touch on her skin like the flare of a fire when a log broke. Something flickered in his eyes, something hot and intense that she'd never seen before. Then at last he drew back. Kate turned and darted away, barely remembering to pull the roller shade on the door to indicate Dixon's was closed.

She raced to the back of the store, through the storeroom, pulled open the door to the kitchen, and hurried inside. She closed the door behind her and leaned on it, breathing heavily, feeling as if she'd run from here to the Notch and back.

And she knew what she looked like. Exactly what she'd looked like.

She'd looked like Reverend Babcock, terrified and scrambling to get away from The Hawk.

# Chapter 5

"What's wrong with Miss Kate?"

"How the hell would I know?" Josh growled as he lifted the keg of gunpowder from the floor to the counter.

His head was aching this morning from a restless, sleepless night spent staring at a book that couldn't exist, a book that made him feel strangely warm and comforted every time he touched it, a fact that made him very nervous.

And thinking about the fact that when he'd touched Kate Dixon yesterday, he'd been nearly swamped with a rush of unexpected and unwanted physical need, hardening his body with a speed that had left him breathless. And he didn't know which seemed more impossible.

Or, he admitted now, which bothered him more.

He glanced at Luke, realizing he'd been sharp with the boy for no reason other than he wasn't very happy about the way his thoughts had been running him in circles all night.

"Sorry," he muttered. And it wasn't until then that what the boy had said truly registered in his mind. Something was wrong with Kate?

He frowned. He knew she'd been startled when he'd touched her; she'd looked back at him like a wild doe frozen with fear. But surely she couldn't still be upset over that, he thought. Could she?

*Why not? You are.*

The answer came back at him as if from that small voice inside his head that warned him when he was headed into trouble. That small voice he'd learned to listen to.

He didn't understand it. It wasn't as if he'd kissed her; he'd barely touched her. And she was hardly the kind of woman who usually caught his eye. But, he supposed, if a man went without a woman long enough, even a touch on the cheek could have an arousing effect. Even if the woman wasn't ... beautiful.

*An arousing effect.* What a pissant description of what had happened to him. He'd gotten so hard so fast he'd nearly groaned out loud. Over the plain, too-tall woman whose husband he'd just killed.

He frowned again.

"What's wrong with *you*?" Luke asked, giving him a decidedly wary look.

Shaking off that fruitless speculation, Josh picked up the hammer he'd put on the counter, and reached for the nails he'd set out to finally fasten down that loose board which had been annoying him every time he walked over it and it twisted beneath his feet.

"I didn't get much sleep," he said.

"Oh."

Luke watched as he knelt down to push against the board, to find the crosspiece beneath. He found it, hammered home a nail, then a second one for good measure. He stood up, tested the board with his foot;

it held steady. With a grunt of satisfaction, he set the hammer back down.

"Did she get bad news?" Luke asked. "I saw Mr. Boardman give her a paper when she walked by the telegraph office. Mr. Rankin says telegrams are usually bad news."

Josh gave the boy his attention then. "A telegram?"

Luke nodded. "I think so. She looked kind of upset when she read it, but she wouldn't tell me what it was."

Josh glanced toward the storeroom, where Kate had retreated and closed the door, saying she had to go over some accounts. He hadn't been sure if she really had work to do there, or was simply avoiding him after yesterday. The thought that it was something else entirely, that perhaps she'd simply received bad news, both relieved and ruffled him, and he wasn't pleased with the combination.

"Maybe it was personal," he suggested.

"I dunno," Luke said doubtfully. "She never gets telegrams, or letters, or nothing."

*No doubt because there was no one who gave a damn about her,* Josh thought grimly. If what she'd told him about her father was true, that he'd given her to Arly Dixon for a pair of boots, it didn't seem likely her family would be sending their condolences on her loss. For that matter, he wasn't sure Kate would tell them, if she even knew how to reach them.

But what had upset her, in whatever message she'd gotten?

"Maybe you oughta go ask her," Luke said. "She'll tell you."

Josh looked back at the boy. "What makes you think she'll tell me?"

"You're grown," Luke said with the fatalistic acceptance of youth. "Grown folks talk to each other. Besides, she likes you."

Josh blinked. "What?"

"Well, she looks at you like she likes you," Luke amended, but Josh wasn't sure he cared for the alteration. "Not like she looked at ol' Arly."

"I hope not," Josh muttered.

"Well, if I'd had to live with ol' Arly, I'd be right happy that someone did him in. An' I'd for sure like the one who did it, too."

"Oh."

That, he supposed, made a certain kind of sense. More sense than what he'd first thought when Luke had spoken of how Kate looked at him. The woman was freshly a widow, after all. She was hardly about to be making eyes at anyone. Especially the man who'd killed her husband, no matter what the circumstances.

Not that it mattered. Widows of any kind weren't his type, although he knew more than one man who wasn't above using a woman's loss to his advantage. But for him, widows were too close to death, and he had too much of that in his life already. He preferred to keep such things purely a business transaction; women he could pay and then leave, without feeling he'd hurt them in any way. No decent woman would have anything to do with him, anyway, nor would he want them to. A woman would have to be a fool to come to care about a man like him, when every moment could be his last. He'd decided long ago women took an unfair share of the pain in this world. He didn't want to add to it.

But something had added to Kate's pain, if Luke was right.

"I'll go see," he finally said. "Watch the store."

Luke lit up at that bit of trust. "Yes, sir!"

He found her sitting on an empty crate, a piece of paper in her hand. She looked up at him, then away, but not before he saw the disheartened look in her eyes.

"What's wrong?" he asked.

For a moment he thought she wasn't going to answer. Then, squaring her slender shoulders, she stood up.

"I have to find other suppliers."

Josh looked at the telegram. "Something to do with that?"

She looked down at the paper in her hand, then crumpled it up. "The Bartons heard that Arly was dead. They don't want to do business with me."

Guilt slammed through Josh, making his voice harsh. "Why? Just because you're a woman?"

She sighed. "A woman alone. And Arly always told them I was . . . stupid. Useless. A nuisance. They don't trust me. They don't think I can run this place."

Josh couldn't think of a thing to say. She was in this fix because of him. But had she really been better off with Arly Dixon alive to abuse her? He didn't know. He didn't feel like he knew much of anything anymore. Except that he never should have stopped in Gambler's Notch, no matter how broke or thirsty for coffee he'd been. He shoved his hair back with one hand, trying to think of what to do.

"If only Fort Bridger hadn't been shut down this year. . . ." Her voice trailed away, and Josh saw her gather herself. When she went on, the determination in her voice sounded forced. "It doesn't matter, I'll find a way. I'll send word to Granite Bluff that they can just turn their wagon around and head back to Rock Springs and—"

"The wagon is already in Granite Bluff?"

She nodded. "It was due here yesterday. But when they heard about Arly, they stopped halfway."

He grimaced; that was his fault, too. If Arly had merely gotten himself killed in a local brawl, word would likely never have reached Rock Springs so quickly. But he'd been killed by The Hawk, and that meant the news spread fast.

He set his jaw. The Hawk had brought this on her; it was up to The Hawk to do something about it.

"Who are these men? Friends of your husband's?"

Her mouth quirked. "I don't know if Arly had any friends. But he dealt with these men all the time. He'd tell them what he wanted, and they'd have the supplies shipped into Rock Springs on the railroad, then bring them here by wagon. It was more expensive, but Arly didn't like to leave here for long enough to go himself."

"I'm sure he didn't," Josh said. The wife who was closer to a slave might up and disappear on him, he added silently.

"Is the load paid for?"

She gave him a puzzled look. "No. Arly always paid when it arrived."

"Do you have the money for it?"

"Yes, I set it aside as soon as we got word it was on its way. . . ." Her eyes widened as if she'd just heard what she'd said, and Josh read her thoughts easily.

"I'm not a thief, Mrs. Dixon," he said wryly.

"No, you're merely a killer," she retorted, a little sharply.

"A fine line, I realize," Josh said. "But still a line. I just wanted to know if you could pay for the supplies."

"Why?" she asked, clearly still suspicious. "What does it matter if they won't deliver them?"

"They won't have to," Josh said.

"What? Why?"

"Because I'm going to go get them."

For the first time in a long time, Josh was grateful for his reputation. It had taken little convincing, once the two enterprising brothers who ran the small freight line realized they were indeed face-to-face with The Hawk, to get them to turn over the supplies. They'd been so glad he was paying for them instead of taking them outright, that they had gladly thrown in the sturdy wagon and pair of healthy-looking draft horses for the extra fifty dollars he'd offered, and had clambered onto the next stage headed back to Rock Springs with every sign of eagerness.

Which meant, Josh thought glumly as he sat in the small, smoky saloon that was crowded even in early afternoon, that he was just about broke once again. He'd had enough for a meal and a drink—the former hadn't been that good, and the latter's quality he was still considering—and not much else.

He was aware of being watched by several pairs of eyes in the room. Warily by most, but with interest by those in the rouged-and-painted face of the woman who had followed an inebriated but happy-seeming cowboy downstairs a few minutes ago. She paused to get a drink at the bar—brandy, Josh noted—asked the bartender something, patted her bright blond hair, and then began to sidle toward Josh.

He should have thought of this, he told himself. He could have passed up that overdone steak and taken care of this other problem. After what had happened with the widow, he clearly needed some female company. And this woman, attractive enough in the way of sporting women, would have taken care of that. But now he had a stomach full of tough beef that was near a sin in cattle country, and an itch he couldn't afford to scratch, unless this woman was cheaper than she looked.

"Evenin'," the woman said, "I'm Lily. Mind if I sit down?"

Josh looked at her for a moment, at the red silk dress cut low over her generous breasts, and tight enough to draw the eye to the curve of her waist and hips. The display was effective, reminding a man of the other differences between man and woman, and encouraging him to do something about it.

Angry with himself for not thinking of this before, he said wryly, "As long as it doesn't cost me anything."

The woman hesitated, then sat anyway. She put the glass on the table in front of her. "Tapped out?" she said, her tone a combination of sympathy and business-like inquiry.

He reached into his coat pocket, pulled out the handful of coins he had left, held back a dollar and tossed the rest on the table. "That close," he said.

She watched the coins fall with a practiced eye; Josh guessed she had the total figured before the one silver dollar rolled to a stop. Then she glanced at the bartender before she looked back at Josh.

"Gus says you're The Hawk."

"He does, does he?"

"Are you? You look kind of young." She gave him a flirtatious smile. "Mighty pretty, but young."

"Only on the outside, Lily," Josh drawled.

She smiled, and as she raised her glass for another sip of brandy, Josh noticed the slight crookedness of the line of the red paint she'd used on her lips.

"So, are you The Hawk?"

"Does it matter?"

"It might."

There was a note in her voice he'd heard before, the tiniest of edges that told him she was one of those women who sought out men like him, men with a reputation. He wasn't sure why they did it. He only knew they seemed to get something out of it that he didn't understand. Nor did he begrudge them; no matter how content some of them seemed with their lives, he couldn't quite believe any woman was truly happy taking any man who could pay the price. But right now he couldn't afford to be choosy. And she was pretty enough, albeit a bit worn.

"Name's Hawk," Josh admitted. "The rest depends on who you ask."

"Well, now," she said as she gathered in the coins and put them in a neat stack, "this might buy The Hawk about anything he wanted."

Looked like he would get that itch scratched after all, Josh thought. He braced himself, expecting an onslaught of heat like the one that had hit him the other day.

It didn't happen. Instead he found himself thinking of drab, baggy dresses that made him imagine the slender body beneath, of hair a much more subtle shade, of skin clean and soft, and a pair of amazing golden eyes not rimmed with dark paint.

He shook his head to rid his mind of the images, inwardly laughing at himself. The woman leaned forward, giving him an even clearer view of what she was offering. She was amply endowed, and he looked at her with some fascination. But no response.

He was losing his mind. Or his manhood, he thought sourly. Between the widow and that damned book, he couldn't even think straight anymore. Here he was, being made an offer he'd be crazy to turn down, the chance to seek the release he'd been dying for just a day ago, with a willing and tolerably attractive woman, the only kind of woman he dealt with, and he couldn't even stir up a trace of interest.

He watched as she finished the brandy, then licked her lips in a suggestive manner that promised him things he hadn't thought about in a long time. His body should have roused to the mere idea, but instead he just found himself thinking that if he left now instead of waiting until morning, he could be back in Gambler's Notch by noon.

Inwardly, he rattled off a string of curses directed at himself and his own stupidity. Outwardly, he sighed. "Some other time," he muttered.

The woman looked surprised. "I don't make that kind of offer to just any man, Hawk."

"Thank you," he said, for the moment meaning it. "But some other time."

She reached over and ran a hand up his arm. For a moment he hesitated, wondering if maybe he could work up some interest after all. Nothing. He wasn't aroused, he was only tired.

"I'd make you happy," she said huskily. "Very happy."

Not likely, Josh thought. But he said, "I'm sure you'd try." He stood up, dug his last silver dollar out of his pocket and added it to the whore's stack of coins. "Buy yourself a night off instead, Lily."

Something flickered in her dark-rimmed eyes, some trace of the woman he supposed she'd once been. "I'll save you a spot on my dance card," she said softly. "Come back and collect it sometime, Hawk."

"Maybe," he said. He picked up his own glass, downed the last swallow, and headed for the swinging doors.

By the time he reached the stable where he'd left the wagon and its load, he'd again muttered every curse he knew. And every vicious word had been directed at himself.

Still swearing, he tied Buck to the back of the wagon. He left the buckskin saddled, just in case, but took his Winchester out of the scabbard and set it on the wagon seat. It had been a while since he'd driven a team, but he supposed he'd remember fast enough. He checked the load, although he doubted anybody would have dared to go near it once it became known it was his.

After a moment's thought, he went back and got his saddlebags as well; the widow had insisted on sending him off with a good supply of jerky and bread that he figured he'd be glad of in a few hours.

"Should have eaten that instead," he muttered to himself as he slung the bags up onto the seat.

They hit with an oddly heavy-sounding thud.

His brow furrowing, he lifted the bags again. There was more than just food in there, he thought, lifting the flap on the heavier bag cautiously. He reached inside, and felt a familiar shape. His breath lodged in his throat. Disbelieving, he pulled it out.

It was the book. The book he'd intentionally left behind, shoved behind a crate in the widow's storeroom.

And he knew damn well it hadn't been in those bags when he'd left Gambler's Notch.

"You gave him all the money you had set aside to pay for supplies?"

Kate nodded at Deborah.

"And he left the day before yesterday?"

Kate nodded again. She could see Deborah calculating the hours to Granite Bluff, and how long it might take to get back with a heavily loaded freight wagon.

"He couldn't be back until late tonight, even if he

turned right around and started back the next morning," Kate said, staring out toward the front of the store where the early afternoon sun was glinting off the glass. She'd done the same calculating in her mind countless times as she'd lain awake last night, wondering how big a mistake she'd made.

And trying not to acknowledge the incredible possibility that this odd, off-center feeling she'd had ever since Josh had left stemmed from a very simple source: that she missed him. She hadn't realized how he'd taken up so much of her life and her thoughts until he was gone, and she found herself wandering aimlessly, pacing, waiting. When she at last realized what she was doing, she'd run from the knowledge just as she'd run from Arly.

When her friend said nothing more, she grimaced. "Aren't you going to tell me I'm a fool?"

"No."

"Aren't you going to tell me I'll never see that money again, or the supplies?"

"No."

Deborah picked up a can of peaches and added them to her basket. Kate sighed. "You are a wonder, Deborah. How do you manage to be so . . ."

"Wise? Discreet? Restrained?"

Kate smiled. It wasn't a particularly happy smile, since she wasn't at all sure she wasn't the fool she'd expected her friend to call her.

"All of those things," she said. "You're the best friend I've ever had."

Deborah looked uncomfortable. "If I'd been a true friend, I would have thought of a way to get you away from Arly long ago."

Kate shook her head. "He would only have hurt you,

too. I couldn't have lived with that. It was so awful when he hurt Luke, because of me, and I—"

"Hush," Deborah said soothingly. "It's over now. Arly's gone, and you don't ever have to worry about him hurting anyone again."

Kate sighed, for the first time wondering if she could live with this, either.

"Do you think he'll have any trouble?" she asked, without stopping to think what her assumption that Deborah would know who she was talking about might imply.

Deborah blinked, then gave her friend a speculative look. "I would think The Hawk could accomplish just about anything he set out to do."

Kate's mouth tightened. "You just don't think he really set out to get my supplies."

"I didn't say that."

"He said . . . he said he wasn't a thief."

"I doubt that he is."

"But I gave him all that money—"

"Kate, Kate," Deborah said, shaking her head, "that might seem like all the money in the world to you, but to The Hawk? I suspicion he gets that much for a day's work."

In that case, Kate thought wearily, perhaps I owe it to him, for he certainly did a fine day's work for me. She saw Deborah give her a sharp look, and tried to smile.

"I swan, girl, you're up and down these days," Deborah said. "I know you can't be sorry to be free of Arly."

"No," Kate admitted.

"I suppose it's wicked to be glad of a man's death," Deborah said, "and the good Lord knows I've seen enough of men dying to wish never to see it again. But if ever a man deserved it, that one did."

"I . . . suppose you're right."

"You know I'm right. You've got a good life to look forward to now. You'll find some good, decent man to marry—"

"No." Kate shook her head positively. "I'll never marry again."

"Now, Kate," Deborah said in a placating tone, "not all men are like Arly. You're young—"

"No," Kate repeated. "Besides, who would want to marry me? Arly only did because he had to. A man wants a pretty woman, or at least one who can who can—"

She broke off, unable to say the words, but knowing she didn't have to; it had been Deborah who had given her the grim news.

"I never said you couldn't have children," Deborah said gently. "Just that it might be very difficult for you to conceive."

Kate wrapped her arms around herself. She'd never wanted Arly's child, had lived in fear of someday having to protect a child from her husband's brutal wrath when she couldn't even protect herself. She'd even been grateful when Deborah had told her a baby was unlikely. But now she found herself lacking in the only thing she could see a man would ever want her for. She certainly would never capture one's attention with her looks.

"You have the store now," Deborah pointed out.

Kate shook herself out of her self-pity. "What?"

"You're a woman of some means now, Kate. That's something to consider."

"I . . . suppose so."

She hadn't really thought of it that way. The idea of a man who would want her just for the mercantile didn't appeal to her, but was it really so different than a man who would want a woman only for the children she could give him? And for that matter, was either any different than Arly, who wanted her to fix his meals, do the work in the mercantile, and submit to him at night?

She shivered, shoving those ugliest of thoughts out of her mind. She didn't have to share her bed with Arly anymore. Never again would she have to face that painful humiliation. With any man. There was no point; the only reason she could see that any woman would participate in that brutal act willingly was for children, and since she—

"Miss Kate! Miss Kate!"

Luke's excited voice was audible before his rapid footsteps. The boy burst in, a grin as big as the Rockies on his face.

"He's back! He's got the wagon!"

Kate stared at the boy.

"Well, well," Deborah said, her voice holding an undertone that suggested she was responding to far more than just Luke's news.

Kate continued to stare at Luke, joy and relief flooding her so completely that she couldn't speak.

"Didn't you hear me?" Luke asked when she didn't react. "The Hawk is home!"

The words sent a ripple of heat through her.

Home. The Hawk is home.

# Chapter 6

Josh was dusty, hot, and tired. His eyes were gritty from lack of sleep, his backside was sore from a night spent sitting on that miserable wagon seat, and his hands were stiff from the unaccustomed task of driving a heavy team. He was generally miserable, and didn't much care who knew it. And he forgot it all a moment later, when he walked into the mercantile and Kate, eyes shining, threw her arms around him.

Instinctively, his arms went around her in turn, and then it hit him in a rush, that wave of heat that had been so strangely absent in Granite Bluff. Kate Dixon had more curves than he'd thought, and he swore he could feel each one. He felt like a boy who'd never had a woman's body pressed against him before, and his own body responded as quickly as if it were true. As if having this particular woman welcoming him back were something he'd waited his entire life for.

He swallowed tightly, trying to brush off that ridiculous idea with the thought that if the widow held him so close like this for another minute, she was going to be in for a big surprise. So was he, for that matter, he thought ruefully as his blood began to surge, then pool low and deep inside him. But for the life of him he couldn't pull away from her.

Kate suddenly seemed to realize what she'd done, and released him hastily. Just as hastily she backed up a step, clasping her hands behind her back as if to assure him she wouldn't do such a thing again. But her eyes were still alight as she looked at him.

"You came back," she whispered.

Her relief was clear, and it added another layer to his exhaustion, frustration, and irritation. He resisted the urge to yank off his hat and hold it in front of him, hiding his half-arousal; better that she knew what she'd done to him. It might keep her from doing it again.

"Of course, I did," he snapped. "Did you think I was going to steal your canned peaches and disappear?"

" 'Course she didn't," Luke put in with a laugh full of a boy's reverence for his hero, and utter unawareness of the other tensions in the room. "But we didn't 'spect you back so soon. Granite Bluff is a long ways."

"You are early," Deborah said mildly.

Only then did Josh realize that both the boy and the dauntless Miss Taylor had been standing there during Kate's unexpectedly enthusiastic greeting. And while the boy might be too young to understand the undercurrent here, he doubted Miss Taylor was. She might be unmarried, but Josh guessed she knew a thing or two.

"I started back last night," he said, less sharply but still gruffly. He glanced at Luke. "Go start on that wagon, will you? Untie the rope, and get that canvas off. I've got a lot of unloading to do."

"You must be exhausted and hungry if you traveled all night," Kate said. "Rest, and I'll fix you something to eat. The drivers can unload—"

"You're looking at the driver."

"What?"

"The Barton brothers seemed in a big hurry to get back home."

"I'll bet they did," Luke chortled happily. "I'll bet they ran like rabbits once they found out they'd tried to cross The Hawk!"

That was close to how it had happened, but Josh merely shrugged. "Get started, will you, boy?"

Luke nodded and darted outside almost as quickly as he'd come in.

"But the wagon," Kate said, looking puzzled. "How will they get it back?"

He grimaced. "They don't. I bought it."

"What?" she said again.

Josh let out a compressed breath; he was in no mood for a long discussion.

"I couldn't very well get the load here without it. You can use it next time you need supplies. Send someone to meet them halfway again. It'll be cheaper."

"Use their wagon?"

"Your wagon," he said, wondering why she didn't understand, she was usually so quick.

Kate frowned. "But what about the horses?"

"They came with the wagon," he said with a tinge of sarcasm. "I could hardly hitch Buck to the thing."

Kate's eyes widened as she stared at him. "You bought the wagon *and* the horses?"

Josh tried to hang on to the last of his patience. "Don't get in a pucker over it. I didn't use your money."

"Well that's a considerable relief," Deborah put in, her tone very dry. "That means they're yours, and *you* can pay for their keep."

Josh wasn't amused. It was suddenly too much, and he was too tired to deal with this abrupt change from delighted greeting to censure. He didn't know why the hell he was doing this anyway, any of it. He should have left the dust of Gambler's Notch far behind by now.

"You said you needed those supplies," he said irritably. "And now you've got them. If you don't like the way I did it, then maybe you—"

"I'm sorry," Kate said swiftly. "I *did* need the supplies, and you saved me having to start all over. And it would be difficult, trying to buy goods when people are stocking up for their trip west."

He hadn't even thought of that, but he supposed few enough folks could afford the two hundred dollars or so each it cost to take the train west, making the big prairie schooners the transportation still most commonly used by those yearning for the land beyond the Rockies.

But Kate had thought of it.

*Arly always told them I was stupid. Useless. A nuisance. They don't trust me. They don't think I can run this place.*

The Barton brothers were the stupid ones, Josh thought, his anger fading as he remembered what Kate was up against. And he owed her. Owed her his life. He understood a little better now why she'd done it, why she wasn't consumed with any great need to see him die for killing her husband, but that didn't lessen the debt any.

He turned his head at the sound of Luke returning, still at a run.

"All done," the boy said proudly.

Josh nodded. "I'll get started unloading."

"I'll help!" Luke was back outside in an instant. Josh shook his head tiredly; the boy's energy was making him feel even more weary.

"Josh, at least sit and rest for a while first. You look so tired."

Kate's concern washed over him like balm, and for the moment he forgot how angry he'd been just a short moment ago.

"I've been sitting," he told her ruefully. "Besides, if I stop now, I may never get started again. Best if I just keep moving."

He turned and walked back outside. Surprisingly, Luke was more help than he'd expected, racing back and forth with the smaller items, bolts of cloth, lengths of stove pipe, and individual cooking pots out of a larger crate Josh pried open for him. Still, it was a lengthy process, and a rough one; the wagon was packed to capacity with a very bulky load.

Josh was shoving a large, heavy crate that he guessed had to contain Art Rankin's shipment of iron for horseshoes to the back of the wagon when Marshal Pike, cheerfully whistling something that sounded vaguely like the refrain of "Beautiful Dreamer," paused in his walk to observe the struggle.

"Well, now," he said cheerfully, "isn't this a sight I never thought to see?"

Grunting, Josh ignored the man and his cheer. He leaned into the crate with his shoulder and managed to shove it a couple of feet. Pike was grinning now, and Josh didn't like the looks of that.

"The Hawk taking to shopkeeping. Why, nobody'd believe such a thing, were I to tell them."

Josh glared at the man over the top of the crate. "Then don't."

Pike tugged at his mustache, still grinning. "I haven't. Leastwise, not yet. Had to come see for myself if it was true, what folks are sayin'."

Josh didn't want to know what folks were saying. He

didn't want anything except to get this done, eat a decent meal—Kate had been cooking something that had had his stomach growling for the past hour—and go to sleep for two days.

"Looks like it's plumb factual, though," Pike said, chuckling audibly now.

With a final surge born of annoyance, Josh shoved the box to the back edge of the wagon. Rankin, he thought, could tote the thing himself the rest of the way. Then he jumped down to the ground and turned to look at Pike dourly.

"All right, Marshal. You're set on telling me, that's clear enough. So what are folks saying, besides that I've taken up shopkeeping?"

Pike glanced at the mercantile, sniffing as if he could detect the aroma of Kate's cooking clear out here. Perhaps he could, Josh thought, wondering if that thick mustache somehow improved the man's sense of smell.

"Why, they're saying it's plumb amazing," Pike said.

Exasperated by this game the marshal was obviously enjoying at his expense, Josh clenched his jaw. Pike had pretty much left him alone up to now, and he didn't want the man angry at him, but he was in no mood to be toyed with.

"What," he said tightly, "is so all-fired amazing?"

Pike grinned widely. "That The Hawk has been tamed by a sparrow."

Kate felt Josh's gaze on her as she served up the meal of chicken and dumplings. It was early, barely dusk, but she'd begun cooking soon after Josh had begun to unload the wagon; she'd never seen a man look so tired before. And he looked worse now after unloading all those supplies and toting them inside, stacking the ones that she had no room for on the shelves in the storeroom, eating away at his already limited sleeping space.

And she felt badly that she'd questioned what he'd done. If he'd felt it necessary to buy the horses and the heavy wagon, then she was sure he'd been right. It certainly wasn't her place to challenge him when he'd been doing her a tremendous favor. Whatever he felt he owed her because of her help in saving him from the hangman's noose, he'd surely more than paid it back by now.

"What's this?" Luke asked as she set a plate before him. She'd invited the boy to stay when Josh had thanked him for his help, saying he'd worked as hard as any man today.

"Chicken," Josh said, rather solemnly.

"And dumplings," Kate added, amused by Josh's tone—chicken was a rarity in this land of beef—and the fact that she thought she'd heard his stomach growl.

"You eat chickens?" Luke asked, looking at his plate doubtfully. "I thought they were just for eggs."

"They usually are, out here," Kate explained. "Back in the States, folks eat them all the time."

"Why?" Luke asked.

"Because there are lots of them," Josh said. "Now eat yours."

Kate sat down as Josh spoke, sounding, she thought, like a father directing his son to be quiet at the table so he could begin his own meal. The thought made her want to smile, and at the same time filled her with a wistfulness she'd never experienced before. She didn't dare contemplate the cause of that feeling, just as she didn't dare think about the foolish, scandalous thing she'd done this afternoon, something she'd never in her life even thought of doing before, hugging a man like that. Yet she'd done it, throwing her arms around Josh in front of both Deborah and Luke, clinging to him, and she just barely a widow.

She'd told herself it was the heat of the stove that had her cheeks so flushed, but she knew it was really humiliation. At first she'd been thankful Josh hadn't talked about it, but then she realized he was probably as embarrassed as she had been, and thinking all kinds of pitiful things of the widow who had treated him so familiarly. She tried to keep her mind occupied with her cooking, because she couldn't bear to think about what she'd done.

Nor did she dare think about the odd sensations that had coursed through her when he had held her against him, when she'd felt the hard, solid male body against her own. Arly had only frightened her with his massive bulk and strength; Josh, while he was much less burly was nearly as tall and seemed just as strong, didn't frighten her at all. At least she didn't think that was the word for the feeling that went through her every time he got close. She wasn't sure what it was, but it wasn't the fear she'd always associated with Arly.

"This is delicious. Thank you," Josh said when he finally slowed after nearly cleaning his plate.

"You're welcome. You more than earned a good meal, both of you, today."

Luke tried to smile around full cheeks. Josh took a swallow of coffee, then asked, "Where *did* this bird come from?"

Kate smiled. "It was a gift from Deborah."

"A gift?"

"She felt bad about what she said this afternoon."

Josh gave her a sideways look. He looked back at his plate, took the last bite of his chicken, finished the last, plump dumpling, then set down his fork.

"She was right," he said at last. "I didn't think about you having to pay for the horses' keep all year, when you really only need them a few times."

"I may need them more," she said wryly, "if the Barton brothers won't do business with me."

"They will," Josh said. "I made that clear to them before they left Granite Bluff."

"See, Miss Kate," Luke said, his first words since he'd warily tested the chicken and found it much to his liking, eating nearly as fast as Josh had. "I told you Josh'd handle it!"

"Yes," Kate agreed, "so you did."

She glanced at Josh, who was staring down at his plate as if the boy's words had made him uncomfortable.

"That new dress in that load," he said suddenly. "I hope it's for you."

Kate blinked. "Me? Of course not. It's for the store."

"You don't like it?"

"Well, certainly, it's very nice, but—"

"Then why don't you take it? Arly isn't running things anymore."

"That would be foolish. It's to sell, not for me. I have no use for new clothes."

"Mesquite," Josh muttered, and Kate flushed at the reminder of their other conversation.

Silence reigned for a while before Luke asked, hopefully eyeing the pot on the stove, "Is there more chicken?"

"You haven't eaten your vegetable yet," Kate said, then laughed when Luke wrinkled his nose.

"My ma used to say that," Luke said.

Kate went very still. The boy had said it simply, with no sign of grief or pain, but the words still tore at her.

"Mine, too," Josh said quietly.

"Really?" Luke looked at Josh, then at his plate, which was empty of the serving of turnips that remained on his own plate. "Is that why you ate 'em?"

Josh nodded. "Since she's not here to remind me anymore, it seems like the right thing to do."

"Oh."

With a resigned sigh, Luke picked up his fork and dug into the cooked turnips. Kate quickly picked up Josh's plate and turned away, fighting the tears that threatened. How could it be that this man she'd always heard of as a cold-blooded killer could be so understanding with a young boy, that he could find exactly the right words to guide him?

She took her time scooping up another serving for him, leaving a small piece for Luke as a reward for eating the dreaded turnips. She had herself under control by the time she turned back. Or she thought she did; Josh still looked at her rather intently when she set the plate back down in front of him. But all he said, after taking another bite, was "Thank Miss Taylor for me."

"Me, too," Luke chimed in, holding out his now empty plate. Kate laughed as she served up the last piece of chicken and last dumpling for the boy, and watched indulgently as he attacked the food as if he hadn't just finished a plateful.

This must be what women wanted, what some of them even had, this quiet peace with a man and a child at your table, hungry after a hard day's work. She'd always looked at cooking as something she'd had to do, as something women just did, a part of the payment for the protection of a man in a harsh world. But watching Josh and Luke eat with such relish gave her an odd sense of satisfaction she'd never known before.

Perhaps, she mused idly as Josh and Luke talked,

some chores weren't such drudgery, if they were done like this, for people who appreciated what you'd done. Perhaps this is what other women thought of when they thought of marrying and having children—

Kate quickly lowered her gaze to her own cup of coffee, praying that her silly, foolish thoughts hadn't shown in her face. She supposed there could be something more foolish than a woman who sat looking at a half-wild orphan boy and The Hawk, and thinking about marriage and children of her own, but she doubted you'd find it in Wyoming Territory. She felt so half-witted she was thankful when they'd finished eating and she could turn her attention to cleaning up.

When Luke had thanked her, and scampered off to check on Buck as the weary Josh had asked him, Kate hastily got to her feet. She set out the pan she used for washing the dishes, then turned to go for the water she'd set to heating before they'd begun to eat. She gave a little start when she saw Josh there before her, reaching to lift the heavy kettle for her. She stared at him while he poured the water into the pan; Arly would no more have thought to help her than he would have thought to thank her for the meal. Especially if he'd been as tired as Josh, not that he'd ever worked as hard as Josh had today.

"I . . . thank you," she stammered out.

Josh merely nodded as he set the kettle down, as if he thought nothing of helping with woman's work. He stood there beside her for a long moment. She looked up at him, noticing the rough stubble of his unshaven jaw, the reddened weariness in his eyes . . . and something else in those eyes, something that made them bright and intense despite his exhaustion. Something that made her very nervous, and reminded her painfully of the moment when, in her joy and relief, she'd embraced him so disgracefully.

"I . . . you should get some sleep," she said, desperate to distract him—and, to be honest, herself—from such thoughts.

For what seemed like an endless moment he still stood there, looking down at her, so close she could feel the heat of him, could almost sense the solidness of him by the way the bare two inches of space between them felt, compressed somehow. She felt oddly as if the room were beginning to spin, and realized she'd forgotten to breathe. She drew in a gulp of air, only to find it didn't ease the swirling sensation in her head.

And then, suddenly it was over. Josh backed up, gave an almost sharp nod of his head, and said a rather brusque good night. And then he was gone, through the narrow doorway that led to the storeroom, closing it with silent care behind him.

Kate let out the gulp of air she'd taken, and fought the puzzling weakness in her limbs that made her tremble. And stood there wondering why she felt nearly as exhausted as Josh had looked.

# *Chapter 7*

J enna Hawk, Josh thought, had been one hell of a
woman. And Kane had been man enough for her,
which was saying a great deal.

*At least she'd been able to save her people.*

At the relentless thought, he slammed the book shut,
barely managing to stop himself from hurling it across
the room. He'd have room to do it, now that he'd had
to move his bedroll into the store itself, in front of the
cast-iron heating stove, because the storeroom was so
full of the supplies for which there hadn't been room
on the mercantile shelves. He wasn't really sure what
stopped him from tossing the book. He still couldn't
explain it, and he still hated things he couldn't explain.

*At least Jenna had been able to save her people.*

That realization—that this woman, this ancestor of
his, had been able to do what he hadn't—had been
nagging at him ever since he'd given up on going back
to sleep and read her story by the light of the kerosene
lamp Kate had provided for him. It was just more proof
to him that after all those years of Hawks breeding
true, it had come down to the one who hadn't. Him.

He didn't understand this at all. He was exhausted,
more tired than he'd ever been, except maybe the time

he'd been riding for Frank Kerrigan's Rocking K. He had gotten pinned down in a line shack during a little disagreement over a small herd of cattle wearing what had once been the Rocking K brand, altered with a running iron to a lopsided Circle R. He'd been awake for three days straight, holding the rustlers off until they'd gotten impatient, and ignoring their orders, had rushed him. He'd taken out three of them and gotten back to the ranch with most of the stock.

But even then he hadn't felt as tired as he did now. He should have slept straight through until tomorrow night, but instead he'd awakened after merely a few hours and been unable to go back to sleep. And the feel of the book in the saddlebags beneath his head was of no help at all in easing a mind that he couldn't seem to slow down.

He'd finally decided either Kate or Luke had to have put the book into the saddlebag before he'd left, and he simply hadn't noticed. He pushed the thought to the back of his mind that there seemed to be an awful lot he wasn't noticing lately.

Luke was the most likely culprit, he thought now. The boy had been fascinated with the damn book. The night he'd first seen it, the boy had spent what seemed like hours trying to follow every branch of the family tree that began with Jenna and Kane, reading every name out loud until Josh was ready to gag the boy with his bandanna.

But then he had decided that listening to that endless list of names was better than hearing that crazy story the boy had read aloud, the one his grandfather had told him so often, about how Jenna had saved the life of a mysterious man of the forest who had made her a promise that in return, her own blood would live on forever. The fact that the bloodline had done exactly that, continued unbroken since that day, didn't make the story any easier to believe, just harder to dismiss.

He wondered now why he hadn't just thrown the boy out. He usually didn't pay much mind to kids, except when they got in his way. They were a nuisance then, following him around, spreading stories that had him doing so many things in so many places he should by rights be a hundred years old instead of twenty-five.

Usually a stern look sent them scurrying away. But Luke was different. Josh couldn't quite bring himself to shoo the boy away. Perhaps because when he looked at him, he saw a bit of himself as he'd been not so long ago: proud, stubborn, and trying to make it alone in a world that seemed to have no place for him.

"Getting soft, Hawk," he muttered, drumming his fingers on the book.

He looked down at the leather cover, remembering Luke's stumbling reading of the incredible story. Josh had been unwillingly fascinated, drawn to Jenna's story in a way he didn't understand. So drawn that he'd read the story himself tonight. And had found the pull becoming stronger, even as he scoffed at the foolishness of the parts about magic and wizardry.

*At least she'd been able to save her people.*

The bitter words rose in his mind yet again. From the time he'd been nine years old, he'd been given a rifle and taught to shoot. Although his mother had been told it was to help supplement their war-shortened food supply, his grandfather had explained to him that the war was very close, and while the fact that they, like many Missourians, had family in both blue and gray, might be of some help should they be visited by troops, they must be ready to defend their home and their women.

Josh, frustrated at being too young to follow his father into battle, had taken to the lessons eagerly, practicing until Gramps had laughingly told him they had to save some ammunition for the real thing.

But when the real thing had come, in the summer of '63, he'd been worse than useless. Despite his grandfather's instructions to stay close while he went into Springfield in search of the latest casualty lists, Josh had been off hunting rabbits when it happened. He'd smelled the smoke first, and started home at a run. He'd heard the faint screams when he'd burst out of the woods, all caution forgotten.

He'd found his mother in the front yard, lying in the middle of her trampled garden. His two oldest sisters were on the front porch, their clothes torn open. His aunt was in the parlor of the big house, her husband's old Sharps rifle beneath her. All were sprawled lifelessly, in grotesque and obscene postures he hadn't completely understood until years later, when he realized what had been done to them. Numb with shock, he'd straightened their bodies, covered them up, and sat down to wait for his grandfather.

It was then that he'd found his youngest sister, twelve-year-old Ruthie, under the high front porch, on her knees, rocking back and forth, staring glassy eyed, muttering "Foxes, foxes" over and over.

Josh knew what it meant; he'd heard about the local guerrilla band of raiders. "They call them Foxes because of the fox tails they tie on their hats," Gramps had told him once. "And they're no better then Quantrill and his gang, for all that they were supposedly formed up to fight them."

By the time Gramps had returned, Ruthie was in the same state Josh had found her in; he hadn't been able to get another word out of her, or even get her to acknowledge he was there. He was crying by then, beyond caring about pride or manhood. But when his grandfather arrived, taking in the grim scene with horrified eyes, Josh had wiped his eyes and stood up to meet him, knowing what he had to do.

"It's my fault, Gramps," he'd said. "I wanted to surprise Mama with a rabbit for supper. The Foxes came. I wasn't here to save them. It's all my fault."

He shivered now, amazed that the old memories still had the power to shake him so. He'd eventually realized that, even had he been there, there was little a ten-year-old boy could have done to stop what had happened.

"You would have died with them, Joshua," Gramps had said that bloody afternoon, "and then where would I be?"

And only much later had he broken the news that Uncle Charles was dead, killed in the fighting at Vicksburg. Josh had known better than to ask about his father; there had been no word for months.

His grandfather had been an incredible man, Josh thought. Comforting his guilt-ridden grandson despite his own pain, and trying futilely to soothe a granddaughter who had retreated so far inside herself she couldn't be found anymore.

He tossed the book down beside him on the floor, resenting that it was stirring up painful memories he'd managed to dodge for years. Remembering the man his grandfather had been only made him more aware of what he himself was not.

Of course, if he quit thinking about that, that left only another uncomfortable subject to dwell on. He hadn't spent so much time in one town since Gramps had taken sick. And he'd come too damn close to dying here to like the place much. So why was he here, on the floor of a place that belonged to the woman he'd made a widow? Why had he pushed himself to near exhaustion chasing down that wagonload of supplies? Why was he still in Gambler's Notch at all?

And most of all, why did every creak of the boards over his head make him wonder what she was doing? And why, when the creaking finally stopped, did the images in his head take such an intimate turn? She wasn't the kind of woman who made men stop in their tracks. She'd said that herself. He thought she was a bit hard on herself to call herself plain—those eyes made that a lie—but she was hardly what you'd call a beauty.

So why was he lying here, wide-awake, wondering if she took her hair down at night, how long it was, and if her nightclothes were as ill-fitting as her dresses seemed to be, or if they perhaps revealed more of that lovely curve of hip he'd noticed that first day?

And why the hell had he turned down the chance to ease this damned ache with that girl in Granite Bluff? She'd been a good-enough-looking woman. And she'd been willing—more than willing—and he could have walked away after without a backward glance. Instead, he'd just walked away.

And it made him more than a little angry that the ache that had vanished in Granite Bluff had come back with a vengeance the instant he'd returned to Gambler's Notch. And it was about to drive him crazy with its fierceness. If he was so damned horny, then why the hell hadn't he been the least bit interested in that saloon girl?

It must have been something about her, he told himself firmly. Perhaps it had been her eagerness to bed The Hawk, without knowing a thing about the man behind the name. That had never bothered him before, but maybe this time. . . .

With a smothered groan, he reached over and picked up the book. Anything would be better that these kinds of thoughts; he'd been far too long without a woman if he was intrigued by one who had nothing in particular to recommend her except a pair of interesting eyes and a certain way of moving.

*You had your chance, last night,* he growled at himself inwardly. There was no reason—except his unexpected lack of interest—why he couldn't have scratched this itch. A man had to take care of those needs, eventually. And the last time had been . . . Cheyenne? Lord, he couldn't remember, except that she'd had red hair he'd discovered was dyed, and had been a bit too bony for his taste. But she'd been enthusiastic enough, although he suspected his reputation might have had something to do with that. Like Lily, she'd been one of those women who seemed to get a strange sort of enjoyment from that kind of thing.

He wondered if Gambler's Notch ran to sporting women. He'd ask Markum tomorrow; although he hadn't seen any girls in the place, most saloon owners found it worth their while to keep a soiled dove or two on or near the premises. That was all that was wrong with him; it had simply been too long. No other reason for him to be wondering what the Widow Dixon wore to bed.

That this conclusion did not give him an answer to his lack of response to the willing Lily was a fact he chose to overlook for the moment. And when that small voice in his head pointed out that he'd been doing a great deal of overlooking lately, he chose to ignore that as well.

Determinedly, he opened the book again. He began to look at the family tree, finding the names Luke had read out loud. It was an odd feeling, to see how the

Hawks had grown, how the line had gone on and on, narrowing in times of hardship or disease, but never breaking. Decade after decade he read, Hawks and their offspring, and theirs, and theirs. On and on it went, each page he turned seeming to pound home to him that he was going to be the one to bring this to an end, that he was the one who would topple the Hawk dynasty.

"Foolishness," he muttered. How did he even know any of these names were right, that any of these people were really his ancestors? This whole thing was unbelievable, the way the book had appeared, the crazy story of Jenna and her warrior, and the wizard. . . .

He nearly laughed out loud. There was no more truth in this than there was in the rest of Gramps's fanciful legends, no matter how this book had come to be in his bag in the first place, or where it had come from. In fact, the whole thing was probably a trick rigged up by that writer he'd run into in Denver last year, who'd taken a notion to make The Hawk the next dime-novel hero.

A slow smile curved his mouth; he was very pleased with this idea. It was much easier to accept than the other crack-brained ideas he'd had. Yes, that writer was behind all this. He'd told the persistent fellow that if he ever saw a book with his name on it, he'd hunt him down and kill him, whether he'd written it or not. Josh had thought the man was convinced, but perhaps not. Perhaps this was the writer's way of trying to convince him he should go along with the idea.

Yes, that was it, Josh thought with a smile. If he poked around hard enough tomorrow, he'd just bet that Mr. Bunting, or whatever his name had been, would come scurrying out from whatever rock he was hiding

under. And he'd make him painfully sorry he'd ever
pried into things that weren't his business.

His smile faded. While someone might be able to
track down his family tree, he supposed, and have it
put into this fancy book, there was one thing his explanation didn't account for, and that was how he'd
known Jenna's story. Hawks might tell the old legends
repeatedly to each other, but they rarely told outsiders.
Gramps had pounded that into him from childhood.

"When you find the right woman, you tell her," he'd
said, making Josh grimace, "because she'll need to
know. Otherwise, you keep this among Hawks."

Well, he doubted such a woman existed, and he'd
certainly never found her, so he'd never told the stories
to anyone. And the rest of the Hawks had been dead
for well over a decade. So how in hell had the writer
come up with the story, down to the details of how
Jenna had found her warrior and lured him out of the
mountains to save her people, in a time and place not
to be found in any history, or on any map?

With a weary sigh, he again tossed the book on the
floor. He was tired of searching for answers to ridiculous questions. He leaned over to the kerosene lamp,
lifting the glass chimney to blow out the flame. He
hesitated when he saw the book had fallen open to the
last page of the tree, the page with the grim record of
deaths, and reached down to close it. His fingers
missed the cover, although he wasn't sure how, and
turned a single page instead.

He stopped, staring at the pages after his branch on
the family tree, pages that he could swear had been
blank. And the first one was indeed blank, as if it had
been skipped for some reason. But the next held one,
short entry at the top of the page. An entry in capital

letters that he knew hadn't been there before. He would have remembered if it had been.

He would have remembered, because of what it said, in that same elaborate, elegant script:

*Joshua Hawk.*

What did you do with a jittery gunfighter?

Kate watched warily as Josh worked the broom with an energy that threatened to wear it out, over a spot near the storeroom door that he'd already swept twice. He'd been on edge all day, and it was making her very nervous in turn.

She'd been surprised by his silence at breakfast after his affable charm with both her and Luke at supper the night before. She'd told herself that he was still tired. She hadn't expected him up at all this morning, and had even been careful not to make any noise, knowing he'd had to sleep in the main room last night. But as noon rolled by, she'd had to admit it was more than that.

Or perhaps this morning she was seeing the real Joshua Hawk, and last night's charm had been an act. She supposed even gunfighters had occasion to be charming, perhaps to lull their targets into thinking they were safe. It was a chilling thought, but then every thought she had about what this man did for a living gave her a chill.

But this was the same man who had pushed himself to exhaustion to retrieve what she'd needed. Who had been kinder, more polite, more helpful, and had worked harder than her husband ever had? How did she reconcile the two? Which one was the real Joshua Hawk?

She looked up as the door opened, grateful for any kind of distraction from Josh's too intense presence.

Luke, who had left at least an hour ago to deliver the monthly supply of preserves and canned peaches to Mr. Meeker, came in as he always seemed to, at a run. He glanced at Josh, who didn't even look up from his sweeping. Luke looked doubtful, then trotted over to the counter where Kate stood.

"Here's the money, Miss Kate, and Mr. Meeker says thank you for . . . remembering him in your time of grief."

The last words came out in a breathless rush, as if the boy wanted to get the message out before he forgot it. That had been very kind of Mr. Meeker. She'd have to make a point of visiting him again soon.

"Thank you for taking it to him, Luke. Here's something for your time—"

"No, ma'am." Luke shook his head, declining the coin she held out to him. "Mr. Meeker, he already gave me somethin'."

"But I always pay you, Luke."

"Mr. Meeker, he said he was payin' this time." The boy grinned. "An' he gave me a dime."

Kate smiled as she put the five-cent piece back in the drawer she'd opened when the boy had come in She would make a point of going to see Mr. Meeker soon, she thought.

Luke glanced again at Josh, who was still sweeping the same spot. Even the boy seemed to sense something wasn't right, because he didn't go over and begin to ply Josh with questions and chatter as he usually did. Instead, he turned back to Kate.

"That man, he surely can talk."

"I'm sure he's just lonely, Luke. It must be awful, to have to be in that room all the time. I hope you were nice to him."

"Sure, I was. I like him. I even visit him sometimes."

"You do?"

Luke nodded. "He doesn't mind. He said so," the boy added earnestly, and Kate's heart ached for the boy who found it such a novelty to have someone who didn't mind his presence.

"I'm sure he's glad of your company," she said.

"He's been a lot of places, and he's got lots of interesting stories," Luke said, "and he lets me look at that old rifle of his, the one he used to shoot buffalo with. And it's not such a bad room. He can see the whole street from that window. Reckon he knows most everything that goes on."

Kate thought it sounded rather sad, watching the world without being a part of it. But she hastily amended that; she'd been part of the world, and there had been many times when she would have given a great deal not to have been. But at least the man didn't treat Luke like he was some kind of wild animal, instead of just a boy who ran a little wild because he had no one to look out for him.

Luke's fascination with The Hawk soon overcame his wariness, and he abandoned Kate for a tentative approach to Josh, stopping a few careful feet away. The boy had been astonished that The Hawk would lower himself to such a menial task as sweeping, but Josh had unperturbedly pointed out that since he was sleeping on the floor, keeping it clean seemed like a good idea. Luke had seen the wisdom in that, and quickly abandoned his opinion that sweeping was beneath him. And now he watched the regular movements of the broom as if fascinated.

"You been sweepin' that spot a long time," Luke said after a moment longer.

Josh kept sweeping, as if he hadn't even heard the boy speak. Luke hesitated, then tried again.

"You were sweeping there when I left."

The broom kept moving, and Josh still never looked up. Kate saw hurt flash across Luke's face, and suddenly she'd had enough; whatever had Josh acting like a caged wolf, it had gone far enough. The boy looked up to him like some sort of hero, and while she was fairly certain a man like The Hawk wasn't the best of idols for a boy, that didn't mean she'd stand by and let the man hurt the boy's feelings.

She stepped out from behind the counter and walked toward them. She put her hand comfortingly on Luke's shoulder as she passed. The boy glanced up at her, his face now a mask of studied indifference. His expression gave her the nerve to keep going until she was close enough to reach out and grasp the broom's handle, stopping the endless motion.

Josh jerked as if startled, instantly letting go of the broom, his head snapping up and his body tensing visibly as his gaze shot to her face.

"If you're going to continue in this mood," she said, "the roof needs fixing."

She saw his right arm flex over his holster, then relax, and realized with a sick little shock that he hadn't just been letting go of the broom, he'd been going for his revolver.

"What?" he said, his brows furrowed, looking merely puzzled while Kate was fighting to keep her heart from hammering its way out of her chest.

Luke was staring up at Josh, wearing an expression Kate was sure was similar to her own, half stunned, half sick.

"You . . . you weren't really gonna shoot us, were you?" Luke said, sounding shaken.

"Shoot you?" His gaze flicked from her to the boy, then back. "Why would I shoot you?"

"Sure looked like you was goin' for that Colt," Luke said, wide-eyed and uncertain.

"Well, she shouldn't sneak up on me like that," Josh said, his mouth twisting in irritation.

"I did not sneak!" Kate exclaimed, her fear shifting to some irritation of her own. "We've been carrying on a normal conversation. You're the one who's been acting like a cornered snake all day, and then ignoring Luke, when all he wanted to do was talk to you."

"Ignoring?" Josh looked puzzled again. He glanced at Luke. "You were talking to me?"

Confusion, then understanding—and relief—dawned on the boy's face. "You didn't hear me?"

The man at least had the grace to look embarrassed, Kate thought. And to be gentle with the boy when he explained.

"No. I guess I'm a little . . . preoccupied."

"What's peroc . . . apied?"

"It means I was thinking too hard," Josh said, his tone wry enough to make Kate wonder just what exactly he'd been thinking about.

"Oh."

He looked at her then. "I'm sorry if I frightened you," he said softly.

"I . . . it's all right."

Josh shifted his gaze back to the boy. Luke studied him for a moment, as if trying to judge if it was safe to go on. Apparently what he saw in Josh's face satisfied him.

"Thinkin' about what?" he asked.

Josh glanced at her again, and unaccountably Kate felt heat rising in her cheeks. She hastily let go of the broom and backed up a step. Josh, moving so swiftly she could barely see the motion, caught the broom handle before it even began to fall. Then he looked back at Luke.

"About that book I showed you," he said.

What was this? Kate wondered. But Josh didn't explain, just kept his gaze on the boy.

"Do you remember seeing my name written in there, Luke?" he asked.

"Sure," Luke said. "Remember, you were on that last line, of that part you said they call the tree."

"I mean anywhere else. On the next page, or anywhere?"

The boy shook his head. "That was the last page with any writin' on it."

"You're sure?"

He nodded this time. "Yep. I looked, 'cause I couldn't figure why there was all those empty pages." Luke looked worried now. "Is something wrong?"

With an audible exhalation, Josh shook his head. "Don't worry about it."

"I liked reading that book," Luke said.

"What book is this?" Kate asked. "And what about a tree?"

Luke turned to her. "It's like no book I ever saw before, Miss Kate. It's got the story of Josh's folks, you know, way back to the very beginning."

Kate looked at Josh curiously. "A . . . family tree?"

Josh's mouth quirked wryly. "Even gunfighters come from somewhere, Mrs. Dixon."

"I didn't mean that." She tried not to blush as he went back to using the formal appellation, and she realized she liked it much better when he called her Kate. "It's just that I've never seen one before."

"I never even heard of one before," Luke said. "But it's real interestin', with all those lines and names, and then the stories."

"Stories?" She'd never heard of a family tree with stories before.

"Yep, I read the one about Jenna and Kane, the very first Hawks, didn't I?" he said, turning to Josh, who was looking decidedly uncomfortable. "Can I read the others sometime? About the other Hawks?"

"Maybe. Just don't be telling anybody about it," Josh said warningly. "Not anybody." He sounded as uneasy as he looked, and Luke's face fell.

The idea of a man like The Hawk carrying around something like a family tree struck Kate as rather whimsical. "I'd like to see this book."

Josh stiffened, so visibly that Kate couldn't help feeling a tiny bit affronted that that "anybody" apparently included her. Then she realized how absurd she was being, to think that a man like Josh would want to share something personal with her. That a man like The Hawk would want to spend any more time with her than he had to to erase whatever debt he felt he owed.

"Speaking of books," she said to Luke hastily, trying to cover her blunder, "we should go back to working on your reading some more."

Luke brightened. "We don't have to hide anymore, do we?"

Kate smiled and shook her head. "No, we don't."

"Hide?"

Something in Josh's tone reminded her she had unthinkingly intruded on his privacy.

"Yeah," Luke explained. "We used to have to hide out in the kitchen late at night, 'cause ol' Arly, he didn't like us reading."

Josh's gaze flicked to her cheek, where the last of the bruise was fading away. Kate kept her head up, refusing to hide it as she wished she could do. She looked back at Luke.

"I have some other books we can read," she said. "I had to keep them hidden before, but now we can look at them whenever I'm not busy, if you like."

"Do they have any wizards and magic in them, like Josh's does?"

She glanced at Josh, startled. "Wizards? Magic?"

Josh shifted his feet restlessly, looking uncomfortable once more. "It's just a story," he muttered.

"I've never heard of a family tree with stories before."

"This one's got 'em," Luke said excitedly. "It's got the tree part, too, but every time it gets down to the last name on the tree, there's a story."

"The last name on the tree?" Kate asked, still looking at Josh, who was clearly not happy with the discussion.

"Just forget it."

His tone was sharp enough that Kate drew back a little, disgusted with herself for again trying to talk to this man as if he was any other man.

"I'm sorry," she said stiffly. "I didn't mean to intrude."

She turned to go back to her work. Josh let out a compressed breath. "Look, I—"

The door to the mercantile slammed open, cutting him off. A man burst in, waving a rifle wildly. Kate smothered a startled cry as Josh reacted instinctively, instantly. He spun toward the door, his Colt in his right hand so quickly Kate couldn't see how he'd done it.

"Josh, don't!" Kate cried. "Luke!" The boy was between him and the man holding the rifle in unsteady hands.

Josh froze.

She could see his gaze flick from the sweating man to the terrified Luke, then back. She held her breath.

He didn't fire.

"Drop it," the man with the rifle ordered.

Kate saw Josh's jaw tighten. "I don't drop my Colt for any man," he said, but he knelt to set it on the floor, his eyes never leaving the man in front of them. That man breathed a sigh of relief. So did Kate; The Hawk had bent for Luke. He'd given up his gun so the boy wouldn't be hurt. Perhaps there was more to him than it seemed.

"Get it over with, mister," Josh grated out. "But get her and the boy out of here first."

Kate's forehead creased, then she gasped as his meaning struck her. He'd given up his gun all right. And he'd done it fully expecting to die for it.

# Chapter 8

"You're safe now, Kate," the man said.

"Safe?" Her voice had risen, sounding nearly like a yelp.

"I heard as soon as I got off the stage that The Hawk had killed Arly, and that he was in here with you right now. I grabbed my carbine and came running."

"Put that *down*! No one is safe with you waving that thing around."

Josh blinked as she issued the order to the man in the fancy suit. People were gathering in the doorway, gaping at the display before them. The man looked uneasy, but didn't lower the rifle. A lock of sandy brown hair fell forward over his brow, and he flipped it back with a snap of his head, but never took his eyes off Josh.

"Yeah, Mr. Hall," Luke said, recovering rapidly from his fright, "put it down. Everybody knows what an awful shot you are."

The man flushed. "Well, maybe I'm not a crack shot, but I backed down The Hawk, didn't I?"

"Oh, for heaven's sake, Alex, only because he was afraid you were going to hit Luke!"

Alex, Josh thought. Alexander? The memory came then, of a name painted on a building.

"You're the lawyer," he said.

"I am," the man said proudly.

"You're also a fool," Josh said sourly. "If that boy hadn't been between us, you'd be dead."

The lawyer held his gaze, hazel eyes unwavering. He was clearly nervous, but he didn't back away, Josh had to give him credit for that. Hall might not be a crack shot, as he'd said, but he wasn't short on nerve.

"You expect me to believe that a man of your ilk would stop simply because a boy got in the way?"

"I expect you to believe the evidence of your eyes," Josh said. "Was there any other reason for me not to drop you where you stood? With witnesses who saw you come charging in here waving that old Sharps around?"

"I would have shot you," Hall pointed out.

"And it would have been your last act."

Hall paled. Then a chuckle came from the doorway. "And you woulda missed to boot, Alex," Marshal Pike said.

Laughter broke out among the group gathered just inside the doorway, a group that had apparently seen the young man heading this way at a run, armed.

"Before you charged in here to rescue the lady, you shoulda made sure she needed it first," somebody called out from the group. Hall flushed. And at last lowered the carbine to his side.

"You're a fine lawyer, Alex," Kate said soothingly. "Isn't that enough?"

Hall cleared his throat. "Well, yes." He cast a wary eye at Josh. "But what *is* he doing here?"

"Working," Josh answered.

Hall blinked. "Working? Working at what?"

"Sweeping," Josh said blandly.

Hall looked from Josh to Kate and back. "Sweeping?"

"Is that a habit with lawyers?" Josh asked. "Repeating things?"

Luke laughed, and Hall flushed again. His sheepish expression clearly showed that he realized he'd made a rather embarrassing mistake.

"Come on, Alex, we'll paint your tonsils with something to wash down that road dust," Pike said.

The clearly embarrassed young lawyer seized the offer quickly. The group continued to harangue the man, clapping him on the back as they herded him toward the saloon and that promised drink, but with the kind of good humor that spoke of liking, not contempt.

Pike lingered in the doorway for a moment, looking at Josh. "That true? You didn't fire on account of the boy was in the way?"

Josh shrugged. He wasn't sure himself why he hadn't shot the man; it had certainly been his first instinct when Alex had burst into the store with that rifle.

Pike seemed to accept his gesture as an answer. "The reverend's been saying you're working here because of killing Arly, and Mrs. Dixon here helping you out." Josh shrugged again. "That'll do, for the town folks," Pike went on. "But you start drawing them in from the territory . . ."

Josh nodded. Pike nodded back, then turned and walked off after the others.

"What did that mean?" Kate asked.

Josh shrugged again. "He was reminding me my welcome here is limited."

"Why?" she asked. "You were freed, and Luke told me the judge's order came through on the telegraph, declaring you innocent of murder."

"No man with my kind of reputation stays welcome in any town for long. Not any town with any kind of lawman, anyway. Pike's just letting me know I have until the men looking to build their own reputations start showing up."

She frowned. "But that's not your fault."

"Doesn't matter."

"But Caleb is a fair man—"

"He's also a good marshal. And a good marshal stops trouble before it starts."

"But it's not fair for you to have to leave because of what somebody else does."

"Worried about me, Kate?" he asked softly, more to see her blush at his use of her name than anything else. She did, prettily. She didn't seem plain at all at the moment, he thought. Nor had she when she'd been so riled at that lawyer fellow. When she got her blood up, those golden eyes fairly snapped. "That lawyer, he a special friend of yours?"

"Alex?" she said, sounding surprised.

"Aww, he's sweet on her," Luke said. "Has been for a long time, but he was too afraid to say anything because of ol' Arly."

"Luke!" Kate exclaimed. "Don't be silly. Of course, he's not."

"Then why did he come in here like a Texas brush popper when he thought you needed help?" Josh asked.

Her color deepened and she turned away from him.

"Told ya," Luke crowed. "Why, he even cozies up to Miss Deborah, 'cause she's her good friend. Now that that ol' bastard Arly's gone, he'll probably—"

"Lucas Mitchell, that's enough," Kate said sharply, turning on the boy. "And I'll thank you not to use that kind of language!"

Luke stopped, staring at her. Josh didn't know if Luke's shock was at her tone, or her use of his full name, which, Josh realized with some chagrin, he'd never asked of the boy. Either way, the boy was startled.

"I'll not have you calling the dead names under my roof," she said. "Arly is gone and buried now, and there's no use in speaking ill of him."

Luke backed up, blinking rapidly. "Why not? He called me the same thing. Said I was nothin' more than a catch colt."

"A . . . what?" Kate asked, in a tone that sounded like she was regretting her irritation with the boy in the face of his obvious hurt.

"It means a colt that comes out of an unplanned breeding," Josh said bluntly, realizing she was embarrassed, but feeling badly for Luke at the same time. He dug into his pocket and flipped the boy a dime. "Do me a favor, Luke. Go check on Buck for me, and give him a good grooming. I haven't had time yet today."

Luke caught the coin, and with a final glance at Kate, turned and ran out of the store.

"Guess we've both been a little hard on that boy's feelings today," he said.

"I didn't mean to be. But Arly's dead. He won't hurt anyone anymore. Let him rest in peace."

"As he let you live in peace?" Josh asked softly. He knew it had been the wrong thing to say the moment he saw her eyes. Anger flared again in the golden depths.

"What would you have me say? That he was a mean, brutal, angry man? That's no surprise to anyone in this town. That he took it out on people smaller and weaker than him? That's no surprise either. That he only married me because it would make it clear he owned me, so if I ran away he could have me brought back?"

"I doubt that was his only reason," Josh said, wondering how Arly had reacted to this fire in her. Had it fired him in turn, or had he, as many brutal men did, felt the need to stomp out that courageous spirit? He suspected he already knew the answer to that.

"No," she agreed, "it wasn't his only reason. There are decent people in this town who were his customers, and he couldn't afford to alienate them entirely by openly keeping a whore."

Josh stiffened. "Don't say that."

"Why? What else do you call a woman traded for a pair of boots because she's the oldest and plainest of four girls, with a father who's afraid he'll never be rid of her?"

"Kate, stop."

She kept on, like a pebble picking up speed as it rolled downhill. "And poor Arly got stuck with her because he was so mean none of the women in town would go near him. He couldn't be choosy—"

He took a quick step toward her, grabbed her arms, and pulled her around to face him. "Stop it!"

"NO!" She screamed it, and instantly began to fight him fiercely, clawing, kicking, twisting. "No, no more!"

The instant he realized what she meant, he released her and backed up. She backed away until she came up hard against the counter. Then she stood there, staring at him, wild-eyed, her breath coming in short, harsh pants.

"Easy," he said, holding his hands up and away from her, palms out. "Easy. I'm not going to hurt you. I'm not Arly, Kate."

He saw her bite her lower lip, as if trying to regain control of herself.

"Easy," he said again, instinctively reverting to the low, soothing tone that had once calmed the girl who had once been his sister Ruthie. "It's all right. It's over, Kate. No one will ever hurt you like that again."

Her breathing slowed, and some of the panic left her eyes. He kept talking.

"I didn't mean to frighten you. I just wanted you to stop talking like that about yourself."

She took a deep breath, and he saw her steady herself with a visible effort.

"You've had a hard time, Kate. But your father was heartless and your husband just plain evil. There's no reason for you to believe a word they ever said about you."

"He . . . hated me. My father. He's hated me since I was eight years old."

"Kate—"

"No. I mean it. He hated me ever since I told a lady who asked where we were from that we'd left Virginia when I was a little girl so Pa wouldn't have to fight in the war."

Josh winced. "Was it true?"

She nodded. "I know it was. I heard them talking about it when they thought I was asleep."

"When did . . . this happen?"

"The year after the war ended. We were in Kansas."

He winced again. In Kansas, a year after the war, blood and emotions had still been running high. He could guess what had happened—a man with obvious Southern speech, who had abandoned his home rather than fight for it, probably amid men who had lost the war but had never surrendered. . . .

"He's lucky he survived," Josh muttered.

"He ran again. That's why he wanted to get rid of me. My sisters were too little to understand, so they couldn't tell anyone."

"Where was your mother?"

Kate smiled, a twisted, dreadful little smile. "Where she always was. In my father's shadow, hiding, hoping he wouldn't come after her."

She was talking again, at least, and not staring at him in that awful, panicked way. That was something, he supposed, even if what she was saying wasn't very pretty. Again it struck him as so very odd, that of the three of them, himself, Luke, and Kate, he was the one who had had the best life.

"I'm sorry, Kate," he said softly.

She seemed to come out of it then, coming back to herself with a suddenness that was visible in the widening of her eyes and the embarrassment in her expression.

"No, I'm sorry," she said. "I don't know what made me go on like that, wasting your time with my sorry past."

"How old are you, Kate?"

A hint of color touched her cheekbones. "I . . . twenty. I know I look older—"

He shook his head. "That's not why I asked. I just wondered how long you'd survived such a life."

She lowered her eyes. "Oh."

"You're a strong woman."

She shook her head wearily, without looking at him. "I'm not. If I had been, I'd have found a way to get away from Arly long ago."

"You tried," he said. Her head came up sharply. "Luke told me," he explained. "He also told me what Arly did to you. No wonder you gave up."

"I didn't!" Her chin was up, her eyes alive again. Josh let out a silent breath of relief; she was going to be all right. "I never gave up. Never. I started saving again, planning again, as soon as I could."

"Like I said, you're a strong woman."

"I'm going to be," she said, determination echoing in her voice, "now. I won't be like my mother, I won't. No one will ever treat me like I'm nothing again."

As if impelled by her own words, she drew herself up straight. "I have work to finish," she said firmly.

He grinned at her, glad beyond what he ever would have expected to be to see the tough, practical Kate back again. "So do I."

She gave him a businesslike nod and retreated to the storeroom. Josh walked over to the broom that had lain forgotten on the floor during the recent encounter. He frowned to himself as he picked it up. Had he really been so lost in thought that he hadn't even heard Luke talking to him? True, he'd been preoccupied, but that kind of preoccupation got a man in his line of work killed.

He heard a slight thump from the storeroom, but no call for help came. He'd discovered Kate was a little touchy about him assuming she needed help when she hadn't asked for it, so he stayed where he was.

This time he finished the sweeping quickly, receiving another sign of how round the bend he'd been by how little he'd gotten swept today. If he kept this up, he'd be dead inside a week, shot while woolgathering, by some other do-gooder thinking to rescue the Widow Dixon. He wondered what would happen to the book when the inevitable came and the Hawk line finally did die out.

He jerked his mind out of the rut it had worn long and deep since he'd found his name written on that otherwise empty page last night, impossibly appearing where nothing had been before. Think about something else, he ordered himself. Anything else. Like maybe just how sweet that young lawyer was on Kate.

That, he thought suddenly, stopping his sweeping,

just might solve his problem here. If the lawyer was genuinely sweet on the widow, and could be persuaded to proceed along that path . . .

Of course. Another husband. A decent one this time, like Alexander Hall, lawyer. That's all that was needed here. Kate would be settled, taken care of, and he could be on his way. Of course, there'd have to be a seemly period of mourning, even for a miscreant like Arly Dixon, but once he was certain the lawyer was going to do the right thing, he could at last shed himself of this town.

Kate and the lawyer. It would work. He knew the townsfolk liked her, had felt sorry for her life with Arly—although not, he thought with more than a little rancor, sorry enough to help her, except for Luke— and would welcome her staying. Not, he amended, that she had anywhere else to go; she certainly couldn't go home to her father.

The question was, would she agree? Did she feel anything in turn for Alex Hall? True, she'd blushed when Luke had said the lawyer was sweet on her, but she could have simply been embarrassed; it didn't seem to take much to make that lovely color rise in her face. He liked that about her. It gave him a clue about what she was thinking.

He'd ask her, he thought. That was the simplest way. He'd simply ask her how she felt, and if he got the right answer, then he'd go have a talk with Lawyer Alexander Hall. Even if he didn't get the right answer, he might have a talk with the man. Surely a man clever enough to become a lawyer could manage to convince Kate she wanted him, now that she was free of the merciless Arly.

He leaned the broom against the shelves behind him, and walked toward the storeroom, only now realizing that she'd been in there without making a sound for some time. He hoped that thump he'd heard hadn't been more ominous than he'd realized, and began to hurry. He stopped in the doorway, relaxing slightly when he saw her upright and seemingly intact.

She was standing beside the small side window, intent on something in her hands.

"Kate," he began, stepping inside.

She gave a little start, half turning toward him. He thought he'd frightened her again, almost to tears, since her eyes looked moist, but her expression wasn't one of fear. Oddly, it seemed almost guilty, as if she'd been caught doing something she shouldn't have, although what it could be here in her own storeroom he couldn't guess.

And then he saw what was open in her hands, and he knew.

It was the book.

"I'm sorry," she said quickly, "but it was on the floor, and I accidentally kicked it. It opened when I picked it up, and I saw . . ."

Her words trailed away. He got an idea of what his face must look like by the way she quickly turned away and closed the book. It was a moment before she looked at him. When she did, her eyes were still moist, and in them was an emotion he couldn't put a name to.

"I apologize, Josh. I had no right."

She held the book out to him. For a moment he studied her face, wondering what had put that odd softness in her expression. Then, at last, he reached out and took the book from her. He felt it again, that odd sense of warmth, of companionship he'd never known before. He glanced down at the cover, wondering how much she'd read. Had she seen the pages with Jenna and Kane's story, that mythical tale of sorcerers and magic? Was she convinced he had descended from a line of nothing less than lunatics?

"I'm sorry about your family," she said quietly.

His gaze shot back to her face. So it was sympathy he'd seen in her eyes. Or pity. She'd begun reading at the end, and seen all the dates of death so painfully close together. His jaw tightened as he looked away. He'd never been able to talk about it, and didn't see himself starting now.

"How awful for you, to find them like that."

His head snapped up. "What?"

"And you were only ten, Josh. Younger than Luke, even. How could you blame yourself?"

"What are you talking about?"

"And your sister . . . how horrible. Seeing it all happen, and being helpless to stop it. No wonder she couldn't live with it any longer. The river must have promised peace to her."

No one, absolutely no one other than he and his grandfather, had known Ruthie had drowned herself. No one.

"And just how," he said, very slowly and carefully, "do you know that?"

She looked puzzled. "I read it. I know I shouldn't have, it's private, but the book just fell open to that page when I picked it up, and I saw your name, and the story, and . . ."

Again her voice faded away. He didn't have to see her expression this time to guess what his face looked like. And he was sure his voice matched it.

"What story?"

She looked apprehensive, but she answered him. "The one about you." She paused. Then she nervously rushed on. "Are you writing it? Are all the dates listed there, after the story, things you're going to put in it?"

"There is no story about me in this book."

Her brows furrowed. "Of course there is. You know there is." Her chin came up as if he'd insulted her. "I don't read as well as I should, but I could read this." As if to prove her point, she gestured toward the book. "It's right at the end there. I mean, it's in the middle of the book, because of all the empty pages, but at the end of the writing."

He shifted the book in his hand to open it. He didn't know what she'd seen, but she was obviously confused. He remembered what Luke had said about her not reading that well, and she'd said it now herself. He wondered if that was what had happened, if she'd been confused somehow. But if she read well enough to teach Luke, who had managed to get through Jenna's story without stumbling too badly, then she

His thoughts came to an abrupt halt as the book fell open in his hand, as if to a page often turned to. But he'd only looked at that page once, last night, and it had sent him into a dizzying whirl of confused thoughts that lasted until Kate had shaken him out of it this afternoon. And his questioning of Luke hadn't helped; the boy's positive statements had only proven what he'd already known—his name had not been there the night before.

But that somehow seemed minor compared to what he was seeing now. Insignificant next to the fact that where last night there had been merely a blank page beneath that graceful script entry of his name, there was now a pageful of the elegant writing, spelling out in grim detail the destruction of the Hawks. Grim details that no one else alive could know. Grim details he'd even managed to forget himself. And following it were dates, dates that were engraved in his mind, dates that marked things in his life he would never, ever forget.

He didn't know which was more impossible, that the story was here, or how it had appeared. Or that it seemed bent on continuing, with that list of dates sitting there like some omen of things to come. It was crazy. He would have thought himself hallucinating had not she seen it as well.

"Josh, what's wrong? You look like you've seen a—" She broke off as he looked up at her. "I'm sorry," she said breathlessly. "that was an awful thing to say."

A ghost? Josh nearly laughed; he could deal with that more easily than he could deal with the impossibility of what he was holding in his hands. At least some people believed in ghosts; the only thing anyone would believe about this was that he been up in the mountains too long.

"Of course it's awful, reliving all that horror. But perhaps it helped, to write it down?"

"I didn't—"

He stopped before the damning words were out. Let her think he'd written it. It would be easier to explain. Now if someone would just explain it to him. . . .

He slapped the book shut. With sharp, determined movements he strode across the small room to his saddlebag and stuffed the book inside, thinking perhaps he should go out and stuff it in the stove at the back of the store instead. Isn't that what they did with things connected to witchcraft and sorcery and wizards? Burn them?

He might do it yet, he thought.

When he straightened up, he found Kate watching him with an odd expression. He waited, unable to think of a single thing to say to her.

After a moment, she said only, "I'm sorry I pried,"

and walked out of the storeroom. Josh looked after her for a while, wondering what she would have said if he'd told her the truth.

He nearly laughed aloud. The truth? He wished somebody had told him the truth long ago. But nobody had. Not his father, not his mother, not his uncle. They'd told him the legends; they'd told him of century after century of Hawk history; and they'd told him all the things to be proud of.

But never once had they told him the damned Hawks were haunted.

# Chapter 9

"Come in, Mrs. Dixon."

Kate winced as she stepped into the marshal's office. "Thank you. But, please, call me Kate."

Caleb Pike looked at her as if he knew exactly why she'd offered him the familiarity of her first name, as if he knew that being called by Arly's name made her cringe inside.

"Of course . . . Miss Kate," he said, much as Luke did, which made her smile.

Pike smiled back. He really was a nice-seeming man. With his long, curling mustache, and his slight paunch hanging over his belt, he hardly looked like a man who could quell a fight among drunken cowboys without drawing a weapon, but she'd heard he'd done it more than once.

"Sit down," Pike suggested.

Kate hesitated. She had hesitated outside as well, not at all certain she wanted to do this. She'd barely spoken to Caleb Pike in all the time he'd been here as town marshal, and most of that under Arly's watchful eye when the man had come into the mercantile.

Once, after Arly had left her face particularly bruised, Pike had threatened to talk to Arly. She'd been terrified this would only earn her a worse beating, and Pike had backed off. And once Deborah had sent for him, that time after Arly had caught her trying to run away. Pike had talked to Arly then, and whatever he'd said had made an impression; Arly had never hurt her that badly again.

It was that that decided her; she sat down in the chair he'd indicated. It felt odd to be here. She still wasn't quite used to the fact that she could come and go as she pleased now. She had to remind herself that if she wished to take a walk, she could; if she wished to talk to someone, she could.

"What can I do for you?"

Kate laced her fingers together in her lap. She had been formulating the question in her mind all the way here, trying to decide how to say it. But now that she was here, all she could manage was to blurt it out.

"You can tell me about Joshua Hawk."

Pike looked thoughtful. He tugged at his luxuriant mustache. At last, he sat on the edge of his desk, a few feet away from her.

"Well, now," he said slowly, "seems everybody already knows all there is to know about The Hawk.

"You mean his reputation. The legend."

Pike smiled. "Sounds like something outta one of them dime magazines, doesn't it?"

"Yes. It does. That's why I'm asking. Most legends are made of half-truths and imagination."

"And you want the truth, is that it?"

"Yes."

"And you think I know it?"

"I think you know more of the truth than anyone else in town."

Pike smiled again. "I may know a thing or two," he conceded. "Exactly what is it you want to hear?"

*I want to know just how awful a thing I've done,* she thought. But she said only, "Is he a killer?"

Pike leaned back. "Well, now, that depends. Lots of men have killed. That doesn't necessarily make them killers."

"It doesn't?"

"Way I look at it, there are those who kill because they're forced to. Given a choice, they walk away. And there are those who, given that choice, kill anyway. Who kill not because it's unavoidable, but because they like it. They take pleasure in it. They're born that way." Pike shrugged. "You ask me, that's a real killer."

"And . . . The Hawk? Which is he?"

"I'm not sure, yet. From what I've heard, he's never been the first to start a fight."

Kate wasn't sure that was a recommendation; she'd seen Arly drive people to making the first move more than once, just so he'd be able to claim later he hadn't started it.

"But he has killed people. Lots of people."

"So they say. I know he's carrying a lot of fame around with him, but . . ." Pike lifted his hands in a gesture expressing indecision.

*He's carrying a lot of pain around with him as well,* Kate thought, remember the horrible story she'd read.

"But what?" she asked.

"I've got a feelin', but I could be wrong."

"What is . . . your feeling?"

Pike shrugged again. "That boy's no born killer. He's good, and he's cooler than most, but he's not cold. Not clear through. Not yet anyway."

Kate didn't know if that made her feel better or worse.

"Funny thing, though," Pike said, as if he were merely thinking out loud, "I got the idea, when he was locked up here waiting on the hangman, that he didn't really mind the idea of dyin'."

Kate stared at the marshal. "What?"

Pike nodded. "He seemed almost relieved. Like a man who was tired of living."

"Tired of living?" Kate's forehead creased. "But he's so young. . . ."

"Twenty-five, the paperwork says. But years don't always tell the tale."

She thought again of the story she'd read in that book, that beautiful, unusual book that he was so secretive about. What had happened to him, what he'd gone through, could indeed make a person older than his years. But still, the idea shook her.

"You think he really . . . wanted to die?"

Pike tugged at his mustache again before saying thoughtfully, "More like he didn't want to live anymore. Leastwise, not like he'd been living."

Kate sat silently, considering this. She knew too well how that felt, to have reached the point of finding death a more pleasant alternative than the life she'd been handed. But she wasn't Josh, didn't have his power, his strength. How much worse had his life been to drive a strong, fearless man like Josh to welcome death?

"Pardon me, Mrs.—er, Miss Kate, why are you asking? Is he giving you some kind of trouble?"

"Oh, no," she said quickly. "Not at all." Not the kind of trouble you mean, anyway, she added silently.

"Well, then, if you don't mind my saying so, there are those in town who think he just might have done you a good turn."

Kate paled. Hastily, she stood up. She searched the marshal's face, looking for any sign of suspicion. She found nothing.

"I didn't mean to upset you, ma'am. It's just that . . . everyone knows Arly was a mean one. And that you had some mighty hard times. Some of us feel we should have done something to help."

"You tried, Marshal. There was no way to help, not with Arly. Thank you for speaking with me."

She was halfway back to the mercantile before her heart slowed to its normal rate.

*That boy's no born killer.*

Perhaps not, she thought. But he'd certainly seen his share of killing, at an age when he should have been concerned only with being a child. If the story she'd read was true, his family had been nearly wiped out by the war. The war her father had run away from.

She turned away from the thought. She didn't think about her father very much, and hadn't for a long time. At first, she'd told herself he hadn't known what he was doing, the kind of situation he was leaving her in. But she knew he had known what kind of man Arly was. She'd heard her mother arguing with him about it, one of the only times in her life her mother had ever dared to dispute her father's decisions.

It was the memory of her mother that hurt. Kate had hoped that just this once, her mother would not give in. But she did, and the Daytons had gone on their way, abandoning their oldest daughter to her fate.

And abandoned was how Kate had felt at sixteen; she'd felt as much an orphan as Luke, which was probably why she'd felt such empathy for the boy, and had sneaked him food, and a pair of sturdy shoes when winter was coming. But she'd soon come to realize that even Luke, for all that he was a child with no one to look out for him, had a better lot than she. He at least didn't have heavy, meaty fists of a drunken beast to dodge—until the day the boy had tried to pay her back by helping her escape, and Arly had caught them both.

She stifled a shiver at the memories, and wondered how long it would take before they went away. She wished they would go now. She had no desire to recall the ugliness.

But Josh apparently did. Why else would he have that book? She supposed it was different if your ugly memories were tied to something big, something momentous like a war. But still, she couldn't see why he would want to remember all the grim details that were in the story she'd read. But he must, or he wouldn't be writing the story down.

It was very odd, she thought, that a gunfighter would write a history of his family. Yet all the writing in the book was the same, so it had to be Josh's. And the family tree, with all those names and branches . . . how had he ever found all that out? She barely knew anything about her family beyond her great-grandparents on her mother's side; her father had never spoken of his own family. But Josh apparently knew the name of every Hawk who had ever lived. How was it possible? Had Josh's grandfather helped him with that, before he died? But how could even he know that?

When she reached the mercantile, she tried to turn away from her scattered thoughts and pull her mind back to business; she had some accounts to go over. Once Arly had discovered she had a knack for numbers, he'd chortled over his good deal, getting a cook, a laundress, a clerk who could keep accounts, and a woman to use in his bed every night, all for a pair of boots. A canny trade, he used to tell everyone, even if the woman wasn't much to look at.

She paused just inside the door when she saw Mr. Rankin standing at the counter, talking to Josh.

"—only enough for one more set of shoes. I needed that iron," he was saying.

Josh lifted a shoulder in a negligent manner. "Now you have it."

"Thanks to The Hawk."

She saw Josh's jaw tighten. "I suppose."

He didn't sound at all happy about it. He looked up then, seeing her in the doorway, and his expression became unreadable. Mr. Rankin turned, and saw her as well.

"Mrs. Dixon," he said in greeting.

She nodded and smiled at the man who had always, even under Arly's fiercest glares, at least been polite to her. "Was your shipment satisfactory, Mr. Rankin?"

He nodded in turn. "I was just thanking Mr. Hawk, here, for getting that load here so quick."

Her mouth quirked wryly. "Having a famous gun-fighter take delivery does seem to speed things up."

Rankin smiled. Josh did not. With a final touch of his hand to his forehead, the blacksmith left and went back to his forge.

Kate turned to look at Josh. He remained unsmiling. She wondered if he was still angry at her for looking at his book. She walked toward him tentatively, pondering apologizing yet again, wondering if would do any good.

Before she could decide, he spoke rather harshly. "I didn't set out to be famous, you know."

She didn't know what to say to that, so she said nothing, just looked at him curiously as she walked behind the counter, wondering what had set him off on this.

"I just . . . happen to be good with a gun, that's all. It's something I can do that men are willing to pay for. When I started, it was just a job. A way to make a living. I never wanted . . . the rest."

"The legend?" she asked softly as she came to halt beside him.

He grimaced. "Some men may like having people be afraid of them all the time. And I admit it has its uses. But I don't *like* it."

"I'm not afraid of you."

She didn't know what had possessed her to say it, although, she realized with some amazement, it was true. And when he looked at her intently, she wished she hadn't said it. And she wished she hadn't come so close to him. But she couldn't seem to back away, either.

"It didn't seem like that yesterday," he said.

She knew he meant when he'd grabbed her and she'd panicked. "That wasn't you I was afraid of. I wasn't thinking. I was just . . ."

"Reacting?"

She nodded. Josh looked at her for a long, silent moment. "How did you survive, Kate?" he finally said, so softly she wondered if he'd meant to say it out loud.

"I got very good at staying out of Arly's way."

Josh shook his head, as if in wonder. "Did he ever know, Kate? Did he ever see that he hadn't ever conquered you, he'd only . . . made you hide?"

She stared at him; that was exactly how she'd thought of her life with Arly, as a time spent hiding, hiding herself in both body and soul, until she would someday be safe to come out again.

"Some men never learn," he said in that same soft voice. "They never see that any creature with spirit is best handled with care. They want to break that spirit, and never see how much more they could have if they fed it instead."

Taken aback by both his perception and the softness

of his words, Kate tried to deny the sudden welling of emotion he'd roused in her.

"It sounds as if you're comparing me to a horse," she said, trying to sound offended. "Or perhaps some other, lesser animal."

"Perhaps," he agreed easily, as if he saw right through her efforts to dissemble. "But as it applies to animals, it applies to people as well. No one with gumption takes easily to having it crushed."

Her head came up. She had to stop this, it was making her feel too . . . She wasn't sure what it was, this heart-pounding, stomach-knotting, hot-and-cold feeling he caused in her, but it had to stop.

"Especially a Hawk?" she asked, hoping to divert him.

He shrugged. "It seems they particularly don't take well to bullies."

"You say that like you're not a Hawk yourself."

He looked away then. "Maybe I'm thinking I shouldn't be," he muttered.

Something in his tone made her regret she'd said what she had. "But you are," she said.

"And I'll be the last," he said, a bitterness in his voice she'd never heard from him before. "The last Hawk. It dies with me." His mouth curved into a twisted smile that echoed his tone. "A grand ending to a centuries-old bloodline, don't you think? A killer who'll buck out in smoke some day? The last of the Hawks, dead in some street, because he couldn't even get himself hanged?"

Before she realized what she was doing, she had reached out and grabbed his hands.

"Josh, stop it," she said, suddenly understanding what had driven him to the same action yesterday.

He stared down at her, so intensely that whatever

she'd been about to say to him died unspoken. The bitterness in his expression faded, to be replaced by something hot and fierce she didn't recognize.

"Kate," he whispered. His voice had changed as well, had taken on an undertone of vibrancy that sent a shiver of that crazy hot and cold racing down her spine.

He lifted a hand and touched her, a gentle finger beneath her chin tilting her head back much as he had before, when he'd tried to tell her some foolishness about her eyes being the same color as that lovely gold ribbon.

But there was something different about this time, something that made her breath stop and her heart seem to miss a beat, then hurry to catch up. She wanted to pull away; she couldn't bear the way he was staring at her, the way his eyes seemed to bore right through her, as if he were searching her soul.

"Josh," she begged, not sure what she was begging for. She told herself it was for him to release her from whatever this hold was he had on her, but when she thought of the loss of the heat of his touch, she was no longer sure.

And then he moved, his hands slipping down to her shoulders. He lowered his head slowly, as if reluctantly, his expression one of a man fighting himself. He drew closer to her, and Kate thought she should move away, but didn't quite know why. She didn't realize until his lips brushed hers that he meant to kiss her.

Her astonishment vanished, overpowered as a jolt rattled through her, a burst of fire and ice that made those shivers she'd felt before seem weak, faint precursors of the sensations that flooded her now. His lips were warm and gentle, and he tasted vaguely of coffee and the peppermint candy she'd seen him sneak more than once. But there was another taste there, something hot and distinctly male, something that made it impossible for her to do what she knew she should do—pull away from him.

She felt herself tremble, felt her muscles go oddly slack; but then all she knew was the feel of his mouth on hers, and the incredible size and heat of him, and the thudding of her pulse in her ears.

She heard a tiny, mewling sound, and realized with some shock that it had come from her. As if in answer, she heard Josh growl, from low and deep in his chest, wild cougar to her helpless kitten.

The sound stopped abruptly, and just as abruptly, Josh broke the kiss and pulled his head away. His movement was short and sharp, and for a moment he just stood there, looking down at her, his lips parted as if he were finding it as hard to breathe as she was. Then he released her, looking at his hands as if he hadn't realized he'd been holding her. He didn't look like a man who was happy about what he'd just done.

She stared up at him, stunned. One hand crept up to her mouth. Shaking fingers touching her lips, lips still tingling from the feel of his.

Josh looked back at her face, and seemed to take in her dazed expression and the trembling of her fingers. His brows lowered.

"Don't look so shocked," he said, as if irritated. "You've been kissed before."

Slowly, unable to speak, Kate shook her head.

Josh grimaced. "You were married," he said, the irritation more discernible now.

She shook her head again. She tried to speak, but her words came out in broken, choppy little spurts. "I . . . Arly never . . . he didn't . . ."

Josh stared at her in patent disbelief. "He never

what? Kissed you? You were married for four years, and he never kissed you?"

"I . . . never . . . like that. Never gentle, and sweet, like that."

Josh's forehead creased. "But he did kiss you."

"In the beginning he did. But when he kissed, it . . . hurt."

He drew back a little. "Hurt?"

She nodded once, or tried to. "He . . . liked it, if I cried out. He said it made him . . . ready."

She saw a shiver ripple through him, saw the look of distaste on his face. She'd disgusted him. She should have realized it would disgust any man, to know what she'd been to Arly, little more than a whore, despite the short, lonely marriage ceremony she'd gone through in front of a drunken Reverend Babcock. Josh was probably sickened that he'd kissed her.

"May he roast in hell," Josh muttered.

Kate went very still, despite the little quiver his words sent through her. Was it possible he hadn't been disgusted by her, but by what Arly had done to her? It seemed impossible, but then, so did the idea of Joshua Hawk kissing her, and she couldn't deny that had happened, not when her lips were still tingling and her fingers still trembling.

Josh turned away from her, and she heard him let out a compressed breath. After a moment of strained silence, he shoved a piece of paper that lay on the counter toward her.

"The telegraph man was in, bought some lamp oil. And Markum came in for some stove pipe. Three feet of it. I wrote it down there. The money's in the drawer."

She stared down at the paper, at the neat printing and tidy figures, trying to compose herself. If there was anything powerful enough to distract her from what had just happened, it should be this. The Hawk working in a mercantile, selling goods like any shopkeeper. For her.

And it wasn't until much later that she realized what else that paper, and the way Josh had written those items and the figures, had told her.

The writing, tidy and precise though it was, bore no resemblance at all to the writing in the Hawk book.

# Chapter 10

"I think it was sweet of Alex."

Kate sipped at her tea, looking at her friend over the rim of the cup. Her Sunday mornings with Deborah had been the one bright spot in her dreary life since she'd come to Gambler's Notch. Even Arly couldn't go against the expected tradition of closing the mercantile Sunday mornings for Reverend Babcock's sermons, although he had always opened in the afternoons. And even Arly hadn't dared to order her not to see Deborah, although he tried to control everyone else she saw; the woman was far too consequential in town for him to set himself up against her. Not only was she the closest thing to medical help the town had, and the daughter of the town's well-respected doctor, Deborah's liking for the expensive tea shipped in from the States had put a lot of coin in the mercantile's till over the years.

Deborah also, Kate thought wryly, had the only chickens in town, and was therefore the sole source of fresh eggs for the store. Arly might have been mulish, but he hadn't been a fool when it came to supplies.

"I suppose it was," Kate said in answer to Deborah's observation about Alex Hall's rush to her rescue.

She didn't add that Alex had also looked a trifle foolish; she knew Deborah liked the young lawyer. In fact, she'd often wondered if Deborah perhaps didn't feel a little more than liking for the man.

"Alex . . . cares for you, you know."

Kate stared at Deborah. That was two people who had hinted at that now. "I barely know him."

"That's because Arly kept you from getting to know anyone," Deborah said, her tone angry.

Kate shifted in her chair uncomfortably. All this bitter talk about Arly, now that he was dead, was growing increasingly bothersome to her. Deborah sensed her unease, and waved a hand in understanding.

"All right, we won't talk about that." A teasing glint came into her eyes. "So, what is it like, having the famous Hawk sweeping your floors and fixing your roof?"

If this change of subject was supposed to restore her serenity, it failed miserably. Kate's hand shook, rattling her cup in its saucer. She steadied it and sipped at her tea again, wondering how she was supposed to answer that.

What was it like? Disconcerting, upsetting, nerve-wracking, unsettling . . . which word should she use? How could she explain what happened when she looked at him? That she seemed to lose track of her thoughts, and often caught herself just watching the way he moved, the way his powerful muscles flexed, the way he had of shoving his hair back with one hand, the way he did everything with an economy of motion that spoke volumes about his strength? Arly had been a big man, and exceptionally strong, but the only thing she had ever watched was which way he was going so she could stay out of his way.

How could she explain the funny feeling she got in

her stomach when Josh looked at her, that odd combination of hot and cold that seemed to radiate out and make her tremble in a way she'd never known before? Arly had make her shake, but it had been very, very different, a reaction born from fear, not . . . whatever this was.

And dear Lord, how could she ever explain what had happened when he'd kissed her?

She ducked her head, terrified that the fact that she had let a man kiss her like that, right there in the store, must be plain on her face.

"Kate?"

She had to get hold of herself. It was bad enough that she wasted so much time drifting off, lost in some foolish reverie about a man she by all rights should despise, or at least be terrified of, but to let him kiss her? A killer. A cold-blooded killer who took money for his killing.

And if she was having trouble fitting that knowledge to the man who'd been under her roof for two days now, it was her own silly fault. Pretty soon she'd be thinking of him only as Josh, and forgetting he was The Hawk, a man paid for his skill with a Colt. Thinking of him as the man with the quick grin that didn't quite reach his haunted eyes, the man who spent time with a boy no one else but Mr. Rankin would bother with, the man who worked harder around the store than Arly ever had. And not the cold, heartless killer she knew he was. The cold, heartless killer he simply *had* to be, or she would be faced with a guilt she didn't think she could bear.

"It's . . . strange," she said at last, a little surprised she could speak at all. "He's not what I expected him to be."

"What did you expect him to be?"

Kate fiddled with the handle of her cup, a delicate piece of bone china painted with a lovely rose pattern. She'd once asked Deborah where the cups had come from. "Another life," the woman had answered, such pain shadowing her eyes that Kate had never asked again.

"Cold," Kate answered at last. "Heartless. Mean, like Arly, I suppose."

"But he's not."

It wasn't a question, so Kate knew Deborah had already decided about Joshua Hawk. She herself wasn't at all certain what her own conclusions were. She only knew that if she'd been wrong about The Hawk, she wouldn't be able to live with herself.

"No, he's not." A cynicism cruelly taught to her by her husband twisted her lips. "Or he hides it well."

"Why should he bother to do that? Everyone knows who he is, what he is. He has nothing to hide."

She liked that about Deborah—she was always so logical, so reasonable; she was always seeing different sides of things. And she understood people, understood them in a way Kate despaired of ever learning.

"But how can it be? How does a man who seems so . . . reasonable, so right-minded, who can act so . . . kindly, become a killer? And for money?"

"Is that what he is?"

Kate looked startled. "What do you mean?"

"Is he a paid killer? Or is he paid to do a job, which sometimes comes to involve killing?"

Kate's startled look faded into thoughtfulness. "I . . . never thought of it in that way."

"This is . . . violent country, Kate. It isn't like back in the States, where there are laws, and plenty of men to enforce them. We can hope it's coming, but it's not here, not yet. So men resort to violence to resolve their disputes. And to men like The Hawk." Deborah shrugged. "Perhaps he kills when the situation demands it, and he's in the situation because no one else would do it."

"I . . . perhaps. I don't know. It seems so awful, but when you put it that way. . . ."

Deborah smiled. "Life would be easier if everything was plain and clear, wouldn't it?"

"I would certainly be simpler," Kate said with a heartfelt sigh.

"For myself," Deborah said, stirring her tea, "I believe I prefer The Hawk's methods to Arly's. At least you know what you're dealing with, and he doesn't try to disguise himself as a pillar of the community while he drinks, gambles, and mistreats anyone weaker or smaller than he. There's a certain honesty in that."

Kate couldn't deny that, so she didn't even try. "I expected Reverend Babcock to rain fire and brimstone down on me in his sermon today." As he would have, she added silently, had he known what she'd done. "But he didn't say a word."

Deborah laughed. "Honey, he wouldn't dare. After what you told me happened when he came into the mercantile Friday, ready to sermonize all over you? He's been busy telling the whole town The Hawk is only doing the gentlemanly thing, unlikely as that might be."

"I think he was a gentleman, once," Kate said. "At the least, very well brought up."

Deborah shrugged. "No one is born a gunfighter."

"Josh certainly wasn't. He has good manners, and he's very well spoken; he's been educated, and he's polite—"

"Josh?" Deborah asked softly.

Kate flushed. "Well, that's his name. Joshua. And he asked me to call him Josh."

"I see."

Something in her friend's tone made Kate's color deepen. "He's working for me. I could hardly call him The Hawk or Mr. Hawk all the time, could I?"

"Kate," Deborah said quietly, "I'm your friend. You can call him anything you like, as far as I'm concerned."

Chagrined, Kate set down her cup and reached to clasp her friend's hand. "I know. I'm sorry. It's just so . . . disturbing to have him around."

Deborah smiled widely. "I imagine it is. He's quite a handsome man."

Joshua Hawk's good looks were something she didn't care to dwell on. And if she didn't stop thinking about that kiss, she'd go utterly mad. As a diversion, she returned to something Deborah had said before.

"You were right, you know. He wasn't born a gunfighter. In fact, his family was quite wealthy. They had a very large farm in Missouri."

"Really? Well, I suppose the best of families have their black sheep."

"I don't think it was like that. His family . . . they all died during the war, except for his grandfather."

Deborah went very still. "All?"

Kate nodded. "Even the women." She hesitated, thinking she shouldn't do this, it was almost like betraying a confidence she hadn't been meant to have in the first place. But she would stake her life—and already had, on occasion—on Deborah's ability to keep her own counsel, and she desperately needed someone to help her make sense of the enigma that was Joshua Hawk.

So she overcame her hesitation and related the horribly grim story she'd read in the Hawk book, feeling herself shiver as if she'd been there when she spoke of the raiders who had raped and murdered their way through the Hawk family.

"I will never understand war," Deborah said quietly when Kate had finished, "but I understand even less the kind of man who uses war as an excuse for his own evil ways."

Kate knew Deborah had seen much of the war, too much, as she'd aided her doctor father in the Northern hospitals. It was why they'd come West, because her father had seen far too much of death, had far too much of being unable to save young lives. But even her grim experience had been once removed; Deborah had dealt with the aftermath, but she'd been safely spared the actual terror. Josh had had to deal with it face-to-face, at an age when he should have been dealing with nothing more than simply growing up.

"He blamed himself," Kate said, "for not saving them."

"But he was just a boy!" Deborah exclaimed.

"Yes."

Deborah looked at her for a long, silent moment. "He . . . told you all this?"

Guiltily, Kate shook her head. "No." She explained about the book, the Hawk history. "That's why you can't ever tell a soul. I should never have looked at it."

"Sounds fascinating. I've seen family trees before, but never one like that, with stories."

"It is unusual. Luke said every time the family tree got down to just one name, there was a story."

"A story about what?"

"That last Hawk, I think. Luke wasn't clear. And Josh . . . didn't like him talking about it."

"I imagine that shut the boy up in a hurry. He's developed quite a case of hero worship for your Hawk."

"He's not 'my Hawk,'" Kate said emphatically.

Deborah lifted a brow at her. "It was merely a figure of speech, Kate, dear."

Embarrassed, Kate sighed. "I'm sorry. I'm a little edgy today. I didn't sleep well last night."

She got to her feet before Deborah could ask why; she was in no mood to explain that she'd spent half the night listening for sounds from downstairs, and the other half trying not to think about the man who was making them.

"I have to get back to the mercantile and start supper." Then, not wanting Deborah to think her haste had anything to do with Josh, she added, "And I have to take advantage of being closed today to count some stock."

Deborah also rose, smiling, and if she was thinking there was anything untoward about Kate's answer, she didn't say a word. "Don't you let Reverend Babcock catch you working on the Sabbath."

Kate's mouth quirked in amusement. "He'd have to stay sober to do that."

Deborah laughed; the reverend's claim that preaching a Sunday sermon dried up a man's throat was chuckled at by everyone in town. "You're right. I think you're safe enough."

Deborah watched her friend go, gave her a final wave, shut the door to her parlor, and slowly turned around. She leaned against the door, still smiling; it was wonderful to see Kate able to laugh, with things to look forward to. She'd watched Arly Dixon try to crush the girl's spirit for four years, and had every day feared that he would kill her in the effort. But Kate had never given in. She'd learned to survive, although she'd often worn bruises from Arly's batterings that made Deborah cringe. And then there were the other attacks, the brutal, ruthless assaults that would have been rape had Kate not been married to him.

Deborah winced at the memories; her father had told her that the physical act of union between a man and woman could be a beautiful thing, but she doubted Kate would believe that. More than once, despite her own terror, she'd sheltered the girl, denying to Arly's face that Kate was there, knowing that if he got hold of her on those particularly vicious nights, Kate would be dead by morning.

Deborah knew most men were not like Arly Dixon, that some were gentle, good men; she'd nursed many of them, men who begged her to get word to their beloved wives. She'd been fifteen when she'd begun helping her widowed father in his overloaded Union hospital, and before her sixteenth birthday she'd lost track of how many men had died in her arms, calling her by the names of the women and children they would never see again, never hold again. Women and children who would be left with only memories and the pitifully small collection of possessions Deborah always sent home to them.

That had been the simple part, the packing and shipping of the belongings. It had been the letters that had been difficult, the letters telling of a loved one's last hours, of his last thoughts of home and family. Each one had been draining, the writing a painful task, but she'd felt compelled to do it. She felt she owed it to each of them, each soldier who died holding on to her, using her as a poor substitute in his final moments.

She wiped at her eyes, amazed that after more than ten years, the memories still had the power to make

her weep. Others had become hardened to the bloodshed, but she never had. Nor had her father. They'd
sold their home and everything in it, and come west
the year after the transcontinental railroad had been
finished, Doctor Franklin Taylor swearing he would
never again amputate another limb without enough
morphine, never again stand ankle deep in blood.

Her own memories were horrible enough; she
couldn't imagine living with the kind of memories The
Hawk carried. But she could imagine how the boy who
blamed himself for his family's destruction had become
the man whose job was the destruction of others.

The knock on her front door was a welcome inter-
ruption of ugly thoughts she seldom allowed herself to
dwell on. She shook her head sharply to clear away the
last vestiges of the hideous images, and went to open
the door.

"Alex!" she said in surprise. She wondered if he'd
waited outside until Kate had gone, too embarrassed
to face her. Judging by his sheepish expression, it
seemed likely.

The young lawyer nodded at her. "Hello, Deborah.
May I come in?"

"Of course."

She stepped back to let him pass. Despite his neat,
dark blue wool suit, clean white shirt and collar, and
freshly combed hair, details she noted with some interest, he looked a little red-eyed. She presumed he'd
been welcomed home in style at the saloon last night.
She didn't hold with too much drinking, but since Alex
overindulged so rarely, she thought she could forgive
him.

*You'd forgive him worse than that,* she thought to
herself ruefully. She knew she had a foolish fondness
for the young lawyer, and knew as well that it would

never do to let it show, not when she was a woman of thirty and he five years her junior. Besides, Alex had a fondness of his own for Kate, and Lord knew the girl could use a good man like Alex. Solid, steady, good-hearted, even handsome, if you liked men who ran to a wiry thinness, with sandy brown hair that tended to fall forward over the brow.

Deborah liked that hair. She liked his warm, kind eyes. And she liked Alex's somewhat shy ways. But she also liked the way he could be roused to high vigor for something he believed in. He was a good man, and he would be good to Kate. They would be happy together.

And she should be happy that Kate would have someone to really take care of her. If Deborah felt a twinge at the idea, it was simply unworthy envy, she told herself sternly. She was far past thinking of that kind of thing for herself. There had never been a time when she'd been helping her father, and it had taken her far too long to get over the horror, and then to grow used to the rough, unpolished ways of the men of the West. By the time she had realized those rough ways often masked good, decent men, it was too late. She was firmly on the shelf, and there she would stay.

"I have coffee on," she said, knowing Alex preferred it to tea, and glad her father had instilled in her the habit of keeping a pot going for the occasional patient needing the stimulation, or the more frequent restless loved one. "Would you like some?"

"Thank you," he said.

He took his usual seat on the medallion-back sofa, one of the few pieces her father had had shipped from the States, as Deborah retreated to the kitchen. Alex often visited her, and Deborah didn't try to fool herself as to why; she was Kate's best friend, and thus the best source of information about her.

She came back with a cup fixed exactly as he liked it, then sat in her chair and refilled her cup of tea.

"How was your trip?" she asked.

"Wasted, I'm afraid. My client seems to have gotten himself killed before I got there."

"Killed? Oh, dear. Over that land claim?"

"No," Alex said wryly, "over a game of poker."

"Oh." Deborah didn't quite know what else to say.

"He didn't even have the winning hand."

He said it with a shrug, and she could tell by his tone that that wasn't what he wanted to talk about. She sighed inwardly, having a fairly good idea what he did want to talk about. Alex stared down at his cup of coffee. Deborah waited, knowing he would get to it in his own time. Alex rarely rushed his words, but what he did say he stood by; it was another thing she liked about him.

"I suppose you heard," he finally said.

Deborah had too much respect for him to pretend not to understand. "Yes."

He glanced at her, and she saw relief that he wasn't going to have to explain clear in his expression.

"What is he *really* doing there?"

It burst from him as if he'd tried to hold it back. Deborah hesitated, considering her answer carefully. She had her own ideas about what was going on between Kate and her new help, but doubted Alex would want to hear them.

"As far as I know," she said at last, "exactly what you've probably already heard."

Alex stared at her. "Surely you don't believe that? That *The Hawk* feels guilty about killing Arly?"

Deborah gave him a thoughtful look. "I think it's Kate he is concerned with."

Alex stiffened. "You don't mean he has . . . intentions toward her?"

So his feelings toward Kate hadn't changed. Deborah didn't know if she was glad or not.

"I mean," she said quietly, "that he feels indebted to her. She did save him from the hangman, when she could have just as easily let him die." Alex apparently had not yet heard about Arly's gun, so she explained what Kate had done.

Alex didn't look any happier, but he nodded. "She couldn't let them just hang him," he agreed. "It isn't in her."

"No. And from what she told me, she did everything she could to get The Hawk to simply leave."

"He wouldn't?"

She shrugged. "He's still here."

Alex's mouth twisted. "Yes. As I found when I made a fool of myself yesterday."

"Alex—"

"I don't know what I was thinking, challenging The Hawk like that. I was worse than a fool."

"No one thinks you made a fool of yourself, Alex." Guessing at his most pressing concern, she added, "Especially Kate."

For a moment he looked hopeful, then sheepish again. "I don't know why he didn't kill me."

Deborah raised a brow. "Kate seems to think it was Luke who stopped him."

Alex looked doubtful, but said, "He was in the way. I suppose even The Hawk might think twice about killing a child."

"I believe you might be surprised at what The Hawk thinks," Deborah said.

Alex's eyes widened. "You sound almost as if you . . . like him."

"Perhaps. Or perhaps I just think it's not always wise to believe everything you hear."

His expression became thoughtful. "You mean about his reputation?"

"My father used to say that reputations had a way of growing on their own, like a snowball rolling down a mountain."

"Are you saying his isn't deserved? That he hasn't killed all those men?"

"I might question the number."

Alex leaned forward, looking at her intently. "Does that really matter, if he is paid to kill them?"

Deborah set down her cup. She delighted in these discussions with Alex, and the way he took her observations as seriously as if she were another man, never telling her not to worry her little head about things that were too troublesome for a woman. Remembering her talk with Kate, she leaned forward in turn.

"Is he, really? Or does he simply take jobs that no one else will do, because the chances are good it will come to killing?"

"Is that what you think?"

"No one seems to know of anyone he was actually paid to kill. Only men aligned against those he worked for."

Alex looked thoughtful. Yet another thing she liked about him; he was always open to a new way of looking at things, and wasn't too stubborn to change his mind. She settled back in her chair, watching with pleasure as he considered what she'd said.

"Well," Alex said at last, "whether he deserves the reputation or not, trouble follows The Hawk, and I don't like the idea of him being so close to Kate."

Deborah smothered a sigh; she knew exactly why

Alex didn't like the idea. "I think that's up to Kate, Alex."

"But she's alone now, with no one to look out for her—"

"Look out for her as Arly did?" Deborah interjected quietly. "Work her half to death, clothe her in rags . . . and beat her if someone is so much as polite to her?"

Alex looked aghast. "You know I didn't mean that."

"I know, Alex," she said soothingly. "But really, can you say she isn't better off alone than with that . . . beast? She has the store, and she can    Alex, what is it?"

He had turned as pale as the bone china cup he held. His warm hazel eyes were wide with distress. "Oh, no," he whispered.

"Alex?" Deborah set her cup down hastily. Instinctively, she moved, doing what she never would have dared had he not looked so disturbed; she went to sit beside him, putting an arm around his shoulders. "Alex, what is it?"

"Deborah," he said, then swallowed tightly and began again. "Deborah, I've done something awful."

"Awful? You? No, Alex, I won't believe it."

"But I have. And Kate . . . she'll never forgive me."

"Kate? What does she have to do with it?"

"Everything," Alex said, his voice full of remorse. "Oh, God, Deborah, I . . . she'll be devastated, and it's my fault."

A chill swept through Deborah. "I think you'd better tell me what it is you think you've done."

He shivered as if he'd felt her chill. It was a long moment, silent and strained, before he began to talk.

He hadn't eaten this well in years, Josh thought. First chicken, now a real Sunday dinner, with all the fixings. Beef tended to get monotonous in this country where it was the main staple, but Kate had managed to make it taste different with the addition of onions, and something else—spices, he supposed. With potatoes and early spring carrots, followed by an apple pie unlike any he'd ever tasted before, he was sure his stomach was more content than it had been in months.

His head, on the other hand, was a muddled mess. She'd not said a word about what had happened between them yesterday. In fact, she seemed determined to pretend it hadn't happened at all. He supposed he should be grateful for that, but he'd be more grateful if the memories would stop flitting around in his mind. Who would have thought kissing the plain little widow would leave a man weak in the knees?

He attacked the last of his meal, determined to act as she was acting, as if nothing at all had happened.

"A meal like that could hold a man for a week," he said when he'd finished.

"Not the way you work," Kate answered. "You've done more around here in these three days than . . ."

She didn't finish, but the implication that Arly hadn't been much for the small chores was clear. Josh supposed the man had left them all for Kate to do. He watched her as she rose from the rather battered table and crossed to the big cast-iron cookstove for the coffeepot. The kitchen was large, running the entire width of the back of the building, and he knew it had been added on in a lean-to fashion after the original building had been completed. "Arly had it built once he had a woman to work in it for him," Kate had told him. "He liked his meals at home, so he only had to leave to drink."

She came back to refill his cup, and when she'd

finished, he asked mildly, "So a killer is capable of honest work?"

She had the grace to blush. "I'm sorry I said that."

His mouth twisted ruefully. "I suppose it's a natural assumption."

She refilled her own cup and resumed her seat at the rickety table. He'd do some work on this thing as soon as he had a moment, he thought.

"Deborah seems to think you're not really . . . a killer. Not like they say you are."

He went very still. "Oh?"

"She thinks you just take jobs no one else wants, and they end up involving killing."

"I see."

"That's not the same as simply killing somebody for money."

"You and Miss Taylor have been talking a lot, haven't you?" His tone was deceptively light.

"Deborah is my friend. She is also a very wise woman. And she helped me—"

She broke off, looking away quickly, and Josh could just imagine the circumstances under which Deborah had helped Kate. He drew in a deep breath. He couldn't have her believing in some make-believe image of him. It was one thing when Luke looked at him like he was some kind of hero—that was the kind of thing boys did. Kate was another matter altogether.

"For that," he said slowly, "and other things, she deserves respect. And she may indeed be wise. But she's deluding herself, and you, if she thinks I'm anything other than what I am." He stood up. "I get paid, and men die, Kate. It's that simple."

"But if you're doing a job—"

"That changes nothing. It's understood, if you hire The Hawk, you expect there to be killing."

"Yes, but it's not like they pay you just go out and kill someone cold-bloodedly—"

"It's true, I've never backshot or ambushed anyone, or killed anybody who wasn't trying to kill me." He leaned over, bracing himself with a hand on the table as he looked at her. "But do you really believe that makes a difference? Yes, I take jobs no one else will take. They won't take them, because they know they'll be called upon to kill or be killed. And most men don't find that easy, so they walk away."

"And you do? You find it easy?"

Josh steeled himself to lie to her. "Yes."

For a long, silent moment she looked at him, and it took more nerve than he ever would have expected to keep looking at those golden eyes.

"Which part is easy, Josh?" she finally said, her voice soft, barely above a whisper and sending a shiver down his spine.

"What?" he finally managed to ask.

"Which part is easy for you? The killing? Or the chance of being killed?"

He straightened up, his brows lowering.

"Will that be payment enough for your family, Josh? When you finally get yourself killed?"

He went rigid, staring at her. He wanted to shout at her, tell her she was wrong, so very wrong. He wanted to tell her she had no idea what she was talking about. He wanted to tell her to stop talking about him at all, to stop thinking about him, and most of all to stop making him think about her.

He turned on his heel and walked out without a word.

# Chapter 11

Maybe he'd head on over to the livery stable and sleep there tonight, Josh thought. He was sure Luke wouldn't mind sharing his space in the hayloft. Maybe he'd finally be able to *get* some sleep.

The more he thought about it, the better the idea sounded. He stepped over his outspread bedroll and picked up the saddlebags that served him as a pillow. Not that they'd been too comfortable of late, not when all he could seem to think of—when he wasn't thinking so damn much about Kate—was that cursed book they held.

Between the two of them, the woman who'd been taking up far too much of his thoughts, and the book that haunted him every moment he wasn't thinking of her, he hadn't had much sleep, and less peace in the last three days.

He'd found himself locked in a kind of absurd tug-of-war—when she took over his mind, when he was thinking too much about the striking color of her eyes, or the way she blushed, when he was reminding himself too often that she was the plain, unremarkable woman he'd made a widow, he would purposely turn his wayward thoughts to the book, that impossible, preposterous book that couldn't exist but did.

But then he would think of how it had changed, how the damn thing seemed to be writing itself, how there were things in it that no one could know, and he found himself shying away from it like Buck shied from a rattler. But the only thing powerful enough to take his mind off the impossibility of the book was the woman, and he was caught in the circle again.

He stared at the bags in his hand for a long time. He didn't want to do this, didn't want to look at the book again, afraid of what he might find.

It was that that finally decided him; he'd be damned if he'd let himself be buffaloed by a book. He opened the bullet-scarred flap and yanked the now too-familiar volume out. He barely noticed the odd sensation this time; his anger overcame it. He dropped the bags as the book fell open in his hands, this time to a story he'd only glanced at before, of the first of his ancestors to come to America, and the only Hawk to survive the trip.

He glanced at the picture of a dark-haired man and the petite but determined-looking woman who stood beside him. Matthew Hawk, the entry said, in the same elegant script used throughout the book. And the woman he'd found, according to the story, a woman who'd brought back his will to live, to survive; Celia Hawk had stood beside her man through the fires of the American Revolution, and after they'd fought to free their country, they'd fought to rebuild the Hawk dynasty. And they'd done it. With the same unflinching courage as the first Hawks.

Drawn by a need he didn't understand but couldn't resist, he went back to the beginning. Back to the very first story, back to the drawing of Jenna Hawk. He looked at her again, this woman with the eyes like his own, this woman of legend, who had lived in a time

so old even the date of her birth was unknown, this
woman who had found a miracle for her people in the
man who stood beside her.

Josh shook his head, trying to fight off the compel-
ling urge that seemed to be overtaking him as he read.
The urge to believe in this nonsense, to believe that
the Hawk legends he'd been raised on were real, not
just a rather fanciful family tradition. The urge to believe in the utter impossibility of this book. The urge
to read every story chronicled here, to study every
branch of the intricate family tree, to know of each
Hawk who had come before him, so he would know
his own place in this incredible history.

*Hawks always breed true.*

He bit back a bitter laugh. He knew what his place
in this history was. He was to be the end, the ignomini-
ous end of a proud line that had endured for centuries.
He wondered what his story would be, how it would
look amid all these stories of brave, dauntless Hawks,
this story of the last one gone bad, of the one who
ended it all.

God, he was believing this. He was standing here
thinking about all this as if it were true, when it had
to be the biggest blazer he'd ever seen. He didn't know
how, or why, but the thing had to be a trick of some
kind. It had to be. Because if it wasn't . . .

With tight-jawed determination, he grabbed a thick
sheaf of pages and turned them over. He wound up on
exactly the page he'd been aiming for, the last of the
family tree. He wasn't surprised; he'd expected nothing
less, not the way things happened with this book.

He stood there for a long time, as the light from the
small window began to fade, staring at the single line,
the last fragile thread of the Hawk family, the final
branch, that bore his name. Finally, with the same

determination that had made him turn those pages, he turned one more.

A shiver rippled through him. He'd half expected it, but it still jarred him like one of Buck's wild bucking sprees when he was feeling ornery.

The first page was still empty, as if left open for some mysterious purpose only the book knew. On the next page, the original list of dates had been replaced, gone as if the wind had blown over tracks in the sand and left the surface clean to be written on anew. In their place were the details of those dates, the markers of death along the trail of a misspent life; his father's death, his grandfather's, the first man he'd ever killed. . . . There were brighter times, dates not connected with death, but they were few, and grew less frequent as the grim story progressed. It was an ugly saga, harsh and ruthless, with little to indicate there was a single worthwhile facet to this last Hawk.

It was the truth. And if it looked all the uglier spelled out, he had no one to blame but himself. He'd chosen this road, and there was—

At a sound from his left he dropped the book, his hand streaking for his Colt as he crouched and spun.

"Oh!"

Kate cried out and jumped back. She dropped the books she'd been holding and stood in the kitchen doorway, staring at him. Josh exhaled audibly. He slid the Colt back in its holster. He stood there, looking at her, cursing himself for being so wrapped up in his own misery that he hadn't realized it was her, hadn't even heard the door open, and cursing her for coming up on him like that anyway. He figured after the way he'd talked to her, she would have gone out the back and up the outside stairs to her rooms, to avoid him.

"I-I'm sorry," Kate stammered. "I didn't know you were in here."

"Never mind," he muttered. "I'm . . . a little edgy."

He walked to the doorway and knelt down to pick up the books she'd dropped. He looked up at her questioningly.

"You keep books in the kitchen?"

"I . . . had to hide them from Arly. The kitchen was the best place. He never went in there unless it was to eat."

He straightened up with the small stack of books in his hands. "Why didn't he like you to read?"

"He said it was foolish, and a waste of time. And it wasn't for women, anyway."

Josh snorted. "More likely he didn't want you finding out you were smarter than he was."

Kate blinked. "That's what Deborah said."

"You said she was a very wise woman."

Color stained her cheeks, and he knew she was remembering how that conversation had ended. Hastily, she took the books from him, glanced around, then stepped quickly across the small room and bent to the floor and picked up the book he'd dropped when she'd come in.

"How did this one end up all the way— Oh. I'm sorry, it's yours."

She straightened and held it out to him. He didn't take it. For a long moment he just stood there, looking at her, at the book she was holding, fighting the ridiculous idea that had come to him. He'd be crazy to do it. She'd think he was crazy if he did. So why was he even thinking about it?

She was looking at him doubtfully, clearly wondering why he didn't take the book from her.

"I didn't look at it again," she said, as if she was afraid she'd somehow angered him by touching it.

"Look at it," he said, before he could stop the words. Her eyes widened. "What?"

"Look at it. At the story you read before."

"But—"

"Just do it, Kate." She backed up a step, and he realized how he had sounded. "Please," he amended, in a gentler tone. "Just the last story."

"Yours?"

His mouth twisted. "Yes."

She studied him for a moment, then pulled the book back. For a moment she fumbled with the other books she held, and he reached out and took them from her. She gave him a wary look, but he nodded at the Hawk volume, and her slender hands moved at last to open it.

She found the blank pages and worked her way back. She paused, her lower lip caught between her teeth in a way that made Josh's stomach tighten as she began to read. After a moment she looked up at him.

"You wrote some more," she said.

He let out a long, compressed breath. "So you see it, too. That it's changed."

"Changed?"

"From what you read before."

"Well, yes. There's more here. You're finishing the story, aren't you?"

He hesitated, knowing how this was going to sound, yet also knowing if he didn't tell someone, he was going to slowly go out of his mind. Luke was too young, Pike would laugh him out of town, Rankin couldn't read it anyway. . . .

"No."

Her forehead creased. "No, what?"

"I'm not finishing it. I didn't start it. I haven't," he said, gesturing at the book, "written any of that."

"Then who did?" she asked simply.

"I wish I knew," Josh said grimly.

"What do you mean?"

Josh rammed his fingers through his hair distractedly. "I mean the damned thing's writing itself. I mean the legend is true. I mean the Hawks are either hexed or insane. I mean I'm going crazy as a loon."

Whether she was reacting to his tone or his expression he didn't know, but after a moment of contemplating his face, she said, "Come into the kitchen and sit down. I'll put on fresh coffee."

She moved around the kitchen with quiet efficiency, firing up the wood stove once more, preparing the coffee to go into the pot. Josh glanced at the small window in the back wall, at the fading light outside, and went to light the kerosene lamp on the table. The routine, ordinary task somehow eased his agitation, as did the fact that Kate thankfully didn't feel compelled to chatter to fill the silence.

But at last, when the coffee was ready, and she had poured him a cup, then poured one for herself and taken a seat opposite him at the table, she looked at him expectantly.

He didn't know where to start. Or even if he should. But he could hardly change his mind now. He'd started this, now he had to finish it.

"That story Luke was talking about," he began. "The one about the very first Hawks?"

She nodded. He hesitated, still not sure what to tell her, or how much.

"What about it?" she finally asked.

"I've heard it all my life," he said, figuring this was as good a place to start as any. "It's sort of a family legend. One of those stories that get fancied up with magic and miracles for children. One of my earliest memories is my grandfather telling me the story of Jenna and Kane."

"That's the first story in here?" She was still holding the book, but looking at him.

He nodded. "Jenna was the first Hawk. She was . . ." He stopped, pondering. Then, still somewhat reluctantly, he told Kate Jenna's story, much as his grandfather had told it to him. When he finished at last, she sat staring at the drawing she'd turned to early in his recounting of the tale.

"She must have been an incredible woman," Kate said, her voice quiet and as heartfelt as if she believed every word of the preposterous tale he'd told her.

"Yes."

Then she looked up at him. "But I don't understand about the book."

Josh laughed ruefully. "Neither do I. I always thought it was just part of the legend, as imaginary as the wizard or magician, or whatever it was that she saved, and the promise that the Hawks would go on forever. I'd never seen the book, my father hadn't, my grandfather hadn't, nor had his father or his before him."

"But . . . you said the legend says it appears only to the last Hawk of the bloodline."

"Yes," he said, sounding bleak. "According to the legend, the last of the Hawks are the only ones blessed—or cursed—by the appearance of the book."

"So it wouldn't have appeared to them, because they weren't the last." She glanced down at the book, then back at his face. "You are."

"I know."

"But why? What are you supposed to do with it?"

He gave her a quizzical look. "You sound as if you believe in it."

She looked down at the book, then lifted it in her hands. "It's here, is it not? You have to believe at least that much. How do you deny what you can see and touch with your own eyes and hands?"

"Don't ask me," Josh said sourly, "I've been trying to do just that ever since the thing appeared."

"It just . . . appeared?"

"In my saddlebags."

He hesitated, then went ahead, figuring at worst she'd tell him he was crazy and to leave for good, which just might solve a couple of his current problems.

"And when I looked at it," he said, "the writing ended with my name on the tree. Only on the tree. It wasn't on that next page."

Kate looked startled, then thoughtful. "That's why you asked Luke yesterday if he'd seen your name in it, isn't it?"

He nodded. Kate's expression didn't change, and Josh didn't know if he wanted to know what she was thinking, or was better off in ignorance.

"But what are you supposed to do with it?" she asked again.

He sighed. "I think it's more what it's supposed to do with me."

"That sounds almost . . . threatening."

"It's not supposed to be. At least, not according to the legend. The book is supposed to help that last Hawk find his way."

She looked down at the book, thumbing through the pages, pausing at the drawings that occasionally appeared, every century or so.

"His way where?" she asked at last.

For the first time in longer than he could remember,

as he watched her long, graceful fingers turn the pages, Josh felt his face heat. It was a moment before he could answer.

"Er . . . his way to no longer being the last Hawk."

She kept going a few more pages, then her hands stopped. Her head came up and she gave him a wide-eyed look. "Wouldn't that mean he would have to . . . have a child?"

He'd had a feeling it wouldn't take her long to make that jump. Wishing now he'd never begun this, Josh nodded. She kept looking at him in that astonished way, and he shifted in his chair uncomfortably. And suddenly he was the one who felt the need to fill the silence.

"That's when it disappears again. When the next Hawk is born, assuring the line will go on. It's all part of the promise the man gave Jenna when she saved his life."

"Aren't you leaving something out?" Kate asked, her voice abruptly very cool. "A child means a mother. Does the book take care of that, too? How?"

"I . . ." Josh felt his face heat again, and groaned inwardly at the thought of anyone knowing The Hawk had suddenly become prone to blushing. "I don't know. They weren't very clear about *what* it does, or how, just the results."

"Oh." Her tone left little doubt of what she thought about that. She tapped the page she'd now turned back to, the page where his name was inscribed. "If you didn't write this, then . . . is it right?"

"Right?"

"Is this the truth? Did your sister Ruth really . . . drown herself?"

His jaw tightened, but he nodded. "The day we got word my father had been killed at Franklin." His mouth twisted. "We didn't even think she'd understood the message. But she did. She walked out that night, straight into the river."

"I'm sorry, Josh."

He tried to acknowledge her, but for some reason the memories were riding him hard tonight and he could only go on.

"Less than five months later, Lee surrendered. On my twelfth birthday," he added, although he wasn't sure why. "Gramps sold everything that was left, which wasn't much, bought a couple of horses, and we headed west."

She glanced down at the first page of his entry again. "Did you really go to all these places?"

He shrugged. "We moved around a lot. Gramps wanted to see as much as he could. Said he just wanted to be on ground war hadn't touched."

"It must have been hard for you when he died."

"He was all I had left," he said, then wished he could call back the words. What was it about this place that made him let his mouth run on like this? First Luke, now Kate. Twice he'd talked about things he never spoke of, to anyone.

"Did you really win your first shooting contest when you were fifteen?"

He smiled at that. "Yep. Down in Abilene. October, end of the trail drive season, they were having a big shindig. Beat a man called Hatch, who'd been the champion in those parts for years."

"Was he angry?"

"Hatch? No. He said it just meant he'd stayed too long in one place, and it was time to move on." He hadn't thought of the lean, rangy man with the thick brush of a mustache in a long time. "Funny," he added, remembering, "he used to talk about taking his winnings and coming up here to Wyoming Territory. But instead I won, and I ended up here." He gave her a sideways look. "Almost permanently."

Kate looked away, as if uncomfortable with the reminder. After a moment, Josh went on.

"Anyway, I won enough money at that shoot to keep us going for a month."

Kate fingered the open page of the book. "And killed a man for the first time two years later."

His smile faded then. "Yes."

"Is it true that that man just came up and hired you after he saw you shoot?"

He didn't want to talk about this, but he found himself answering her anyway. "I was broke. Hadn't eaten in a while. He offered me double his cowhand's pay to stand guard on his stock. He'd been having trouble, and expected more."

"And it came?"

"It did. They thought because I was young I was the weak link. Their mistake."

"And the next time?"

"He tried to backshoot my employer," Josh said curtly. "I stopped him."

"Then how—"

"No." He cut her off. "We're not going to sit here and chew over my no-account life."

"I thought we were trying to . . . understand this," she said, toying with a page of the book.

He stood up and shoved a hand through his hair again. "Understand? It appears out of nowhere, it adds bits and pieces to itself, writing things no one still alive could know. . . . How do you understand that?"

"I don't know." She gave him a sideways, nervous look that made him realize he'd sounded a little agitated. "It's your legend."

He sat down again. He looked at her across the table. "I didn't mean to be so . . ."

He shook his head, not knowing what to say. Uncomfortable again, he reached out and picked up the top book of the four she'd been carrying when he'd scared them out of her hands. It was an often-read volume, judging by the wear on the cover and the corners. When he looked at the title printed on the spine, he smiled.

*"Moby Dick?"*

For an instant she cringed; then she drew herself up. "Is there some reason I should not read it?" she said, a defiant undertone in her voice.

"No," Josh said gently, "not anymore."

The air of defiance faded, to be replaced by chagrin. "There is a reason," she said with a sigh. "I can't. At least, not well enough."

"You read well enough to teach Luke."

She lowered her eyes. "We read . . . simpler things."

He leaned across the table and handed her the time-worn book. "This isn't that hard. Just take your time. Try. Perhaps I can help."

"Oh, no, I couldn't. Not in front of . . . you."

"Me? I'm just a hired gun-toter, remember?" He grimaced, nodding at the book. "Besides, this seems rather . . . appropriate. Captain Ahab was mad, as I recall."

"You don't really think you're—"

"I know I will be, if I don't think about something else for a while. Read. Please."

After a long, silent, rather strained moment, she did. She read, floundering at first, then more easily. Her hesitation over the longer words tested his admittedly rusty memory of a story read long ago, but her enthusiasm for the tale made him smile inwardly.

When after a few pages she came to a halt, he looked over at her.

"I wish I was better at this," she said.

"You're doing fine."

"You . . . went to school, didn't you?"

He blinked. "Yes. Back in Missouri. At least, until the schoolhouse became a hospital, and our teacher left to go North. Then my grandfather taught us at home. He used to be a teacher himself."

"Us?"

"Ruthie and me." He was glad his voice was steady, because Kate looked at him as if she was searching for signs of distress. "Rebecca and Amanda were older; they'd already finished school."

"Your . . . sisters went to school?"

She said it so longingly it made him look at those days he'd so often hated, trapped inside a classroom when he yearned to be outside, as perhaps a privilege rather than the punishment he'd thought it at the time.

"Yes," he said, "they did."

"My father didn't hold much with schooling, especially for girls. He said a man needed to know how to read and figure numbers, so he wouldn't be cheated by those that can, but girls . . ."

She let her voice trail away as she lifted one shoulder in a shrug.

"Then how did you learn to read?"

"In one of the towns we lived in for a while, there was a reverend. Not like Reverend Babcock, but a real, living and believing reverend. A good man. He taught me. Told my father that all of God's children should be able to at least read the Lord's words. My father was a God-fearing man, and didn't dare to go against him."

"And you've kept on yourself?"

"I try. Deborah helps when she can, but she's always

so busy, I hate to ask her. It's hard, because I don't know if I'm working some of the words out right."

"You do fine."

"Still, I wish I could have gone to school. There's so much I want to learn, to know about."

Ruth had had that same kind of eagerness, that same kind of quick intelligence that had made her look forward to the lessons Josh had so dreaded. For the first time he began to look at what he'd considered the curse of his childhood as something to be appreciated.

"Maybe . . . I could help. While I'm here, anyway," he amended, wondering what had possessed him to say it, to offer to do something that would force him to spend even more time in her distracting company.

Kate blushed furiously. "Oh, no, I couldn't ask that."

"You didn't ask," he said, a bit irritated at her instant rejection. "I offered."

"But you—"

"I what?" An edge had crept into his voice. "I can read. Fairly well. That's all you need, isn't it? Or are you still afraid of me?"

That, as he'd expected, did it. Her head came up. "I'm not afraid of you."

"Then it's settled." She looked at him warily, and with an effort he softened his tone. "I helped Ruthie, when Gramps was busy."

"You did?"

He nodded. "She loved to read. Anything. Everything." He had kept it long buried, this memory of the lively, quick mind lost behind the vacant stare of the girl who had once been his sister Ruthie. "My grandfather used to tell me you can find the whole world and more in books."

"*And more . . .*" she said slowly. Then she reached

out to touch the dark blue cover of the Hawk book. "Like this."

Josh exhaled slowly. He'd needed this break she'd given him, this respite from the chaos of dealing with an impossibility that had apparently turned into reality. But nothing had changed. The Hawk book hadn't vanished as it had appeared, leaving him free to blame the entire occurrence on some mental lapse perhaps brought on by too many legends heard and too much time spent alone in the mountains of late.

He watched her as she toyed with the book, watched her long, slender fingers touch the gilt edges of the pages, stroking them as if she like the feel. He studied the twin semicircles of her lowered lashes, noticing the thick softness of them. Her eyes, he thought, were really more than just striking, they were beautiful. It was as if all the beauty that in other, more classically lovely women had been divided among their features, in this woman had been poured into those eyes, making them so clear and gold and haunting that they were impossible to forget once you'd seen them.

He didn't know how long he'd been sitting there, watching her as she slowly turned the pages of the book, but when he realized that he was wondering what it would be like to have those long, lovely fingers sliding over his skin in the same slow, torturous way, he yanked his gaze back to his now-empty cup.

A few moments later, he sensed rather than saw her sudden stillness. He raised his head. Her hands were no longer moving. She was staring down at the book that was open before her, to the last page where the elegant lettering ended about halfway down. And she had gone very pale.

His heart seemed to slam up into his throat and for

an instant he couldn't breathe. He tried to say her name, but it came out as an odd sort of croak.

He saw her eyes move, but she didn't raise her head. She looked at the top of the page and began to read again, with that intensity he'd seen before as she worked her way through the printed text of the other book. He knew when she had finished by the shiver that visibly rippled through her.

"Kate?" He finally got it out past the tightness.

At last she looked up at him, those golden eyes full of both fear and awe. She opened her mouth as if to speak, then closed it again. With a little shake of her head that told him she was having the same trouble speaking he was, she slid the Hawk book across the table to him.

He didn't want to look, because he was afraid he knew what he'd see. It was impossible; the book had been here on the table between them, unmoved and untouched, long enough for dusk to fade to black. It was impossible, but still he had to force himself to look. And the moment he did, he knew his fear had been well-founded.

The book had changed.

It had caught up to the present. It now spelled out the dates and the story of each of his killings, including every grim detail, yet somehow making them sound not as bad as he knew they were.

It even told of his weeks spent up in the mountains, examining his life, making himself remember each of the men whose death he'd caused, comparing himself to his father, and his grandfather, and seeing himself come up sadly short.

All of it was true. Right down to the smallest detail, the book was accurate. He didn't know how it had been done, and right at this moment, he wasn't sure he cared. Because it was the last entry that held his attention now. The last entry that seemed to mock him, both in what it said and the taunting promise that it wasn't the final entry, that there would be more to follow, whether he liked it or not.

The last entry, telling him he'd met the woman who was going to make sure the Hawks continued as promised. And it was dated the day he'd ridden into town.

He looked across the table at Kate. The only woman he'd met on the day he'd arrived in Gambler's Notch.

# Chapter 12

"What the hell are you doing?"

Kate jumped at the sharp inquiry, and spun around. It took her a split second to realize it wasn't directed at her. Josh was in the storeroom doorway, glaring into the small room.

Kate hurried toward him, and saw Luke inside the storeroom with what appeared to be Josh's Colt cradled in his hands. He must have come in as he often did, through the back kitchen door. She felt a twinge of guilt; Josh had only taken his gunbelt off for breakfast because she'd told him it made her uncomfortable at the table, and he hadn't yet put it on again since they'd been back in the store.

"I was just lookin', honest! I didn't hurt it!" Luke exclaimed, panic in his voice as Josh strode across the room toward him.

"You *never* handle another man's gun without asking him."

Josh's anger was clear in his voice. He lifted his right hand, and Kate saw Luke cringe away.

"Stop!" she cried out, reacting instinctively. "Don't you dare hit him!"

Josh froze as Kate's voice came at him from behind.

He looked over his shoulder at her. She ran past him to stand beside Luke, putting her hands protectively on the boy's shoulders.

"Hit him?" Josh asked a little belatedly.

"He didn't mean any harm," Kate said, her voice shaking.

"Maybe he didn't." He lifted his hand again, taking the Colt from the anxious boy. "But he could have hurt himself, or anybody else around."

"I was only holding it," Luke protested.

"The notch of that hammer is filed so close you practically don't have to pull the trigger," Josh said harshly.

Kate was appalled, but held her ground. "That's still no reason to hit the boy. He didn't know."

"Hit him?" Josh gave her a bewildered look. "I just wanted . . ."

His voice trailed away, and his gaze shifted from her to Luke, as if he were remembering the way the boy had cringed away when he'd moved his hand. His gaze flicked back to Kate, and she knew he was remembering the moment when he had grabbed her and she had panicked, screaming and fighting him.

He looked back at Luke, then slowly knelt in front of the boy, so he was looking up at him.

"I wasn't going to hit you, Luke," he said softly. "I just wanted to get the Colt away from you."

"I wouldn'a hurt it," the boy mumbled.

"I was worried about you, not this," he said, gesturing with the six-shooter. "And Kate. What if you'd dropped it and it had fired?"

Luke looked properly chagrined. "I didn't think of that."

"When it comes to weapons, thinking's the most important thing you have to do." He paused, looking at the boy's troubled face. He didn't look at Kate again, but she felt the intensity of his next words as if he had. "But I'd never hit you, Luke. I don't hold with hitting those who are smaller or weaker than I. That's a coward's way."

Luke swallowed. "Arly used to say he was just doin' what I had no father to do, and I oughta be grateful."

Josh's jaw tightened. He muttered something Kate couldn't hear, but she suspicioned it was a comment guaranteed to speed Arly on his way to whatever hell he was bound for.

Convinced now that Josh meant what he said, Luke looked at him curiously.

"Didn't your father ever beat you?"

"Whipped me, yes, when I had a hiding coming. But he never beat me, not like you mean. Nobody has the right to do that, Luke. Nobody."

After a moment, the boy nodded. Kate tightened her hold on the boy's shoulder, and he glanced up at her.

"Do you have something else to say?" she hinted.

Luke looked puzzled, then his expression cleared. "Oh." He shifted his gaze back to Josh. "I'm sorry. I shouldn't have touched your things."

Josh stared at the boy as if nonplussed; then a wry smile curved his mouth. "Apology accepted."

"I hope you'll accept mine as well," Kate said.

Josh's gaze shot to her face. "What?"

"I apologize for thinking you would strike him. That was Arly's way. And as you . . . reminded me on Saturday, you are not Arly."

"No," he said quietly, "I'm not."

He looked at her silently, and so steadily, that Kate began to feel uncomfortable. Hanging between them was the knowledge of the Hawk book, and what it had said. After he'd read it, he had been by turns disbelieving, scornful, and furious. When he pointed out that by the date's implication, the woman the book mentioned was her, she'd been stunned. And then, when she realized that was no doubt the reason for his scorn and fury, she'd been humiliated by the realization that the idea was so repulsive to him.

She had made her escape upstairs, castigating herself every step of the way for even caring what such a man thought of her. For even thinking about such things, no matter what kind of man Arly had been, when she was barely a widow. She had slept little that night, but that wasn't new; she hadn't slept soundly since Joshua Hawk had come to Gambler's Notch. Breakfast had been a strained meal, eaten in silence except for her request that he remove his gunbelt, which he had done grudgingly, but without comment. By the time they'd finished, the atmosphere that was already tense between them was almost unbearable, and it hadn't changed all morning.

Hastily, she turned back to the boy.

"What did you need, Luke?"

"Nothing," the boy answered. "I just had a message for Josh."

"A message?" Josh asked as he buckled his gunbelt on. "From who?"

"Mr. Meeker."

Josh settled the holster against his right thigh, and the cartridge belt around his lean hips with absent, practiced motions that told Kate the task was as familiar to him as putting on his coat.

"I paid up my bill," Josh said, "so what did he want you to tell me?"

"Not him, I mean old man Meeker," Luke said.

"I think Mr. Meeker, Senior, might be a nicer thing to call him," Kate corrected mildly.

"All right," Luke said agreeably. "Anyway, he said to

tell you"—Luke's brow furrowed with his effort to get the message right—"that he saw Robards ride in early this morning."

Josh, who had been testing the slide of the Colt out of his holster, went very still.

"Robards?"

Luke nodded. "That's the name he said. He made me repeat it, so's I got it right. Said you'd understand."

For a long moment, Josh said nothing. He slid the Colt back into the holster. Then he asked, "This Mr. Meeker, he have a first name?"

"I don't know." Luke glanced at Kate, who shook her head.

"I'm afraid I don't know his first name, either," she said. "I've only met him once or twice, when I've delivered a basket to him. And I've only heard him called Mr. Meeker, or Henry's father." She studied Josh for a moment. "This Robards . . . is he a friend of yours?"

Josh's mouth twisted wryly. "Not exactly."

"How would Mr. Meeker know him?" she asked. "I don't think he ever gets out of his room."

"Robards," Josh said, his tone dry, "has a face you don't forget. A man once took offense at something Robards said about a member of his family, and re arranged it for him. From what I hear, it didn't teach Robards any manners."

He pulled the Colt out again, this time checking the load. He pulled a single cartridge from the belt and slid it into the empty chamber in the cylinder.

"What did you do that for?" Luke asked, his eyes bright with interest.

"Always keep your hammer on an empty chamber. Nothing looks more foolish than a man who shoots himself by accident."

"Oh. But why did you load it now?"

Josh reholstered the weapon, answering somewhat absently, "You don't walk around with only five beans in the wheel with a man like Robards around."

Luke's eyes widened. "Is he a bad man?"

"If you like living, you don't ever turn your back on him."

Luke looked up at Josh, then down at his Colt, then back at his face. "He's here after you, isn't he?"

Kate gasped. Josh looked at her, giving her a look that made her shiver.

"Is he? After you?" she asked, shaken.

"Probably."

"But . . . why?"

"To try and take The Hawk, why else?" Luke said excitedly.

"Luke!" she said sharply. "That's hardly something to be excited about."

"Sure it is, Miss Kate! We'll get to see The Hawk in action! Get to see—"

"Get to see him kill someone, or be killed himself?"

Luke gaped at her. "Be killed? The Hawk? You might as well go barkin' at a knot as wait for that to happen! No one's gonna beat you, right, Josh?"

Josh looked down at the boy, but Kate had the strangest feeling that he wasn't really seeing Luke at all. "Sooner or later, there's always somebody who beats even the best."

"Not you," Luke insisted.

Josh shrugged. "We'll see."

Kate shook her head in horror. "You can't mean to just go out there looking for this man?"

He gave her that look again, that look she imagined had been the last thing seen by the men he had killed. *She's deluding herself, and you, if she thinks I'm any-*

*thing other than what I am.* His harsh, almost angry words came back to her with jarring intensity.

"What would you suggest, Kate?" he asked with deadly softness. "That I wait until he finds me, then maybe shoot up your mercantile here, and leave you with the mess to clean up?"

"You can't be sure that's why he's here," Kate said desperately.

"Oh, he's here for me, all right. That last job you read about in the book? Down near Denver?"

She remembered the story the Hawk book had recounted, of the three men who had tried to rob an ore wagon from one of the local silver mines. They had had the bad judgment to pick the one guarded by The Hawk, and two of them had paid for the mistake with their lives.

It hit her then. Her eyes widened. "Robards . . . is the third man?"

Josh nodded. "And one of the others was his brother. If he didn't come to Gambler's Notch looking for me, he'll be looking as soon as he finds out I'm here." He glanced at Luke. "Which probably won't be long."

Kate knew it was true; Luke had been bragging up Josh's presence in Gambler's Notch to anybody who would listen.

"But that doesn't mean you have to go out looking for him, make it easy for him to find you! Surely if you told Marshal Pike—"

"I don't send another man to do my fighting for me. If I did, I'd never work again."

Something snapped in Kate. "You mean you'd never kill for a living again! There are some who would count that a blessing, you know!"

"There are some who would count my being killed a blessing," he said grimly. Kate stared at him, something in his expression giving her the oddest feeling that he put himself among that number.

He turned on his heel and started toward the front door. After three steps he halted, as if considering something. Then he turned and strode rapidly past her back into the storeroom. When he came out, he was holding the Hawk book.

He crossed to the small stove. She had just stoked the fire, so the small door was still open. Before either she or Luke could react, he shoved the book into the flames.

Luke cried out something Kate couldn't hear over her own exclamation of shock. But Josh ignored them both. He watched until the book was engulfed, the pages curling into ash. Then he turned again on his heel, and strode out into the noon sun.

Robards was uglier then he remembered, and Josh was reasonably certain he was just as mean-spirited and arrogant. He knew it had put a serious bend in Robards's pride that even at odds of three to one, they hadn't been able to take Josh. In fact, he guessed that probably bothered the man more than the death of his brother.

He also guessed that Robards hadn't changed his ways; he'd meant what he'd said to Luke about not turning your back on him. So when he left the mercantile, he headed down the narrow alleyway to come up to the back of Markum's saloon. He still spent the occasional evening there, slowly building the stake that would take him out of Gambler's Notch. He'd spent most of what he'd won before on his room and Buck's care, but now that he had a roof over his head he didn't have to pay cash for, things would move faster.

He was grateful for that; he'd about come to the end of his rope in more ways than one in this town.

Robards had been where he'd expected him to be, at the bar, already downing what looked to be the latest in a few shots of Markum's cheapest trade whiskey. As usual, he was wagging his chin, and as usual, not saying much.

Josh checked the slip of the Colt in the holster. He'd try to dodge this, but he had little hope of being successful; Robards was too downright mean. But he'd promised Pike, so he would try. Besides, while he wanted out of Gambler's Notch, he wanted to leave on his own terms—and in his own time—not because Pike had ordered him out.

He walked to the end of the long bar and touched his hat brim in greeting to Markum. Markum's hasty, almost furtive glance toward Robards and then back to Josh told him the man had been asking about him. Josh nodded in understanding.

"I paid a lot of money for this saloon outfit," Markum said, rather mournfully as he wiped a rag over his catalog-ordered bar.

Josh nodded again, understanding the man's fear that the rather ornately carved mahogany piece would soon be scored with bullet holes.

"I hope you don't have to replace anything," Josh muttered as he glanced around. There were only a few men in the place at this midday hour, and only four that he recognized—Rankin, no doubt cooling down from a morning's work at the forge with a beer; the reverend, who seemed to need no excuse to drink; the telegraph operator; and Henry Meeker. They were all watching Josh warily, and he half expected them to scramble out of the place at any second. Josh saw movement at the front door of the saloon, then at the window, and a glimpse of blond hair told him Luke was outside, watching. He only hoped the boy would stay outside, where it would be relatively safe.

Belatedly, although he'd always seemed to Josh a little slow in the head, Robards noticed Josh's presence. The man's fingers tightened around his now empty glass.

Josh nodded to him. "Been a while, Robards. Let me get that refilled for you."

The man's eyes narrowed, although it was hard to tell between his scarred brow and his right cheek, left looking permanently swollen by the man who had rearranged the bone beneath it while administering his lesson about insults and family loyalty.

"Hawk," the man growled, "I heard you was here."

"And now you see. Hugh, how about that drink for this fellow. On me."

Markum complied, but poured the whiskey gingerly, as if he were offering it to a coiled rattler. Close enough, Josh thought. At his nod, Markum poured a shot for him as well, although Josh made no move to pick up the glass.

Robards seemed puzzled by his hospitality. He glanced downward, as if to reassure himself Josh was indeed armed.

"Why you buyin' me a drink?"

"Why not? We're old . . . acquaintances."

"You know I come here to kill you."

Josh suppressed a sigh; the man just wasn't going to make this easy. "You're just going to have to wait. I promised the marshal here I wouldn't go hunting trouble."

Robards snorted. "You takin' orders from some town marshal now, Hawk?"

Josh shrugged. "He's a tough hombre. I wouldn't want to have him after me."

"You should be worryin' about me being after you, Hawk. You shot my brother—"

"After he shot that driver. In the back."

Robards stiffened. "Are you callin' my brother a back-shooter?"

"I'm sure it wasn't intentional," Josh said mildly. "I'll bet Martin was no more a back-shooter than you are."

And that, Josh thought, was God's pure truth. Robards looked at him suspiciously, obviously struggling to understand if there had been something in that placating— on the surface—answer that he'd somehow missed.

"You still killed my brother, Hawk. And I owe you lead for that."

Josh shook his head slowly. "Take the drink, man. It was bad luck, and poor shooting on your partner's part."

"My brother's dead. You killed him."

*I tried,* Josh thought. *I really tried.*

"Yes," he said. He reached out and picked up the glass in front of him with his left hand. "And he had it coming."

He saw Robards's eyes track the movement of his hand with the glass, and saw the second when the man decided. He'd known it would happen; the man was the type to wait until he thought he had his opponent at a disadvantage.

Josh moved the instant he read decision in the other man's eyes. His hand streaked for his Colt. A fraction of a second later, Robards drew. Josh had him dead to rights before he even cleared leather. But he didn't shoot. He didn't shoot, and he didn't quite know why.

A low whistle echoed in the room as Robards backed off, hands held out from his sides. Josh heard an ex-

cited yelp that could only have come from Luke. He
set the untouched glass back on the bar.

"You've got one chance to live, Robards," Josh said,
low enough so that only the man with the twisted face
could hear him. "Take it and ride out."

Without a word, the man began to back away toward
the door. Josh watched him, gun still drawn. Even when
Robards scampered through the door and disappeared,
he was slow to slide the Colt back into the holster.

"You want that drink?" Markum asked, eyeing the
shot of whiskey Josh had put down. Josh shook his
head. "Good," Markum said fervently, lifting the glass
and draining it himself in a single gulp as there was
the noisy clatter of youthful footsteps at the door.

"Did you see that, Mr. Rankin?" Luke crowed as he
ran into the room and skidded to a halt at Josh's side.
"He didn't even have to shoot. That man just turned
yellow and ran."

"I saw, boy," Rankin said. The blacksmith stood up,
giving Josh a considering look. "I also saw he went a
long way to avoid that fight."

"Don't tell me," Josh said grimly, "tell the marshal.
He's not going to be happy about this."

"I might just do that."

"Well"—Babcock also rose, looking a trifle discom-
fited—"I don't care for the kind of people you're bring-
ing into town, Mr. Hawk. I don't care for it at all."

"I'm not particularly happy about it myself, Reverend," Josh said.

"First you shoot one of our citizens—"

Josh turned on the little man. "I don't notice anyone
around here doing a lot of mourning for Arly Dixon."

Babcock flushed. "Well, perhaps Mr. Dixon wasn't
one of our more popular residents—"

"He was one mean son of a bitch," Rankin said bluntly.

"Well, yes, but—"

"And he beat his wife nearly to death," Josh said, his voice infused now with deadly menace. "And the only person with guts enough to try and help her is this boy here." He put a hand on Luke's shoulder. "That doesn't say much for the men of this town."

"Why, what do you—" Babcock began, red faced.

"Where the hell were all you fine men when she needed help?"

"That's fine for you to say," the telegraph operator, a tall, skinny man appropriately named Boardman put in. "You're The Hawk. Any of us tried anything, we would have wound up like those four men who tried ·to help old Happy Jack Morco's wife down Ellsworth way. Shakin' hands with St. Peter."

"So you let him get by with it? You couldn't even find the guts between all of you?"

Boardman shut up, and even Babcock looked uncomfortable.

"He's right," Rankin said. He glanced around at the others. "We all knew what was going on, that Arly was hurting that girl, hurting her bad. And we did nothing, said it wasn't our business what a man did with his wife. But we were wrong. We should have done something long ago."

From the taciturn Art Rankin this was close to a speech, and the other men stayed silent. They looked at each other, then at Josh. Then they looked at Luke, somewhat ashamedly. The boy was looking up at Josh, pride at the implied praise glowing in his young face. Josh smiled back at him; whatever hurt he'd done to the boy's feelings this morning, it was obviously well forgotten now. He reached out and tousled the boy's hair, wondering where this sudden burst of affection for the wild kid had come from. Maybe he was just seeing himself—

The instant he heard the steps behind him he knew he was in trouble; Robards had followed his lead and come in from the back. Josh pushed Luke down to the floor. That moment's delay cost him. He heard the crack of gunfire in the same instant he felt the sting at the top of his left arm. He heard another shot as he stepped clear of the sprawled Luke. This one went wild.

He drew, concentrating on accuracy rather than speed. It gave Robards a chance for one more shot, but Josh wanted the man down before Luke or someone else got hurt. This was his fight, not theirs. The shot came. Missed. Josh fired for the first time. A look of shock came across Robards's distorted face. He stared at Josh. He looked down as his six-shooter fell to the floor. He crumpled without a word.

Josh stood there, staring down at the body. Thirteen, he thought dully. The Hawk had another to his discredit.


"It's fine," Josh protested. "I've cut myself shaving worse than—"

"Quiet," Deborah said, and continued to clean the wound. Luke had come running for her, although she'd already been on her way when she'd heard the gunfire. One man was far beyond her help, and she'd had to track Josh down at the marshal's office to treat him.

Marshal Pike was watching the proceedings with every evidence of interest as Deborah began to lay out bandages.

"Art tells me you gave him more than one chance to walk away. Even offered to buy him a drink. That true?"

Deborah paused as Josh looked at Pike. "I gave you my word, Marshal."

"Henry Meeker told me the only reason you got hit at all was because you pushed the boy out of the way."

Josh shrugged.

"Hold still!" Deborah ordered. "You'll start this bleeding again, and I just got it stopped."

"Don't argue with her, son," Pike drawled. "And don't let that pretty face fool you. She's a determined woman when it comes to doctorin'."

Josh grimaced. "I can see that."

Deborah fought against blushing. "Caleb Pike, you go spread your palaver somewhere else. Pretty face, indeed."

"Indeed," Josh said.

Deborah gave him a startled glance. Josh smiled at her in a way that made her lose the battle against the heat that threatened to rise in her cheeks.

"You're a fine-looking woman, Miss Taylor," Josh said, looking at her with a puzzlement that went a long way toward convincing her of his sincerity. "Surely you know that?"

Deborah thought she'd never felt so embarrassed—and so pleased—before in her life. Nor had she ever been at such a loss for words. So she said nothing, but went back to her bandaging of the ragged but shallow furrow Robards's bullet had left in the flesh of Josh's upper arm.

Pike looked at Josh for a moment longer before he said, "Guess I'll go on over and see to the body."

Deborah felt Josh go very still. "No charges?"

Pike shook his head. "Seems clear enough. Lots of witnesses, and they all say the man tried to back-shoot you. He fired three times, you only once. And that you saved that boy's life and got that"—he gestured at Josh's bloody left arm—"for your trouble." But then he added sternly, "But I'm warning you again, Hawk.

That's two men you've killed in my town. Now, I'll give you that Arly brought it on himself, and this one probably had it coming to him, but I don't like bodies scattered around. Makes folks nervous."

"Makes *me* nervous," Josh muttered.

Pike chuckled as he left the office. Deborah finished her bandaging, then stepped back to assess if it would hold. Josh thanked her, and asked what he owed her.

"A dollar, and to stay out of shooting scrapes."

"I *tried* to stay out of this one," he said as he pulled out a silver dollar and gave it to her.

"I know you did. If you hadn't, it would have been two dollars."

Josh grinned at her, then leaned over and reached for his bloodied shirt. For the first time, now that she was finished with her work, Deborah saw him as a man, not a patient. A man with a grin that could turn a woman's mind foggy. A man with a nicely broad chest, solid shoulders, and a flat belly. He was taller than Arly had been, and leaner, more fit, and much more pleasing to the eye.

To the female eye, anyway, Deborah thought as she watched him pull on his shirt. It was no wonder Kate had been on edge for days now. Having this under your roof—and literally under your feet at night—would be enough to distract any female alive. Unlike most women, she'd seen her share of near-naked men while helping her father, so perhaps it took more to impress her. Joshua Hawk impressed her.

He wasn't to her taste, of course. For the little it mattered, she much preferred the wiry quickness of, say, Alex Hall.

Alex.

Alex, who was no doubt at this moment with Kate.

"Does Kate know you're all right?" Deborah asked.

Josh paused in the buttoning of his shirt with the bloodied sleeve. "For all that she'll care right now, yes. She was waiting in front of the store when I was headed here."

"Luke told me she knew you were going into a fight."

"Yes."

"He said she tried to talk you out of it."

Josh gave her a sideways look. "Most women feel that way about bloodshed."

"Yes, we do. Especially when people we care about are involved."

Josh drew back, and Deborah saw the wariness in his eyes as he looked at her. She sensed he wanted to ask what she'd meant, and she sensed as well he wasn't going to do it. She wondered if it was because he didn't want to know, or if perhaps he already did.

"She'll be fine," Deborah said with planned casualness. "Alex is with her."

Josh stiffened again. Then he turned away quickly, picking up his gunbelt and buckling it on. But Deborah hadn't missed that flicker in his eyes, telling her that whatever attraction to this man Kate was fighting so hard, the feeling was mutual.

Deborah sighed inwardly; truly, the last thing Kate needed in her life was another difficult man. And this man, she thought, could be the worst of all. Kate's father had ignored, then all but sold her; her husband had beaten her . . . but this one would break her heart. How very ironic, Deborah thought, that the man who was kindest to her could be the one to at last break that valiant spirit.

"I suggest you stay away from her for a while," Deborah said. "She's going to have enough to deal with."

Josh turned back sharply. "What do you mean?"

"I mean the reason Alex is with her."

"I thought he was with her because he—" He broke off, and for a moment Deborah could have sworn she saw a faint hint of color tinge his cheekbones. "What do you mean?" he asked again.

"Just don't give her any more grief to handle," Deborah warned, meaning it.

Josh studied her for a long moment before, without another word, he walked out of the marshal's office.

And Deborah wasn't the least bit surprised when he headed directly for the mercantile.

Josh slowed when he saw the shade pulled down over the front window of the store, the dark, heavy cloth making the white letters spelling DIXON'S DRY GOODS—GROCERIES stand out. He tried the front door; locked.

He stood there for a moment, then glanced back toward the marshal's office, wondering what Deborah Taylor had meant by saying Kate was going to have enough to deal with.

He walked around the side of the building, glancing up the stairway that led to her rooms. She rarely went up there during the day, but after what Deborah had said . . .

He'd try the kitchen first, then upstairs. And if she wasn't there or wouldn't talk to him, he'd go to Deborah and make her tell him what she'd meant. He'd—

The kitchen door opened at his first touch. The young lawyer and Kate were seated at the rickety table he hadn't gotten around to fixing yet; the lawyer in *his* chair, Josh noted. He stifled the spurt of irritation that shot through him, thinking wryly that it was far past time for him to get out of this place if he was getting testy over a simple thing like who sat in the widow's chairs.

Alex looked up as he stepped in, and hastily got to his feet. Kate never moved.

"I'll have to ask you to leave, Mr. Hawk." Alex moved to block Josh's way.

"Lawyer," Josh said, "I just had to kill a man who gave me no choice. That tends to make me downright touchy. I suggest you get out of my way."

Kate made a tiny, barely audible sound of distress that felt like a knife digging into Josh's gut.

"This is not a good time to bother her," Alex said, standing his ground. He was tough enough, Josh conceded, and reined in his spiraling temper.

"I hadn't planned on bothering her," he said. Then, prodded by the young man's proprietary air, he added, "I live here, remember?"

Alex went rigid. "Whatever debt you feel you owe, I wish—"

"Wish away, lawyer. Just think real hard before you do, in case you get it."

Kate still hadn't moved, and Josh was beginning to feel concerned. He walked toward the table.

"Kate?"

When she didn't look up or speak, Alex tried again. "She's just had some disturbing news. Please leave her alone."

Josh found himself clenching his jaw, hating the genuine concern in the lawyer's voice. "You bring that . . . disturbing news to her?"

Alex flushed. "Well . . . yes, but I—"

"Then maybe it's you who should leave her alone."

Alex said something in protest, but Josh ignored him. He lifted the chair the lawyer had vacated and put it down beside Kate. He sat, barely a foot away from her. He kept his gaze fastened on her, even when Deborah came in the door, clearly having followed him from the marshal's office.

"Kate?" he repeated.

She looked up at last, and Josh's breath caught at the despondency in her eyes. Driven by a need he didn't stop to analyze, he grabbed her hands.

"Kate, what is it?"

"Arly," she began.

"What about him?" he prompted when she didn't go on.

She looked around her, at the kitchen they sat in, but Josh sensed she was seeing much more. Then her gaze came back to his face.

"I was such a fool, to think that things would be better. That I'd finally have something of my own."

"You do," Josh said. "You have this place—"

He stopped when she laughed; it was a painful, harsh sound. "I have nothing," she said. "Nothing."

"You don't have to tell him anything, Kate," Alex said. "He's not involved in this."

Josh's gaze flicked to Alex. "Oh, yes, I am," he said gruffly.

The lawyer opened his mouth again, but when Deborah hushed him, he fell silent, his expression troubled. Josh sensed it was more than just the fact that he was sitting here holding Kate's hands in his. He looked uneasy, almost . . . guilty. Josh shoved that realization to the back of his mind; he'd deal with that later. Right now Kate was all that mattered. He turned back to her.

"Kate?" he said for a third time, but for the first time realizing that her fingers had curled around his, and that she was holding on tightly, as if she needed the contact. "What are you saying?"

"Arly had a will. It's not mine. None of it is. He left it all to someone else."

# Chapter 13

"So that's why you looked so damned guilty," Josh muttered, glaring at Alex.

"I know perfectly well this is my fault," Alex said, glaring back at Josh.

He turned to Kate, his expression distressed.

"Kate, I swear, when I convinced Arly to make a will, I had no idea. I tried to change his mind, to tell him he simply had to make some provision for you, but he was . . . he was so . . ."

"I know what Arly was," Kate said. "It is not your fault, Alex."

"But if I hadn't pushed him," Alex said, pacing the kitchen anxiously, "if I hadn't been so eager to establish myself here as a lawyer with anyone who would hire me, he never would have done it." He turned when he reached the stove and started back. "You could try and fight it, Kate. You were his wife, and maybe his brother will agree that you should at least get—"

"No, Alex," she said wearily.

"I had no idea he had a brother in St. Louis," Deborah put in.

Kate took a deep breath to steady herself. "I knew. Arly used to talk about him, when he was drunk. Called him a mean, rotten . . ." Her voice trailed off; even now she couldn't repeat the words.

"*Arly* thought his *brother* was mean?" Deborah sounded shocked. "Land sakes, I don't even want to think about what kind of man a man like Arly would consider mean."

"He hated him," Kate said. "He said Will used to beat him, when they were little."

In fact, he'd whined it, often, in the blubbering, drunken state that Kate generally welcomed, because it meant he would soon pass out. And Arly unconscious was an Arly who wouldn't be looking for someone to take out his anger on.

"I think that's why Arly was . . . like he was," she said. "Partly, at least."

"That's no excuse," Deborah said shortly. "Alex, stop that pacing." The lawyer stopped.

Kate sighed. "It doesn't matter now. It's too late. I know I was less than nothing to Arly, but—"

"Kate—" Alex began.

"Are you going to tell me it's not true? When it's clear that Arly would rather see the brother he hated get everything he owned than me have anything at all?"

"Kate, I'm sorry," Alex said.

"Don't be sorry," she said tiredly. "It's no more than I deserve."

"Stop it," Josh said sharply. "Don't say that. You don't deserve this."

Kate nearly laughed. If ever she'd doubted she understood irony, that doubt was gone now. What could be more ironic than Josh, of all people, defending her when she'd finally been called to account for what she'd done?

"Thinking to benefit from someone's death has to be

a mortal sin," she whispered, "and that's the very least of my sins here."

"Whatever you get out of Arly Dixon's death, you've more than paid for," Josh said, his voice tight.

She almost told him then. She sat there, looking at him, thinking how different he was from the cold-hearted killer she'd expected The Hawk to be, and she almost told him. But her nerve failed her. She couldn't, not now, not in front of them all. She just couldn't. Nor would she humiliate herself by showing how frightened she was.

She glanced up at Alex, who still looked decidedly uncomfortable. Poor man, he thought this was all his fault, when in fact it was hers; she'd brought this retribution down on herself.

"How long do I have?" she asked him.

"What?"

"How long before I have to leave?" she clarified.

Alex winced. "I . . . Kate, we don't even know what Arly's brother will do. You may not have to leave at all. He may not even want the place."

"Maybe he's dead," Josh put in bluntly, sounding almost hopeful.

Kate winced at that, but kept her eyes on the young lawyer. "How long, Alex? I have to . . . to think. I have to decide what to do."

Alex sighed. "I had to notify him right away, Kate. You understand that, don't you?"

"You mean he already knows?" Josh said sharply.

"I wired him Friday," Alex said reluctantly. "It's my duty as a lawyer. I had to."

"Before you even told Kate?" Deborah asked. At her sharp tone, Alex looked inconsolable.

"I understand, Alex," Kate said softly.

"Nothing is legally his until he arrives and signs the necessary papers," Alex said anxiously.

"And anything the store makes until then will be hers?" Deborah asked, her tone kinder this time.

"Well . . . unless the brother chooses to argue that, I don't see why not."

"Just don't go planting the idea, lawyer," Josh said ominously.

Alex winced, but said nothing, guilt still contorting his expression. "Is there . . . someone we can get in touch with?" he asked. "Your family?"

Kate shook her head. "No. No one." She hated saying it, knowing that everyone would know she had no place to go, no one to turn to.

"Of course, you can stay here until we hear from him," Alex said. "And that may take a while."

"You're always welcome to stay with me, Kate, for as long as you need. But he may be willing to just let you stay on in the store," Deborah said hopefully. "If he lives in St. Louis, perhaps he has family there, ties that would make it impossible for him to leave."

Kate shook her head, refusing to hope. "Then he would simply order the place sold, wouldn't he?"

"Maybe," Alex agreed reluctantly. He rubbed a hand over his face as he shook his head. "If only I'd—"

"Please, don't blame yourself, Alex," Kate said. "If anyone is to blame, it's me."

"You?"

Again she resisted the urge to confess. Having Alex find out the truth would be bad enough, but having Josh find out what she'd done to him would be worse. So very much worse. Kate buried her face in her hands, trying to stop the shivers that were threatening to overtake her.

Josh stood up suddenly, shoving back his chair, making a loud, scraping sound on the uneven wood floor. Kate's head came up.

"That's enough," he said, his tone nothing less than an order. Alex started slightly before turning his head to gape at him. Deborah drew back from him slightly, a speculative look on her face. Kate stared at him, not moving.

"You've delivered your 'disturbing news,' Hall," he said. "Go do whatever it is lawyers do after they've brought someone's life down around them."

"Do you think I'm happy about this, Hawk?" Alex exclaimed angrily.

"I think," Josh said coldly, "that what you feel isn't important right now. Get out."

Alex drew himself up straight, although Josh still topped him by six inches. "I'll leave when Kate asks me to leave," he said.

Josh's mouth curved up at one corner. "You've got sand, Hall, I'll give you that. Or else you're stupid."

"You think what you want of me," Alex said with a wave of his hand. "But Kate may want legal advice—"

"Like Arly did?" Josh said.

"Stop it, both of you!" Kate leapt to her feet. "Just stop it."

She looked at them, from Josh to Alex and back again, a little wild eyed. Then, with a tiny cry she couldn't quite stop, she turned and ran out the door. She kept running until she was around the corner and heading up the stairs, and didn't stop until she was inside and had the door closed and locked behind her.

Josh was right, she thought as she stood there, gasping for breath. Her world was coming down around her, and it was her own wicked fault. Not because of Arly; Arly had been courting his fate for years. She just couldn't feel guilty about that, not after surviving four years of that man's hell. It would never have happened if Arly hadn't been the cruel, vicious man he'd been.

But Josh . . .

"Oh, please," she moaned aloud, "I didn't know. I didn't know."

Her plea died in the silence of the room she'd so quickly emptied of all signs of her husband's presence. She sank to the floor, wrapping her arms around herself, trying to stop the trembling.

She had known there would be a price to pay. No one did what she'd done and didn't pay. But she had judged it worth it, then. But that had been when she had thought she would be the only one to pay the price. She could have lived with that; it was better than dying at Arly's hands.

But she'd made one mistake, one enormous mistake in judgment. An unforgivable mistake.

And there was no living with that.


"He said what?"

Luke took a deep breath and let the words tumble out again. "He said if you were of a mind to come thank him for the warning about Robards, to just forget it." Luke's face scrunched up in an expression that told Josh the boy didn't like delivering this part. "He said he didn't want to see you."

"Oh?" Josh paused in his cleaning of the Colt to look at Luke.

"I don't think he's afraid of you," Luke said. "He might be in that wheelchair, but he's been in a fight or two, and he's still got that rifle."

"You like him, don't you?" Josh asked.

Luke shrugged. "Guess so. He's nice to me, and he's been places, like I'd like to do someday." Luke looked up at him calculatingly. "He doesn't look like you, but he kinda reminds me of you."

Josh lifted a brow. "Me?"

Luke nodded. "Not just 'cause he's been so many places, or been in fights . . . he just sort of . . ." The boy gave up with a grimace. "I dunno. He just does."

This shadowy Mr. Meeker was becoming more interesting by the minute, Josh thought. The warning about Robards alone would have caught his curiosity; the caution to stay away only intensified it. But for now, he thought, he'd do as the man wished. He went back to his task. He'd give Kate a little longer, he thought. Until dark. He'd let her hide out in her room until then, but no longer.

He finished with the Colt and began to reload it. His movements tugged slightly on the wound to his arm, but the pain was merely an annoyance, not incapacitating.

He didn't quite know what he was going to do now. He'd only been staying to make sure she was settled, that she would be all right. He'd planned on making the store as solid as he could, doing the repairs her husband had been too busy drinking and abusing her to do, and if necessary pointing out to Arly's suppliers the wisdom of business as usual with Arly's widow. He'd done most of that. But now, he wasn't sure what he was going to do.

"Josh?"

"Hmm?"

"Would you teach me to shoot?"

Josh went still. Then he methodically finished reloading, looking only at the Colt as he checked that the hammer was resting on an empty chamber, and then slid the weapon back into the holster. Finally he looked at Luke.

"Why?"

The boy looked nonplussed. "Well . . . 'cause a fellow has to know how to shoot."

"Why?" Josh repeated.

Luke's brow furrowed. Finally he said, " 'Cause there are bad men like Robards around."

"Knowing how to shoot isn't going to change that. It never has."

"But if you know how to shoot, you can get them before they get you."

Josh's mouth twisted wryly. "The smart thing to do is to make sure they don't *want* to get you."

Luke sighed. "I guess that means no, huh?"

Josh stifled a smile at the boy's downcast expression. "I'd say you're a little young yet."

"How old were you?"

The memories welled up, sudden and vivid. Too close to the surface these days, Josh thought as he fought them down. "That was different," he managed to say after a moment. "That was in the middle of the war."

"But if I'd been able to shoot, I woulda killed ol' Arly a long time ago, before Mr. Hall messed up, and Miss Kate wouldn't be in trouble now."

Josh wasn't surprised at the boy's knowledge; Luke seemed to know everything as soon as it happened. "Killing a man is not something to take lightly, no matter who or what he is, Luke. You carry it forever, and it doesn't make for easy sleeping at night."

Luke looked at him, wide-eyed. "Even after you've killed a lot of men?"

Josh's jaw tightened. "If the day comes when it doesn't bother you, then you're dead yourself. You may still be walking around, but you're dead inside, and it won't be long before the rest of you follows."

For a moment Luke looked at him as Kate had, when she'd said those words that had haunted him ever since. *Will that be payment enough for your family, Josh? When you finally get yourself killed?*

"Are you . . . dead inside?" the boy asked.

How many times had he nearly wished for that, wished he was already at that state when the killing no longer tormented him? How many times had he wished he could just kill and walk away without feeling, as others seemed able to do? Even killing Robards, devious back-shooter though he was, hadn't been easy, just a necessity.

"Not yet," he answered Luke grimly, "but I'm working on it."

"She hates me."

"No, she doesn't."

"She's still locked up in her rooms, and she won't even talk to me."

"She needs time," Deborah said. "She's had a tremendous shock. She won't talk to me, either, but I know she doesn't hate me."

"She hates me," Alex repeated. "How could she not?"

Deborah stifled a weary sigh. Alex had been pacing her parlor for the past hour, seemingly on the edge of tearing out large portions of his sandy hair. She was worried about Kate, but right now Alex concerned her more.

"Because she's not that kind of woman, Alex."

He plopped down in his accustomed spot on her sofa. "But if I hadn't given him the idea of doing a will, if I hadn't told him a man of property should have one—"

"Tell me something," she said, interrupting his flow of self-recriminations, "if you went to a brand-new town, and found that the owner of the largest business there had no will, what would you do?"

"Advise him that he needed one, of course. But that's different."

"Why?"

"Because of Kate!"

"You didn't know her when you wrote up Arly's will."

"I still should have refused to draw up that will for Arly, once I knew what the terms were going to be. I should have never have—"

"Alex, is it a lawyer's job to tell his client what he wants?"

"No, but—"

"Did you do what your client asked you to do?"

"Yes, but—"

"Then you did your job as a lawyer, Alex."

"I just failed miserably as a man," Alex said.

Deborah rose abruptly to her feet. "I've heard quite enough of this, thank you."

Alex blinked, apparently nonplussed.

"Alexander Hall happens to be a friend of mine," she said sternly, "and a man I happen to think very highly of. I'll not have anyone speak ill of him in my home."

Alex gaped at her.

"Not even you," she added pointedly.

She stood there glaring, looking at him for all the world as if he were a total stranger who had just insulted her dearest friend. And suddenly Alex saw the humor in it, and his mouth began to twitch. And then he was laughing, hesitantly at first, then uproariously. And Deborah began to smile. She sat down in her chair once more.

"Deborah," he finally gasped out, "you are a treasure. And I'm proud to have you count me as your friend."

Deborah's smile became slightly stiff. His friend.

That's what she was best at, it seemed, being everyone's friend. Kate, Alex, shy Mrs. Boardman, they all came to her to talk. Even the marshal had occasionally dropped by under the guise of checking on her since her father had died, and stayed to probe for advice on how to handle this person or that in the town she'd lived in longer than he had.

She was confidante for half the town, but it seemed there was no one for her to confide in in turn. Not that she could, she thought, chastising herself for her selfish thoughts. How could she ever confide to anyone what sensible, settled Miss Taylor secretly longed for in the night?

"Deborah? What's wrong?"

She gathered her composure. "Nothing, Alex." Then, choosing the topic she was certain would divert him, she added. "I'm merely worried about Kate. What can we do to help her?"

Alex looked down at his hands. "I've . . . been thinking about little else. And I think . . ." He hesitated, his voice sounding odd. After a moment he went on. "I think the best thing would be for her to marry again."

So, Deborah thought, he'd come around to it at last. She did her best not to appear downcast as she made herself cast aside the last of her foolish daydreams. She felt guilty for even thinking about her own silly hurt feelings when Kate's entire life was in chaos.

Alex was probably right, it would be best for Kate to marry again, now that she had lost the store. There was little else she could do in town, or in any other town, for that matter, not as a woman alone.

Still there were things to consider.

"She's barely a widow, Alex," she said. "It's hardly proper for her to be thinking about marriage so soon. Even if her first marriage had been . . . a pleasant one."

"Well, it certainly wasn't that," Alex muttered. Then, in response to her point, added, "It would have to be long engagement, of course." He studied her for a moment. "She could . . . stay with you during that time, couldn't she? Even if it was . . . a long while?"

"Of course. That's wisest, don't you think? Gives a couple a chance to know one another, to be sure you're doing the right thing."

"Yes," Alex said, with the air of a much older man, "I've seen too many folks very unhappy because they'd married too soon, without really knowing the other person, you see."

"And then one day they're surprised to find they don't even like that person."

"Exactly," Alex exclaimed, apparently delighted at her understanding. "People need to take time, so they're not surprised later."

Deborah nodded. "They need to talk, to learn about each other."

"Precisely. I mean, look at you and me—we've talked for hours. I know how you feel about so many things, and you always understand me."

"Yes," Deborah said, her throat growing tight.

Couldn't he see what this was doing to her? Was he really so blind to her feelings as to not realize she even had them? Did everyone in this town think her so firmly an old, settled spinster who had no needs, no desire for anything more out of her life?

"And you make me laugh," Alex went on, seemingly as oblivious as she'd feared, "and see sides of things I never thought of. And you laugh, too, even if the story I tell you isn't really so very funny. And I know that you like that special tea, and you know how I like my coffee."

"Yes," she said tightly, "yes, I do."

"And I can talk to you about anything. That's important, isn't it?"

"Very. A . . . husband and wife should be able to talk about anything."

He was tearing her heart out, and he didn't even know it, Deborah thought. She wondered if he would even care. Of course, he would, she thought. Alex was a kind, caring man. But he would be horribly embarrassed if he ever guessed that his confidante, a woman five years older than he, and at thirty far too old to be entertaining such notions, harbored a secret fondness for him that went beyond the bounds of friendship. And she guessed that Alex had had more than enough embarrassment for one week.

"Deborah?"

His questioning tone told her she'd failed to respond to something he'd said.

"I'm sorry, I was . . . thinking," she said. "Did you ask me something?"

"Er . . . yes." He was wearing a rather militant expression, and Deborah braced herself. "You don't think . . . I mean, that man is still there . . . You don't suppose Kate . . . ?"

"What are you asking, Alex?"

"She doesn't *care* about that man, does she?"

"Josh?" Deborah asked, using the name purposely, although she wasn't certain of her motivation, or whether it was of the purest kind.

"Josh?" Alex gaped at her. "You call *The Hawk* Josh?"

"Well, it is his given name," she said blithely, a tiny bit pleased, albeit meanly so, to see him disconcerted a little.

"But he's—"

"A very charming man."

"Charming? My Lord, Deborah, this is The Hawk you're talking about!"

"So it is." She allowed herself a little more enjoyment at having rattled the usually very proper Alex into the oath. "But the only men I've personally seen dead by his hand it appears have tried to shoot him in the back."

Deborah paused, thinking she was acting the fool, going on like this. But then Josh's words echoed in her mind: *You're a fine-looking woman, Miss Taylor.* It gave her back her courage, and she went on in the best tone of female appreciation she could manage.

"I think he's a very handsome man."

"Handsome?" Alex almost yelped.

"Very." Deborah smiled, enjoying this in a purely feminine way she'd never known before. "That dark hair, those blue eyes, that jaw. And he's tall, and strong—"

Alex leapt to his feet. He stared down at her. "Deborah, what has gotten into you?"

She relaxed in her chair as if this were a perfectly normal conversation. "Perhaps it's just nice to meet a man who treats me like a woman instead of a sister."

Alex glowered at her. "Just what *has* he done?"

"Why nothing, Alex. He's been a perfect gentleman."

"Look, I know you have some idea that he's not the bad man some say he is, and perhaps there's something to that, but you can't seriously think . . ."

"Think what, Alex?" she said sweetly.

"Whatever it is you're thinking!" he roared.

*I'm thinking,* Deborah realized in wonder, *for the first time in my life, that perhaps it isn't too late for me after all.*

# Chapter 14

"Open the door, Kate."

"Go away."

"No."

"Go *away*."

"Open it, Kate. Or I'll take it down."

Josh listened to the silence from the other side of the door. It was dusk, in fact nearly dark, and she was still holed up inside her room. He hadn't heard a sound since she'd run from them, not even the familiar sound of her light footsteps above his head. She'd gone to ground like a wounded fox seeking her den, and if he left her there, Josh was afraid she'd simply curl up and bleed to death inside. That valiant spirit would drain away, finally crushed by this final blow delivered from beyond the grave.

He backed up a step, ready to keep his word to take the door down if he had to. He'd fix it later, after he was sure she was all right. He picked his spot on the door, next to the knob, where the faded-to-gray paint was peeling the worst. He'd thought about painting the whole damn place, but he'd discarded the idea simply because it meant he'd probably be here another month, and he didn't want that.

Hell, he didn't want to be here another day. His life had started to fall apart in Gambler's Notch, and was only getting more confused, and he wanted the place far behind him as soon as he could manage it. But he had to see to this first, had to know she was all right.

He set himself to kick the door. He wasn't about to use his shoulder—it was still too sore from his encounter with Robards this afternoon, and using the right shoulder would put him with his back to the room, and he couldn't quite bring himself to do that, even knowing it was only Kate inside.

He gathered himself, but in the instant before he delivered the blow, he heard the faint sound of footsteps on the other side of the door. He lowered his foot back to the small landing, and waited. After a moment, he heard a slight metallic sound. Then more footsteps.

Nothing happened. After a moment, he reached down and tried the doorknob; it turned. He opened the door. When nothing happened again, he stepped inside.

He'd wondered what the place looked like, if the home Arly had provided for his wife was as paltry as the clothes she wore. The room was dim. Kate had not lit a lamp in the fading dusk, but even so, Josh could see that if anything, it was worse than he'd imagined. Although painfully clean and tidy, there was little comfort here, little sign even that a woman lived here.

The only furniture was a worn small sofa, a single chair at a table even more battered than the one in the kitchen, and a large humpbacked trunk. The floor was bare wood, without even a rag rug to cushion it. A single kerosene lantern sat on the table, and a smaller version of the cast-iron stove that was in the store sat midway down a side wall, cold and empty despite the chill in the air now that the sun was dropping behind the mountains.

On the other side of the stove was an iron bed. Large enough to accommodate a man the size of Arly Dixon, but with little room to spare. Josh stared at it for a moment, wondering if the man's viciousness had carried over into this part of their marriage as well, but in his gut he knew there was little chance it hadn't. The images that leapt to life in his mind, of Kate at the mercy of the brutal Arly in that bed, made him nearly ill as he turned away from it.

By now his eyes had adjusted, and he finally saw her, huddled in a battered rocker he hadn't seen at first, by the single small window in the back wall. He pulled the door shut behind him and walked toward her.

"Kate," he began.

"Don't. There's nothing to say."

He stopped in front of her. The faint light from the window spilled over her, lighting her hair with a kind of halo, and casting her features into contours of light and dark. It was not, perhaps, a pretty face, he thought, not in the way of other young women her age, but it was a face with its own kind of beauty, the beauty of strength and spirit.

And it made him feel sick inside to see her look so defeated.

"There's everything to say," he said. "You can't just give up."

"I was a fool, and now I'm paying for it."

"You are many things, Kate, but not a fool."

"If you really knew some of the things I am, what I've done . . ."

Her voice trailed away. She looked at him then, her eyes wide with something that looked almost like guilt, although he couldn't be sure in the dim light. He must be wrong, he thought, she had nothing to feel guilty about. But he needed to see her, to look into those golden eyes until he was certain she was all right. He walked over and lit the lantern on the table, trimmed the wick, then came back and crouched in front of her, bracing himself with his hands on the arms of the rocker.

"Kate, no matter what you think you've done, you don't deserve this."

"You don't know what I deserve," she said, an edge of desperation in her tone. "Josh, I—"

She broke off abruptly. He wondered what she'd been about to say; he'd had the strangest feeling that more than once she'd been about to tell him something, but had stopped herself. This was just the latest.

"What is it, Kate?"

"I . . . Nothing."

He knew it was a lie, but he couldn't bring himself to press her for the truth, not now, not when she was so vulnerable. He wished he could think of something to distract her, to take her mind off what had just happened. But all he could think to do was try to reassure her.

"You'll be all right. We'll think of something."

He meant it. There had to be something to do about this. He just wasn't sure what it was, not yet.

"You've done more than enough," she said. "You don't need to worry about me."

As if he could stop, Josh thought ruefully. He only wished he could. He'd probably spent more time worrying about this woman than he'd spent worrying about anything. Except maybe that damn book.

He stood up, hoping he'd found the distraction he'd been looking for.

"You're late," he said.

She looked up at him. "What?"

"You're late," he repeated. "We're supposed to be reading by now."

He heard her sigh, a soft, wistful sound, but she didn't speak.

"Come downstairs, Kate. We'll join up with that crazy captain again."

She shook her head. "It won't change anything."

"No, it won't. But it will take your mind off of this trouble. Gramps used to say a man could lose all his troubles in a good book."

He held out a hand to her. She stared at it for a moment, then at his face. Then, slowly, she lifted her hand to take his. His fingers curled around hers, and he felt the faint pressure as she clasped his in turn. She was a tall woman, but her hand felt delicate and fragile and soft in his. He liked how tall she was, he thought. She was a woman to stand beside a man, not hide in his shadow. She just didn't know that. Yet.

And her touch sent a burst of heat through him that made him remember with vivid clarity how her mouth had felt under his, soft and warm and giving, with a sweet innocence that had startled him until she'd given him the harsh explanation that she'd never been kissed with gentleness before.

He felt the pressure of her hand increase as she rose to her feet. And just that quickly she was bare inches away, and the memory of that kiss was beginning to send fiery little licks of heat along his nerves. It didn't matter why of all women it was this one, not now. It didn't matter why, despite his long bout of celibacy, despite the fact that most men would call her plain, despite how they'd met and all the complications that meant, he could only seem to respond to this woman.

It didn't matter what the book had said, or how instinctive and fierce his rebellion was against the idea that
a woman—this woman, it seemed—had been chosen
for him by a fate that seemed to take special delight
in playing with the Hawks.

All that mattered was that she was here, looking up
at him with those incredible eyes that glowed in the
lantern's light, and that he wanted to kiss her again
more than he wanted to take his next breath. And he
seemed to have lost the will to stop himself.

Her lips parted on her next breath, and Josh was
lost. He had to kiss her, had to taste that mouth that
was as sweet as the honey her eyes reminded him of.
He simply had to. He thought she would dodge away
when he lifted his hands to her shoulders and pulled
her close, but she didn't move.

He meant to go gently, slowly, but at the first touch
of her lips beneath his, he forgot all his good intentions. Only remembering what she had told him kept
him from plundering the depths of her mouth as he
longed to do. But he captured her mouth, savoring the
softness of her lips, the taste of her, and when she
didn't draw back, flicked his tongue across her lips.
When they parted at the first touch of his tongue, he
nearly groaned aloud.

It was all he could do not to plunge his tongue forward into those honeyed depths, taking what he
wanted so badly, but not for anything would he add to
her painful memories. So he probed gently, stroking
the inner edges of her lips, tracing the even ridge of
her teeth. He heard her make a tiny sound of surprise,
and felt her tremble.

He slid his hands up over her shoulders to her neck,
threading his fingers into her hair, marveling at the
thick, silken, rich feel of it, belying the plainness of

the color. He wanted to take out all the pins he could feel, wanted to see it cascade down her back, wanted to see just how long it was, this smooth, satiny mass.

"Kate," he murmured against her mouth. "Open for me, Kate."

"Josh," she whispered back, the movement of her lips against his as she said it made a shiver ripple through him.

She went still, as if she'd felt it. That tiny sound came again, and she gave him the entry he'd asked for. He traced her lips again, then explored farther, deeper. When he stroked his tongue over hers, she gave a little start. He felt her fingers digging into the muscles of his arms, sending out a jagged little barb of pain from his injury. He ignored it; nothing mattered now except the incredible, enticing allure of the woman in his arms.

He was spiraling out of control, his body making it clear that now that it had decided to cooperate, it was doing so thoroughly, almost painfully. As if it wanted to make up for all the months of neglect at once. He was already as hard as the barrel of his Colt, and about as ready to go off. He tried to clamp down on the urgent need that seemed to be consuming him, but then Kate moved, pressing herself against him, as if she intended to caress his rigid flesh with her body. The rising, boiling tide swept through him, so powerful he thought it unstoppable.

In the back of his mind was the knowledge that there was a bed less than a dozen feet away. But at war with that knowledge was the thought of what had no doubt happened to her in that bed, at the cruel hands of Arly Dixon. And no matter how badly he wanted to, no matter how hot he was, he knew he could never take her there, not with the images that would haunt her.

He wanted no ghosts between them, not the ones she carried, or his own. He—

"Kate? Kate!"

The shout, and the hammering on her door made Kate jump, breaking the kiss. For a long moment Josh looked at her, seeing the rise and fall of her breasts beneath the ill-fitting dress as she took in quick breaths, seeing the heat in her eyes that told him she'd not been thinking of brutal kisses, told him that she'd been caught up in the swirl of sensation just as he had.

"Kate!"

The lawyer, Josh realized belatedly. The metallic click of the doorknob turning and releasing echoed in the charged silence, and he remembered that, in his worry about her, he for once hadn't locked the door behind him. Reluctantly, in the instant before the door swung open, he let her go. She swayed on her feet, and for an instant he almost did the same. He shook his head sharply, as if that would clear away the odd weakness he was feeling in his knees.

Alex Hall stepped into the room, calling Kate's name yet again. When he saw them, he came to a halt, staring.

"So it's true," he said. "You are here."

"Obviously," Josh said coolly. He'd learned early on to mask whatever he might be feeling; betraying himself to an opponent was a good way to get himself killed.

The lawyer looked at Kate. If he guessed what had caused her flustered air, he didn't say anything. "Kate, I know you're upset, and you have a right to be. And I know he probably pushed his way in here, but you shouldn't allow him to be here in your . . . room with you, alone."

Josh stiffened. "And if I wasn't here, you'd be alone with her now."

"That's different," Hall said.

"Why?" Josh asked, his voice going very soft.

"Because I care about her welfare, and you . . ."

The lawyer's voice faded as he suddenly seemed to take in the details of the scene he'd walked in on. Kate's tousled hair, the brightness of her eyes, the slight swollenness of her lips . . . and if the man had any kind of eyes at all, Josh thought ruefully, the fact that he was still so aroused he could hardly stand up.

"And I what?" he said, softer still.

"Josh, stop." Kate's voice quavered slightly, but was audible enough. She looked at Alex. "He didn't push his way in here, Alex. I let him in."

"I . . . think I can see that," Hall said, his glance flicking from Kate to Josh and back. "Kate, Kate, you don't know what you're doing, what kind of man this is."

"And just what kind of man am I, lawyer?"

Hall drew himself up to his full height, set his jaw, and met Josh's gaze. Josh stifled a flicker of admiration for the smaller man.

"Apparently," Hall said, "you are the kind of man who leads on one woman while he's . . . trying to trifle with another."

Josh blinked. For one of the few times in his life he was completely taken aback. "What?"

"Mrs. Dixon and Miss Taylor are respectable women, and I'll thank you to leave them both be."

Josh heard Kate gasp in surprise, but didn't look at her. "Miss Taylor?" he said in astonishment.

"Deborah?" Kate echoed, in a tone that nearly matched Josh's.

"Just because she's a woman alone doesn't give you

the right to ride in here and make eyes at her, and fill her head full of nonsense," Hall said vehemently.

Josh barely managed not to laugh. "If you think any man could fill Miss Taylor's head with nonsense, then you're a bigger fool than I thought, Hall. That is one levelheaded woman."

"And she's my dearest friend," Kate put in, an edge in her voice. "And if you weren't the blindest man in the entire country, you'd see that she—"

Kate stopped suddenly, in the manner of one who has just realized she was about to say something she shouldn't. Josh studied her for a moment, then the lawyer. A possibility occurred to him, and he wasted no time in testing it.

"She's a plumb handsome woman to boot," he drawled. "And smart, steady, loyal. A man could do a lot worse."

"What man?" Hall said, glaring at Josh.

"Why . . . any man with sense," Josh said blandly.

Josh sensed Kate move, and glanced at her. She was staring at him as if she was trying to decide if his words should bother her after the passionate kiss they'd just shared. He wasn't sure what he was going to do about this unexpected, unwanted attraction, but he was sure that he couldn't add to her pain, not right now. Slowly, turning his head so the lawyer couldn't see, he winked at her. Her eyes widened, but an instant later understanding filled them. Understanding, and a glint of mischief that made him want to grin, he was so glad to see it. He had a feeling Kate had had little chance to play in her life.

"Sense," she said thoughtfully. "Mr. Rankin has sense."

"Art?" Hall blurted in amazement, as if this had never occurred to him.

Josh nodded. "He thinks Miss Taylor's a fine-looking woman, too. And then there's Marshal Pike."

"The marshal?" Hall yelped.

"Why, just this afternoon he said she had a pretty face," Josh said cheerfully. "But he's a mite old for her, I'd say. She'd be better off with a younger man."

"You mean . . . a man about your age?" Kate asked, with every appearance of innocence. Josh caught the twinkle in her eyes, and was again barely able to stop himself from grinning sillily back at her.

"That seems about right," Josh agreed.

Hall gaped at him. "But you . . . you're no older than I am."

Josh shrugged. "I'm sure a woman as clever as Miss Taylor wouldn't hold that against a man, if he were lucky enough to catch her eye."

"And smart enough to realize it," Kate put in, in rather pointed tones.

Hall seemed stunned into silence, his eyes slightly distant and unfocused. Josh glanced at Kate. She smiled at him, shyly but with obvious pleasure, her own problems forgotten for the moment in the merriment of their mutual teasing of the young lawyer. Josh returned the smile, glad to see the old sassy Kate back, the defeated, weary girl he'd found when he'd come up here banished, at least for now.

"Was there something you wanted, Alex?" she asked.

"What?" Hall seemed to come back to himself then, focusing on her. "Oh. Er, yes, yes there was."

"What?" Kate prodded gently when he didn't go on.

"I . . . er . . ." He looked like a man who was no longer quite so certain of a course of action he'd once been sure of. With an effort that was visible, he went on. "I think that there is a solution to your problem."

Josh could have kicked the lawyer as he saw the

reminder of her situation take the enjoyment from her eyes, leaving them shadowed once more. And when she spoke, the animation was gone from her voice.

"What solution?"

His gaze flicked to Josh. "I'd rather not talk about it in front of him."

Josh frowned. "I'm not going anywhere until I'm sure she's all right."

Hall set his jaw again, stubbornly. The man had more nerve than sense, Josh thought, wishing he could simply dislike the lawyer. But he had to admire the way he refused to back down, even when it was clearly the wisest thing to do.

"And if Kate asks you to leave?"

Josh looked at Kate. "If she asks, then I'll leave. Are you asking, Kate?"

She sighed, sounding weary. "It doesn't matter. Just tell me what this solution is, Alex. But if it's to fight Arly's will, then the answer is no."

"It's not that. It's much . . . simpler. And better. Really. You'll be able to stay here, and you won't have to work, at least not like you do now, and no one will ever hurt you like Arly did ever again, I promise you that."

The words came in a rush, as if the lawyer wasn't certain he wanted to say them and had to hurry to get them out before he changed his mind. Josh's frown deepened. Kate looked doubtful.

"I wish that could be true," she said.

"It can be, Kate," Alex said, sounding more certain, but not looking it. Premonition rattled through Josh like the shaking of the earth he'd once felt in California.

"How?"

The lawyer took a deep breath.

"Marry me."

# Chapter 15

He'd thought of it himself. He'd thought it was a fine idea, the solution to all his problems. Not to mention a fine way to foil that damned book's prediction. He'd even considered Alexander Hall, lawyer, as the ideal candidate. And he'd been ready to shake the dust of Gambler's Notch the moment the lawyer seemed set on the right path toward the widow.

So why the hell was he so all-fired huffed about the fact that exactly what he'd wanted to happen had happened? Why wasn't he already packed and heading for the stable, ready to saddle Buck and hit the breeze? Why had he spent the night lying awake on his bedroll, trying not to think of Kate actually married to the man?

And the fact that Kate had seemed utterly shocked, and that none of the lawyer's fine reasons why she should marry him seemed to impress her, should have worried him. If she turned the man down, who knows how long he'd be stuck here. But for some reason, he'd found himself pleased, even when she'd told them both to leave her alone and give her time to think.

Time to think. Kate might want it, but to Josh it seemed he'd had far too much of it lately. His mind hadn't been so tangled up since he'd been a boy and

Gramps had made him read those old epic poems and then tell him what they were about. But even Homer seemed simple compared to the complexity his life seemed to have taken on now.

Maybe he should just leave. There was nothing more he could do. Surely Kate would see sense and marry Hall, and Josh could safely be on his way. Of course she would, he assured himself. He would pack his few possessions and head out this morning. There was no reason not to.

He gathered up his two extra shirts, the best of which Kate had washed for him on Saturday, before he'd told her not to bother, as he had no intention of attending Reverend Babcock's sermon given in the parlor of the Grand Hotel. He set them down on the chair that held the kerosene lamp he used at night, and added the heavy woolen undershirt he wore during the winter to the pile. He set his vest on top, glanced out the window at the brightly sunny sky, and tossed his black frock coat down on his blankets, to be rolled up in the bedroll. He added his razor and the small mirror he used for shaving on the trail to the pile of shirts and vest.

It made him feel better to be taking some action, to be going through the task of packing. He was really going to get out of this town that had nearly been his last stop. He'd done all he could, and he was tempting fate to stay any longer. He'd nearly died twice in Gambler's Notch; only a fool would give the town a third shot at him.

He stepped over the blankets, heading for the saddlebags that still served him as a makeshift pillow, although Kate had offered him at least another blanket to use. He'd declined without telling her why; the fact that he preferred not to get too comfortable, and therefore too deeply asleep, was something he didn't feel like explaining to her.

Yes, it would be best if he just hightailed it on out of here, he thought as he knelt to pick up the bags. And if it took him a while to forget what it had been like to kiss her, if he spent a long time looking for that sweet fire in another woman, then it was what he deserved for dallying with the woman he'd made a widow. He never should have kissed her in the first place, never should have—

Still crouched, he whirled at a sudden sound, reaching swiftly for his Colt. The outside door to the kitchen, he thought. The door he'd unlocked only a few minutes before. Gun in hand, he took two steps toward the inside storeroom door, then stopped. He knew the quick, light steps that were coming from the kitchen—Luke. He reholstered the Colt as he heard the second door open, then heard some faint thumping as the boy made his way through the now crowded storeroom. The lever handle of the inside door lifted, and the door swung open. Very slowly.

"Josh?"

The boy had learned quickly not to approach without warning, Josh thought. "Come in, Luke," he called out, although he wasn't really in the mood for the boy's garrulousness.

But for once the boy didn't seem disposed to idle chatter. "Where's Miss Kate?"

"She hasn't come down yet."

Luke looked up at him from under lowered brows. "Is it true?"

"Is what true?"

"Did Mr. Hall really ask her to marry him?"

Josh gaped at him. "Boy, you could put the telegraph to shame. Where did you hear this so fast?"

Where normally he would have been pleased at Josh's words, now Luke merely shrugged. "Nobody watches what they say much in front of a kid. Is it true?"

"What makes you think I know?" Josh asked warily.

"Mrs. Boardman says you were there," Luke said, gesturing upward toward Kate's rooms. "Says she told Mr. Hall you were with Miss Kate and he went runnin'. Like he was gonna rescue her again."

"I believe that's what he had in mind," Josh admitted wryly. "He's very . . . fond of Kate, you know."

"Is she gonna do it? Is she gonna marry him?" The words came in a rush; clearly the boy was upset.

"I don't know, Luke."

"She won't," he said in the overly positive tones of someone trying to convince himself. "I know she won't."

"Luke," Josh said slowly, "Hall's a good man. He made a mistake, but he admitted it, and that takes sand. And he's stood up to me more than once, and for a man who doesn't carry a gun that takes—"

"But why would she marry *him*?"

Josh felt like a man floundering on the edge of quicksand. "A woman alone has a hard life out here, Luke. Marrying again might be the best thing for Kate to do."

"But you said yourself, he doesn't even carry a gun. He couldn't protect her or nothing, not like you."

Josh went still. "Me?"

"Well . . . sure," Luke said. "You like her, don't you?"

*Like her.* Josh had liked a few women in his life, and he knew that wasn't the word for what he felt for Kate Dixon. What the right word was he didn't know, but it was considerably more complicated than simple liking. The ground that was keeping him from that quicksand felt like it was about to crumble.

"Don't you?" Luke asked again, somewhat anxiously. "You wouldn't have stayed if you didn't, would you?"

"No, I wouldn't," Josh agreed reluctantly.

Luke looked relieved. "If you were to marry her, nobody'd ever dare be mean to her again."

Josh felt as if he'd tripped and fallen face first into that quicksand. Unbidden, the memory of the book, the book he'd burned to cinders in the cast-iron stove in this room, came back to him, the book that had told him he'd met the woman who was going to make sure the Hawks continued as promised.

Marry Kate? Marry her, and have the right to kiss her to distraction any time? Marry her, and have the right to ease that aching need she roused in him all night if he wanted to, every night? He nearly shivered at the idea, before the reality of his life quashed the response of his body.

Marry her and watch her wonder every time he walked out the door if he would come back?

"Don't go getting any wild ideas, boy. I'm not the marrying kind. Nor would any woman with an ounce of sense marry me."

And he wasn't about to marry her and end up fulfilling the damned prophecy of a haunted book he didn't even believe in.

He turned on his heel and went back to his work. He knelt at the foot of his blankets and began to roll them up. He heard Luke's footsteps behind him. He glanced at the boy in time to see him frown at the neat pile of shirts topped with razor and mirror.

"What are you doing?"

"Packing."

"Why?"

He had had, Josh decided, about enough of the boy's

constant questions. "Because I'm getting shed of Gambler's Notch once and for all."

Luke gaped at him. "You're leaving?"

"Soon as I get packed and go saddle Buck, I'm riding out." Just saying it made him feel like there was some hope it might be true.

"You're just going to leave?"

The boy sounded so incredulous Josh felt a qualm of guilt. "It's time. It's past time."

"Why?" Luke asked, sounding bewildered now. "I thought you liked it here. I thought you liked Miss Kate, and Mr. Rankin, and . . . and me."

*Damn.*

Josh stood up and turned to face the boy, thinking he'd faced down armed men with less churning in his stomach. Luke looked up at him, his brown eyes wide with confusion. But already Josh saw the beginnings of a mask of indifference stealing over the boy's features. He'd been abandoned before, he knew what it was about, and it was clear he was determined not to let on that he cared. Josh knew that feeling all too well.

On impulse, Josh reached down and grasped Luke's arms. He swung the boy up to sit on the counter so he could look at him eye to eye. It took some effort; Luke wasn't small for his age. The boy was so startled by this action that for a moment his indifference faded.

"I do like you, Luke. I like you a lot. But I have to keep moving. I should have been gone the day they let me go."

"But why? Marshal Pike said you could stay—"

"For a while. He knows that men like me can't stay in one place too long. It's not healthy. For anyone."

"But you said you were gonna stay here until Miss Kate was all right—"

"She'll be fine. She'll marry that lawyer, and have a

good life." He tousled the boy's hair. "And she'll always look out for you, Luke. She's that kind of woman. A good woman. Solid. Strong."

"Then why don't *you* marry her? Then you could stay, couldn't you?"

"That's not a very good reason to marry someone."

Luke's mouth twisted into a surprisingly adult grimace. "I don't know why folks get married anyway. Why do they, Josh?"

*Damn,* Josh thought again. He wanted to say hell if he knew, but somehow that didn't seem the right thing to tell the boy.

"Lots of reasons," he said, stalling.

"Miss Deborah says I shouldn't reckon that ol' Arly and Miss Kate were really married. I mean, they were, all legal and all, but she said that wasn't what it's 'sposed to be like."

"That," Josh said fervently, "is God's own truth."

"My ma and pa, they used to hold hands all the time. And they were always kissin'. And sometimes they'd just look at each other for the longest time."

"Mine, too," Josh said, his voice suddenly tight.

"Sometimes . . ." Luke swallowed visibly. "Sometimes I can't remember what they looked like."

Josh closed his eyes for a moment. How many times had that happened to him, how many times had he been struck by panic because their faces were fading from his memory? How many times had he blamed himself for that?

"I know," he whispered. He opened his eyes to look at Luke. "And that's scary, isn't it? Like all you have left of them is fading away."

Luke nodded, staring down at his toes in the shoes Kate had given him.

"Do you feel like . . . like you're bad, because you can't remember?"

The boy's head came up swiftly, and Josh saw the boy's fear in his eyes, just as he had once seen it in his own.

"It's not what they looked like that's important, Luke," Josh said, struggling to remember what his grandfather had told him when he'd been where the boy was now. "It's what they were to you, how they loved you, and each other, and you loved them. That's what matters, and as long as you never forget that, you'll never forget them. And as long as you never forget them, they're never really gone."

When he saw some of the fear subside in the boy's eyes, Josh felt like he'd come through some kind of battle. For a long time the boy was silent, but at last he nodded.

"I'll never forget them," he promised.

"I know you won't."

Luke studied him for a moment. "Did your ma and pa love each other?"

A memory long denied flashed through Josh's mind, of a long-ago morning when he'd awakened before dawn, frightened by some childish nightmare, and had scuttled down the hall to his parents' room. It hadn't been until years later that he'd understood the significance of the fact that they'd been naked together in their big bed, understood the meaning of the frequent heated glances that preceded their disappearance for short "naps" in the middle of the day.

"Yes," he whispered, "yes, they did."

Luke looked at him solemnly. "Is that what it should be like? Bein' married, I mean."

"I . . . Yes. But it only happens that way for very few, boy," he added silently.

"Then Miss Kate can't marry Mr. Hall," Luke said positively. "She doesn't look at him like that. She only looks at you."

"Luke—"

For the first time ever, the boy interrupted him. "And you look at her, too. I've seen you."

Josh opened his mouth to deny it, but he knew it was useless. He did look at her. Far too much.

"You look at her like my pa used to look at my ma."

"Sometimes that isn't enough," Josh said gruffly, "Sometimes there are other things that . . . get in the way."

"What things?"

Josh took a deep breath, wishing he'd just told the boy to go away before he'd gotten himself into this.

"You saw what happened with Robards, Luke," he explained. "There are a hundred more like him out there. You can't ask a woman to live with that."

"But . . . you're the best. You beat that man."

"And someday, someone will beat me."

Luke shook his head vehemently. "Not you. Not ever. You're The Hawk."

Josh reached out and grasped the boy's shoulders. "Everybody dies, Luke, and gunfighters sooner than most. Someday, somebody will come along who's faster, a better shot, or who gets the drop on me. Or I'll get careless—"

"No!" Luke jumped down from the counter, dodging away. "No, not ever," he cried out again, backing up as he stared at Josh, wild-eyed.

The boy stumbled over something on the floor behind him. Arms flailing, he struggled for balance, and before Josh could reach him, went down in a heap. Angry and embarrassed, the boy kicked out at the object that had caused his fall. Then he stopped as if frozen, staring at the floor.

Josh knelt beside the boy, fearing he'd hurt himself, although it had looked like a harmless enough tumble. But the way he was sitting so still, as if he were afraid to move, just staring at—

Josh's breath caught as he at last saw what it was that Luke was staring at. It lay on the floor beside his bedroll, where it had skittered away when Luke had kicked it. It looked as it had always looked. As if it had never been gone. As if it had never been touched.

As if he'd never consigned it to the stove's flames and stood there and watched it burn.

The Hawk book.

Kate held the book gingerly in her lap. Luke had nearly run her down as she'd come in the kitchen door, clearly frightened by the sight of the book all of them had seen go up in smoke, and frantic to get away from it. Josh was sitting on a chair beside her, elbows on his knees, looking at it as if he wanted to run away like the boy had. She wasn't at all sure she didn't want to do just that herself.

And none of them had had the courage to look inside it. She wasn't even sure she liked holding it. She'd wished for something to distract her from the predicament she was in, from Arly's final betrayal to Alex's astonishing proposal. It appeared that wish had been answered.

*Wish away, lawyer. Just think real hard before you do, in case you get it.*

Josh's words to Alex echoed in her mind. She should have heeded that warning herself. She'd hardly been prepared for the incredible story Josh had told her, of this book and its connection to his family, and how the stories he'd grown up with had told of its appearance to each of the Hawks who were the last of the line. It had been frightening enough to see the changes inside the book, and she'd been fighting not to remember Josh's insinuation that the woman mentioned had to be her when she knew it couldn't be, for the very simple reason that she could not have the children the book foretold. But this . . . this was beyond even frightening.

"How can this be?" she finally asked, not even caring about the thinness of her voice.

"I don't know."

"But you . . . burned it."

Josh grimaced. "Do you think I don't remember?"

"No, but . . . we saw it happen."

"I know. I watched it. I smelled the leather burning. I saw the pages curl, then turn black and crumble. It burned. I know damned well it burned."

She didn't even cringe at the curse; Lord knew she'd heard worse from Arly, with far less provocation. "Then how—"

He jumped to his feet. "I don't know!"

She gave a little start, her fingers tightening around the book involuntarily. Josh let out a harsh breath. He raised a hand and ran it through his hair. Kate found her fingers curling for a different reason, as she wondered what it felt like, that long, dark, thick mane, which reminded her in turn of the way he'd threaded his fingers through her hair when he'd kissed her last night. . . .

"I'm sorry," he said. "I didn't mean to—"

"It's all right. You certainly have reason enough to be . . . edgy."

"That's no excuse for yelling at you," he said, looking

at the book rather than her as he spoke. "You've had enough of that in your life."

His empathetic words, even delivered in such an off-hand manner, tightened her throat, and she felt her eyes brim. His image was blurry as she saw him sit back down. She blinked rapidly, and tried for a lighter tone.

"This part was never in the stories?"

He went very still. Slowly, he lifted his gaze from the book to her face. In his eyes was a distant look, as if he'd focused inward, or on some long-ago or far-away place.

"Yes," he said finally, very softly. "Yes, it was. Gramps said the legend says . . . the book won't be left behind. That it can't be destroyed. That it will always reappear. That it follows the Hawk blood, legitimate or not, and whether it's welcomed or not."

She found it hard to believe that anyone would welcome such a thing.

"I suppose, when people believed in witchcraft and such, it might be easier to . . . believe this really happened," she said slowly, "but welcome it?"

Josh shook his head, his jaw tight, his lips compressed. Then one corner of his mouth twisted wryly. "I hope that boy can keep his mouth shut for once. Reverend Babcock already thinks I'm the devil's born son. If he hears about this . . ."

Kate shivered.

"That would be ironic, wouldn't it?" Josh said, sounding on the verge of laughter. "Escape the noose only to wind up . . . what, burned at the stake?"

"Don't joke about things like that!" Kate exclaimed.

"Honey," he said softly, the unexpected endearment completely unnerving her, "if I don't joke about that, then I have to think about what happened with that book, and I don't have any answers for that."

It took her a moment, as that sweet word rang in her ears, to compose herself enough to answer him. "Except . . . what your grandfather told you."

"Yes."

"And that's . . ."

"Impossible. Believe me, I know that."

"But it happened. You burned the book, and now it's here. As if it had never been even singed."

"Yes."

He sounded so strained, Kate thought. And why wouldn't he? How did one deal with this? It frightened her, and it wasn't her family that was apparently being haunted by this book, and had been for generations.

It took her a moment to recognize the odd feeling that crept through her then, a sort of longing that weakened the fear's hold on her. Then she realized it was a wish that she'd come from a family like that, a family with a great sense of its own history, a family that passed that history down from generation to generation, a family which held together despite adversity, a family which would never think of abandoning one of their own to a man such as Arly Dixon. . . .

She felt the intensity of Josh's eyes on her, felt a tension as if he were waiting, barely breathing, and realized that in her reverie she'd opened the book. She nearly slammed it instantly closed again, certain she didn't want to know if it had changed once more, as it had practically beneath her fingertips the last time she'd seen it. She'd worked very hard at putting that out of her mind, trying to convince herself she had simply not seen that part of the book before, or had misread it, just as Josh had misinterpreted the part he thought had referred to her. Deep down she'd known it wasn't true, but she'd had no other explanation for what had happened.

And now? Now she had an explanation, but it was one she couldn't accept.

"I can't believe it either, Kate," he said as if he'd read her mind. "But what other explanation is there? The thing appears out of nowhere. I leave it here, and it shows up in Granite Bluff. The story in it changes right in front of us. And you and Luke both saw me put it in the stove. You know it burned. I know it burned. But here it is."

"You're talking about . . . magic."

Josh sighed tiredly, as if he'd slept as little as she had last night. "I suppose so."

"I don't believe in magic."

"Neither do I."

She fiddled with the gilt-edged pages of the book, riffling through them with her fingers as if it were just an ordinary volume.

"I don't believe in magic," she repeated, "because no one ever wished harder than I did to be saved from my life with Arly. I wished and I prayed every day, and I didn't care if redemption came from God, or the devil, or . . . or that wizard in this story. I still would have taken it."

As she mentioned the story, she opened the book to that page, to the picture of Jenna and Kane. And again she felt the tug of longing, to be a part of such a family, to know her ancestors back to, if what this said was right, before history was even written. She wondered if Josh even appreciated what he had, if he—

*I didn't care if redemption came from God, or the devil, or . . . or that wizard in this story. I still would have taken it.*

But her redemption hadn't come from God, or even

from the devil. It had come from Josh. Joshua Hawk, one of the Hawks that wizard had blessed. Or cursed, as Josh had ruefully said.

She opened her mouth, once more on the verge of telling him the truth, of ridding herself of the burden of the secret of what she'd done. But another thought stopped her short.

Her redemption had come from Josh. Did that mean the magical intervention she'd wished for had truly happened? Had it not been an accident that The Hawk had come to Gambler's Notch?

Kate shivered; she was cursed herself if she began to think in such ways.

"I know, Kate," Josh said. "I feel the same way. It's impossible, but it's there, in your hands. How else do you explain it?"

"I can't."

She stared down at the book, at the drawing of the woman who had begun it all. A woman. A woman had done this. The thought that it had been a woman who had founded a dynasty that would continue unbroken long, long after her lifetime, made Kate feel oddly proud. And it appeared that none of the Hawks were bothered by this. Josh himself had had nothing less than pure admiration in his voice when he spoke of her.

Only when she turned a page and the long, rapidly expanding family tree of the Hawks began, did she realize that she'd read the entire story of Jenna and her warrior. And Josh had just sat there the entire time, watching her.

"I . . . I'm sorry," she stammered. "I didn't mean to read it again, but it was just so . . . interesting, and I could read it so easily—"

"Don't apologize."

Josh stood up rather abruptly. Leaving the book in her hands, he turned and walked across the kitchen to the storeroom door. He pulled it open, then looked back over his shoulder at her.

"Kate?"

She bit her lip, steadying herself before saying tentatively, "What?"

"Marry your lawyer."

She stiffened. Pain shot through her, and she fought not to let it show; he'd only kissed her, after all. And a kiss from a man like The Hawk meant little. Especially when given to a woman like her. She didn't know why he'd done it, only that she would be a fool to believe it held any kind of promise.

Slowly, she rose with all the dignity she could muster. "I married once because I had no choice. I paid for it every single day afterward."

"It doesn't have to be that way. Hall isn't like your husband was. Give him a chance."

It was good advice. She was certain it was. It was only that it wasn't what she wanted to hear, Josh advising her to marry Alex Hall. It took more effort than she cared to admit, but she answered him levelly.

"I will not marry again simply because I'm alone, or because some man happens to . . . pity me."

Josh looked at her for a long, silent moment. Then he gestured at the book. "Read it," he said. "Read all of it. Maybe it will . . . help you make up your mind."

More likely it would drive her out of her mind, Kate thought as he left her alone. But she was drawn to the book as if it were indeed magic. She paged through the pages of slanted lines and carefully printed names, Hawk after Hawk after Hawk. She followed the lines as they narrowed, dwindled, until only one name remained. The last Hawk.

She turned the page. Looking back at her from a drawing just like the one of Jenna and Kane was another couple, this time a tiny, lovely woman standing next to a man whose resemblance to Josh was more than passing. Their story began on the opposite page, and without any thought of putting the book down, she began to read.

She read them all, the stories of all the last Hawks. And each one told of that Hawk fighting against believing in the magic, fighting the reality of the book she held in her hands. And fighting other things as well, she thought; the Hawks seemed to be well represented in whatever war or crusade was happening at the time.

She paused over the story of Matthew Hawk, the first Hawk to come to America. His story was as tragic as the others. His family had died on the long journey, leaving him as the last surviving Hawk. Yet amid the fires of the war for independence, he had found a woman to love—as all the Hawks did, eventually, it seemed—and the Hawk blood had pulsed on.

It was Matthew who had speculated that the book was meant to assure that the last Hawk didn't give up, that it was a reminder of all the Hawks who had gone before, and who would be forgotten if the family died away. As for the how of the book, Matthew had been as wary and baffled as every other Hawk. Apparently none of the Hawks cared much for the idea that they were touched by magic.

Kate couldn't believe she'd even thought that with any kind of seriousness. But in each tale of the last Hawk finding his way with the help of the book, she'd read of their disbelief, their skepticism, and oddly, that fellow feeling made her somehow more receptive to the idea.

Smiling ruefully at herself, she began to turn the pages again, reading the names of Matthew's children, their children, and then their children, on and on, as the Hawk family began to grow and expand anew. But this time, the period of peace and growth was shorter than usual, less than a hundred years, and the abruptness of it, when the expanse of names plummeted to two, then one, gave her a feeling of loss as strong as if she carried the name herself.

She looked at that single, final line, the one that bore Josh's name for a long time. The last Hawk.

Who was she, this woman he would find someday, a woman to love, as the others had? She knew he'd been wrong, that there was no way the book could have meant her, despite the fact that it claimed he'd met her the day he'd arrived in Gambler's Notch, and Josh had said she was the only woman he'd even seen that day.

No, he would find a woman worthy of the Hawk name. A woman with whom he'd rebuild the dynasty that had been nearly destroyed by the savagery that had swept the country, dividing families as it had divided the Union. Who would she be, that woman, the woman strong enough, smart enough, beautiful enough to win the heart of The Hawk? Would their story someday grace the pages of the Hawk book?

Kate smothered the pang that thought brought her, just as she'd smothered the pain that had threatened to swamp her when Josh had told her, with every evidence of absolutely meaning it, to marry Alex. If only she could smother the memory of his kiss, the kiss that had made her understand why some women didn't dread them. The kiss that had made her wonder if there could be another way in bed as well, a way that was kinder than Arly's brutal habits. Josh had been

aroused in that way; she'd felt the hard readiness of
his body, had known what it had always meant before.
But Josh hadn't forced her, hadn't taken what he obviously wanted.

Convulsively, she turned the page, thinking that even
the consternation of finding the book changed yet
again would be better than this longing ache. It was
impossible that the thing still existed at all, so what
did a few changes inside matter? She made herself
look. She read the entry about the mysterious, un-
named woman again, laughing at the very idea that it
could be her; she wasn't meant for the kind of life that
got recorded in books, especially one that appeared to
have a magical life of its own.

She read on, and found herself barely reacting when
she saw that the pages at the end of the story, Josh's
story, had indeed changed again. She saw that the book
again showed a list of dates, as if promising parts of
the story still to come. But none of it mattered, not
after she'd read the final entry, dated barely three
weeks away.

That final, ominous entry that left her cold with fear.
*May 1870—Gunfighter Joshua Hawk buried in Gam-
bler's Notch, Wyoming Territory.*

# Chapter 16

Kate stared at the items on the counter: the jerky, the small sacks of sugar, and Arbuckle's coffee beside the neatly tied bedroll. And at the saddlebags that sat beside them, packed with Josh's belongings, just enough room left on one side for the foodstuff on the counter. A movement from in front of the store caught the edge of her vision and she looked that way. Buck stood at the hitching rail beside the water trough, saddled and waiting. The only conclusion to be drawn was obvious.

Moving slowly, Kate set the book down beside the sack of Arbuckle's.

She raised her gaze to watch Josh, who had just graciously handed Mrs. Boardman, who looked by turns repelled and fascinated by the idea of a notorious gunfighter serving as a store clerk, her change. The woman cast a curious look at Kate, but merely nodded and scurried out.

Josh headed toward her. Kate said nothing, because she couldn't force a single word out of her mouth. Josh came to a halt, glanced down at the supplies that sat beside his saddlebags, then back at her face. Still she couldn't speak.

"I paid for all of it," he said after a moment. "The money's already in the drawer."

Kate flushed, jarred out of her speechlessness. "I never suggested that you hadn't."

"Then what were you thinking?"

"I . . . you're packing," she said unnecessarily.

He looked at her steadily, his face a mask of indifference, an expression she hadn't seen for a while; she wasn't happy it had returned.

"Yes," he agreed.

It took every ounce of what little nerve she had to ask evenly, "You're leaving?"

"Yes."

It was short, terse, and without emotion. He was looking at her as if he expected her to . . . to what? Plead with him? Beg him to stay? She drew herself up; Arly hadn't left her much, but she still had some pride, even though she'd had to keep it deeply buried while her husband was alive. And she would not beg any man again. Not for anything. Ever.

*But, oh, I'm going to miss him.*

Kate paled, the words ringing so loudly in her mind that for a moment she feared she'd said them. But it was true, she would miss him. Miss his slow, lazy smiles, his quiet support, the warning look that came into his eyes whenever anyone didn't treat her with what he considered proper respect. She'd never had anyone to stand up for her before, not really, and it had been a heady experience. But it was over now, and best forgotten.

As were kisses given by a man with a lot of experience in moving, but not much in staying put.

Not, Kate thought, that he had much choice, now. She drew in a deep breath. "Then you've already read it."

"Read what?"

She indicated the book on the counter. "Is that why you wanted me to read it? So I'd know why you were leaving?"

Josh frowned. "I wanted you to read it so you'd know . . . some marriages can be good. Even happy."

He'd wanted her to know that? Why? So she'd be willing to marry Alex, and he could go on his way, knowing the woman he'd widowed was safely taken care of?

And what would he do if he knew the truth about her widowhood? Kate quailed inside at the thought. What would he do if he knew what she'd done?

He would hate her. He wouldn't just be indifferent to her, or be kissing her out of pity or worse, he would hate her. How could he not? He would hate her, and he'd leave Gambler's Notch without a backward look. He'd be off to find the one who could win his heart, someone woman enough to hold him.

As, apparently, he was about to do anyway. If she'd fostered any silly hope that the book had been even a little bit right about the woman fated for The Hawk, she'd certainly learned her lesson now. But it was better that he leave now, like this, for his own sake . . . and, thankfully, without knowing what she'd done. And if it was cowardly for her to hope that he would never find out, then that's what she was.

But still . . .

"Happy?" she said suddenly, the words coming despite her effort to hold them back. "If you marry for love, you mean? Not like it would be if I . . . did as you said and married Alex . . . but to marry as the Hawks do? Like"— she had to swallow to keep her voice from breaking before she went on—"you will, someday?"

The indifferent mask was back. "No. I won't. I'll be the last Hawk that breaks the chain, that ends the unending, that breaks the spell. Whatever you want to call it."

The impassivity of his voice chilled her. "But it doesn't have to be—"

"No man in my line of work marries, unless he enjoys the idea of leaving a widow behind."

"So you *have* read it," Kate said.

"I've read it."

He opened the flap of the saddlebag that still had room, and then picked up the sack of sugar. Unable to stop herself, she reached out and touched his hand. As if startled, he froze, his gaze shooting up to her face.

"You will be careful, won't you? Come May?"

"What?"

"I know it sounds crazy, and that you . . . we don't really believe in this, but still, you will be careful?"

"I'm always careful. A careless gunfighter doesn't live very long."

She supposed that was one of the truest things ever spoken. And as he was leaving, he would no doubt be safe, but still, the entry in the book prodded her into persistence.

"I know it says Gambler's Notch, but it could happen anywhere, so no matter where you are in May, you'll be careful?"

He stopped in the process of adding the sack of coffee to his bags. "What says Gambler's Notch? And what does May have to do with it?"

"That's when it's dated, next month. Didn't you notice?"

He went very still. "That's when what is dated?"

"The last entry," Kate said, frowning. Why was he looking at her so strangely?

He looked from her to the book, which lay closed and perfectly normal looking on the counter. Then he looked back at her face.

"Are you saying that there is an entry in that book dated May of 1878?"

"The last one," she repeated. "You must have—" She broke off, her eyes widening as she at last realized the reason for his intensity. "It . . . wasn't there? When you read it last?"

He shook his head. Slowly, he reached out and slid the book across the counter toward him. His expression changed slightly the moment he touched it, the intensity in his eyes abating somewhat, as if simply touching the book eased his agitation about it. He lifted it to rest on its spine, and opened it.

Had it been any other book, Kate would have been surprised that it opened to exactly the right page. She wasn't surprised at all now. She watched Josh's face as he looked at the list of dates . . . and saw his eyes stop when he reached the last one. Other than that, there was no sign that what he read there had any effect on him at all. His expressionless mask never slipped.

"I looked at it after Luke tripped over it and took off running this morning," he said without looking up, almost idly. "I looked at it carefully, because I knew it couldn't be the same book. I'd watched it burn." He looked up at her. "This wasn't written there then."

"But it is now," Kate whispered.

His mouth twisted. "Yes."

He looked back down at the page that foretold his death. He studied it for a long, silent moment, as if the secret of the book, its arrival, its apparent resurrection, and its constant changes were somehow revealed there.

Then she saw his dark brows lower. He looked up at her. "You thought I was leaving . . . because of this?"

Something in his tone made her tense. She nodded.

"You think I'm leaving because this book says they'll bury me here?" He sounded astonished.

"You must," Kate said, puzzled at his reaction. "If you go now, you'll be far away by May, and then—"

He stared at her. "You sound like you believe this thing is true."

"It's been true up to now, hasn't it?"

"What happened to 'we don't really believe in this'?"

"This is different. You can't take a chance."

"A chance?"

"That it might be right."

"Why?" He sounded merely curious.

"Josh," she exclaimed in exasperation, "it's your *death* it's reporting! You have to get out of Gambler's Notch."

"It also says the Hawks will go on. If I die, how does that happen? It's contradicting itself."

Kate frowned at that. "I don't know. Maybe that can only happen if you heed this warning."

"Or maybe the whole thing is nonsense."

"But you can't take that chance. What if it's wrong about that, but right about this?"

For a full minute he stood there, just looking at her. Then, slowly, he shook his head.

"But May is only three weeks away! You'd be crazy to stay here—"

"No, Kate."

"Why?" She indicated his saddlebags with a sweeping gesture. "You were going to leave anyway," she pointed out.

And why had he been leaving? she wondered, thinking of this for the first time. If he'd been packing before he'd ever known about the ill omen in the book, why? Had she been right in her guess, that he assumed she would marry Alex, thus removing from him any lingering sense of responsibility? Was he truly so very anxious to get away?

"I was leaving on my own terms. This"—he pointed at the book—"changes that."

Her pondering forgotten, Kate stared at him incredulously. "You mean you were perfectly willing to go before for no real reason, but now that there is a real reason, you won't?"

"I had my reasons for leaving."

"Then you still do. Even more now. What could be more important than avoiding dying?" she exclaimed.

He looked at her steadily, in a way that made her remember that kiss upstairs last night, made her wonder what would have happened had Alex not come bursting in on them. She wasn't naive enough to think that Josh's condition, the hardening of that malest part of him, meant anything more than that he, as Arly, and she supposed all other men, had been seized with the urge to take the closest available woman. No matter that it was too-tall, too-plain, strange-eyed Kathleen.

Color flared in her cheeks, and she saw Josh's sudden intake of breath, as if he'd known exactly what she was thinking. She lowered her gaze swiftly, wondering if this had happened to him before, if some plain, simple woman had looked at him that way. She wondered if that was why he'd kissed her, if that was why—

"You have to go," she said quickly, desperate to tear her thoughts out of that painful rut. "You were going anyway. So do it. Get out of here, Josh."

"No. I still have work to do." His voice sounded a little rough, as if he were having to force out the words.

"Work you were perfectly willing to walk away from a moment ago," she pointed out, his contrariness helping dispel the memories and restore her irritation, although it did little to ease the quaking of her knees; she couldn't believe her own temerity in arguing with him.

He looked a bit sheepish, but he didn't try to deny her words. He only shrugged. "I was wrong. I'm not finished here."

"If what the book says is true, you'll be finished, all right," she snapped, regaining her anger now in the face of his senseless contrariness. "Finished and buried."

"You really want me to run, from some words in a book? A book that's a mirage that can't really exist?"

She leaned over and slapped the book shut, picked it up, and shoved it into his belly so hard and fast he grunted in pain and surprise. Then she slammed it back down on the counter with a loud thud.

"It doesn't exist?"

"You know what I meant," he said, rubbing his stomach gingerly.

"You told me it's all true, everything in here that's been written about you. About your family being divided by the war, and how your grandfather kept both sides together under the same roof. About your father going to fight with the Union army, while his brother wore rebel gray. About what happened to your mother, and your aunt, and your sisters."

She saw his jaw tighten, but she couldn't seem to stop now. In some part of her mind she was aware of the utter insanity of what she was doing, trying to face down Joshua Hawk. She never would have dared this with Arly; she had little doubt that she would have been dead by now had she even begun to talk to him like this.

But Josh wasn't Arly. He wasn't like Arly in any way, despite his reputation as a cold-blooded killer. Arly, much more than Josh, had deserved that cold-blooded label. The vague thought that she had her answer to why a killer could make her feel the way he did flitted through her mind. The thought that it was precisely because he *wasn't* a killer. And that on some deep, instinctive level she knew that, or she would never have risked standing up to him like this.

"You said it was true," she went on, feeling reckless now, "what it says about how you and your grandfather came west together after the war. About how he died of cholera. And how you won all those shooting contests, and first hired out your gun. You said all of that was true. Did you lie?"

"No! But that's past. It happened. This"—he gestured at the book—"is the future. There's no way that book can . . . know what hasn't happened yet."

Kate gaped at him. "There's *no way* it can even exist, but it does!"

"I'm not being run out of town by a damn book!" he shot back.

"All right, stay! Stay and get killed. I'll have them bury the book with you."

"You do that," Josh snapped.

She stared at him, not sure whether she was feeling furious or sick. "It's true, isn't it? You really do want to die."

"What?" he exclaimed.

"Marshal Pike was right. He said you didn't want to live anymore, not like you'd been living."

Josh drew back a little. "He said that?"

"He said that when you were in jail, waiting . . . that you didn't seem to mind the idea."

Josh's mouth quirked. "Knew that old coot was

smarter than he looked," he murmured. Then his brows drew together. "And when did he tell you this? And why?"

"It doesn't matter. You're going to prove him right, aren't you?"

"I'm not going to take to my heels because this damn book says I'm going to die here," he said emphatically. "Now I've got work to do."

"Not here you don't."

He blinked. "What?"

"I don't want a man who's too contrary to save his own life around here."

"Contrary?" He sounded offended.

"You were ready to ride out, until somebody said that's what you should do."

"I don't take orders from anyone." He grimaced. "Or anything."

"Then I have no use for you here."

He stared at her, as if astonished. "Are you firing me?"

"If that's what it take to get you to see sense."

"Fine," he muttered. He scooped up his saddlebags and slung them over his shoulder. He picked up the bedroll and strode out from behind the counter.

"You forgot something," she called out, picking up the book.

He half turned, and she heaved it at him. He moved instinctively to catch it. He glared at it, then at her. Kate watched as he turned and marched out the door. He went down the steps to the street and turned right, past the water trough.

And as he passed the trough, she heard the splash as he tossed the book into the water.

He should have looked for Luke, Josh thought as Buck settled into that smooth, single-footed pace that made him the easiest-riding horse he'd ever slapped a saddle on. The boy had been pretty upset this morning. And then that damned book had scared the liver out of him.

Not, Josh thought wryly, that it hadn't done pretty near the same to him.

He should have done this sooner, take the rangy buckskin out for a ramble. The horse had been fretting, Luke had told him, cooped up in a corral for so long. It would clear his head of some of this foolishness as well; he'd been cooped up too long himself, playing storekeep. Maybe all he really needed was room, some space around him, and things would start to become clear.

Maybe.

It had been a very strange feeling, he mused, to see someone, even a young boy, upset that he was leaving. Usually his departure from any town was welcomed by most, the occasional dance hall girl who feigned heartache notwithstanding.

He wondered if Luke would be glad he wasn't gone yet. Although he should make it clear to the boy that this was only a delay in his departure. But at least he'd have the chance to say good-bye. Unexpectedly, there were a few people in Gambler's Notch he'd like the chance to say good-bye to; that had never happened before. Even the marshal, he thought wryly. And Art Rankin. Maybe even the intrepid Miss Taylor.

The thought of the dauntless Deborah Taylor made him wonder. Was she really, as Kate had hinted, sweet on that lawyer? And if so, what was he doing proposing to Kate? He was a fine one to be accusing Josh of dallying with two women at the same time. And was he really fool enough to let a little thing like her being a trifle older than him interfere? She was an uncommonly fine woman, any man could see that. Or should. Of course, if it were true, his hope that Kate would marry Hall could hurt Deborah.

Josh sighed. Life had been much simpler when he'd been alone, no one and nothing to think about but himself and staying alive. How had he ever lost that simplicity? When had things become so complicated?

Buck tossed his head and snorted. Josh recognized the signs; the powerful horse had had enough of the leisurely pace. And a good, fast, high-loping charge across the flats held a certain appeal for him as well; maybe it would blow some of the fuzziness out of his head. Clapping his Stetson down firmly, he let Buck loose. No urging was necessary; the buckskin had had too little freedom to run in the past three weeks, and romping in the stable's corral barely took the edge off.

Setting him in a circling course that would bring them back into Gambler's Notch from the opposite direction, he let the horse run until he'd worked up a good sweat, but reined him in before he was tuckered. The last thing he wanted was to be caught with a run-out horse. Buck was still ready to run, and Josh had to keep a firm hand on the reins to keep the horse single-footing again. Near a thick stand of cottonwoods about a mile from town he pulled the horse down to a walk, and by the time they passed the telegraph office at the edge of town, the buckskin was cooled out.

He only wished he could say the same for himself. He was no closer to any answers than he had been when he'd ridden out.

At the stable he led Buck inside and unsaddled him. He was about to start rubbing the horse down when a piece of straw drifting down from above warned him he wasn't alone.

"You want to come down out of there, Luke?"

Silence greeted him.

"I was kind of hoping you wanted to talk. That infernal book has me awful twitchy."

There was the sound of movement against the boards of the loft over his head.

"I'd be grateful if you were to come down here and keep me company. I don't want to be alone if that thing shows up again."

A blond head popped out over the edge of the loft. "Where is it?"

"Darned if I know," he said honestly. "I dumped it in the water trough, but I don't have much hope it'll liquefy any more than it burned."

Luke scrambled down the pegs driven into the upright beam that served as a ladder. He brushed at the straw that clung to him, casting sidelong glances at Josh.

"Are you really scared?"

Josh shrugged. "It's natural to be scared of something you don't understand," he said. "And I sure don't understand how that book does what it does."

Luke let out a breath of relief, obviously deciding that if The Hawk could be scared, he could, too. "I'm scared, too. Is it really magic?"

"I don't know, Luke. I truly don't know. I don't know what else to call it, though."

There was a long silence before the boy spoke again.

"Is there good magic and bad magic?"

Josh paused in his work on Buck's withers. "I suppose, if it exists at all, it'd be like luck, with good and bad. Why?"

Luke sighed. "I was hoping there'd be some good for Miss Kate."

Josh couldn't quarrel with that hope. "She surely is due some good luck."

"She doesn't want to marry Mr. Hall, I know she doesn't."

Josh knew it, too, with even more certainty than the boy; Kate had made that clear.

"She'd have to kiss him, and she don't like kissin'," Luke said.

Didn't like kissing? Josh busied himself below Buck's shoulder, so Luke couldn't see his face. She'd curled his toes and brought him to the boil faster than any woman he'd ever touched, and she didn't even like kissing?

"What . . . makes you think that?" he finally managed to ask.

"I seen her, when ol' Arly'd grab her and start kissing her."

He didn't want to know, but he couldn't seem to stop himself from asking. "What happened?"

"She'd fight him something awful, till he started to get mean. Then he'd drag her up the stairs, and all the folks'd start looking at each other real funny."

Josh's stomach knotted. God, what had she endured at the mercy of those brutal hands, that massive body? How had she survived it? And why hadn't anyone helped her? How had they let it go on for four awful years?

And if that lawyer cared enough about her to propose, where the hell had he been? Did he think that marrying her now would make up for it? Even if he was the gentlest lover in creation, it wouldn't—

With a sudden jolt, Josh realized he didn't care for the idea of Kate married to Hall any more than he cared to think of her life with Arly Dixon. And the image of Kate in Hall's arms, of her kissing the lawyer as she'd kissed him, of the two of them intimately entwined, Alex Hall taking all the sweetness she had to give, spending himself in the honeyed depths of her body, started a slow rage inside him.

His first instinct was to find the young lawyer and thoroughly settle his hash for even thinking about Kate as his. Only that he had to admit—reluctantly—that he kind of admired the sometimes foolish, but never cowardly man stopped him. That, and the fact that he had no right whatsoever to do it.

"—wish somethin' good happen," Luke was saying, yanking Josh out of his useless anger, "so's she wouldn't have to marry him, or leave."

"Maybe she won't have to leave," Josh said.

Luke shook his head. "If ol' Arly's brother's as mean as he was, he'll be mean to her, too, when he gets here."

Josh looked at the boy over the buckskin's back. "What?"

"He'll make her go away, or he'll hurt her, like Arly did."

"Luke . . . you said 'when he gets here.' Do you mean . . . he's coming?"

The boy nodded miserably. "Mr. Boardman, he got the answer to Mr. Hall's telegram."

"And Arly's brother is coming here?"

The nod, even more miserable, came again. "In a couple of weeks."

A couple of weeks. That would put it about May first.

May, Josh thought, was going to be an interesting month.

# Chapter 17

She never should have relented. She'd fired him, and she should have kept it that way.

"Kate? Are you all right?"

Kate looked up to see Deborah, standing in her open doorway, watching her curiously. She flushed as she realized she'd done it again, had been so lost in her thoughts about Josh that she'd been standing in a daze on Deborah's porch, without even knocking at the door. Long enough for her friend to notice and come see what was wrong.

"I swan, Deborah," she exclaimed, "that man is the most bothersome, unsettling—"

"So you've said," Deborah interjected with a smile that was almost a grin.

"Hello, Kate."

"Oh!" Kate's breath caught at the quiet, solemn greeting; she hadn't realized Alex had been standing right behind Deborah. "I . . . Hello, Alex," she ended rather lamely, now furiously embarrassed at her outburst. "I'm sorry, I didn't see you."

An odd look flashed in the young lawyer's eyes, as if she'd said something far more significant. The expression was replaced by one she couldn't define but that looked almost like relief. She looked from Alex's face to Deborah's faint blush, and suddenly felt very awkward.

"I'm sorry," she said. "I didn't mean to . . . intrude."

"I was just leaving," Alex assured her, with a glance at Deborah that Kate thought rather pointed.

"I'll see you this evening, Alex," Deborah said.

Alex nodded, glanced at Kate almost furtively, then bid them both a hasty good-bye and walked past Kate and down the porch steps.

Kate watched him go, then turned back to Deborah. "I truly didn't mean to—"

Deborah waved her hand. "It's all right, dear. It's time for our Sunday tea, and I wouldn't miss that. Besides," she added with a pretty blush, as she waved Kate inside, "he's coming back for supper."

Kate stepped through the doorway, then turned to stare at Deborah. She knew her friend had fixed supper for Alex before, but never had Deborah acted so strangely when talking about it. She was acting like . . . like . . . Kate's eyes widened as a possibility struck her.

"Is Alex . . . I mean, are you . . . Did he . . ." She gave up, afraid she would hurt her friend if she was guessing wrong.

"He's been here a lot in the past few days," Deborah admitted, her color deepening. "In fact, ever since Josh stopped by just as he was leaving Wednesday afternoon, he's been quite . . . attentive."

Kate blinked. "Josh . . . was here?"

Deborah nodded. Her brow furrowed. "He said his arm was bothering him, but it seemed fine."

Kate frowned. "Where he was . . . shot? He's been doing a lot of heavy work, and we've been unusually busy for the past few days, but he wasn't acting like it hurt him."

An oddly pleased expression flitted across Deborah's

face before she said, "It really wasn't that serious a wound." Her brows lowered. "And he acted very . . . odd, while he was here. Restless."

"Restless," Kate said wryly, "is a good word for it."

Kate followed Deborah into the kitchen, where she set out the cups while Deborah took the steaming kettle of water and filled the graceful little teapot that matched them. She hadn't told her friend about her attempt to fire Josh, because there wasn't any way to explain without telling about the book, and she had no right to do that. Not that it could be explained anyway, she thought ruefully.

And it didn't matter anyway; Josh had stubbornly refused to be fired or to leave. He'd continued to work around the store, and she hadn't had the heart to tell him to go sleep in the barn with Luke if he was so determined to stay. Besides, she admitted, she would miss dreadfully the evenings when he kept his promise and helped her with her reading—when he told her she was really much better than she thought, because she could work out what unfamiliar words meant by the way they were used. His quiet praise warmed her in a way she'd never known before.

As did the soft, gentle, good night kisses he gave her each evening after their reading, kisses she knew she shouldn't allow, but awaited too eagerly to prevent. Kisses she knew she was foolish to believe in, coming from a man who'd been ready to ride out of her life mere days ago. But she was so fascinated with the idea that a kiss could be gentle, that a man could be aroused yet not act, could want to mate, yet not force it, she couldn't bring herself to stop him.

And if she were to be honest, she had to admit that, much to her shock, she *liked* the way his kisses made her feel. She liked the odd, tingly sensation, the warmth that flooded through her, the feel of his hands, strong yet light on her arms as he held her, on her cheeks as he tilted her head back. She liked it all, and she was stunned by that fact.

And too often she found herself wondering if the rest of the act between man and woman could be as different as Josh's kisses. Could a man truly be gentle then, too? Or were all men brutal when seized by lust? Would Josh use . . . that part of his body as Arly had, cruelly, painfully? She knew he got as hard as Arly had; she'd felt him more than once when he'd kissed her. It had frightened her at first, until the second night when she'd frozen in his arms, and Josh had whispered quietly to her that he would never do anything she didn't want him to do.

Want? Was it possible? Could a woman truly want such a thing? She would never have believed it. Until Josh's kisses made her shiver with pleasure instead of quake with fear.

"Kate?"

She came back to herself with a start, and her hands flew to her cheeks as she became aware of the heat there, not from a blush this time, but from her own wayward, wanton thoughts. She mumbled something to Deborah as she hastily busied herself with the cups, trying desperately to bury those wicked thoughts.

They were seated with the tea poured before Kate, determined to stay off the subject of Josh, gathered her nerve and asked, "Is Alex . . . upset with me?"

"Because you told him you wouldn't marry him?"

Kate's eyes widened. "He told you?"

"That he proposed? Yes. But I already knew he was going to."

"You knew?"

"I guessed," Deborah corrected. "He felt very responsible for what happened with Arly's will."

Kate sighed. "I know."

"There can be good marriages, Kate. My parents were very happy, before my mother died."

Why did it seem everyone was trying to convince her of this? And using their family to do it? Surely Deborah didn't want her to marry Alex, not when she cared for him herself.

"Why would I want to marry again? I know I . . . have no place to go right now, but to marry just to . . . have a place to live, or someone responsible for me seems . . ."

Deborah started to speak, then hesitated. Then, after a deep breath, she said quickly, "The marriage act can be . . . pleasant, too."

Kate stared at her friend, all her wayward thoughts coming back in a rush.

"Don't be shocked," Deborah said, blushing. "I know it's not proper of me to say, being a spinster, but . . . some of the wounded soldiers, I had to read their letters to them. At first Father wouldn't let me read . . . that kind, letters from their wives that talked about . . . that. But in the end, there was no one else to do it."

Kate was stunned at the thought that other women perhaps had wicked thoughts similar to her own. "They really . . . wrote about . . .?"

Deborah nodded. "And some . . . were quite . . . blunt about missing their husbands. And . . . such intimacy."

So it was true, Kate thought wonderingly. It could be different. It must be, for those women to truly long for it, for no woman could ever desire the kind of thing Arly did, but Josh . . .

*I'll never do anything you don't want me to do.*

Josh's whispered words rang in her head, and she wondered if she was a fool for believing them. Was it possible? Could a man really . . . stop himself, as Arly had always said was impossible? Could the act she had come to dread really be something . . . pleasant? Something a woman might even . . . like? Could it—

"I only tell you this," Deborah said, clearly still embarrassed and wanting to explain, "because I know Arly was . . . a callous, cruel man. And I know, better than anyone, Kate, what he . . . did to you. It would be enough to make any woman fear the marriage bed."

"I know not all men are like Arly," she said. "Some are gentle and kind."

She thought she saw Deborah's lips tremble for a moment, but then her friend's head came up and she said steadily, "Alex is like that."

Kate looked at Deborah for a long moment, wondering if she dared say that part of her reason for turning Alex down was knowing Deborah cared for him. Kate hesitated, knowing she could embarrass her horribly. But she couldn't just let it go, not when her friend was so obviously willing to sacrifice any chance at her own happiness for Kate's sake.

Then Deborah spoke again, as if to thoroughly change the embarrassing subject.

"I'm glad you took his advice not to make any hasty decisions, until Will Dixon arrives. We could be misjudging the man."

"I doubt it," Kate said.

"Then you'll just move in here," Deborah said simply. "At least until you decide what to do."

"Perhaps," Kate said cautiously. She didn't like the idea of taking charity, even from her dearest friend, but she knew also that she might not have any choice.

She saw Deborah open her mouth to insist, and spoke quickly to forestall her.

"I know you . . . care for Alex," she began.

Deborah blushed, and lowered her gaze, confirming what Kate had always suspected. But then Deborah's head came up, and she frowned. "That isn't why you said no, is it? For you know I'm simply being foolish. I'm far too old for that kind of—"

"Don't be silly. You're *not* old."

"I'm thirty, Kate. Alex is no older than Josh."

"And it was Josh who said a woman as clever as you wouldn't hold that against a man, if he were lucky enough to catch her eye."

Deborah stared at her. "Josh . . . said that?"

Kate nodded. "He said you were handsome, smart, level-headed, loyal—"

"So is a good dog," Deborah said, her tone wry. But her blush betrayed her as she asked, "Just when did he say all this to you?"

"Oh, not to me. To Alex."

"Alex?"

It came out as a yelp, and for the first time since Kate had known her, Deborah looked utterly disconcerted. And despite herself, Kate smiled. It was wicked of her, she supposed, but it was nice to see someone else at a loss for a change. Besides, she hated it when Deborah called herself old, as if her life were nearly over, when Kate knew she'd given up so much to help others.

"He told him how Marshal Pike said you were a fine-looking woman, too," she added, just to see her friend's eyes go wider. Kate smothered a smile as she went on. "And Alex didn't like hearing it much. He didn't like much of anything Josh said."

And she'd been so pleased at what Josh had done.

She would have felt awful had she actually blurted out what she knew Deborah would hold as her closest secret, but Josh had quickly discerned the meaning behind her words and had proceeded to rattle Alex out of his complacency about the one who had for so long been his confidante, yet whom he seemed never to see as a woman.

Could that be why Josh had come here? Deborah had said his injury had seemed fine. Had he purposely come when Alex had been visiting, to remind the lawyer that there were men in Gambler's Notch who indeed saw Deborah as a woman, not just a friendly, understanding ear?

But that made no sense. The only reason she could see for him to do that was if he wanted to see Alex and Deborah together. But he'd told Kate flatly she should marry Alex. But then he'd started that dizzying string of nightly kisses, each one longer than before, each one hotter, each one giving rise to more of those wanton, lustful thoughts that both astonished and mortified her. But she wasn't foolish enough to believe he meant anything by it; he'd made his feelings clear enough about that, as well. So what did he want? Why did he continue to kiss her like that? Simply because she let him?

Surely not because he wanted to, not her, not tooplain, too-tall Kathleen. Although Arly had told her often enough one woman was the same as another when the need was upon a man. Perhaps that was it. But if so, why hadn't he forced himself on her? Why did he seem content to kiss her and then let her walk away, in fact even hurry away, when she knew he was—

"Kate? What *is* wrong with you? You've been miles away all afternoon."

"I'm sorry, Deborah," she said, meaning it. "I know I've been woolgathering all day. It's just that—"

"Josh is a most bothersome, unsettling man."

Kate sighed. "Yes. Yes, he is."

Deborah sighed, the first time Kate had ever heard such a thing from her. "It seems we've both done something very foolish, haven't we?"

Kate knew she had done more than one foolish thing recently, but Deborah? "I doubt you've ever done anything foolish in your life," Kate said.

"Perhaps." Deborah sighed yet again. "But for the first time I'm not certain that's something to be glad about."

"Do you mean Alex?" Kate asked gently. "Did he . . . say something?"

"Not really. But he . . . acted differently." Deborah grimaced. "But if Josh said that to him . . ."

"Don't blame Josh. I started it," Kate said. "You're a wonderful woman, and if he's too blind to see that, then it was time someone opened his eyes."

"I'm sure you only meant to help, but I should be far past harboring any tender feelings for a man, especially one so much younger."

"You're *not* old," Kate said firmly.

"I'm older than Alex. Too much older."

"Five years isn't that much," Kate said, although she knew it was. "Why, if he were five years older—"

"But he's not. It is the way it is. Just as . . . Josh is who and what he is. We've both come to . . . care for impossible men, haven't we?"

Kate's breath caught. She knew what word Deborah was avoiding, and it made her head reel. She felt an odd trembling begin, and hastily set her teacup down in its saucer. Was that what she'd done? Had she really—and oh, so foolishly—fallen in love with Josh? With The Hawk?

The absurdity of it, of quiet, plain Kathleen in love with a man like Joshua Hawk, nearly made her laugh out loud. But she bit it back, knowing it would be a painful, whimpering laugh, and would reveal more than she wanted even to her dearest friend.

"No," she whispered. "I don't . . . I can't . . ."

"Kate," Deborah said quietly, "the whole town knows how late the lanterns burn in your store. And how late you're going upstairs."

"We've been reading! I told you that."

"Yes. And I believe you."

"But they don't, is that it? Don't people have anything else to do than . . . than—"

"Talk about The Hawk being tamed by the sparrow?"

Kate stared at Deborah. "Is that . . . what they're saying?"

Deborah nodded. "They seem . . . rather proud of it, in a strange kind of way."

Kate shook her head, bewildered. "I don't understand. I haven't . . . tamed him. How could they think that *I* could?"

"Perhaps not everyone sees yourself as you do," Deborah suggested.

"But they can't really believe that we . . . that I . . . I mean, Arly's barely cold, and—"

"Arly Dixon," Deborah said sharply, "doesn't deserve a minute of mourning from you."

Kate's mouth tightened, and she bit her lip as she looked at her friend. Deborah sighed a third time.

"I've seen a lot of ugliness in life, Kate. I've seen a lot of good men die far too soon. Some were hardly more than boys, boys who had never really lived. It teaches you a different way of looking at things. Save your mourning for those who deserve it."

"And your love?" Kate asked softly. "Who do you save that for?"

"I don't know," Deborah whispered. "With all the regrets about wasted love, and love never experienced, that I've heard with dying breaths, I've begun to wonder . . . perhaps we're the biggest fools for saving it at all. Perhaps it's meant to be gambled, not hoarded, awaiting another chance that may never come."

Deborah lowered her gaze, and Kate suddenly knew that, however wise she might be, Deborah no more had an answer for this confusion than she herself did.

"We're in a fine fix, aren't we?" Kate whispered.

She was thinking that an understatement as she walked slowly back to the mercantile in the long shadows of late afternoon. Surely she wasn't that witless, to have fallen in love with a man she hardly knew, when she'd just barely survived a husband she'd just buried less than a month ago? A man with a reputation like The Hawk's?

But she was fairly certain now that that reputation was blacker than the truth, that while he may have killed, he didn't do it in cold blood or from ambush, as Arly had tried, or Robards. So perhaps she was merely witless and naive enough to become infatuated with the first man to stand up for her, the first man to go out of his way to help her. . . . The first man ever to kiss her with tenderness.

She had to stop thinking about those kisses. She had to stop wondering about whether he would kiss her again tonight. She had to stop her even more wicked thoughts about what it would be like to go beyond kissing.

She tried to crush those extraordinary wonderings with the memories of the loathsome, ugly nights spent with Arly, but the logical part of her brain refused to cooperate; it simply kept telling her Josh was not Arly, that he was nothing like Arly, and that she had the mere fact that he was still here, let alone the sweetness of his kisses, to prove it. And now she had more, the proof of longing letters written to beloved husbands by loving wives.

*Perhaps it's meant to be gambled, not hoarded. . . .*

And perhaps Deborah was right. Perhaps you only got one chance. Perhaps if you didn't take that chance when it came—

She thudded into a large but oddly yielding body and smothered a gasp.

"Excuse me, Mrs.— Er, Miss Kate."

"Marshal Pike," she exclaimed. "I'm sorry. I wasn't watching where I was going."

He nodded at her. "You looked a mite preoccupied."

"I'm sorry for bumping into you," she repeated.

"Didn't hurt none," Pike assured her. He seemed to hesitate a moment before going on. "I heard about your trouble, Miss Kate. I'm sorry to hear that Arly's as mean dyin' as he was livin'."

Did everyone in town know this, too? Kate wondered. Had she always been the subject of so much talk, and had just never known it before, because she never spoke to anyone unless it was under Arly's watchful eye?

"I thank you for your sympathy, Marshal," she said, a little stiffly.

He nodded slightly, touching the brim of his hat as if he was about to move on. Kate stepped to one side to let him pass, but he hesitated again.

"I'd best get over to Markum's place," he said.

Kate looked at him, puzzled; why was he telling her?

"Fella named Carter rode in this evening. Heard it might be Jackson Carter."

Kate was even more puzzled; the name meant nothing to her.

"Just gonna make sure he intends to move on. Reckon one gunfighter in town is enough."

Kate's eyes widened then, and as if her reaction was the sign he'd been waiting for, Pike touched the brim of his hat again and moved on.

Another gunfighter? Surely not another one looking for Josh, like that awful Robards man. But the marshal must suspect that he was, or why would he have told her?

Why indeed? she wondered as she began to walk again. Why had he told her? Had he done so knowing she would tell Josh? Was that what Pike had wanted? For her to warn Josh? It seemed an unusual act for a town marshal, to warn one gunfighter of the arrival of another.

But perhaps not. Gambler's Notch did seem to have taken a shine to their temporary resident. Once they'd been sure he wasn't going to let lead fly every time he turned around, they'd become fascinated. Men and women alike—although she doubted it was for the same reasons—came into the mercantile more often than ever before, seemingly attracted by the novelty of seeing The Hawk in such unexpected surroundings, doing such mundane tasks as stocking shelves and selling papers of pins to women who were half frightened, half thrilled by his presence, and more than a little enraptured by his easy charm.

*One gunfighter in town is enough.*

She stopped dead. She'd been so busy pondering the puzzle of why Pike had apparently sent a warning, that she'd nearly forgotten the warning itself. And what it could mean.

*May 1878—Gunfighter Joshua Hawk buried in Gambler's Notch, Wyoming Territory.*

It wasn't May. Not for another two weeks. But that didn't necessarily mean Josh was safe. It could mean only that he wouldn't die until then. Deborah had told her stories, awful stories of wounded men who lingered in agony for days on end before the blissful darkness of death had finally claimed them.

Not Josh. Surely not Josh. She couldn't bear the thought of him lying in agony, couldn't imagine him dead, not Josh. Luke was right, no one would ever best The Hawk.

But what if someone did? What if this Carter was the man who would bring an end to the Hawk dynasty? Especially since Josh didn't seem at all disposed to stop it from happening?

She began to move again, to walk, then to run. She ran as if it had somehow already happened, as if she would reach him too late, as if somehow he'd already been vanquished, as if she would never again know the sweet, gentle touch of his lips on hers.

As if she would never know the answers to all her wild imaginings, to all the questions, all the needs his touch had aroused in her. Would never know what came next, after the luscious flow of warmth that flowed through her when he touched her, after the tiny licks of flame that leapt along her nerves when he kissed her.

"Josh," she whispered as she ran; it came out as an urgent plea, and she knew Deborah had been right. For better or worse, and there was little question as to which it was, she had fallen in love with The Hawk.

The front doors of the mercantile were still closed,

the shades still down; no one, it seemed, had needed anything on this Sunday afternoon. Hardly surprising; everyone in town, it seemed, had been in several times this week, stocking up on things they'd never seemed to need before—what Art Rankin was going to do with that piece of lace was beyond her.

She hurried around to the back of the building, and pulled open the kitchen door, holding her breath despite the fact that she'd run so far.

He was there.

He was there, leaning back in a chair, his feet up on the newly repaired and steady kitchen table, obviously quite alive and relatively well. She let out her breath in a rush.

For a long moment neither of them moved. She stared at him from the doorway; he held her gaze from his seat. She was so relieved that her imagination had been so wrong that for a moment she couldn't speak.

And then she saw what he'd been doing. Saw what was in his hands, looking just as it always had, rich and elegant—and utterly undamaged.

The book he'd thrown in the water trough.

# Chapter 18

If he hadn't thought it futile, he would shove the damn book right back into the stove again, Josh thought as he stoked the fire against the oncoming evening chill. Spring was waging its usual confusing battle with summer here at the foot of the mountains, with the occasional day like today where both combatants seemed worn out and left the field for a last gasp of winter before summer set in.

"Has it . . . changed again?" Kate asked from the storeroom doorway.

"You mean besides showing up on the counter in front of me, dry as the Sonora desert, and without a single blurred letter?" he asked wryly. "No."

"Oh."

She sounded almost disappointed, he thought. "Were you hoping it had?"

She came in quietly, pulling the storeroom door closed behind her. "I was hoping perhaps that last entry had been . . . a mistake."

Josh chuckled almost bitterly. He tossed the book down on top of his bedroll. "If you're going to believe in the thing at all, I'd say mistakes aren't likely."

As if stung by his attitude, Kate's chin came up.

"Then perhaps I should warn the reverend he'll need to be ready for a funeral service."

He wanted to smile at her sass; she'd come a long way from the quiet, frightened woman she'd been a mere two weeks ago. But he knew she wouldn't appreciate the sentiment, so he restrained himself.

"If the book is right," he pointed out, "what makes you think anything I do can change it?"

"But if you're not here. . . ."

He shrugged. "So I get killed somewhere else, and dragged back here to be buried."

She stared at him, shaking her head slowly. "How can you be so . . . calm about it? Don't you care at all that you could die? That all the people who've come to . . . to like you, will have to watch them bury you?"

Had she been about to say something else? Was it not really the people of Gambler's Notch, who had inexplicably seemed to have shifted from being wary of him to being proud, that she was concerned for?

"Is that what you're worried about, Kate? That you're going to have another funeral to go to?"

"What makes you think I'd go?" she snapped.

Abruptly, she spun away from him, but before she turned her back, Josh was certain he'd seen the sheen of tears in her eyes. Slowly, and as quietly as he could, afraid she might bolt, he moved toward her.

"I'd like to think maybe you'd miss me, just a little."

She whirled back on him. "Miss you? You talk about dying as if it were nothing more than taking a walk, you insist on staying here after a warning like that"—she gestured angrily at the book—"and then you expect me to miss you?"

Josh stood there, looking at her, at the wire-drawn tension of her slender body, at the glitter of those honey-gold eyes, and wondered that he could ever have thought her plain. Had it been that this woman who was facing him down now, as if she hadn't an ounce of fear in her, had merely been buried by her husband's relentless presence? Had this ardent spirit always been there, just hidden by the timid demeanor she'd had to adopt to survive, much as a less well-armed animal had to blend into its surroundings to survive amid bigger, stronger predators?

"No," he said at last, "I don't expect you to miss me. I don't expect anyone to miss me."

He said it in such an offhand, careless tone that the words lacked the self-pity they might otherwise have held.

"Josh . . ."

"I knew a long time ago," he said with a shrug when her voice trailed away, "that I'd end up being nothing more than some other gun's stepping-stone to a reputation some day."

He heard a slight sound, as if her breath had caught in her throat.

'Someone like . . . Jackson Carter?"

Josh went very still. "And just where did you hear that name?"

"Marshal Pike. He said he'd heard that he rode into town this afternoon."

"Well, well. Jackson Carter." His lips pursed thoughtfully. "I don't suppose the marshal mentioned if he rode in alone?"

Kate shook her head. "No. But he only mentioned Carter."

Josh rubbed a hand over his chin. "Carter always rides with company. Wonder where they are?"

"Who is he, Josh?"

He took one look at her expression, wide-eyed and fearful, and knew he shouldn't have said anything.

"Just somebody to watch out for," he said.

And that was like calling a hurricane a slight breeze, Josh thought. If there was any man out there he thought might be able to take him, it was Jackson Carter. They'd met before, but never when either of them had a reason to go after the other. But now . . . now there was the small matter of Carter having been riding with that bunch of rustlers he'd had the run-in with back on the Rocking K. It had been Carter's orders the rustlers had disobeyed when they'd rushed the line shack he'd been holed up in, and three of them had died for their mistake. But Carter had always been the kind to take such things personally.

He hastened to distract Kate before she could ask more questions he didn't want to answer.

"Aren't we supposed to be reading? What's next?"

They'd finished the whale hunting tale last night, and Kate had been so excited, her eyes had shone so, that he'd been hard pressed to leave their good night at a kiss.

But then, stopping at a kiss had somehow become the greatest effort of his life. Every night he swore he wouldn't kiss her at all, because it was too damned hard to stop. And every night the simple joy that glowed in her face was a lure he found irresistible.

He knew what the town was thinking, knew what they assumed was going on in the mercantile after dark, when the lamps burned late. And he'd been surprised at their reaction when he'd taken care to let the truth be known for Kate's sake; they had seemed almost disappointed at such a tame explanation as reading. And knowing people's penchant for gossip, he was sure many of them had chosen to continue to believe in what they'd already decided rather than the much less interesting truth.

What had surprised him was that they didn't seem to hold this belief that he and Kate were carrying on against him. Or even Kate, who was in a much more precarious position than he. People expected no better from a man like The Hawk.

People, Josh thought, were very unpredictable.

"I don't feel like reading tonight," Kate said suddenly.

Speaking of unpredictable, Josh thought. He looked at her curiously; he would have sworn she looked forward eagerly to their sessions. Her reading had improved dramatically even in such a short time. She'd only needed a little guidance. And very soon he was sure she'd be as adept at reading as she was at numbers.

"I thought you wanted to read *Little Women*."

"No. I'd rather . . . ask you something."

Damn, Josh thought. She was going to start in on him again, about not heeding the warning in the book.

"Ask me what?" he said warily, although he was sure he knew what was coming.

"Why do you kiss me at night?"

Josh gaped at her, unable to believe he'd heard right. "What?"

"Why do you kiss me at night?" she repeated.

"I . . . It . . ." He wet lips that were suddenly dry and tried again. "What kind of a question is that?"

"One I'd like answered. Is it pity?"

"Pity?" Josh exclaimed. "Of course not. Why would you think that?"

She shrugged negligently. "I've heard some men have . . . ideas about widows."

Josh's mouth quirked. "Usually widows who have been widows for longer than a month." And certainly not widows who were married to men like Arly, he added silently.

"Then is it because you feel . . . obligated?"

"I've never kissed a woman in my life because I felt *obligated*," Josh snapped.

"Then why?"

Exasperation seized him. "Did it ever occur to you that I might just kiss you because I *want* to?"

To his chagrin, Kate just looked at him thoughtfully. "I suppose that could be. Arly used to say any woman would do, if a man was in enough need."

"I would greatly appreciate it," Josh grated out, "if you would *never* compare me to Arly Dixon again."

"Oh, I didn't mean to compare you," Kate said quickly, in a reassuring tone that somehow did little to reassure him. "You're nothing like Arly. Why, I even *like* your kisses."

His anger drained away, disappearing like spilled water on desert sand. How could he be upset at a woman who looked at him so earnestly and told him she liked his kisses? Especially when all he wanted to do was grab her and kiss her right now, kiss her until she sagged against him again, until she made that tiny sound in the back of her throat that had nearly driven him mad every night this week.

"Kate," he said, a warning tone creeping into his voice as she began to tread very, very close to dangerous ground; he'd had to rein in his urges far too many times already to welcome another go-round.

"Does a man only kiss a woman nicely, like you do, if he doesn't . . . ?"

"Doesn't what?"

"I mean, I know no man could truly . . . want, Arly's leavings—"

"You're not Arly's leavings," Josh snapped.

"I only meant that I know I'm not the sort of woman men like to look at anyway, and that's the kind men want to kiss, but you've kissed me, and—"

"Stop talking like that—"

"—I just wanted to know if that's why you kissed me so nicely, because you didn't . . . you know."

"No, I don't know. A man should always kiss a woman nicely," Josh said, starting to feel a little beset.

Kate looked puzzled. "Then how does a woman know what to expect?"

"What to expect?"

"How does a woman know if a man is just kissing her because he wants to kiss her, or because he wants to . . ."

When she trailed off yet again, Josh let out an exasperated breath. "Kate, what in blazes are you talking about?"

"I don't want to say what Arly always said," she explained patiently, as if to a child. "It was so crude and ugly, but Deborah said it didn't always have to be that way, and I hope she's right, but I don't know. . . ."

She finally ran out of steam. And Josh finally realized what she meant. "Kate," he said carefully, "are you talking about sex?"

She gave him a grateful look. "Yes. I know that when the need is on a man, any woman will do. But if kisses are always supposed to be nice, how does a woman tell if it's that, or just . . . a kiss, like yours?"

Josh stared at her for a long, silent moment. *Damn you, Arly Dixon,* he swore inwardly. *How could you not see the beauty hidden in those eyes, how could you not see the treasure of that dauntless spirit? Or did you, and is that why you tried so damned hard to break her?*

"Is that what you think, Kate?" he asked softly. "That

when I kiss you good night, it's *just* a kiss? Maybe no more than a handshake?"

Color flared up in her cheeks. "Isn't it? I mean, I know . . ." She lowered her gaze, and he saw her swallow tightly before she stumbled on. "You get . . . like Arly did, but you don't . . . you never . . ."

He assumed she meant she'd known he was aroused when they kissed—it would be hard for her not to know, when it made him harder than he could remember being in his life, but what had she expected him to do about it? Grab her and throw her down while he had his way with her?

A cold tightness knotted up his stomach. No doubt that was exactly what she'd expected.

"You mean I never forced you?" he asked softly.

Head still lowered, she nodded.

"Only a coward forces a woman." He reached out and lifted her chin with a gentle finger. "No matter who she is to him," he added, anticipating the answer he saw in her eyes. "Even . . . no, especially, his wife."

Kate looked at him with an expression of wonderment.

"I kiss you because I want to, Kate. And if . . . things were different, if I wasn't who I was, I'd want everything you would give me."

"Give . . . ?" She sounded as she had looked, full of wonder at a new idea.

"I may not know much about it myself," Josh said, "but I remember my parents, Kate. They loved each other. My father would have cut off his arm before he would have hurt my mother."

Kate stared at him for a long, silent moment. Then, "Did you mean that? That you . . . wanted more? From me?" She sounded astonished.

"I meant it," he said gruffly. "But I also meant it

when I said I'd never do anything you didn't want me to."

"I heard . . . Someone told me that . . . it can be . . . pleasant. What happens . . . between a man and woman."

Josh nearly groaned; her wonder coupled with the innocent sensuality of her words sent the need he'd been battling for days surging through him in a wave that nearly staggered him.

"It can, Kate," he said fervently. "Oh, it can."

She swallowed again. Josh thought with a lurch in his belly that she wore an expression like a gambler who'd decided there was little left to lose. And when she spoke, she nearly brought him to his knees.

"Show me," she said.

"Kate," he said, or tried to; it came out as more of a croak.

"I know I'm being . . . awfully bold. Forward. But I'm not the kind of woman men . . . offer for. Any kind of offer. And now I don't even have the mercantile to recommend me. I don't know what else to do."

"Stop—" His protest at her belittlement of herself wouldn't come out past the tightness in his throat; he could only guess at what courage it had taken for her to offer herself like this, when she thought herself so undesirable. He swallowed and tried again. "You don't . . . mean it."

She trembled slightly, but her jaw was set. "For four years, Arly told me what I meant, what I wanted, what I was to do. And for the rest of my life before that, my father told me what I wasn't to do, what I couldn't do. I promised myself if I was ever free, it would never happen again."

"Kate, I'm not the kind who stays around. That lawyer wants to marry you, and even if you don't want him, there are others—"

"Did I ask you to stay? Did you ever think that maybe . . . maybe that's part of the reason why? Besides . . ." She gulped, then went on in a rush, "the book says you'll be dead soon."

He grimaced. "All the more reason this is crazy."

"I've never done anything . . . crazy before. Maybe it's time."

"But . . . why?"

She gave him a look that was desperate but determined. And it struck him then, the irony of it; he'd been aching for her for days on end, and now that she seemed to be offering exactly what he'd been dreaming about, he was trying to talk her out of it.

"Because I think Deborah was right," she whispered. "It's meant to be gambled, not hoarded."

His brows furrowed. "What is?"

She shook her head. Then she drew herself up rather stiffly. "I know I'm not anything to look at, and I understand if you don't want—"

He cut her off with a growl. "Oh, I want, all right. And I'm damn tired of hearing you say that. But why me?"

"Because . . . I know you can be gentle. Because no one has ever made me feel the way you do. Because no one has ever made me want to know if it can be something other than cruel. Because you won't . . . talk about it. Because you're going move on to find the woman you're supposed to find. You won't stay and try to own me, and I won't have to face you every day . . . after."

God, all those reasons; how long had she been thinking about this? Had all his nights spent in painful longing not been as solitary as he'd thought?

"I thought I was supposed to die," Josh said, seizing on that somewhat desperately.

"And if you do . . . I'll never know. I'll always wonder."

"The lawyer," he began, but stopped when she shook her head.

"He doesn't make me feel all tingly inside just by looking at me. He doesn't make me forget to breathe."

Josh nearly forgot to breathe himself. "I don't understand," he said slowly. "After . . . your husband, you should be . . . running away from this, not after it."

"You're not Arly," she said simply, using his own constant reminder to defeat him. "And I need to know that . . . not all men are like him. Or I'll be afraid the rest of my life."

His head was reeling. His body was already thoroughly aroused to the possibility of getting what it had been clamoring for for weeks now, and the cold, calculating part of his mind was telling him he was crazy for resisting an offer freely made, but his gut was tied up in knots; Kate had been hurt so much already.

But she'd said she knew he'd ride on. That he wouldn't stay. She'd even seen that as positive, not a negative reason for this wild idea. She'd taken every objection he could have placed before her and turned it around.

Except one.

"Kate . . . what if you . . . get pregnant?"

She paled, and despite knowing it had had to be said, he wished he could call back the words. She lowered her head, and he saw her hands plucking at the folds of her faded calico dress.

"I . . . won't," she said at last. "Arly, he . . . twice after he . . . got really angry . . . I lost babies. Deborah says I probably won't . . . that I can't . . ."

So the bastard had taken that from her as well, Josh thought. Damn him.

"So you see," she said, her voice steadier now, "I knew all along I wasn't the woman in the book. But I thought . . . perhaps that wouldn't matter to you. Men need—"

"Men need," Josh agreed, tight jawed, "but only boys *take*."

She was silent for a moment, honey-gold eyes searching his face. He wasn't sure what she saw in his expression, but she lowered her head.

"I'm sorry. I was a fool to think you would want . . ."

She turned away. As fast as if he were drawing his Colt, before he even thought about it, he reached out and took her arm, stopping her. He turned her around, gently but purposefully, and pulled her against him.

"I want," he repeated, his voice a little thick. "I've wanted ever since you faced me down with more nerve than half the men I've ever known."

She stared up at him. He lowered his head swiftly, taking her mouth without preamble, sparing only a moment to trace the soft line of her lips with his tongue before he probed forward, tasting again the sweetness that had been torturing him every night. He tilted her head back, threading his fingers once more through the thick mass of her hair, suppressing a shudder as he wondered yet again what it would feel like trailing over his skin.

He deepened the kiss, careful not to crush her lips, yet unable to go slowly. She seemed startled, then a sigh escaped her as she seemed to go soft in his arms, soft and warm and willing.

He probed deeper, searching, until his tongue met the hot, wet velvet of hers. She made that sound, that tiny, throaty sound that sent a shiver down his spine and made his already aroused body surge to full attention.

He shifted his hips, pressing himself against her, knowing she had to be able to feel him even through the layers of cloth between them. He heard her gasp, and pressed harder, rubbing this time.

Then, with the greatest of efforts, he broke the kiss.

"Be sure, Kate," he said between the panting breaths he couldn't seem to stop. "And if you're not, say so now, before I carry you upstairs and—"

"No!"

Josh shuddered. He'd known she'd change her mind, that she'd drop this insane idea as soon as she was confronted with the reality. Kate might think she wanted to know what sex was like with someone less brutal than her late husband, but thinking and doing were two different things.

He made himself release her, and backed up a step.

"I didn't think you really wanted this," he muttered.

"No," she said again, then added hastily, "I mean . . . I do, but . . . not there."

Josh stared at her. "What?"

"Not in . . . his bed."

All his breath left him in an audible sigh. "Ahhh, Kate."

"I don't want to be reminded of him. Ever." She looked up at him, her eyes wide with so many emotions Josh couldn't begin to name them all. He knew then that he was lost; he didn't need her words to convince him. But when they came, when she looked at him with those eyes and pled softly, he resolved that he would do whatever he could to make her plea come true.

"Make him go away Josh. Make him go away forever."

# Chapter 19

"Leave it on."

Kate looked at Josh in surprise. "You want the lamp on?"

He gave her a look so hot she nearly gasped aloud. "I want to see you," he said.

She did gasp then. "Arly always said . . . this was only done in the dark—"

"We wouldn't be here if I was Arly," he said softly. "He forced you. I want you willing, wanting. He was fool enough to hide you in the dark. I want you in the light. He took his own pleasure, and cared nothing at all for yours. I want you to learn that it can be *more* than good between a man and a woman."

His words rocked her, and Kate held her breath as he took that last step toward her. He'd done everything she'd shyly asked, he'd locked the back door, checked the shades, and of his own volition restoked the fire and added half the store's stock of blankets to his bedroll, trying to make it as comfortable as possible. He'd even taken off his vest, and then his precious Colt, although he kept it close to hand.

But then he'd made it clear he had his own ideas about how to proceed.

"Take down your hair, Kate."

She blinked, startled. "What?"

"I've wanted to see it for so long. Please."

The soft, quiet plea made her shiver; she felt more helpless in the face of his gentleness than she'd ever felt when facing Arly's cruelty. She'd been able to deny Arly, though it had often cost her dearly; she was powerless to deny Josh.

She reached up and began to pull out the pins that held the tight bun at the back of her head. She felt the moment when the heavy weight of her hair shifted, and it spilled down over her hands to her waist. She heard Josh let out an audible breath.

He reached out, slowly, stroked his fingers over her hair, then threaded them through the long mass, pulling some of it forward over her shoulders.

"It's beautiful. It feels like silk. I knew it would."

She stared at him, disbelieving; it was plain, brown hair, not dark, not light, nothing special. She lowered her hands to her sides, afraid he would see them shaking.

Then, as if in time with the pounding of her heart, he began to unbutton the high neck of her dress. She lowered her eyes in humiliation, for the first time in longer than she could remember embarrassed by her poor, shabby, and worn clothes.

"He kept you in rags," he said huskily, as if he'd read her mind. "I'd dress you in silk and lace."

She laughed nervously. "I'm not a silk-and-lace kind of woman."

His hands stopped for an instant, and Kate held her breath again as his fingers slid inside the opening he'd made, stroking across her skin.

"Perhaps not. You've silk of your own," he whispered.

She shivered as he undid more buttons, slowly, so slowly.

"Why . . . why are you taking so long?" she whispered, her voice shaking.

"Because this is half the pleasure," he said, his fingers taking a very long time at the tiny buttons over her breasts.

Kate went still, trying to absorb yet another startling idea, that a man could find pleasure in anything other than the act itself. But there was no denying the expression he wore as he continued to tug at the buttons, nor the fact that he lingered over her belly, then below, so close to that part of her that she knew she would soon have to surrender to his will.

That she thought of that without the fear of bruises to follow was a measure of how much she had come to trust him. She knew it would hurt—it always hurt—but she was beginning to see why women apparently tolerated the pain for the closeness. That must be the good part Deborah had spoken of.

But when the buttons of her dress were all loose and he moved to slip the bodice of the dress from her shoulders, she instinctively tightened, holding the thin, faded calico to her body as if it were a shield.

"Anytime," Josh said softly. "Anytime you want to stop, you say so and we stop."

"But . . . once you start . . ."

"I am not Arly, Kate," he said again. "Nor am I a boy who can't control himself. No matter how much I want you, I'll stop."

She didn't know which stunned her the most, that she believed he truly would stop if she simply asked him to, or the other astounding thing he kept saying.

"You . . . want me?"

He groaned, a low rumble from deep in his chest that

made her shiver. He grasped her left hand with his right, and slowly pulled her hand down his body. He placed her palm over the hardness that strained against his pants. Instinctively she tried to pull away. Arly had never wanted such contact; he'd wanted only to drive himself into her and spend himself as quickly as possible. But Josh's hand was still holding hers, and turned her movement into an inadvertent caress of that rigid flesh. He groaned again, deeper now, and when she hastily looked up at him, she saw his eyes had closed, as if he wanted to concentrate solely on her touch.

He removed his hand to again grip her shoulder, but the startling thought that he might welcome such touching made her leave hers where it was. Carefully, always ready to pull away quickly, she repeated the motion that had been unplanned before. Josh groaned yet again, and she felt his hips shift, pressing himself against her hand as if he indeed sought more of her hesitant caress.

She did it again, a longer, firmer stroke this time, and when he let out a throttled sound and his fingers tightened on her shoulders, a thrill she'd never known before rippled through her. And this time, when his hands moved to push the dress off her shoulders, she didn't stop him.

She heard him suck in a breath as he looked down at her. Belatedly she realized she had on one of her oldest cotton chemises—not that any of them were new—and that it was worn so thin it might as well not exist as far as concealing anything. She didn't, couldn't look at herself; she knew too well that he could see every curve of her breasts, and the darker rose circles of her nipples. Nipples that felt oddly tight, like they did when she was very cold, or in the days before her woman's time.

He had her single, equally worn petticoat untied before she realized what he was doing; Joshua Hawk was no stranger to women's underclothes, it seemed. She stood there in her thin chemise and underdrawers, shivering more from emotion than cold; the healthily stuffed wood stove had warmed the room nicely.

"Good God," Josh said, reverently rather than profanely. "Maybe Arly wasn't crazy as a loon after all." Kate looked at him quizzically. "If the men in this town had known how lovely you are under those baggy dresses, he'd have had to fight them all for you."

Kate stared at him. Lovely? Her? Plain, too-tall, strange-eyed Kathleen? He was mocking her, he had to be. Yet she could see nothing in his face except honest admiration, nothing in those vivid eyes except a fierce need that was like Arly's in its urgency, yet tempered with a gentleness she'd never known before.

His hands moved, and her eyes instinctively followed the motion as he began to work at the buttons of his shirt. It took her a moment to realize he was going to take it off, and her gaze shot to his face. He shrugged the shirt off, then stopped in the act of dropping it to the floor. His brows lowered as he took in her startled expression.

"What's wrong?"

She shook her head mutely, so stunned by the naked expanse his chest she couldn't speak. Lord, she thought wickedly, she'd never realized a man could look so . . . so . . .

Josh let out a compressed breath. "Let me guess," he said wryly. "Arly never got undressed?"

She shook her head again. He was beautiful, she thought in shock. She'd never thought a man could be beautiful, but he was. He was so big, so strong, yet at the same time he'd been so gentle with her, and that made him even more beautiful to her.

"Did he undress you?"

Heat flushed her cheeks in a rush. She couldn't tell him, couldn't describe how Arly had merely pulled her nightdress up, draping it over her head so, as he'd so often told her, he wouldn't have to remember how homely she was.

"He . . . said it wasn't fitting," was all she could manage to say. Josh growled something unintelligible. Suddenly possessed of a recklessness she didn't understand, she added "But I'm glad. He didn't . . . look like you. He was soft, and . . . and ugly."

"Stop talking about him. Stop thinking about him. He's gone, Kate. He'll never touch you again."

He pulled her hard against him, and Kate let out a startled gasp at the feel of him as her hands came up against his bare chest. The first sensation of incredible heat, then of sleek skin taut over hard muscle, and dusted with just enough hair to make her fingers itch to move. Unlike Arly, who had been covered with a pelt of coarse hair—

*Stop thinking about him.*

And then Josh was kissing her again, hard and deep yet gently, coaxingly, and she couldn't think of Arly, of his ugliness, his cruelty. She could only think of herself, and Josh, and what he was doing to her, the incredible feelings he was causing in her.

His hands slipped up from her hips, over her ribs and up to her breasts. Instead of kneading them cruelly, he cupped them tenderly, lifting their weight in a way that nearly made her dizzy. She felt her nipples draw up even tighter, until she wanted to cry out, although she didn't know for what. And then, as if he'd known, Josh gave it to her. His thumbs moved upward to rub over the stiff peaks. Darts of fire shot through her, and she did cry out then, cried out in shocked pleasure; she'd never known such pleasure from that part of her was possible. All she'd ever known from Arly was pain from his roughness.

*Stop thinking about him.*

Josh broke the kiss, and Kate couldn't help the little sound of loss that escaped her. But then he did something shocking. He lowered his head to her breasts and one after the other captured the nipples he'd just been teasing with his lips and flicked them with his tongue, hot and wet through the thin cotton.

"Josh!"

It burst from her helplessly as she stared down at his dark head. What was he doing, suckling her like a babe? Did he get some pleasure out of this? Could he possibly know how it made her feel? Why did she feel it so low and deep inside her, as if there were some unseen connection between her breasts and that hollow place Arly had invaded but never really filled?

*Stop thinking about him.*

Josh's head came up then, and at her first look at his face she had to believe; his eyes were hot and his lips were parted as if he wanted to continue this forever. And Lord help her, she would let him; she'd never felt anything so lovely.

"Remember what I said about going slow?" Josh asked, his voice oddly thick. She nodded, a little frightened by his intensity. "Forget it," he said.

She braced herself, knowing the gentleness was over, that now he would become as all men, rough, urgent, and in a hurry to hammer himself into her body until he reached his release. She told herself this was enough, that this was all the pleasure a woman could expect. More. It was certainly much more than she'd ever felt with Arly—

*Stop thinking about him.*

She gasped as Josh swept her off her feet. But he held her gently, cradled her easily, as if she were something precious, as if she were the tiny, normal-sized woman she'd always longed to be. But then she heard the rending of thin, worn cloth as Josh tore her undergarments away. Fear struck her as she lay naked in his arms; even Arly was too practical to damage her shabby clothing in his haste to take her. Had she been wrong? Would The Hawk be as savage as his namesake?

And then he was putting her down, laying her atop the pile of blankets as carefully as if he thought she might break. He knelt beside her, first looking at her, then touching her with such gentle care and reverence it almost made her weep. She forgot her embarrassment at being naked before him as his hands slipped over her, caressed her, stroked her, as if he truly thought her as lovely as he'd said.

She knew she wasn't. There were places where Arly had marked her permanently, but even that didn't seem to bother Josh; he merely kissed the marks, slowly, lingeringly, as if to ease that long-ago pain.

He cupped her breasts again, and bent his head to her. Even before his mouth closed over one nipple, she felt her pulse leap in anticipation of that burst of heat, and when it came she couldn't help herself, couldn't stop the utterly wanton response of her body as it arched, thrusting her breasts upward to him.

"Katie, Katie," he murmured against her soft flesh. "Yes, that's it."

Kate trembled. No one had ever called her that; Arly never spoke, in fact had barely seemed to know or care who she was. Nor had she ever heard a voice that sounded like Josh's did now, deep, rich, hot and husky. He laved her breasts, teasing the crests to a hardness that seemed almost unbearable. She couldn't seem to stop the unseemly undulations of her body, and barely noticed his right hand sliding down over her belly until his fingers parted her and she felt him probing where no one had ever touched her before. She gasped in shock, reflexively clamping her thighs together.

"It's all right, Katie," he said soothingly. "Relax, just let me touch you."

"But Arl—"

She broke off suddenly. Yes, Arly would never have touched her there, had been interested only in how fast he could get inside her. But again, Josh was not Arly. *Stop thinking about him.*

Josh returned his mouth to her nipple and drew it deeply into his mouth. That heat rippled through her again as he pulled at the nub of flesh she'd never known could give such pleasure. He moved to her other breast and repeated his actions, and it wasn't until she felt the slow, circling motion of his fingers between her thighs that she realized she had indeed relaxed them.

Before she could clench her legs together again, a jolt of sensation shot upward from beneath Josh's hand, seemed to collide with the little darts of fire from his mouth at her breast, and together settled into a molten, spreading pool of golden warmth.

"Oh!" The exclamation escaped her before she could stop it. "What are you doing?"

"Showing you," Josh said, then went back to teasing her nipples as he circled that tiny knot of flesh she'd never realized was there before.

She didn't know what was happening to her. His caress wasn't so forceful that it should build such awful, wonderful pressure. He just kept doing it, that slow, circular stroking, and she found herself wanting to arch that part of herself toward him as she had her breasts, and the wanton thought both thrilled her and shamed her. It seemed he was barely touching her, yet the urgency began to build, to grow until she was fairly writhing.

She was vaguely aware that she was sprawled open before him in a most indecent manner, but she couldn't seem to care. Nor could she care when she realized that the tiny, mewling sounds she'd been hearing were coming from her. Nothing mattered except the growing ache inside her, and she wondered how she could feel so swollen and so empty at the same time.

He increased the pressure of his touch just slightly, and Kate cried out at the much greater surge in her urgency. She had to hurry, had to reach . . . what, she didn't know. But she knew that Josh knew, and convulsively lifted her hands to tangle her fingers in the long, dark thickness of his hair, for once not even thinking that Arly never would have allowed such a thing, because this was a place Arly had never taken her.

And suddenly Josh's fingers were moving faster, and then faster still, until she was moaning helplessly, thinking she would die if something didn't happen, if this awful, wonderful pressure didn't ease.

Her body went suddenly rigid as the sensations changed, from heat streaking from beneath Josh's hands and mouth to a strange sensation that seemed to come from within her. It started as a small ripple, then a swelling pulse. She felt Josh move away and cried out his name, but he came back to her swiftly, settling himself on top of her. She realized he'd shed the rest of his clothes, but couldn't find it in her to be shocked at her first real sight of a naked man. All she could think of was the unexpected revelation that, even naked and aroused, a state that should have terrified her, she still thought him not just handsome, but beautiful.

She felt no fear, only that rush of hot, shuddering sensation when Josh levered himself between her legs. She felt the insistent probe of his maleness, but she didn't care that the pain would come now, as it always did; anything was worth this glorious feeling.

But it didn't hurt at all. Instead he slid into her as if meant to, easily, yet at the same time filling that hollow empty place so completely that she nearly wept out her joy. And then he began to move, to thrust into her, and still there was no pain.

Instead, that fullness burst into a wave that grew ever larger, ever more powerful as it swept through her. She felt a strange, powerful clenching in that deep, low place, an intense, rhythmic movement of muscles she'd been unaware of until now, muscles that seemed to be clasping . . . Josh. He was buried deep inside her, she could feel him, but there was no pain as her body seemed to be trying to draw him in even deeper, as if he were some long lost part of her returned at last.

"Oh, God, Katie . . . yes." Josh's voice was harsh, yet Kate thought it beautiful. "Katie-eee."

He thrust harder, but he slid in and out of her so easily she felt only a sweet, luscious friction instead of pain, the pain she'd always thought to feel. And just as the incredible sensations that had swept through her began to fade, she felt Josh go rigid. His back arched, he ground his hips against her, and she heard a low, strangled groan break from him. She stared up at him through the lingering haze of her own unexpected ecstasy, watching in wonder as his head lolled back, his eyes closed, and his face drew taut with pleasure.

He cried out her name once more, and it seemed to Kate the sweetest sound she'd ever heard. He shuddered, then shuddered again, and then she felt the hot, searing pulse of him inside her. Josh collapsed atop her, his head cradled on her shoulder, and she heard the quick pants of his breathing as she felt the rapid movements of his chest. But still he held her, his arms cradling her as he murmured things she couldn't believe he was saying, things about sweetness and beauty no one had ever said to her before.

For the first time in her life, pinned beneath a man, she did not feel trapped, did not feel overwhelmed with the need to escape. In fact she found a strange enjoyment in the feel of Josh sprawled atop her, especially as he continued to hold her as if he truly wanted to.

She lifted her hand, then hesitated. But need overcame her, and she moved to touch again the surprisingly silky thickness of his hair. Instead of drawing away, he made a sound almost like a purr and snuggled into her shoulder. She stroked his hair then, loving the way it felt under her fingers. When he still didn't protest, she let her reach extend until her fingers were brushing over the skin of his shoulders, skin that seem almost too sleek and smooth for a man.

For a long time they lay silent, until Josh stirred and slid to one side, telling her he was too heavy for her. She didn't protest, although she didn't agree. Especially since he still kept his arms around her. After a few more silent moments, he chuckled, a small rueful sound that made her smile without knowing why.

"I guess I showed you. I just didn't count on showing myself at the same time."

"Showing . . . yourself?"

He lifted his head, and in his face she saw, to her

amazement, a touch of the same wonder she herself had felt.

"How good it can be," he said.

Kate's eyes widened. "You mean . . . it was different . . . for you, too?"

His mouth quirked into that lopsided grin that always made her insides take that tumble. And he proceeded to tell her exactly how different it had been. And then he proceeded to show her all over again.

And she never once thought of Arly.

Groggily, Josh wasn't sure what had awakened him, a fact that worried him, since he usually awoke alert and aware. But that feeling only lasted for a moment; he felt the soft warmth of Kate beside him, and memories of last night swamped him, pushing everything else out of the way like a flash flood clearing its path. He didn't remember how many times they'd made love; he only remembered how each time was more incredible, as Kate grew certain he wouldn't hurt her and became braver, freer, bolder.

He'd never been with a woman who'd responded to him so sweetly. In fact, since he'd never been one for seducing respectable women, had rarely been with one who hadn't been paid, and the fact that he knew Kate didn't know enough to be pretending only heightened his exhilaration. Knowing that he'd given her pleasure where she'd once known only pain and humiliation made him feel a pride he'd never experienced, had never even known was possible.

She stirred in her sleep, and instinctively Josh reached to cuddle her near, to savor the closeness. And froze. Never had he done such a thing, never had he craved a woman's closeness once his need had been assuaged. But he craved Kate, not just for the unex-

pectedly powerful physical release he'd found, but simply to hold her and feel her warmth. Simply to know
she was there, within reach. To know that if he woke
her, as he had more than once during the night, she
would look at him with that sleepy little smile and
welcome his touch.

To know that strong, determined Kate had wanted
him enough to risk this, had wanted him enough to
give him the chance to prove he wasn't like her brutal
husband. To know that despite the scars she bore, ugly
souvenirs of Arly Dixon's brutality, the marks that had
made him want to weep for what she'd been through,
she had trusted him to be different. To know—

A rattle from the back door of the kitchen brought
him upright. The sound brought back to him the noise,
forgotten until now, that had awakened him. The front
door, he realized now, was still locked.

"Josh?"

Kate's voice was husky with sleep, and were it not
for whoever was at the door, it would have tempted
him to show her that mornings could be as sweet as
the nights.

Morning. He glanced at the old clock on the high
shelf above the kegs of nails, barely readable in the
dim light. A good hour past the time Kate normally
opened the store. And the shades were still down, sig-
naling to the entire town of Gambler's Notch that
something wasn't as usual.

"Miss Kate? Josh?"

Luke's call came to them faintly from the back door.
Josh sensed Kate's sudden stiffness as she awakened
fully and became aware of where she was. She sat up
swiftly, and he caught only a glimpse of her breasts,
the full, rounded flesh he'd caressed so thoroughly last
night, before she grabbed at the blanket he'd pulled

over them and clutched it to her. He hoped it was merely because of Luke's imminent intrusion, and not that she was embarrassed to be with him now, or ashamed of what they'd done.

Impulsively he leaned forward to kiss her, a brief brush over her lips that left him wanting more even as he knew he couldn't have it now.

"I'll keep him busy," he said softly. "Get dressed."

The grateful smile she gave him, clear even in the faint light, both pleased and relieved him for the same reason. It told him that it was indeed Luke she was worried about, not that she was ashamed.

Quickly, he scrambled into his clothes, aware she was watching him, glad she wanted to but sorry he couldn't take advantage of the fact at the moment. Then, as if she'd realized she should make some similar move herself, she reached for her underclothes and began to tug them on. He didn't dare watch her; he didn't have that much faith in his restraint at the moment. He hastily tucked in his shirt and fastened his pants. He grabbed up his Colt in a reflexive action that was automatic.

"I was worried," Luke said when Josh opened the door for him. He trotted in, then turned to watch Josh curiously as he strapped on the Colt, but said only, "Miss Kate's always open by now, but the shades were still down and the door was locked. Is she sick?"

"No. We were . . . taking inventory," Josh said, fighting the urge to grin sillily at the boy.

"In . . . ventory? What's that?"

"It's when you count what you have," Josh said, thinking that for the first time in a long time it might be possible for even him to have something worthwhile. He'd never dared think of such a thing before, had always been certain riding on was the only way for him. But now, with Kate's scent clinging to him, with the memories of her in his arms fresh and vivid and powerful in his mind, he wondered if maybe, just maybe—

"Oh." Obviously bored by that idea, Luke hastened to impart his news. "There's another man lookin' for you," he said excitedly.

Josh sighed. He'd forgotten this little detail in his silly thoughts. Just as he'd forgotten it last night during all those hours of pleasure found in Kate's arms. There would always be another Carter, another Robards.

"He's talkin' real big about how he's going to kill you," Luke exclaimed. "And he's got a bunch of men with him."

"Carter," he said with a nod.

Luke's eyes widened. "You already know?"

"Knew he was in town. The rest only figures."

"He's over at the saloon now. Made Mr. Markum open up early. Told him he'd shoot the place up if he didn't."

"Be a shame to put a bunch of holes in that fancy mail-order saloon outfit of his," Josh drawled.

"Hello, Luke."

Kate's voice was soft, husky. Josh had been so absorbed in reluctantly admitting the impossibility of the idea that had come to him that he hadn't heard her come in. That seemed to be happening a lot lately, and there was no surer way to get himself killed. He wondered how much she'd heard.

He glanced over his shoulder at her, and nearly smiled at how she looked. Her dress was neatly buttoned, her expression composed. But there were two spots of high color on her cheeks, and several wisps of her hair had already broken free of her hasty attempt at her usually severe bun.

And for the first time in his life he truly wished, not for the end of his life, but that he could change it. That somehow he could have a second chance, a chance to make things different, so that it wouldn't be impossible, so that he could stay with Kate, or take her with him, if she truly had to leave Gambler's Notch. She was tough in a quiet way many wouldn't understand, in a survivor's way. She was generous enough to have worried about the welfare of an orphan boy even when her own life had been a daily battle. She had the courage to risk herself in an act that had before only brought her pain, because she had somehow hung on to the belief that not all men were brutal and cruel. And when she had, she'd given him the sweetest night of his life.

The color in her cheeks deepened, and Josh could only guess what his expression must look like, how it must have reflected his thoughts. She quickly turned to Luke.

"Do you want some breakfast?"

Luke shook his head. "I ate hours ago," he said, causing Kate to blush even more deeply. "Are you gonna open up the store?"

"I . . . yes. I just did."

"Good. Mr. Rankin wants some sugar. He ran out for his coffee this morning, and he was snarlin' like a bear."

Josh smiled inwardly. Until he saw that Kate's hands were shaking.

"You go tell Mr. Rankin the store's open, will you?" he asked the boy.

"All right," Luke said, turned, then stopped. "You won't fight that Carter without tellin' me, will you? I want to watch!"

"Luke!" Kate exclaimed, horrified at the boy's blood-thirstiness despite her upset.

"I don't doubt you'll be one of the first to know," Josh said truthfully.

Appeased, the boy trotted toward the now open front door.

"Kate," Josh began soothingly, turning to her. Kate shook her head a little frantically, and dodged back into the kitchen.

Josh started after her, but before he had taken more than a step he heard Luke yelp as if in pain, then yell Josh's name, sounding frightened. Josh whirled and ran to the door. He saw Luke sprawled face down in the dirt in front of the store, just past the water trough. Josh's gut knotted and he dashed outside, wondering if some runaway horse or wagon had hurt the boy.

He knelt beside him. Gently he turned the boy over. When he saw Luke was weeping, he let out a sigh of relief; if the boy could cry, he couldn't be hurt that badly. He opened his mouth to reassure the boy.

The voice came from behind him, and Josh's words to Luke never came. He froze. Every instinct that had become dulled in his peaceful time here leaped back to life. He'd been right to wonder about the gunfighter riding in alone.

He ticked them off in his head. A man on the board-walk in front of the saloon. Another near the livery stable. A third behind him in the alley beside the mercantile. And the man in front of him. He was trapped.

He cursed himself; he'd let himself get lazy here, let himself ease up. Now it seemed he would pay for his foolishness with his life. It was going to happen exactly like the damned Hawk book had said.

Slowly, he rose to face Jackson Carter.

# Chapter 20

"Let the boy get out of the way, Carter," Josh said.

Carter lifted a brow. He hadn't changed much, Josh thought. Still tall and rail thin, still so blond his hair appeared almost white, and still with the most lifeless pair of eyes he'd ever seen that weren't on a vulture.

Slowly, Josh reached down and pulled Luke to his feet.

"I'm sorry, Josh," the boy said, tears still spilling from his eyes. "I didn't want to call you, but he made me, he—"

"It's all right, Luke. You run along now and—"

"No!"

"Go, Luke. Now."

"But—"

"Now," Josh repeated, and gave the boy a gentle shove. Luke gave him a distressed look, but started to back away. "Get," Josh snapped, aware that Carter was known for his volatility, not his patience. Luke ran then, jumping up onto the boardwalk in front of the hotel.

"Very touching," Carter said.

Josh ignored his words and his sarcastic tone. "I see you brought help. Still can't face a man one to one?"

Carter shrugged. "And I'll outlive you. Starting today."

Josh had known it was useless; Carter cared little about the fairness of the fight, only that he was the one to walk away. He would shoot him down right here, armed or not. All he could do now was hope that Kate stayed inside. He didn't relish the idea of her watching him die here in the street, and terror gripped him at the thought of her being possibly hit by a stray bullet. And with Carter's cohorts surrounding him, the possibility seemed all too real.

He thought he could take Carter. He'd seen the man in action down in Colorado, and while he was fast, he was also hasty, and not always accurate. But he also knew few men got the chance to draw at all; Carter's habit was to let one of his men wound his opponent first, then finish him off himself.

Carter glanced around, as if to assure himself everyone was in place. The other three men held their rifles at the ready, and Josh knew that this was it.

Odd, he thought. He'd faced death before, and had always felt almost neutral about it. Pike—and Kate—had been right: when he'd been awaiting the hangman, he'd almost welcomed it. But now . . . now he was thinking of all the things he would miss if he died now. More nights in Kate's arms. More days watching her change, bloom, now that she was free of her husband's shadow. Hell, he'd even miss Luke. He'd never thought much about kids, but now that he'd never have any of his own, unlike the book said when it said he'd met the woman who . . .

His mind jolted to a stop. He knew he was down to moments left alive, but time seemed to slow to a crawl.

*The woman who was going to make sure the Hawks continued as promised.*

The book had said nothing more than that. He'd

thought it a contradiction at the time, this promise of the continuation of the Hawk bloodline and the prediction of his death. There was no way both things could be true. Unless . . .

Unless Kate was already pregnant.

What if last night . . . what if somehow, despite what she'd said, it had happened? What if even now she was carrying his child? What if the next Hawk was already growing inside her? Was that what the book had meant? That he would die, but the Hawks would go on?

His grandfather's words about the book came back to him. *It follows the Hawk blood, legitimate or not. . . .*

Carter was staring at him. Fine time to start having regrets, Josh thought ruefully. He heard noises from behind him and across the street. The stable door slid open, and Art Rankin peered out. Josh gestured him back; he was too close to Carter's man. Rankin backed up, but the stable door didn't close.

He heard another sound, from inside the mercantile. Any sense of time moving slowly vanished at the thought of Kate stepping outside into this. Even if she hadn't heard Luke's yell, she'd be back in the store soon, and she couldn't help but realize something was going on. And if she came out to look . . .

His mind began to race, to do what he should have been doing all along instead of mooning over senseless longings—looking for a way out. He could take Carter, and maybe the man in front of the saloon, before he went down from the shots from the man behind him in the alley. And should he get lucky and survive that, there was still the one by the stable to make sure he didn't get up again.

"Let's get it done, Carter," he growled.

"In a hurry to die?"

"Maybe I'm just in a hurry to take you with me."

Something flashed in Carter's dead eyes. "Believe it. No matter what your backshooters do, you're coming with me to hell."

Carter backed up a step, shoving his coat back to free his six-shooter. His gun hand twitched, but he still didn't make his move. Josh willed himself to ignore everything except the man before him. Ignore the man who would no doubt put a slug in his back the minute he went for his gun. Ignore the other men who would pump lead into him until he stopped moving.

"You can meet up with your thieving, cattle-rustling friends there," Josh said, prodding, wanting this over before Kate wound up in the middle of it. "I hope for your sake these boys are less cowardly than your usual friends. But then, birds of a feather—"

"Son of a bitch," Carter snapped.

The man moved then, clawing at his gun. Josh's hand streaked downward. He heard a shout. He cleared leather. From another direction came a howl of pain. The distinctive report of a Henry rifle came from behind him, although he hadn't seen one. He waited for the impact. For the pain in his back. It didn't come. He heard a noise to one side, from the mercantile as Carter fired. A puff of dirt erupted at Josh's feet; Carter had again shot too soon. Josh leveled his Colt and pulled the trigger. Flame spat. Smoke from the black powder curled. Carter doubled over, began to fall. In a crouch Josh whirled toward the livery stable, and the closest threat. He heard the boom of a shotgun, then another rifle shot. Then silence.

Silence.

No more shots. And he was still standing. And, as far as he knew, unhurt. It was impossible.

Slowly, he straightened up. The man beside the livery stable was already sprawled in the dirt, his hands clutching his bloody head. A heavy draft horseshoe lay beside him in the dirt, and standing over him was a grinning Art Rankin. The man who'd been on the boardwalk lay dead against the wall of the saloon as if tossed, giving Josh proof that he had indeed heard the big Henry buffalo gun.

Only one man left unaccounted for. Colt still in his hand, Josh spun toward the alley beside the mercantile. The fourth man lay there, staring sightlessly at the sky. The gaping wound in his chest told the tale: A shotgun left little doubt.

Then his gut finally delivered the message it had been trying to get to his brain since he'd heard that last noise—the door opening, he realized now—from the mercantile. Slowly, he turned to face the store. And saw Kate standing there in front, shotgun at her side. She looked back at him, chin up, as if daring him to say anything.

He'd gotten Carter, but expected to die doing it. Yet all three of Carter's men were down. He was unhurt. And he'd had nothing to do with it. He tried to take a step toward her, but couldn't seem to do it.

"Reckon we ought to send somebody out to the river to round up Marshal Pike," Art Rankin said as he strolled over, having tied up the only one of Carter's men left alive.

Josh stared at the blacksmith. The man had risked his own safety to help him. As had whoever had blasted the man at the saloon. And as Kate had, stepping out with her dead husband's shotgun to once more save the life of the man who had killed him.

"Why?" was the only word he could manage.

"I hate stacked decks," Rankin said with a shrug.

"I . . . thanks, Art."

"My pleasure." Rankin grinned. "Always knew all that horseshoe pitchin'd come in handy some day."

"Josh! Josh!"

Luke's yell was, Josh was sure, audible for miles. The boy raced toward them, skidding to a halt barely a yard from the downed Carter, seemingly undisturbed by the death surrounding him.

"Did you see that shot Mr. Meeker made?" the boy asked excitedly. "Knocked that man at the saloon right off his feet!"

Meeker. Again. To hell with the man's desire for privacy; Josh wasn't going to let this one pass. People were appearing now. Boardman's gangly figure was visible in the doorway of the telegraph office, and Henry Meeker was peeking somewhat gingerly out of the hotel doorway.

"And that was some nice shootin' by Miss Kate," Rankin said, smiling at her.

Luke's eyes widened. Only then did he seem to take in the rest of the grim tableau, the other dead man and the shotgun Kate still held. He turned to stare at her, awe and admiration clear in his face.

"You shot him, Miss Kate? Really?"

"It's not something I'm happy about, Luke." Her voice was flat, oddly emotionless.

"It's nothing for anyone to be happy about," Josh said, finally able to speak again. "Killing is ugly, even when . . . they ask for it."

"But better them than you," Luke said, unperturbed.

"Hard to argue with that, son," Rankin said with a laugh. "I'll round up some help and we'll get this vermin out of the street."

Josh blinked. Most towns, he'd be considered the vermin that needed removing. He wasn't sure how it had happened, but it was different here. He looked back at Kate. She met his gaze for a long, silent moment, then turned and walked back into the store.

He caught up with her just inside.

"Kate—"

"Don't. I don't want to talk about it."

"But what you did—"

"I said I don't want to talk about it."

"Kate, you saved my life. Again."

For some reason this seemed to heighten rather than ease her obvious distress.

"Please. Just . . . leave me alone. I need to . . . to think."

Josh thought he understood. She'd just killed a man for the first time, and she was shaken. Anyone would be. A woman especially. Kate even more so. He wasn't certain of the wisdom of leaving her alone right now, but he was less certain of the wisdom of pushing her. So, reluctantly, he let her go.

"Is she all right?" Luke asked anxiously.

"I think she will be. But she needs to be alone right now. Killing someone isn't . . . a good thing to do, Luke."

"But you do it."

"And I hate it," he said honestly. "And sometimes I hate myself because of it."

Luke stared at him. Before the boy could ask the questions Josh saw building, questions he knew he couldn't answer, Josh hastily changed the subject.

"Take me to this Mr. Meeker of yours, will you?"

"But he said—"

"I know. Take me anyway."

They were halfway to the hotel before Luke looked up at Josh and said hesitantly, "Did I do wrong? I was worried, there were so many of them—"

"It's all right, Luke."

"He was already ready for them anyway. Had that big buffalo gun of his loaded and was sitting in the window. He doesn't miss much in town."

"I've noticed."

This town, Josh thought, was a most confusing place. They'd let him stay instead of running him out, and now three of them had saved his life, when most would have let him and Carter kill each other and count it a gain all around.

Henry Meeker was conspicuously absent as they walked into the hotel. Josh supposed after the anxiety of the morning, the aptly named man had retreated to the saloon for fortification. It didn't matter; it was Henry's apparently ill-named father he wanted to see. Twice now the unseen man had helped him, and he wanted to know why.

Luke led the way up the stairs at a run, and turned to head toward the front of the hotel. He knocked, but didn't wait for an answer to open the door. Josh followed the boy inside. He'd half expected Luke to trumpet his arrival, but the boy remained quiet, as if remembering the man's request not to see Josh.

"I didn't figure you'd stay away this time, Hawk."

The man in the wheeled chair still sat by the window, his back to the room. All Josh could see was that he'd been tall, was still lean, and had dark hair flecked with gray.

"I owe you my thanks."

"You owe me nothing."

"You saved my life. I'd say that's a sizable debt."

"You want to pay me back? Don't waste the rest of your life."

He knew that voice. Knew that cultured voice with the slight Southern inflection. It was about the only thing Josh was certain of; where or when he'd ever encountered the man escaped him. Along with a lot else; he hadn't even begun in his own mind to deal with the seeming second miracle of life he'd been handed in Gambler's Notch.

"You've helped me twice," he said instead. "I'd like to know why."

"Old times' sake," the man said, confirming what Josh had already guessed. But Luke was startled, and after a hasty glance at Josh, ran over to Meeker's chair.

"You know Josh, Mr. Meeker?"

"I did. Once."

Slowly, with hands that were thin yet obviously still strong enough to wield the big Henry with deadly accuracy, Meeker wheeled his chair around. Josh stared at him, at the eyes he'd never forgotten, the thick brush of a mustache that hadn't changed at all except for the flecks of gray.

"Hatch," he whispered.

"Robert Hatch . . . Meeker. You can see why I dropped the name."

"Hatch," Josh repeated, a smile curving his mouth.

"You've come a long way since Abilene, boy. Not sure I like the direction, though."

"I'm not sure I do, either," Josh admitted, still stunned to see the man he'd beaten in that first contest so long ago, the man who had been so tall and straight and strong, reduced to the gaunt, crippled figure before him.

"Your grandfather?" Hatch asked.

"He's dead. Nearly ten years now."

"I'm sorry. He was a good man."

"Yes, he was." Josh eyed the wheeled chair. "What happened to you?"

"I started down the same path you did. I wasn't as lucky. Or as good."

"You were always as good." Josh shifted his gaze back to the thin man's face. "How long?"

Hatch shrugged. "Few years back."

"Henry really your son?"

The other man's mouth quirked. "Much as I dislike admitting it, that he is." He gave Josh a considering look. "I always had in mind he'd grow up more like you."

"I thought you didn't like the direction I've been going."

"And neither do you, you said. But you've got the brains and the grit to change. Before you end up like me."

"Hatch—"

"That's a good woman, that Kate Dixon. She deserves better than what she got with that bastard Arly."

Josh didn't question the man's knowledge; he suspected Luke had something to do with it, but it didn't really matter how he knew. "She deserves better than what she'd get with me."

"Maybe you should let her decide that."

"I got lucky this time. Next time . . . well, that's nothing to ask a woman to live with."

"Make sure there is no next time."

Josh grimaced. "It's not that easy."

Hatch lifted one thin shoulder in a half shrug. "You take that girl and get out of here, to somewhere they never heard of you, and men like Robards and Carter aren't coming after you like the scavengers that they are."

Josh let out a compressed breath. "I wish . . ."

"Don't wish. Do it. You've got another chance, boy. Don't waste it."

He almost made it sound possible, Josh thought later, as he walked back to the mercantile after a long afternoon of talking with Hatch. At Josh's suggestion,

Luke had remained behind; Josh needed to talk to
Kate, and didn't think she'd talk very easily with the
boy around.

By the time they'd finished the meal Kate had silently fixed and placed on the table, he was beginning
to wonder if she would even talk to him. She'd changed
her clothes at some point during the day, and her hair
was pinned back as tightly and primly as ever. She
looked as she always had, but her movements were
quick, sharp, and forced, and he sensed a new tension
about her, a tension that was building.

He helped her clean up, trying to think of a way to
broach the subject of what had happened this afternoon. When she left the kitchen and walked back into
the now closed store, Josh gave up looking for a subtle
approach. He followed her into the store, took her by
one arm and turned her around.

"Talk to me, Kate."

Mutely, she shook her head. Josh had the feeling
that there was more bothering her besides what had
happened this morning. He could only hope it wasn't
what they'd done last night.

"I know you're upset about killing that man—"

"Oh, dear God," Kate moaned, and Josh felt a shudder go through her. He pulled her close, and after an
instant of resistance, she sagged against him. He heard
her gulp, and shudder again.

"It's all right, Kate. It's all over now."

"No," she said, in a tight little voice that tore at him.
"It's not over. It will never be over."

He couldn't deny that, not when he was haunted by
his own ghosts. So he said nothing, just made soothing
noises as he stroked her back. At last she gave in to
the sobs that he guessed she'd been fighting all day.
He'd never seen her cry, even when her future had

been ripped away from her, and her tears seared him like acid. She wept until the shadows faded into darkness, until he knew she had to be exhausted.

He wasn't sure what to do next. She needed rest, but he couldn't bring himself to even suggest that she go to the bed she'd shared with her husband. Yet to suggest she stay with him seemed . . . wrong somehow.

At last he unrolled his blankets, added the extras they'd used last night, and set her gently down on them. She didn't protest; in fact, she seemed almost numb when he began to undress her. He left her undergarments, shed only his own shirt, then settled down beside her and pulled her gently into his arms. He held her for a long time, feeling her quiver as if she were still crying, but no tears came. He held her, fighting his own weariness, until she at last drifted to sleep.

He was startled when he awoke in the darkness to feel Kate clinging to him, an urgency in her grasp that brought him fully alert in a rush.

"Kate?" he asked softly.

"Please," she whispered. "I know I shouldn't, but I . . . I want . . ."

Her voice trailed away, but her softly yearning tone left him little doubt as to what it was she wanted. His body hardened with a swiftness that took his breath away at simply the idea of losing himself in her sweetness again, but his mind was crying out that there was something wrong, in her voice, in her clinging, something he should know. But then, hesitantly, she began to touch him, to slide her hands over his chest and her fingers over his nipples, in the way he'd finally convinced her last night was all right, and he couldn't think of anything except the heaven she was offering him once more.

The moment he moved to kiss her, Kate seemed to go wild in his arms, kissing him back with an eagerness that stunned him. She followed his lead and probed into his mouth with her tongue, sending darts of heat shooting through him. Swiftly he tugged away her worn chemise and pantaloons, swearing inwardly that someday he'd see that she had the finest of linen and lace. He didn't linger on what that thought implied. He couldn't, not when she was touching him like this, with undisguised eagerness.

He stroked his hands over her with a matching eagerness he couldn't deny, and she writhed as he touched her, and caressed him in return in all the way she'd shown her. If he realized there was a touch of desperation in her movements, the knowledge was soon lost in the maelstrom of sensation she was causing. He'd never known a lovemaking as fierce, as powerful as he'd experienced with her last night, but now she seemed intent on showing him that that had been merely the beginning.

He found himself responding to her urgency with a rising need of his own. It was fierce, fiery, and beyond his control. And he found he didn't care, didn't care about controlling it, didn't care about anything except Kate and the passion that exploded between them.

He tugged at her hair, freeing it, uncoiling the silken length of it. She reached for him, and he shoved away the rest of his clothes heedlessly, and urged her seeking hands down his body. She took his wordless hint and curled her fingers around him, beginning to stroke him in the way he'd taught her last night, but with an eagerness that made his breath catch violently.

"Kate," he gasped, "I . . . I don't want to hurt you. . . ."

"You won't," she murmured against his chest. "Not you, Josh. Not you."

He felt the hot, wet dart of her tongue as she tentatively tasted his skin. This final sign that she truly wanted him sent him over the edge. But he still knew he was nearly out of control, and not for anything would he frighten her, bring back memories of another man out of control in another way.

With a throttled growl of need, he reached for her. He pulled her on top of him, settling her hips over his, then urging her to sit up. Kate stared at him, clearly startled.

"What . . . what are you doing?"

He groaned as she moved; knowing she hadn't meant it as a caress didn't lessen the fierce clenching of his body.

"You . . . you have to do it. You're driving me too wild and I don't want to hurt you," he repeated, his voice nearly breaking as she moved again, unintentionally stroking his rigid flesh with her body. His hips jerked involuntarily, thrusting himself upward against her.

Her cheeks flamed, and her eyes widened. Her voice was barely a whisper as she said, "Me?"

He saw her shock, but saw as well a flicker of shy yearning in her eyes. She might be stunned by the idea, but she wasn't afraid. He tried to talk but couldn't, not when he could feel her feminine heat, not when a move of merely inches would put his aching flesh inside her. Instead he guided her, carefully, gently, even though his body was screaming out for him to hurry, to bury himself in her sweet warmth before he died of wanting it.

When at last she realized exactly what he wanted, her color deepened even more. But she didn't pull away, didn't retreat. And when she began to cautiously, hesitantly lower herself onto him, the slowness of her movements nearly undid him. He clenched his jaw as her slick heat gradually enveloped him, so slowly he nearly cried out with his growing urgency. Only the growing look of wonder on her face as she, for the first time in her life, controlled the pace, kept him from rolling her onto her back and driving home in the savage thrust his body was clamoring for. And when she at last settled down atop him, taking all of him in one last easing of flesh into flesh, he did cry out, her name, in a voice he'd never heard from himself before.

He showed her the movement, urged her with his hands on her hips into the slow rocking that flexed him deep inside her. As much as he loved the feel of this, looking up at her, watching her breasts sway slightly as she moved against him, was making it nearly impossible for him to hold back the tide boiling up inside him. Her hair fell forward, brushing over his skin, feeling as soft as he'd always imagined it would. It screened them both, as if hiding them from the world. He knew he wasn't going to be able to last much longer, and slipped a hand down between their bodies to find and stroke that tiny knot of flesh that made her quiver.

Kate cried out his name at the first touch of his fingers, and began to move faster. Josh gritted his teeth and fought to hold on, quickening his circular caresses, reaching up with his other hand to pluck both her nipples into tight peaks, groaning thickly as he felt an answering ripple in the hot, female flesh that was clasping him so tightly.

And then Kate's head went back sharply, her body curving like a bow. He felt it begin for her, felt the first shuddering convulsion of those deep, powerful muscles. His hands shot back to her hips, pulling her hard against him. Then he was lost, swept up by the coaxing of her body, and his fingers dug into her soft flesh as he arched beneath her, growling out her name as he poured himself into her in a burst of heat and light and sensation that left him panting and utterly drained.

She collapsed atop him, trembling. She murmured his name, and he just managed to lift his arms to hold her. He cradled her there for a long, quiet time, drifting in some wondrous place he'd never known existed, where there was more sweetness than he'd ever dreamed of and anything seemed possible. Even a life of peace for The Hawk.

He slept for a while, then woke when she stirred. It was deep night now, and this time they made love slowly, gently, with less of the urgency but more tender passion. And he thought the sound of his name as it broke from her in the moment her body shuddered to completion the sweetest sound he'd ever heard.

He didn't know how much time had passed before he could bring himself to speak. He knew she wasn't asleep; he could feel the flutter of her lashes against the skin of his chest when she blinked. He wondered if he should just let it go, and hope she was over it now, that somehow the heat of their passion had seared away the ugly memories of having killed a man. But deep down he knew better; it didn't go away so easily and who knew that better than he did?

"Kate?"

"Hmmm?"

She sounded calm enough. But he didn't want to bring it up again, if she had somehow come to terms with what she'd done.

"Why do you suppose Art . . . did that?"

She went still, and he almost wished he hadn't said anything at all. But he knew it would haunt her forever if she thought she'd had another choice.

"It wasn't a fair fight," she said after a long moment.

"Carter believed in sure things, not fair fights," Josh agreed. "And this would have been a sure thing, if not for Art. And Hatch." He tightened his arms around her. "And you."

This time she seemed to stop breathing.

"It's true, Kate, I would have been dead, if you hadn't shot that man."

"Don't."

"I know you don't—"

"Please, stop."

"Kate, you saved my life. For a second time. Allowing you to let it fester inside you would be a poor way to pay you back."

She'd gone beyond still; she was rigid in his arms. Then, suddenly, she yanked herself away from him and sat up. He could hear her suddenly quickened breathing, and even in the dark he could fairly feel the tension radiating from her. Hastily, he rolled over and pulled open the door of the stove, tossing in fresh wood until there was enough light from the fire to see her. She was kneeling on the blankets, staring at him, shy Kate for the first time seemingly heedless of her nakedness.

"Kate, listen to me. I know it seems awful, but you made the choice you had to. And I'm damn glad you did. I owe you—"

"Owe me?" Her voice was high and strained. "Do you want to know what you owe me?"

"Kate—"

"You owe me for being in this to begin with. You

owe me for being in jail. You owe me for having to fight Arly. For having to kill him."

"What?"

"I did it to you, Josh. I set Arly on you like he was a dog. I knew you'd kill him."

Josh rose to his knees. He had that same sensation as in the street, that feeling of time slowing to a crawl. "What are you talking about?"

"After we met . . . that first day, I found out who you were. The notorious Hawk. Arly was already suspicious. He always was, of any new man in town. It was . . . easy."

A chill was setting in, a chill unlike any he'd ever known. "What was easy?"

"I told him . . . you talked to me nicely. Smiled at me. That you . . . touched me. I knew what he would do."

Her hand crept up to the cheek that had been so badly bruised. Josh forgot to breathe. He felt as if he'd caught one of Buck's wilder kicks in the gut.

"You . . . used me to . . . kill him?"

"I couldn't bear it anymore. And you were The Hawk. A cold-blooded killer. At least that's what I thought. I didn't think one more death would mean anything to you. I never dreamed you were . . ."

She broke off. She lowered her gaze, as if she could no longer meet his eyes. As if she'd only now remembered her nudity, she grabbed up one of the blankets and held it in front of her.

"It doesn't matter why," she said, her tone utterly weary. "I did use you. Because I didn't know you then, I didn't think it would matter to you."

"The gun Luke found," he began.

She didn't pretend not to understand. "I put it there,

then told Marshal Pike it was missing. I knew he'd find it, and let you go."

Josh sat back on his heels. Dixon *hadn't* been armed. "So you did lie for me." He was amazed at the steadiness of his voice; his gut was in turmoil.

"No. I told you I didn't. I lied for me, because I couldn't bear to see even The Hawk hang for freeing me. I couldn't live with that."

He remembered all the times he'd thought she was about to say something, tell him something, but had stopped herself. He guessed he knew all too well now what that something was.

"Maybe you should have thought of that first," he said, his voice tight.

Her head came up then; whatever he felt about what she'd done, he couldn't fault her nerve.

"I should have thought of many things. But I thought past nothing but my own salvation. And I used you to buy it."

She gathered up her clothes, then rose unsteadily to her feet. "And I used you tonight as well, to try and take away my guilt and shame, to burn it out of me." Her voice began to shake. "But not even this," she said, gesturing at the blankets, "can burn it away."

She walked away through the storeroom door. Josh stared after her. He fought the nausea roiling in his stomach. Dreams shattered around him, dreams he hadn't even known he'd had until now, when they lay in shards, taunting him with his own foolishness.

At last he reached for a blanket himself, wrapping it around him as if the wool could somehow ward off an iciness that came from within. Then he realized the naked feeling had nothing to do with clothes; it was his soul that had been stripped bare, and there was no defense for that.

# Chapter 21

"I don't understand," Kate said.

Deborah smiled indulgently at her friend as she handed her the money for her basketful of ribbons, jams, canned peaches, and the peppermint sticks she'd discovered Alex had a weakness for. She added a cooking pot she didn't really need, one of the few Kate had left.

"Did you think everyone in town had run out of everything at the same time?"

"I . . . didn't think of it at all. I guess I've been . . ."

"Distracted? I know, dear." Kate had been more than distracted, Deborah mused. She'd been lost in a world of her own, and Deborah thought she knew quite well what was going on in it. "You have been putting all the money in Alex's safe, haven't you?"

Kate nodded, her expression still bewildered. "But why? Why would they all do it?"

"Perhaps because everyone in Gambler's Notch knows we should have done something to help you long ago."

"You put them up to it, didn't you?"

"Me?" Deborah shook her head. "It was Josh's idea."

Kate paled. "Josh?"

"He's the one who explained to everyone that anything the store made before Arly's brother got here would be yours. And suggested if they had any buying to do, they do it now."

Kate looked utterly stricken, and it didn't take much for Deborah to guess why.

"He'll come back, Kate."

Kate shook her head. "He won't. Not after what I did to him."

Deborah shook her head in turn. The day Alex had told her, after learning it from a disconsolate Luke, that Josh had vanished in the night, she had gone to the mercantile to check on Kate. She'd found her friend huddled in the rocker in her shabby room, and had gently pushed until Kate told her the story. All of it.

"He'll get over that. He knows about doing what you have to do to survive. He'll realize you were desperate."

"He's gone, Deborah. He won't be back. I know it. I used him horribly, because I thought he was cold, a killer. . . ."

"We all thought he was."

"I was so wrong. He's nothing like . . . his reputation."

Deborah sighed. She didn't know what to say. She wanted to believe Josh would be back, but she was a little bit afraid that her own happiness was coloring her thoughts.

"Don't give up on him yet, Kate."

"Why would he come back?"

"Because he loves you," Deborah said simply. "And you love him."

Kate stared at her. "No! No, he doesn't . . . I don't . . ."

"Whatever you say, dear."

"You just want to believe that because of you and Alex."

Deborah blushed at this sudden turning of the tables. She hadn't said anything to Kate, but in a small town like Gambler's Notch, it was hard to hide the fact that Alex had been at her house every evening since the night Josh had taunted him into recognizing his own feelings.

"I'm sorry," Kate said remorsefully, "I didn't mean to be rude. I'm very happy that you and Alex are . . . together. It's just that—"

"I understand. Besides, I'm not all that sure Alex and I are together."

"But you're—"

"Still older than he is."

Kate reached over the counter and grasped Deborah's hands. "Don't, Deborah. You deserve to be happy."

"So do you."

"No. Not after what I've done. But you've done nothing but good for people—"

"Kate, stop, you're being too hard on yourself. We all know what your life was like—"

"Miss Kate!" Luke's call was quickly followed by the clatter of footsteps as the boy ran in. "Miss Kate, he's here! Ol' Arly's brother, he just got off the stagecoach."

*Well, he'd wanted out of Gambler's Notch.*

Josh rolled over, shifting the saddlebags beneath his head, trying to find a comfortable spot. That damned book had more sharp edges than seemed possible. He'd pondered trying once more to destroy it, but burning it and drowning it hadn't been very effective. He'd considered leaving it behind, then decided that wouldn't do any good either, and packed it, figuring that was less disconcerting than having the damn thing show up again out of nowhere. Although it had remained relatively placid of late; nothing had changed since the entry documenting his burial in Gambler's Notch.

Perhaps, now that that had been averted, the book had nothing to say, Josh thought wryly. Maybe he should have left it behind. It might have stayed this time. Kate had seemed so fascinated by it, he should have left it for her.

He just hoped he hadn't left her anything else. The thought of her pregnant with his child made him feel . . . he wasn't sure what. So he tried not to think about it.

Two nights. Two nights, that's all he'd spent in Kate Dixon's arms, so why was he finding it impossible to sleep without her? Why had he spent the past week in this rocky little campsite at the base of the notch that had given the town its name, as if crossing over to the other side and losing sight of the clustered buildings was some irrevocable choice he wasn't ready to make?

He shifted the bags again. And then again, with a sigh of exasperation as he rolled over on his back and stared up at the predawn sky through the canopy of ragged-edged cottonwood leaves.

So she'd used him. What did it matter? Didn't everyone? Wasn't that how he made his living? And God knew she'd paid him. She'd paid him in a different coin, but she'd paid him. With her soft lips and sweet body she'd paid him a thousandfold more than he ever would have charged her for getting rid of the likes of Arly Dixon.

So why was he in such a frenzy over this? Why was he still here at all, why hadn't he lit out for somewhere, any place that didn't have a tall, golden-eyed woman who persisted in haunting him despite his fury at her?

And the fact that a small voice in the back of his head kept telling him he didn't have any right to be angry didn't help any. Whatever else she'd done, she'd saved his life twice. Maybe she'd felt she had to plant the gun, but she hadn't had to risk herself to take out Carter's man. But she'd done it. And he didn't know why.

Just like he didn't know why she'd given herself to him. Had she done it out of some feeling of guilt, or indebtedness? Had she traded herself to him the same way her father had once traded her for a pair of boots? If so, did she now consider them even?

The thought did nothing to ease his mind. In fact, it made him ache in a way he'd not felt since his grandfather had died in his arms.

He rolled over yet again, giving the saddlebags another shove. He'd been wrestling with this for a week, and was no closer to resolving his jumbled emotions. He was angry, but wasn't sure he had the right to be. He was glad to be out of Kate's disturbing presence, but he missed her. He was glad to be shed of Gambler's Notch, but he was still lingering within sight of it. He was glad to be on his own again, but he regretting not having said good-bye to Luke, to Art, to Hatch—

And he was going slowly crazy, waking up in the night and reaching for Kate as if he'd been with her for years.

Dawn streaked the sky, shooting across the land to hit the wall of the Rockies. When the pink-streaked indigo brightened to cobalt, then clear morning blue, he finally sat up, rubbing at gritty, weary eyes. Thinking next time he'd use his saddle as a pillow and maybe get some sleep, he shoved the saddlebags off the edge of his bedroll with an angry swipe of his hand. The top bag flipped open, and the book slid out.

"Got something to say?' he muttered, half mockingly, half seriously.

He doubted it. It had been unchanged for two weeks now, but he picked it up anyway. Maybe he'd completely ruined that old wizard's spell. His mouth twisted wryly.

*Leave it to me,* he thought, *to be the Hawk that broke the chain, the Hawk that took generations of history and brought it to an end.*

He spent a long time looking once more at the drawing of Jenna and Kane, feeling as if he should apologize to them for making such a mess of things. For a moment he almost wished Kate was pregnant, that the Hawks would somehow continue, for the sake of these two courageous people. But the thought of what she would face if it were true made him feel ashamed of the selfish urge.

Unless, of course, he stayed. Unless he went back and . . . and what? Married her?

*If you were to marry her, nobody'd ever dare be mean to her again.*

Luke's words echoed in his head, followed swiftly by Hatch's fervent recommendation.

*You take that girl and get out of here, to somewhere they never heard of you, and men like Robards and Carter aren't coming after you like the scavengers that they are.*

He nearly laughed aloud. As if any woman would marry him, even if he were to want to marry the woman who'd used him to . . . to what? Save her own life?

Disgusted with the furrow his thoughts seemed to be endlessly plowing, he flipped to the middle of the book with a sharp motion. All he had to do was stay alive for another couple of weeks, until June, and he'd know this whole thing was a farce. That last entry would be proven wrong, he thought almost defiantly as he turned to the page that held the grim prediction.

It was no longer the last entry.

The book had changed again.

He didn't want to read it. He didn't want to know what ridiculous new prediction was going to be written there. He started to close the book, thinking he'd bury the damn thing under the biggest rock he could move. And then something caught his eye.

It wasn't his story anymore.

It was Kate's.

He read of her indifferent father, glad to get rid of the daughter he thought so plain as to be unmarriageable. He read of the four years of utter horror her marriage to Arly Dixon had been, both day and night, a harsh tale that confirmed much of what he'd already guessed and added grim details he would rather not have known.

And then came the fateful day when he had walked into her life. He was beyond questioning how the book knew. He merely read.

*It was an innocent encounter, barely a word spoken, but Dixon refused to believe it. He resorted to his usual method of persuading his wife to say what he wanted to hear; his fists and his boots. Screeching his accusations, he battered her. When she refused to give in, he grew more furious. His accusations became threats, then evil, vicious promises of what he was going to do to her, of how he was going to mark her body, how he would take her until she was bloody from it, so that she would never again forget who owned her.*

*Kate tried to hold out, but she was hurting so.*

*What if she gave him what he wanted? Wouldn't it serve him right if he was fool enough to challenge The Hawk? Another blow, so hard it made her dizzy, coupled with the horrible images his words invoked, broke her heroic resolve.*

*"All right," she cried out. "He talked to me. He was nice to me. He touched me. Is that what you want to hear?"*

*She'd done it, she realized, when the enraged Arly left at last. She had said the words that would send her husband after a man who would very likely kill him. She thought she should go after him, try to stop him, but instead she merely sat on the floor where Arly had thrown her, nursing her aching ribs and face, waiting, admitting in her pain and humiliation and exhaustion that she prayed The Hawk would indeed put an end to this torture. It was her only hope. She didn't think she could survive another night like the one Arly had promised her.*

*She sat huddled against the wall, waiting. And the hollow, despairing ache inside her grew, until it seemed to go beyond the boundaries of her body and encompass her soul. And she decided then that if Arly came back, she would end it herself. One way or another.*

The words halted there. Josh shut the book sharply, a shiver rippling through him. He shivered again, feeling a strange emptiness inside, as if he were experiencing himself what Kate had felt that night. He felt weighted down, as if her despair had become his. It was an appalling feeling; while he'd been weary enough not to fight death when he'd thought it had come for him, had even welcomed the idea, he'd never been so broken as to actively seek it.

He was still sitting there, the closed book cradled in his hands, when Buck's sudden alertness, head up and ears swiveled toward the trail below the camp, warned him. Instantly he rolled out of sight behind a large boulder to his right, and held his breath until he heard the sound of a horse on the narrow path.

He was gauging whether he had time to go for the Winchester, his preferred weapon in this kind of terrain, when Buck, surprisingly, whinnied softly.

Someone the big buckskin knew. And trusted.

"Josh?"

Luke. Josh let out a compressed breath, half relieved and half irritated; if he'd been someone else, the boy could have gotten himself killed.

"Over here," he said, coming out from behind the boulder.

The boy, astride one of Art Rankin's horses, looked at first relieved, then subdued. He slid off the horse and stood there for a moment, just looking at him. Josh supposed Luke hadn't forgiven him for riding out without a word. He couldn't say he blamed him for that.

"How'd you find me?"

Luke shrugged, masking his hurt with a boy's studied offhandedness. "Mr. Rankin said he saw you ride out to the west. And Marshal Pike's been talking about seein' smoke up here now and then."

"So you figured it was me?"

"I figured I'd look."

"Look, Luke, I didn't mean to just ride out like that, but . . ."

"You and Miss Kate had a fight. I know."

Josh blinked. "She told you that?"

"Not 'zackly. She said it was her fault, that she did something awful to you, so you left."

The simple explanation hit him hard on the heels of the ghastly story he'd just read. "It . . . wasn't her fault. Not really."

"I know."

Josh blinked. "You know?"

The boy shrugged. "Miss Kate just couldn't do nothin' awful. 'Specially not to you."

"Luke, my friend, you are wise beyond your years," Josh said softly.

Luke gave him a look that was adult enough to prove his words. "Are you still my friend?"

"I hope so."

"Are you still Miss Kate's?"

There was a tone of desperate hope in the boy's voice that made Josh stiffen. "Why?"

"Are you?"

He thought again of the book and its gruesome tale, of all the times he'd felt Kate had started to tell him something and been unable to bring herself to do it, of the story Luke himself had told him of her attempt to escape . . . and of the vicious bruise that had been Arly's final legacy. He thought of the scars that marked her body, scars that had made him cringe inwardly at the thought of what she'd gone through. And then he thought of the scars that didn't show.

*She didn't think she could survive another night like the one Arly had promised her.*

She'd had no choice. She'd been utterly, completely desperate, and she'd used the only tool she'd had left to her, a man who, for all she knew, was the heartless killer his reputation bespoke, to whom one more killing would mean less than nothing.

She'd had no choice, but she blamed herself anyway, blamed herself not for the death of her brutal husband, but for what it had done to the man who had killed him.

She'd had no choice.

"Yes," he said suddenly, "I'm still her friend." *If she'll have me as one,* he added silently.

"She needs help." It burst from Luke urgently. "Ol' Arly's brother's here, an' he's bigger and uglier and meaner'n Arly was."

Josh went very still. "When did he get here?"

"Couple of days ago."

"What's he done?" Josh's stomach knotted. "Has he . . . hurt her?"

"No, but he called her awful names because she let you stay in the store after you killed Arly. And he said some things I didn't understand, but Miss Deborah says they were really nasty, about Miss Kate and you."

*I'll just bet he did,* Josh thought grimly.

"And he made her leave."

"Leave?"

"He put a new lock on the door upstairs. And he wouldn't let her take anything with her, not even her clothes."

"Didn't anyone stop him?"

"They tried, Mr. Rankin, and Mr. Hall. But that man, he chased 'em off with Arly's shotgun."

"What about the marshal?"

"That man Mr. Rankin hit, turns out he was deserter. He had to go turn him over to the army. Didn't get back until today."

"Where is she?"

"She's staying with Miss Deborah. But she's talking about leaving, and I don't want her to, Josh. Not her, too."

The implication made Josh flinch. "I'm sorry, Luke. I didn't . . . want to leave."

The boy shrugged, in an offhand gesture Josh himself had used so often at that age to mask the hurt inside. "Mr. Meeker—Hatch—told me when you first came I shouldn't count on you stayin' around."

And he'd fulfilled that prediction, hadn't he? Josh thought bitterly.

"Come on," he said abruptly. "Help me break camp so we can get back to town."

They were halfway there before Josh asked, "Does Kate know you came after me?"

Luke gave him a sideways glance, that strangely adult look still in his eyes. "No. She woulda been really mad if I'd told her."

Of course, she would, Josh thought. How else would she feel? He'd accepted her own assessment of her guilt, when in fact his life was built on far more grievous sins. He'd judged her when he had no right, thought only of his own pain when he should have been remembering hers, and then he'd deserted her when she needed his help the most.

"Mr. Rankin know you have that horse?"

"He lets me ride him," Luke said defiantly with a deft evading of the question Josh had to admire.

"Better get him back soon as we get in," Josh recommended.

"I will," Luke said. Then, after a moment of studying Josh's face, he asked, "Are you gonna leave again?"

"I don't know, Luke." And that was nothing less than the truth, Josh thought.

When they pulled up behind Deborah's house, out of view of the street, Josh looked over at the boy.

"Do something for me. After you take that horse back, you find out where Dixon is. Keep an eye on him, but stay out of his way, out where I can find you, all right?"

Luke nodded eagerly, as if glad to have something to do. Josh watched him go, then braced himself to knock on the door of Kate's best friend, an indomitable woman in her own right.

It was only a moment before the door swung open.

"Well," Deborah said, looking him up and down, "It's about time. Over your sulking?"

Josh felt himself flush.

"Oh, I'm not saying you haven't the right. But you cut it a little fine."

"Is she here?" Deborah nodded. "Is she all right?"

"That's a matter of opinion," Deborah said.

"Luke said he hadn't hurt her—"

"Not physically, if that's what you mean. But I'd say being told she could stay in her home if she wanted to provide *everything* she'd provided for Arly, without benefit of marriage, carries its own kind of pain."

"Son of a bitch," Josh muttered, then grimaced. "Sorry," he began, but Deborah waved him quiet.

"Don't apologize. I quite agree."

"As do I."

As he spoke, Alex Hall came up behind Deborah and rested his hands easily on her shoulders. Josh's gaze flicked from the lawyer's hands to his face, where he found the distinct glower of a protective male, something he recognized because he was feeling a bit that way himself at the moment. It was yet another new experience for him, as were so many others since Kate had come into his life.

Josh looked at Deborah then, and saw the soft glow of feminine happiness in her eyes. As he'd once seen it in Kate's eyes. He glanced back at the lawyer.

"Figure out those five years don't mean as much as you thought?"

Deborah blushed, and lowered her eyes, but Alex

met his gaze steadily. "Odd though it may seem," the lawyer drawled, "considering the mess you've made of things, I thank you for that . . . lesson."

Josh blinked. "The mess *I've* made?"

"Only a fool would ride out on a woman like Kate if, as someone once said to me, he was lucky enough to catch her eye. So what are you going to do about it?"

Josh's jaw tightened. "What do you expect me to do? I'm a gunfighter. I draw men like Robards and Carter like carrion draws flies. And one day one of them will be faster."

"Well," Alex said, rubbing his chin thoughtfully, "I suppose getting killed would be one solution."

As had happened all too frequently lately, Josh had no answer for that. "Where is she?"

"Resting," Deborah said succinctly and pointedly.

Josh's eyes narrowed. "Resting? That's all?"

"I told you she's not hurt. But she's very tired. A lot has happened to her, and she's facing a lot of difficult decisions."

"Why didn't anybody stop him?"

Alex flushed, but he met Josh's gaze head on. "You've seen my ineffectiveness with a gun. Against a shotgun I would only wind up dead."

"Sorry," Josh muttered, not even reluctant about his admiration for the lawyer anymore. "You're right . . . Alex. You stick to lawyering. The future's going to be yours, I think. Men like me are on our way out."

"Or on your way to change," Alex suggested, looking pleased at Josh's switch to his given name.

"Maybe." Josh turned to Deborah. "You're not going to let me see her, are you?"

"I will let Kate decide if she wants to see you. Later."

"Fine," Josh said, feeling more edgy by the moment.

"I'll go find Will Dixon and explain a few things to him."

"He doesn't carry a sidearm," Alex said in a calm, merely informational tone. "At least not a visible one. Wouldn't surprise me if he kept a derringer handy, though. And he keeps that shotgun of Arly's handy when he's in the store."

A little surprised at the lawyer's demeanor—and his realization of what Josh would need to know—he thanked him before he turned on his heel and headed toward the street.

He found Luke across the street from the saloon, watching the doors intently.

"He's in Markum's?" Josh asked.

Luke nodded. "You gonna kill him?"

For once the boy didn't look eager to witness bloodshed, and Josh wondered if what had happened here on the street of Gambler's Notch had cooled his ardor for violence.

"Not if I don't have to," he answered.

Luke hadn't understated things, Josh thought, as he stepped into the saloon and immediately saw his quarry. Judging by his reflection in the fancy bar's mirror, Will Dixon was bigger and considerably uglier than his dead brother. He didn't know who'd given Dixon the scar that slashed across his throat, but Josh had the feeling before this was through he'd regret that the wound hadn't been fatal.

As for the meanness, he didn't doubt that, either; he'd seen kinder eyes on a grizzly. If this was what Arly had grown up with, it was no surprise that he'd been what he was, or liked to work out what must have been a lifetime of ineffectiveness on people who were unable to fight back.

Markum groaned as he looked up from behind the bar as Josh walked across the room.

"Easy, Hugh," Josh said with purposeful cheer, "I haven't put a hole in your fancy bar yet, have I?"

"No," Markum agreed, with a quick flicking glance at the hulking man who was slowly turning from the bar to face Josh, "but there's been five funerals since you've been here."

"I won't make it six unless someone makes me," Josh said, still not looking at Dixon, who now had his back to the bar and was watching Josh with beady-eyed curiosity.

Markum had the half shot of whiskey that was Josh's usual fare already poured by the time he reached the bar.

"Where've you been?" Markum asked, still sounding a bit testy.

Josh grinned. "Miss me, did you?"

Markum's mouth curved reluctantly. "You do liven things up a bit, Hawk."

Josh sensed Dixon freeze, but ignored him. "Always aim to please," Josh said affably. "But I came back because I heard you've got a new resident here. Big, ugly fellow."

Dixon stiffened, but again Josh ignored him.

"One who doesn't know how to treat a lady," he went on. "And thinks he can get away with it."

Markum groaned aloud as Dixon pushed away from the bar.

"Fine talk," the big man said, "from a gunslinger who shoots unarmed men."

Slowly, Josh turned to face Arly's brother. He swept his coat back and kept his gun hand clear, just in case the lawyer was wrong about Dixon's armament.

"You speaking to me?"

Face-to-face, Will Dixon's eyes were even colder and tinier than his brother's. And they hadn't missed Josh's movements.

"Going to shoot another unarmed man, gunhawk?"

"I don't know," Josh said conversationally. "Am I?"

His tone seemed to anger the hulking man even further. "You killed my brother."

"Yes."

"I don't care what that marshal says, Arly never carried no gun."

Josh couldn't dispute that, not after what Kate had told him. So he said only, "Defending your brother, even though he hated you?"

Anger flared in the man's eyes, eyes so dark Josh couldn't really tell what color they were. His hand crept up to the ugly scar, and suddenly Josh knew who had given it to him. Pity they hadn't killed each other young, he thought.

"He was still my brother," Dixon declared.

"Yes. And like you, he preferred beating up women and children who couldn't fight back."

"You mean that slut my brother bought, who spread her legs for you before Arly was even cold? She got what she had coming to her. And she'll get worse before I'm through."

Josh went very still.

"And your brother got what was coming to him," he said in that deadly quiet voice the people of Gambler's Notch had come to know. "And so will you if you do one, tiny little thing to harm Kate. If you so much as look at her, I'll gut shoot you and leave you to die in the street."

"You're welcome to try, Hawk." Dixon puffed out his already considerable chest. "Come by *my* store anytime. I'll be waiting. And when you're dead, I'll spread that slut's legs myself, and show her what a real man is like. I'll use her until there's nothing left."

It took every bit of Josh's self-control to let the man walk out alive. Only the fact that he wasn't sure he was armed made him do it. But he knew now that what he'd told Luke was a moot point. He would have to kill Will Dixon.

"Make sure he keeps his bar bill paid," he said to Markum, watching the doors swing after Dixon swaggered out. "He's not going to be alive long."

# Chapter 22

"He's . . . here?" Kate stared at Deborah and Alex. "He came back?"

"He never was very far away," Deborah said, explaining where Luke had found Josh camped.

"And apparently he made it quite clear to Will Dixon this afternoon what would happen to him if he continued to bother you," Alex added.

"I don't understand why he came back," she said, feeling more confused than ever. "Why would he do that?"

"I think you do understand," Deborah said softly, "but you're afraid to believe." Kate glanced from her friend to Alex, then back. "Yes," Deborah said, correctly interpreting her look, "I was afraid, too."

Alex, sitting beside Deborah on the sofa, slipped his arm around Deborah's shoulders. "You and Josh made me realize what a fool I was being, to let such a silly thing stand between us. Don't let—"

A rap at Deborah's front door interrupted him.

"I'd guess that's for you," Deborah said. "Alex and I were about to go for a walk anyway. A very long walk."

"We were?"

"Of course we were. Out the *back* door."

"Oh." Alex blinked. "Oh! Of course we were."

The rap came again, sharper this time, and Kate looked at the door with trepidation. She turned back to Deborah, just in time to see her friend vanish through the kitchen, Alex on her heels.

"Kate!"

Dear Lord, it really was Josh. She hadn't really believed it, could see no reason why he would come back, why he would try to help her, after he'd found out what she'd done. But he was here.

He rapped again, sharper yet. She wanted to run. In a very different way, she was more afraid of facing Josh than she'd ever been of facing Arly's fists. That was only physical pain, this . . . this was something she'd never felt before.

But she couldn't run. Whatever else she'd done, she couldn't run. Not from Josh. Taking a deep, steadying breath, she made herself walk to the door. She smoothed down the one dress she now had, only because she'd been wearing it when Will had thrown her out. Deborah had supplied her with fresh underthings, but she was too tall for any of her friend's dresses. But she should be used to this by now, looking shabby. And Josh had never seen her any other way.

Except naked in his arms. She bit her lip to fight off the stinging, beautiful images that came to her then. And the memory of the morning she'd discovered that she wasn't carrying his child, further proof that she would never be able to. She had met the realization with sadness rather than relief, despite the awful problems it would have presented.

She forced herself to move. With a hand she couldn't keep from trembling, she opened the door.

It had only been a week, but she felt as if she hadn't seen him for months. He stood there on Deborah's porch, looking at her in a way it took her a moment to recognize. And then it came to her—he was looking at her in a way that matched the way she was feeling inside, as if he'd been hungry for the sight of her in the same way she'd been for him. It seemed impossible, but she couldn't deny the heat in his gaze. And when he stepped into the room and closed the door behind him, she found herself holding her breath.

For a long moment he continued to just look at her. She couldn't speak; it was taking every bit of her strength to keep from trembling. But when he finally spoke, soft and low, she lost that battle.

"I'm sorry, Kate. I know now you didn't have any choice. There was nothing more you could have done, any more than I could have done anything to save my family."

She barely kept back a moan.

"I know what my reputation is. You had no way of knowing I was . . . anything else than what they said I was." He lifted one shoulder negligently. "If I am."

"You are," she whispered. "You are. I had no right to do that to you—"

"You were just trying to survive."

She stared at him, unable to accept that he truly believed that. Her trembling intensified as she struggled with the fact that he was here, that he'd come back. Would he have, if he still blamed her, if he hated her for what she'd done?

"You don't . . ."

"Don't what? Blame you?" he asked, as if he'd read her thoughts again, as he seemed to so many times.

"Yes," she whispered, eyes searching his face.

"You did what you thought you had to do." His brows lowered slightly. "Just like . . . one day a long time ago . . . I did what I thought I had to do."

He said it as if he'd just realized it himself. And when Kate looked up at him, for an instant she caught a glimpse of the boy he'd been then, haunted by his past, so alone after the death of the last member of his family, and hungry, more than a little scared . . . and he'd turned to using the only talent he thought he had.

"Josh," Kate said, rather urgently. She raised her hand, reaching toward him hesitantly, unsure of her welcome despite his words. He reached out to take it.

"Kate, I—"

"Miss Kate!" Luke didn't bother to knock, just threw the door open. "He's throwing your things in the street. Yellin' and saying nasty things."

Josh stiffened. "Stay here," he ordered Kate.

"He's got that shotgun of Arly's, too, Josh," Luke added excitedly.

"Josh, don't." She touched his arm. "It doesn't matter. I had so little. . . ."

"That's not the point."

"Please, it's only some clothes, and they're hardly worth keeping anyway—"

"I've had my fill of men like the Dixon brothers. It's time this one learned to keep his filthy mouth shut."

Fear mixed with exasperation seized her. "Are you *determined* to make that book's prediction come true?"

He looked as if he'd forgotten about that. Then he shook his head. "I'm not going to die now, Kate. Not at the hands of the likes of another Dixon."

"Will Dixon is as bad a man as Arly ever was, except that he's a better shot with that shotgun. And he's even readier to use it."

"I'll be back, Kate."

She watched him go, wondered if she should, as Luke had the instant Josh was out of sight, disobey his

order to stay here and follow him. But she sensed that
if Arly's brother saw her, the situation would only go
from bad to worse. She had to trust that Josh knew
what he was doing. That The Hawk wouldn't be bested
by a brute like Will Dixon.

And she wondered if this was what happened to
every woman fool enough to fall in love with a man
who made his living with a gun.

*Are you determined to make that book's prediction
come true?*

*Getting killed would be one solution.*

Josh frowned as he made his way down the wide,
single dirt street of Gambler's Notch toward the com-
motion in front of the mercantile. He didn't know why
all this talk of death was sticking in his mind; he had
no intention of letting himself be taken by Will Dixon.

"—she's never done anything to you!"

The sound of Art Rankin's angry voice broke in on
his thoughts, and the sound of Dixon's fired his anger
back to a high boil.

"She's a lying slut who let the man who murdered
my brother stay under his roof, let him screw her!"

"It wasn't murder. Arly had a gun. They found it."

Boardman, Josh thought in shock. He didn't know
the man had it in him. Maybe there was hope for the
people of Gambler's Notch yet. His gaze narrowed as
he walked the last few yards toward the mercantile,
and he saw the small pile of clothing tossed in the dirt
at Dixon's feet. True, Kate's clothes weren't much, but
they were all she had.

Both Rankin and Boardman caught sight of him, and
looked so relieved he had to stifle a wry smile. *You
boys have a lot of faith in me,* he thought. *More than
Kate, anyway. She assumes I'm going to die out here.*

"Been waiting for you, Hawk," Dixon sneered, gesturing with Arly's shotgun. "Thought you might want your whore's clothes. Pick 'em up."

As if he'd been trained to servitude, Josh knelt to gather a dress, then the worn undergarments that sparked memories he couldn't afford right now.

"Well, now, so this is the great Hawk. Heard folk hereabouts saying he'd been tamed by that ugly little sparrow, but I didn't believe it. Reckon I should have."

Josh was aware of Boardman gaping at him, and Rankin staring thoughtfully, but looked at neither man. Nor did he look at Dixon, even when the big man began to snigger as Josh walked around him to pick up the worn calico dress that lay in the soft dirt behind him.

"Now, I was hopin' you'd make a fuss. I was lookin' forward to being the man who finally killed The Hawk."

Josh moved swiftly then, from behind Dixon. He grabbed the barrel of the shotgun and forced it downward. Dixon yelped and tried to pull it away from him, but he was a split second too late. His hand on the butt of the steel, Josh had the end of the barrel jammed against the ground. Dixon struggled, but without leverage couldn't match Josh's hold. Josh saw his hand move toward the triggers.

"I reckon," he said in that deadly quiet voice, "that you should think about just what would happen if you fired this thing right now. If you're lucky, it'll only take your leg off when the barrel peels open sideways. And maybe your hand, too."

Dixon had gone very still, and Josh pressed his advantage.

"But you just go ahead and pull that trigger, Dixon. As big as you are, you'll make a fine piece of cover. I'll never know the thing went off, except by the blast. And you screaming, of course."

"You bastard," Dixon snarled. But his hand quit moving.

"I'm many things, but that's not one of them," Josh said. Then, as if merely curious, he added, "I wonder just how badly you would get chewed up. Maybe I should find out."

He slid his own hand down toward the triggers. It was a bluff; he couldn't pull the triggers himself without risking his own hand, but he was gambling Dixon didn't think that fast.

He was right.

"Son of a bitch!"

Dixon abandoned the shotgun and dove sideways—right into the mud at the base of the water trough.

"I'd say you misjudged your direction a little," Josh observed mildly, as both Boardman and Rankin burst into laughter. Dixon's face flushed. Josh broke open the shotgun and pulled out the shells. He pocketed them, and tossed the gun back to the ground.

"Luke?" he called.

The boy scrambled out from behind the trough where he'd been hiding and came racing over. Josh bent and whispered something to the boy. His eyes lit up; he nodded and ran into the store. He came out moments later with a bundle in his hands. Josh pulled some coins out of his pocket and tossed them into the mud beside the fuming Dixon.

"I believe that's more than the price of the new dress," he said. "But you can keep the change. Buy yourself a new shirt."

"I'll kill you, Hawk, I swear it!" Dixon bellowed. "Next time I see you, you're a dead man!"

He left Dixon swearing in the mud, and Art and Boardman laughing as they returned to their work.

"That was great, Josh," Luke exclaimed as he scampered along beside him. "Would the shotgun really have blown up?"

"With the barrel jammed into the dirt? It wouldn't have been pretty."

Luke chattered on excitedly as they walked back toward Deborah's. They were passing in front of the saloon when Marshal Pike stepped out. Josh looked at the man warily; he hadn't seen him after the incident with Carter and his men, but he was willing to bet the man hadn't been happy to have three more dead men to deal with.

"Expected you back a little sooner."

Josh blinked. Where was the order to get back out of town?

"I see you've already met Arly's brother," Pike added.

"You . . . saw?"

"Been watching through the window here," the marshal drawled. "That was a right smooth bit of work."

"Thanks."

"It won't stop him, you know."

"I know."

"You've made a powerful enemy." Pike tugged at his mustache. "Watch your back."

"Always."

Josh watched the marshal walk away, wondering why he hadn't delivered the expected warning.

"Maybe you *should* have killed him," Luke said.

"Probably."

At his weary tone Luke's eyes widened. "Will he . . . will he try to kill you?"

"Probably."

*Getting killed would be one solution.*

*Are you determined to make that book's prediction come true?*

The words echoed in his head again, and he didn't know why they kept coming back. They were like that damned book, haunting him.

The book.

*May 1878—Gunfighter Joshua Hawk buried in Gambler's Notch, Wyoming Territory.*

*I was lookin' forward to being the man who finally killed The Hawk.*

The book's prediction and Dixon's declaration—born of ignorance, Josh thought; no man in his right mind would want the kind of notoriety that made others want to kill you just for the sake of building their own reputation—joined Alex and Kate's words, circling in his mind like buzzards over a carcass.

*You take that girl and get out of here, to somewhere they never heard of you, and men like Robards and Carter aren't coming after you like the scavengers that they are.*

Was there such a place? Anywhere? Was there anyplace far enough away to keep those men off his trail, short of hell itself? Would it do any good? Or was the book's prediction destined to be the truth?

His steps slowed. He felt the shotgun shells in his pocket. He pulled them out, looking at them speculatively.

If he believed in the book, he had to believe in all of it, he thought. And if he believed the book was right about his death, here in Gambler's Notch before the end of this last week of May, then he had to believe it was right about the Hawks as well, that they would continue. Which meant . . .

Which meant Kate was already pregnant. With his child. The mere thought nearly staggered him.

But she'd said she couldn't be, thanks to Arly's beatings. Which meant he couldn't be going to die. Didn't it? His mind was whirling so fast he couldn't begin to sort it all out.

"Josh? Are you all right?"

He muttered something at the boy that was supposed to be reassuring. Luke looked at him doubtfully, but Josh was too distracted by his thoughts.

If the book wasn't right about his death, then what? If he wasn't going to be buried here in Gambler's Notch, his grave to probably become a place of minor fame for as long as it took people to forget he'd ever existed, then didn't that prove the book was a . . . joke? A bad magic trick perpetrated by some long-dead wizard who perhaps had had one too many cups of mead before muttering his incantation?

But it had been right about so much. . . .

*May 1878—Gunfighter Joshua Hawk buried in Gambler's Notch, Wyoming Territory.*

His eyes widened. He stopped in his tracks.

"Josh?" Luke had stopped beside him, looking up at him with some concern.

"You go on, Luke. Take the dress to Kate. Tell her I'll . . . see her later."

"But—"

"Go, Luke. I need to go see Hatch."

"Oh." Then, brightening, "Can I come up later?"

"You do that."

Luke grinned, and hastened off to deliver the new dress. Just as well, Josh thought; Kate would most likely throw it back at him.

He trotted across the street, warily watching his back, knowing he'd made a deadly enemy by humiliating Will Dixon in public. Henry Meeker gave him a wary nod as he stepped into the lobby of the Grand

Hotel. Josh returned it as he took the stairs two at a time.

He opened the door when Hatch answered his call.

"Saw that move you pulled from the window here," Hatch said with a grin as he wheeled his chair around to face Josh. "You haven't lost your touch."

"Have you lost yours?"

Hatch lifted a brow. "Mine?"

"Time was, you knew more about every kind of gun made than any man alive.

"Time was," Hatch agreed.

Josh tossed him the two shotgun shells. "I hope you still do," he said.

Then he sat down and began to talk. And when Luke arrived some time later, the boy quickly found himself pressed into service as a messenger. And eventually, one by one, several members of the population of Gambler's Notch made their way to the Grand Hotel.

Kate's heart was pounding as she stood in Deborah's parlor, smoothing her hands over the folds of the first new dress she'd had in years, the first dress that had actually fit her in just as long. It was the dress Josh had suggested she take when it had arrived at the store. She hadn't wanted it then, but she accepted it now with an odd sense that it was a symbol of some kind, of a new life she was about to begin.

Barely ten minutes after leaving yesterday, Luke had returned bearing the unexpected gift of the dress and the thankful news that Josh was all right. The boy had been full of admiring excitement at The Hawk's handling of the big bully, and she herself hadn't been able to stop a small tug of selfishly pleased amusement at Will Dixon's very public embarrassment.

But Josh hadn't come back. She had been nearly

frantic by the time Luke had returned again, this time with a message from Josh. The message that had brought them to this pass today.

"Everything will be all right, Kate," Deborah said soothingly.

Kate wished she could believe that. But that ominous entry in the Hawk book haunted her, and she wondered with dread if this might be the day it came true. But she smiled at the couple standing beside her, unable to dim her friend's obvious joy with her own fears.

Alex and Deborah had quite given up worrying what anyone else thought of the inappropriateness of the young lawyer courting a woman older than he. It did Kate's heart good to look at them even as she wondered what her own future held.

She sighed heavily. Was she being a fool yet again? Was she placing too much faith in a few moments of exquisite pleasure in the night? She shook her head, as if that could rid her of the painfully sweet images.

No, she told herself firmly. It wasn't just that. It was the evenings spent reading, the days spent working companionably side by side. It was the way Josh treated her, with a respect and consideration so ingrained in him she knew it was automatic, that it was as natural to him as the constant cruelty had been to Arly. As it was to Arly's brother.

She shivered. Half the town had heard Will Dixon swear he would kill Josh on sight. And the entire town knew that he was savage enough to do it. In only four days in Gambler's Notch, he'd made his late brother look gentle by comparison; at least Arly had been drunk and only semiconscious half the time.

"It's noon, Kate. Let's go for that walk."

She shivered again, but nodded. Alex held the door

for Deborah and Kate, then closed it behind them. It was a bright, sunny day, a harbinger of the summer to come. As they walked, Kate tried to see it as a good omen, but so little had gone right in her life, she couldn't seem to find the faith to believe it. Or to hope that somehow things had changed, simply because a man called The Hawk had come into her life.

They were in front of the hotel when she heard Will Dixon roar. Her heart seemed to leap into her throat, cutting off her breath. She looked at the mercantile that had once been the center of her life, in time to see Josh coming out the door. He stepped out into the street, and walked toward the saloon. He never even looked at Kate, or at Art Rankin, who was standing outside the stable, or at Marshal Pike, who was in his office doorway, arms folded across his chest, covering his badge.

Seconds later, shotgun in his hands, Dixon charged out onto the boardwalk. Josh didn't turn.

"I told you you'd be a dead man if you came back here!"

Dixon's bellow made Kate shiver yet again. Josh kept walking, his back to the infuriated man. Dear God, was it really going to happen? She saw Marshal Pike move, stepping down into the street.

"Turn around, Hawk! Or are you afraid to face me?"

Josh took another three steps. He stopped, glanced around as if to be sure of how far he'd come. Then, slowly, he turned around. Dixon moved then, stepping off the boardwalk. Josh tensed as if to move, but when Dixon stopped in the street in front of the mercantile, Josh stayed where he was.

"Why didn't you just backshoot me, Dixon? You're the type. Just like your brother was."

With a howl of rage Dixon lifted the shotgun. In the

same instant Josh's hand flashed down toward his Colt. The sound of the six-shooter was lost in the blast of both barrels of the shotgun going off at once.

As the echo died away, Dixon stood there, gaping stupidly. The others stared. Kate cried out despite herself.

Joshua Hawk was facedown in the dusty street.

Before anyone else could move, Marshal Pike was there. A second later, Art was beside him, both of them huddled around Josh's body, almost hiding it. Dixon moved, but the marshal gestured him back warningly. Pike looked at Art, and shook his head. Art looked back at Kate.

"Keep her away," he called to Alex. "His head's practically blown off."

Kate couldn't help the scream that escaped her. Alex gripped her arm to steady her. She watched mutely as the marshal pulled off his coat and spread it over the body. She stood there staring.

The legend of The Hawk had ended. As the book had predicted, The Hawk had died in Gambler's Notch.

# Chapter 23

"It was a nice funeral, wasn't it?" Luke said.

"Very," Kate agreed.

"Reverend Babcock even said some nice things, didn't he?"

"Yes, he did."

She tugged at the short jacket of the new traveling dress she'd bought, a pale yellow, fine wool trimmed in lace that was decidedly unwidowlike and lit her eyes to the gold Josh had once told her they were.

"An' Mr. Rankin made a really nice marker, didn't he?"

"Yes," Kate agreed yet again.

"I like that part about 'Here lies the no-no . . .' "

"Notorious," Alex supplied.

"Yeah! 'The notorious gunfighter known as The Hawk,' " Luke finished with a wide smile.

"Hush, Luke," Kate cautioned; the train platform was too full of people for her taste, and too many of them could hear the boy. The engine let out a hiss, and she looked around a little nervously.

"Notorious is the word, all right," Alex said. "Frank Boardman telegraphed every newspaper for five hundred miles around. Pretty soon Will Dixon will be famous as the man who killed The Hawk."

Kate winced.

"Not worried about that bully, are you Kate?" Alex asked.

"Of course not. I hope someone like Carter or Robards comes after him tomorrow. But I still hate the sound of that."

"Sorry," Alex said, but he was smiling.

"I wanna see the engine again!" Luke exclaimed as another warning hiss of steam came.

"You just mind the time," Kate warned, and the boy bobbed his head as he went to examine the huge wheels and the steam pistons that drove them.

Deborah threw her arms around her friend. "You take care now. And you will write me"—she glanced with shy pride at Alex—"*us* when you get settled?"

"Of course."

"Are you sure you have everything you need? Your new clothes? Money?"

Kate nodded, answering the oft repeated question yet again. "I packed all three dresses. I can even afford to buy more in San Francisco, if I want. There's the money from the store, and from Marshal Pike."

A soft smile curved her lips as she remembered thanking the people of Gambler's Notch for their subtle help, and recalled how the crusty marshal had blushed when she'd thanked him for turning over the five hundred dollars reward money that he'd discovered had been out on Jackson Carter. And she'd silently added another thank you; she had a fairly strong feeling the marshal had guessed the part she'd played in Arly's death, but he'd never spoken of it, to her or anyone else.

"And you can travel in comfort," Alex said. "A stateroom will be much nicer than one of those passenger cars. You'll be in San Francisco, in luxury at that new Palace Hotel, before you know it."

"Perhaps you'll want to stay there," Deborah said hopefully, "rather than go on to that Seattle place. I don't know why you settled on that, anyway."

*And I couldn't begin to explain it to you,* Kate thought.

The whistle blew, and Kate knew it was time.

"Luke!" she called, afraid the boy would still be hanging on to the side of the engine as the train pulled out. The boy's head popped into view from between the locomotive and the coal car. "Now," she called, and he nodded and began to clamber down.

Then she turned back to Alex and Deborah.

"Thank you . . . for everything," she said, her eyes beginning to brim.

"Don't thank us," Alex said gently. "Just be happy, Kate."

She hugged him then, thankful for Deborah's sake for Alex's solid, strong goodness. Then she hugged Deborah again. And when the conductor's final call came, she gestured to Luke and stepped aboard the train. With a final wave, she turned her back on her friends, afraid she would begin weeping if she looked at them any longer. She couldn't help wondering if she would ever see them again. She made her way down the narrow passageway to the compartment labeled with the number five. She opened the door and stepped into the small stateroom.

The moment she was inside, a man's strong arm came around her from behind, and she was pulled hard against a solid, muscular body. She gave a startled cry, a cry which died in her throat as she was turned around and pair of hot, eager lips claimed hers.

"Josh," she murmured against his mouth, slipping her arms around his neck.

His hands slid down her back, pressing her even harder against him. His tongue probed her mouth, and when he withdrew, she returned the favor. He shuddered when her tongue slipped past the even line of his teeth to taste him.

She could feel the thick, hot ridge of his arousal through the fine wool of her new dress. She shifted her hips, caressing him, and he shuddered again as his hands crept up to cup her breasts. She made a soft, tiny sound, a sound of welcome, of joy, and it was echoed in the rumble rising from deep in his chest as he spoke her name.

"Are you gonna kiss all the way to San Francisco?"

Luke's voice, sounding innocently curious, broke the spell.

"Maybe," Josh said gruffly, making Kate smile.

"And maybe," she added, "all the way to Seattle on the boat."

Luke groaned. "This is gonna be a boring trip."

With a stifled sigh that made Kate smile again, Josh released her. He didn't back away, however, but stood behind her, and heat and color stained her cheeks as she realized why; he was still obviously aroused, and was hiding the fact behind her skirts. She would tease him about that later, she thought. Much later, she thought, the anticipation of being alone with him again increasing the heat infusing her.

"Don't go thinking that because you did such a good job back in Gambler's Notch you're running things now," Josh said sternly.

Luke only grinned. "I did do good, didn't I?"

Josh relented and grinned back. "Yes, you did. You

sneaked those shells Hatch doctored up into that shotgun slick as can be."

"Well, Mr. Rankin helped," Luke said generously,
"pitchin' that fit over that new anvil he never really
ordered, he kept ol' Arly's brother real distracted."

"I'm just grateful it worked," Kate said fervently.

"Barely a scratch here and there," Josh said, still
grinning. "Hatch knows what he's doing. Lightened
those loads just enough for that distance. Nearly as
much noise, but not much range."

"It scared me for a minute," Luke said.

"Me, too," Kate agreed, shivering at the memory. "It
all seemed so . . . real."

"Especially since you'd been expecting it to happen
anyway?" Josh suggested quietly.

She couldn't deny that. " 'Joshua Hawk buried in
Gambler's Notch, Wyoming Territory,' " she quoted
softly.

"Is that really what made you think of it?" Luke
asked. "That line in the book?"

Josh nodded. "Not died. It never really said that.
Just 'buried.' "

Luke laughed. "Folks'll come from all over to see
your grave. An' you're not even in it."

"A fact I'm very thankful for," Josh said wryly.

"Bless Deborah for thinking of the reason you
couldn't be put on display like some . . . some . . ."
Kate shook her head as words failed her.

"I know," Josh agreed. "That would have been hard
to pull off. But since—how did Boardman put it in
those telegrams? 'The Hawk's face was left unrecogniz-
able by the shotgun blast that killed him—' "

He stopped when Kate shivered. "I don't like hearing
it, even now." Then, curious, she looked at him. "You
said that like . . . like The Hawk was someone else."

Josh shook his head. "He's someone I've left behind. Forever."

Kate smiled. "We've enough money for a good start."

He nodded. "And enough for something else."

"What?"

"I wired ahead, Kate. There's a minister in the next town. We'll be there just long enough for him to marry us."

Her eyes widened in shock. Josh looked suddenly doubtful.

"Didn't you . . . you didn't think we were just going to . . ." He took an audible breath and tried again. "I would never expect you to . . . just come with me. You knew I meant for us to get married, didn't you? I mean," he added hastily, "if you'll have me."

"I . . . " She swallowed tightly.

"I know you've no reason to trust in marriage, Kate. You've been hurt badly, and it would take an exceptional man to make you believe it's worth trying again, and I'm hardly that—"

"Aw, she knows you're different from ol' Arly, don't you Kate?" Luke said confidently.

She still couldn't speak. Josh was looking more doubtful by the moment, but she still couldn't force any words past the lump in her throat. Luke, on the other hand, was studying her intently, as if wondering why she wasn't answering. Finally he nudged Josh.

"I think you're supposed to say as how you like her a lot and such first, aren't you?"

Josh looked suddenly sheepish. "You're right. I bow to your superior wisdom, Luke. Now why don't you . . . er, go check on Buck while I take care of that. He'll be restless in that freight car for a while."

Luke looked hesitant.

"We'll still be here, Luke," Josh said gently. "We're . . . family now."

The boy flushed, but smiled at the same time. Then he turned to go.

"Luke?" Josh called. The boy looked back. "Remember, we're borrowing your name for a while."

Luke grinned. "I'll remember, if'n anyone asks." He pulled open the door, then looked back again. His eyes went from Kate's face to Josh's, then back. "Thanks for . . . askin' me to come with you, an' live with you in this Seattle place. It'll be almost like havin' my folks back again," he said in a rush, then was gone, closing the stateroom door behind him before they could respond.

For a long moment Josh and Kate just looked at where the boy had been, clearly moved by what he had said. Finally, Josh put his hands on her shoulders and turned her to face him.

"I don't have much to offer you, Kate, except myself, and that's not much. I don't have a trade, but I'll learn one. The book says . . . we'll do well in Seattle."

She smiled at that. They'd both given up questioning the magical book; it had been right every step of the way. When they'd needed a place to go, where no one had ever heard of or would recognize The Hawk, an entry had appeared as if in answer to their need. It had told of the last of the Hawks moving to the young, raw, lumber town on the north coast of the Pacific, and flourishing there.

"And I swear I'll never use a gun to make my way again."

"I haven't much to offer you, either," she said, the first words she'd been able to get out. "You know it's likely I can't have children—"

"We have Luke. We'll make him a Hawk in everything but blood, and that will be enough."

"But—"

"You have everything I want. And more than I ever thought to find." He swallowed visibly. "I love you, Kate."

"Oh, Josh." The tears that had been threatening brimmed over now. "I never thought I could love anyone. I was afraid to even try. But I love you."

"Will you, Kate? Will you marry me, and try to make a family out of the three of us?"

"I will, Josh," she breathed. "I will. And we'll be a family, Josh. A good one."

She went into his arms then, and he held her so tightly she felt any remaining doubts slide away. He kissed, gently at first, then more urgently, until at last he lifted his head and muttered, "I wonder how long Luke's going to be gone?"

"Long enough," Kate said a little breathlessly, "if we hurry."

Josh looked down at her, a lazily pleased smile curving his mouth as heat flared in his eyes. But then, slowly, the passion seemed to ease, and he lifted a hand to cup her face as he shook his head.

"No, I don't think so," he said softly. "I want the next time to be with my wife."

Kate blushed.

"But until then," he added conversationally, "there are a few other things I'd like to do."

"What?" Kate asked, wary of the teasing glint she saw in the eyes that were as blue as the Wyoming sky.

"I'll show you," he said, reaching for her again.

And it was much, much later that they heard Luke's plaintive exclamation from the doorway.

"You really *are* gonna kiss all the way to San Francisco, aren't you?"

Josh sat up sharply, wide awake, the vividness of the dream as astounding as it had been every night this week.

"Josh?"

Kate's voice was sleepy, and he tried to reassure her. "Go back to sleep, honey."

She sat up beside him. "Was it that dream again? About the man named Jason?"

He took a deep breath, then nodded. "It's so . . . real. He looks so much like me, but . . ."

"But what?"

He looked at her, saw her eyes gleaming in the glow of the moonlight through the window. The small cabin he'd built when they'd arrived, on a hill overlooking the island-dotted waters of Puget Sound, was a home now, with a room added on for Luke, and a kitchen for Kate. The main room, as it had always been, was a library, filled with shelves long before they'd had the books to put on them. But they were filling up; in the two years they'd been here, their collection had grown rapidly. The small newspaper Josh had begun was doing well, and had developed a reputation for honesty. He'd found a different way to fight battles similar to those he'd once fought with a gun.

"But what?" she prompted gently when he didn't go on.

"He's . . . a little older, I think, and he dresses . . . differently. And he's in a strange place."

"A strange place?"

"I can't explain it. I get the feeling he's from here, Seattle, I mean, but in the dream, he's somewhere else. And he's . . ."

"He's what?"

This was going to sound crazy, Josh knew that, but what could possibly be crazier than what they themselves had been through? He took a deep breath and plunged ahead.

"I think he's the last Hawk. But in another time."

Kate blinked. "Another time?"

He nodded. "Later than now, I think. There are strange things around him, but I can't see them clearly. All I can really see is him. And a woman."

"A woman?"

"Yes. Dark hair. Sassy." He grinned. "She's the one who calls him Jason, and she's giving him a lot of trouble. But then Hawk women always do that to their men."

"Hush," Kate said, elbowing him as she giggled.

"He's fighting the book, Kate."

She went very still then. "It . . . came to him?"

"Like it did to me. And he's fighting it just as hard. I can feel it, in the dream. I can feel . . . his confusion, his pain. As if I were there, watching him."

"I wish we could help him."

Just like that, she had accepted it, and wished to help. Josh drew her into his arms and held her close, blessing the book, Jenna's wizard, or whatever fate had brought them together. She drifted back to sleep in his embrace, but Josh lay awake for a long time, that other Hawk's face still vivid in his mind.

At last, in the faint light of dawn, he got up. Pulling on his denim pants, he walked barefoot out of their bedroom into the main room, shivering a little against the damp chill. The beauty of this paradise had a price that seemed sometimes to consist of endless wet days. He stoked the fire so it would be warmer when Kate got up.

Then he crossed the room to a bookshelf that held only one volume, and picked it up. It no longer gave him that odd sense of warmth and companionship, but Josh suspected it was his own life that had changed. The cold was gone, banished by a golden-eyed woman, and he no longer needed the comfort of the book.

He took it out to the kitchen, where he lit a lamp, then fired up the stove and started a pot of coffee, fighting off yawns. As the coffee was brewing, he sat down at the table and opened the book.

As always, he smiled at the picture that had appeared on that empty, skipped page before his story began. It had emerged on the day of their wedding, that hasty, in transit, but no less heartfelt ceremony held under a spreading stand of aspens beside the train platform. It was the same kind of drawing that appeared throughout the book, as if the artist who had captured Jenna and Kane had somehow been witness to their own joining.

And perhaps, he thought with wry acceptance, he had.

He thought about him again, that other Hawk of his repeated, vivid dreams, thought of what he must be going through. What he must have felt when the book appeared out of nowhere, and haunted him until he was forced to believe in it. In every dream it felt stronger, that last Hawk's resistance, and Josh felt a strange kinship with this man he would never know. Hawks really did breed true, he thought. Even when they didn't believe it themselves.

*I wish we could help him,* Kate, his ever generous Kate, had said.

He looked at the book thoughtfully, remembering how it had come to him. Then he got up, poured a cup of the fresh coffee, and thought some more. It might work, he thought. It just might work. He would try, anyway. There was nothing to lose.

He had just finished when Kate wandered sleepily into the kitchen and leaned over his chair to nuzzle his neck. It was early yet—Luke was still asleep, and the dawn quiet was pleasant, now that the rooms were warm. He reached back to give her an awkward hug.

"What are you writing?"

He showed her. "I don't know if it will work, if you can put something in the book and have it . . . go with it, but I thought it was worth a try."

"So you wrote him a letter? This man in the dream?"

Josh nodded ruefully. "Crazy as a loon, I know."

She shook her head. "It's not, if it will help him avoid some of what we went through."

Again, that incredible acceptance, born of a love he'd never thought to find in his life. The past two years had made him realize that no matter how bleak things looked, you could never give up, because around any corner could be the reason for it all.

"What did you say to him?" she asked.

He handed her the note he'd written. She began to read it out loud, because that had become their habit as they continued what was now a family tradition of reading to each other every evening. Just the sound of her soft voice as she read warmed him even more than the fires he'd stoked.

*I don't know who or where or even when you are, or if this will ever reach you, but if I can spare you some of what I went through, I must try. If you are reading this, you are the last Hawk. If you are like me, you are fighting, as all the last Hawks have fought. Don't. The legend is true. The book is real.*

*Jenna and Kane Hawk are forebears to be proud*

*of. I hope that, whoever you are, you might even find something in me to be proud of, little though there is. Don't let it end. It does matter. Jenna and Kane and the others deserve to live on in you.*

"*I wish you luck, and Godspeed.*

*Joshua Hawk*

Kate's voice broke on his name, and she let the letter drift from her fingers back to the table.

"I love you, Joshua Hawk."

Amused and touched by her sudden emotion, he shifted his chair and pulled her down on his lap. "And I love you, Kathleen Hawk."

She snuggled against him with a tiny sigh. Smiling with the contentment that never seemed far away when he was with her, he reached around her and folded the letter. He flipped open the book, but was unsure where to put it. Finally he turned to his own page, the last page with any of the elegant, mysterious writing, the page that documented their wedding and their settling in Seattle. He would put it there, he thought, and hope that somehow—

He went very still.

He looked at the last entry, which for two years had been about their wedding, and their move here to the town Josh knew was about to boom. It had been that way until minutes ago. Until, he thought, Kate had come to him.

He read it again. And then a third time.

"Josh?"

He knew she had felt his sudden stillness.

"Kate, I . . . are you all right?"

She sat up on his lap, looking down at him curiously, and he wondered just how strained he had sounded.

"I'm fine," she said. "I told you, I'm just a little tired lately. Whatever was making me so sick went away."

"I know what was making you so sick. And it didn't go away."

She blinked. "What?"

"Deborah was wrong, Kate. Or maybe you just needed . . . time to heal. Or maybe it's that old wizard at work again."

"What are you talking about?"

"Our son, Kate. Our son."

She looked puzzled. "Luke? What about him?"

"No, not Luke. Yes, he's our son in all the ways that matter, and always will be. But I mean . . . a baby, Kate. You're pregnant."

She paled. Slowly, she shook her head. He'd known she mourned the impossibility of it; she'd told him that, except for his love, she wished she could have his child more than anything in the world. He'd assured her it didn't matter, and he'd meant it, but now the idea filled him with sheer joy. She would have to be careful, the entry said, but in the end . . . they would have a son.

But Kate didn't believe him.

"The book has never been wrong, has it, Kate?"

Mutely, she shook her head.

"Then read about our son."

He nudged the book toward her. And watched her face as she read. Disbelief, doubt, then hope flashed across her face like the morning sun clearing the mountains and darting across a meadow of wildflowers.

She lifted her golden gaze to his face. "A baby? Our baby?"

He nodded. "Trust it, Katie. It's true. You know it is."

She pressed a hand to her heart, and he knew she was feeling the same welling joy that was making his chest ache.

"Our son, Katie," he whispered. And suddenly, with a flash of certainty whose origin he didn't question, he picked up the letter he'd written and added, "And this man will be his . . . a few times great-grandson. Another last Hawk. And it will begin again."

He tucked the letter between the pages almost reverently.

"And again," she whispered, awe tingeing her voice as she watched him.

He nodded. "Forever. For the first time, I really believe that. It will go on forever."

He felt Kate shiver, and tightened his arms around her. "A baby," she repeated again and again in wonder. Josh found himself just grinning sillily.

After a long time, Kate lifted her head to look from the book to his face. "This means . . . the book will go away, doesn't it."

Her words weren't a question, but Josh nodded. "When the baby is born. That's how it's supposed to work. It records the name, and vanishes. Until he"— he pointed at the letter—"needs it."

They both stared at the book, at the family tree begun again, their own names at the top, awaiting the next entry. The name of their son. Kate laid a hand on her still flat belly.

"I . . . know what his name should be," she whispered.

"You do?"

She turned her golden-eyed gaze on his face and nodded.

"What?"

She smiled, a tiny, half-smile that made his heart turn over and made him want to take her right back to bed.

"Jason," she said.

His eyes widened. He had a sudden, vivid flash of that other man, that last Hawk who was yet to come. The one who would fight the same battle he had fought, just as hard, just as stubbornly.

Jason.

It was perfect.

Josh threw back his head and laughed. And with an inward salute to his descendent yet unborn, he swept up in his arms the woman who would make it possible, and followed the urge he'd denied before.

And as he carried her back into their room, he spared one last thought for the man in his dreams.

*Good luck, Jason Hawk, whoever, wherever . . . whenever you are. You're going to need it.*

# CELEBRITY TOPAZ MAN
# MICHAEL O'HEARN

**Michael O'Hearn is the current—
and three-time—Mr. Universe and
has won California state championships
in both judo and powerlifting. Mike
is also very involved with children,
regularly touring the country and
encouraging them to stay drug-free.**

**Visit the Topaz area on our website
http://www.penguin.com**

# WE NEED YOUR HELP

To continue to bring you quality romance
that meets your personal expectations,
we at TOPAZ books want to hear from you.
Help us by filling out this questionnaire, and in exchange
we will give you a **free gift** as a token of our gratitude.

- Is this the first TOPAZ book you've purchased? (circle one)

     YES          NO

  The title and author of this book is: _____

- If this was not the first TOPAZ book you've purchased, how many have
  you bought in the past year?

     a: 0 - 5     b 6 - 10    c: more than 10    d: more than 20

- How many romances in total did you buy in the past year?

     a: 0 - 5     b: 6 - 10    c: more than 10    d: more than 20 ____

- How would you rate your overall satisfaction with this book?

     a: Excellent    b: Good    c: Fair    d: Poor

- What was the main reason you bought this book?

     a: It is a TOPAZ novel, and I know that TOPAZ stands
         for quality romance fiction
     b: I liked the cover
     c: The story-line intrigued me
     d: I love this author
     e: I really liked the setting
     f: I love the cover models
     g: Other: _____

- Where did you buy this TOPAZ novel?

     a: Bookstore    b: Airport    c: Warehouse Club
     d: Department Store    e: Supermarket    f: Drugstore
     g: Other: _____

- Did you pay the full cover price for this TOPAZ novel? (circle one)

     YES          NO

  If you did not, what price did you pay? _____

- Who are your favorite TOPAZ authors? (Please list)

- How did you first hear about TOPAZ books?

     a: I saw the books in a bookstore
     b: I saw the TOPAZ Man on TV or at a signing
     c: A friend told me about TOPAZ
     d: I saw an advertisement in_____magazine
     e: Other: _____

- What type of romance do you generally prefer?

     a: Historical    b: Contemporary
     c: Romantic Suspense    d: Paranormal (time travel,
         futuristic, vampires, ghosts, warlocks, etc.)
     d: Regency    e: Other: _____

- What historical settings do you prefer?

     a: England    b: Regency England    c: Scotland
     e: Ireland    f: America    g: Western Americana
     h: American Indian    i: Other: _____

- What type of story do you prefer?

  a: Very sexy           b: Sweet, less explicit
  c: Light and humorous    d: More emotionally intense
  e: Dealing with darker issues   f: Other

- What kind of covers do you prefer?

  a: Illustrating both hero and heroine     b: Hero alone
  c: No people (art only)                d: Other_____

- What other genres do you like to read (circle all that apply)

  | Mystery | Medical Thrillers | Science Fiction |
  |---|---|---|
  | Suspense | Fantasy | Self-help |
  | Classics | General Fiction | Legal Thrillers |
  | Historical Fiction | | |

- Who is your favorite author, and why?_____
  _____

- What magazines do you like to read? (circle all that apply)

  a: *People*             b: *Time/Newsweek*
  c: *Entertainment Weekly*   d: *Romantic Times*
  e: *Star*                f: *National Enquirer*
  g: *Cosmopolitan*      h: *Woman's Day*
  i: *Ladies' Home Journal*   j: *Redbook*
  k: Other:_____

- In which region of the United States do you reside?

  a: Northeast    b: Midatlantic   c: South
  d: Midwest      e: Mountain    f: Southwest
  g: Pacific Coast

- What is your age group/sex?    a: Female   b: Male

  a: under 18     b: 19-25     c: 26-30     d: 31-35    e: 36-40
  f: 41-45        g: 46-50     h: 51-55     i: 56-60    j: Over 60

- What is your marital status?

  a: Married      b: Single     c: No longer married

- What is your current level of education?

  a: High school        b: College Degree
  c: Graduate Degree    d: Other: _____

- Do you receive the TOPAZ *Romantic Liaisons* newsletter, a quarterly newsletter with the latest information on Topaz books and authors?

  YES            NO

If not, would you like to?    YES      NO

Fill in the address where you would like your free gift to be sent:

Name: _____

Address: _____

City:_____ Zip Code: _____

You should receive your free gift in 6 to 8 weeks.
Please send the completed survey to:

Penguin USA•Mass Market
Dept. TS
375 Hudson St.
New York, NY 10014